THE
DUNGEONEERS

THE DUNGEONEERS

JOHN DAVID ANDERSON

WALDEN POND PRESS

An Imprint of HarperCollins*Publishers*

Walden Pond Press is an imprint of HarperCollins Publishers.
Walden Pond Press and the Skipping Stone logo are trademarks and
registered trademarks of Walden Media, LLC.

The Dungeoneers
Copyright © 2015 by John David Anderson
All rights reserved. Printed in the United States of America.
No part of this book may be used or reproduced in any manner whatsoever
without written permission except in the case of brief quotations embodied
in critical articles and reviews. For information address HarperCollins
Children's Books, a division of HarperCollins Publishers, 195 Broadway,
New York, NY 10007.
www.harpercollinschildrens.com

Library of Congress Control Number: 2014949457
ISBN 978-0-06-233814-3

Typography by Erin Fitzsimmons
15 16 17 18 19   CG/RRDH   10 9 8 7 6 5 4 3 2 1
❖
First Edition

In memory of Niru Shah, an adventurer, hero, and rogue
who taught us all what to treasure most

"Give a man a fish, and he will eat for a day.

Teach him to fish, and he will eat for a lifetime.

Teach him to steal, though, and he won't have to eat fish every day for the rest of his life."

—*Darrius Snowthorn,* The Rogue's Encyclopedia, *Volume One*

1

HIDDEN TALENTS

Colm Candorly had nine fingers and eight sisters. He was born short the finger and quickly learned to make do without it. He would trade five more of them and the better portion of his toes for a moment of peace and quiet.

They came in bunches, the girls, as if they couldn't bear to be alone, even for a moment. Triplets first, then a set of twins bracketing each side of the Candorlys' only boy, and finally the baby, Elmira. Mrs. Candorly insisted little Elm would be the last, but Mina Candorly was an indisputably healthy woman with biceps the size of house bricks and hips the width of an oxcart, who loved her husband very much and her children even more, so no one was holding their breath. Least of all Colm.

Except when they made him. Hold his breath, that is. The *sisters*, that is . . . pinning him down near the meadows outside the Candorly farm and thrusting handfuls of pollen-packed posies into his face until he turned red and blew snot all over himself. It was their idea of torture.

"They do it because they love you," his mother would say. "You're their little brother."

Which was true for the five older ones, but not for the three who came after. They treated Colm like a child despite the fact that he was twelve already and taller than most of them (save the triplets, who were well into their teens). Only baby Elmira deigned to leave him alone, though she was nearly walking already and would soon join her sisters in their daily persecution of the only boy in the house. Already they used her to trick him, making her cry by pinching her legs so that he would come check on her, and then cornering him so they could braid his hair. Colm had learned to keep it cut short. A flop of wheat-colored locks trimmed close by his mother's only shears, hard to stick a ribbon in.

"Don't complain to me," Colm's father would tell him. "You only have to live with them. Try raising them. They are more cunning than wolves."

Some days, Colm would have preferred the wolves.

It was a daily gauntlet he was forced to run—the cutesy names and the rolling eyes, the stealing of his underwear (he once found it hanging on the fence for the whole village of Felhaven to see), the incessant giggling about nothing funny at all. Girls were like that, he discovered. Colm spent most of his time in hiding, lurking in shadows, escaping into the

2

nearby woods, always planning for his next escape. Tiptoeing through the back door. Hiding in the cupboard, scrunching his body and wedging beneath the usually empty shelves. Covering himself in leaves as a disguise and holding his breath as the gaggle of Candorly girls traipsed by. He could count on both hands the number of times they locked him in the cellar (fewer than ten, at least), until he taught himself to pick the lock using a hairpin that he kept hidden beneath the stairs.

Not that he was completely innocent. He teased them mercilessly at the table, where the presence of parents kept their retribution in check. He had learned to pilfer small items from his sisters' dressers and the secret wooden boxes they stashed under their beds. He had even learned to steal the pins and combs right out of their hair. He used these little treasures as collateral, wards against future torture. "Let me go and I will give you back your brush." "Give me back my pants or you will never see your rag doll again." He loved them, of course; they were his sisters, and the torment was just their idea of affection and family bonding, but it still taught him a few tricks in the arts of subterfuge and avoidance. With so many sisters, it was simply a matter of survival.

For Colm's parents, the challenge was of a different sort. Feeding a family of eleven on a shoe cobbler's salary required the most precarious balancing of coin. Rove Candorly, Colm's beefy, rough-skinned father, was an industrious man, handy with nail and awl, well respected by the villagers of Felhaven and many of the neighboring villages besides. Everyone in a twenty-mile reach enjoyed the comfort of a well-stitched sole, and the wax candles beside Rove Candorly's workbench always seemed burned to the nub from long hours he spent huddled over split heels and busted boot toes.

But it wasn't always enough, and the Candorly children, from Carmen down to little Elm, made do with what little they got. Each of the girls had precisely two outfits—though a shared skinniness not inherited from either parent allowed for trading between them. The rooms were cramped, the triplets commanding one, both sets of twins sharing another, and the baby cribbed alongside her parents. Only Colm had his own room—the benefits of being an unmarried man, his father told him—though it was little more than a closet, with just enough space for a hammock, a shelf, and a trunk. He had a window, at least, that he would often stare out of for hours. And his boots were in top-notch shape.

Still, for all of their wanting, the Candorlys found contentment. Mina Candorly and her capable daughters tended to the small garden and doted over the chickens and twin cows (most everything Candorly came out in twos or more). The older girls brought in extra coin through stitchcraft, and Cally, the fourth oldest (or fifth depending on how you looked at it) had discovered a hidden talent for baking, often spending the whole day in the kitchen whipping up concoctions to sell down on the square. Even Celia, the second to arrive of the second set of twins, did her best to keep the Candorly spirit up, though her mischievous smile and infectious laugh did little to fill the larder.

4

For his part, Colm helped his father when able. The hope was that someday soon Colm would apprentice with his father, and then would be able to take over the family cobbling business when Rove Candorly was no longer able. Colm was certainly nimble fingered enough for the cobbler's trade, lithe and lanky like his sisters, adept at picking up and tinkering with small objects. Colm was obviously cut out for finer work than farming or blacksmithing; his frame and mind-set called for something requiring concentration and dexterity. The problem was, he had absolutely no interest in shoes. He would stand at his father's workbench thinking only of the nasty, noxious, boil-crusted feet that the shoes were pried off from, and his stomach would churn. Colm's father had lost his sense of smell long ago.

Yet Colm knew he shouldn't complain. His parents were doing their best. There were many nights when he would sit and listen to them pooling the family's earnings, counting coin by coin. Often necessities turned into luxuries. Some nights Celia would sneak into his room and the two of them would eavesdrop, cheeks pressed to the wood door, eyes on each other, listening to the clink of copper on copper, followed by his father's gruff resignation.

"I think we might have to do without sugar this week," Rove Candorly said one night after they'd sent Colm and the girls to bed and Celia had tiptoed down the hall into Colm's closeted space.

"Cally will be disappointed," Mina Candorly replied. "I suppose we can send the girls to gather honey, though you

5

know how Celia feels about bees."

It was the same conversation as the week before, except then, instead of sugar, it was soap. And butter the week before that. There was always something they wanted and couldn't have. Beside him, Colm's sister shuddered. Her nearly strawberry-colored hair fell down the back of her nightgown, chaotically curled. During the day she always wore it up, bundled and tacked into place with her favorite silver butterfly pin, the only thing she owned of any real value. Celia was a firebrand, with a temper that didn't seem to come from either side of the family, and she was often the one found stranded in a tree that she was skilled enough to climb into but not out of, or torturing the chickens by chasing after them. She was once caught putting rotten eggs in the toes of everyone's shoes. Of all his sisters, Colm liked Celia best.

Celia turned and whispered to him, "I'm not going near any bees." Colm shushed her. She was so good at getting into trouble; she needed to learn better how to stay out of it.

"I just don't see how we will make it work." Colm's father sighed. "There are only so many feet in the world, Mina. And each of 'em only ever wears one shoe at a time."

"Then people will just have to start having more children so that you can shoe more feet," Colm's mother said brightly. Somehow his mother's voice was always cheerful, even when discussing dire subjects. Colm heard her drag the weary cobbler out of his chair, telling him there was nothing to be done about it tonight. Colm listened for their door, then turned and slumped against his own.

"It's not that I'm afraid," Celia said, slouching beside him. "I just don't like getting stung, is all."

"No. You're not afraid of anything," Colm teased her.

"I'm not afraid of *you*," she said, punching him in the arm. Then she gave him a fierce hug and slipped out of his room.

It didn't pay to fret, but on nights like these, Colm couldn't help but lie stretched out in his hammock and think about how unfair it was that there were nobles born with purses already in their fists, swaddled in fine silks and never needing to work in their whole life, while his father grew calluses on top of calluses mending shoes, hoping for a tip that didn't come as often as it should. Colm lay back and imagined a world where you didn't have to scrabble for every last coin. Where you could just take whatever you wanted whenever you wanted, without anyone the wiser.

He knew it was possible. There were tavern tales—though to Colm they sounded more like myths—of men and women, warriors, gallant knights, and studied wizards, who ventured far into the unmapped wilderness, into the caverns and hollows leading deep beneath the ground, to vast subterranean passageways riddled with no end of vile and nasty creatures— goblins and ogres and spiders so big they bit your head off to feed to their young and wrapped your body in silk for leftovers. Trolls and giants and wolves and dragons and warlocks and hundreds of other foul fiends that might give a grown man nightmares, all lurking in endless corridors capped with enchanted doors. A host of unspeakable horrors, all guarding the same thing.

Treasure.

Endless treasure. Gobs of it. Heaps of it. Silver and gold and gemstones that had never seen the light of day, mined and hoarded, kept in chests stacked twenty high. Colm had heard several stories of poor sots who ventured into dark and dangerous places and came back rich as lords.

Or didn't come back at all.

But to Colm, they were just stories. He had never met anyone who had even seen a goblin, let alone stolen its gold. Such places were far from Felhaven, some of them across mountain ranges or vast oceans, nearly impossible to reach. There was no fabled treasure to be had here, unless you counted the collection of worn stones that Elmira insisted could grant wishes. Once, several years ago, when he was first learning to help his father, a man had come in with a pair of well-worn boots in sore need of repair. He looked much like the characters described in Colm's stories, from the scabbarded sword to the scabbed knuckles and the sack thick with coin that he used to pay in advance. Colm was certain this man had seen the kinds of things he had only read about, but before he could ask, Rove Candorly had sent his son back to the house on some trivial errand. By the time Colm returned, the man was gone.

No, there was no hope of finding adventure here. There were no dungeons near Felhaven, not that he was aware of, anyways. There was no fabled treasure, only farmlands.

But there was money.

After all, not everyone had eleven mouths to feed. Some people only had the one, and had more than enough to feed it with. There were still lords and ladies in town with fat velvet purses, bags bursting with silver, dripping from belts like ripe apples. Gentlemen with billowing satin pants and pockets plump with gold. Girls with pearl necklaces too tight to be comfortable. He had seen fine gentlemen reach into silk bags so heavy they could barely hold them, just to give his father a single coin for a half day's work. Sometimes it just didn't seem fair how much of it was out there, sitting in pockets, gathering lint.

If only you could get it.

From the room next door, he heard one of his older sisters cough.

Seysha was sick.

She was the one heard coughing in the night. By morning she was shivering and sweating both. Mina sent the older set of twins to fetch Felhaven's resident healer, while Colm stood by Seysha's bed with the rest of the family.

It wasn't the first time. Seysha was one of the triplets—the second to emerge—and thus one of the three who suffered the most from strange illnesses. The rest of the Candorly clan was hardy as hickory, but the three oldest sisters were waifs. Skinny even by Candorly standards, and pale, hair more their

9

father's tarnished gold than their mother's fiery red. It was inevitable that every few months or so, one of them would fall victim to some infection and be bedridden for a week.

The healer would visit, trailing her wooden cart of unguents and herbs—garlic and ginger root and witch hazel and others with more potent properties whose names she never said. She would chant and blow smoke and generally fill the house with a noxious fog, and then she would give Colm's parents a jar of paste or a bottle of some black stuff the consistency of pudding and charge them a pocketful of silver. The old crone was no wizard—not that Colm knew what one of those looked like either—though her potions and poultices were worth the steep price.

It took most of the morning to find her. But hardly any time at all for her to work her own special kind of magic. Seysha would be fine, the healer said after she'd finished rubbing her chest and neck with some oily liniment and placed a cool cloth on her head. The medicine should be enough, but it was possible she might need more, that the illness could linger. Or that she might need something even stronger (meaning, Colm knew, even more expensive).

Colm saw the look in his father's eyes: relief that his daughter's ragged breathing had steadied, but soon replaced with other concerns. The money he paid for that little bottle of glurpy syrup could have fed the lot of them for a week. Rove Candorly paid the healer out of last night's meager stack, then kissed his daughter's forehead and ran all ten fingers through his bushel of hair. "I guess I'll be in the workshop," he said, and turned to leave.

Colm stood between his mother and oldest sister. He listened to his father slam the back door and head out to the barn. He would work until his eyes failed him and he started hammering his own fingernails. He would probably ask for Colm's help at some point, but maybe not. Rove Candorly was a proud man. He could handle any hardship. He would work clear through the night, mending every boot still sitting on the bench. Then he would travel into town to drum up even more business, pointing to floppy soles and busted stitching, offering a discount and promising a one-day turnaround. Colm had seen it before.

So many nights spent mending the holes in their socks, patching the holes in the roof, his father out at his bench, refitting the fine leather boots that noblemen had had made from deer hunted in their own private forests. This week the family would go without sugar and soap both. And probably butter and meat, unless his mother broke down and decided one of the chickens wasn't worth her eggs. He looked at Celia, hair carefully coifed already this morning, kneeling with her other sisters beside Seysha's bed. He wondered what would happen if she got sick. If they all got sick. There weren't enough busted boots in Felhaven to pay for that much medicine, and if there were, his father only had the two hands.

Colm looked down at his own hands, nine slender fingers, then back at his sisters. It wasn't fair, he thought to himself.

11

There had to be a better way.

"I'm headed out too," Colm said to no one in particular, then slipped away before his mother could say anything.

He went to his room, slid on his boots, and then escaped out the back door. He sneaked past the barn without his father noticing. It wasn't difficult. He had eight sisters who stalked him religiously. He was used to having to be stealthy. He was used to not getting caught.

On the way out, he deftly tucked an apple into his pocket for breakfast.

The town square was busy, as it always was during the day. Rove Candorly worked out of his home, but most of the merchants and artisans who settled in Felhaven had set up shop in the center of town. Straw-hatted farmers haggled over the price of wheat and carrots. Bakers, butchers, dressmakers, and perfumers ushered passersby through their doors with spritzes and tugs. Children much younger than Colm huddled together in the dirt, making up games that mostly involved chasing after pigeons. Today a minstrel had set himself up in the very center by the fountain and was strumming out some long-winded tale about a one-handed swordsman who wandered the world in search of the villain who had behanded him. Several dozen people crowded around to listen. Colm found an empty bench on the outskirts. The sun was working hard today, snaking its way beneath Colm's torn cloth shirt. And yet when he lay down tonight, he would shiver under his one blanket.

Colm sat and sweated and watched.

That was the first step, he guessed. To watch and take note. So many years of spying on his sisters had at least taught him patience. Riches weren't hard to spot, but Colm needed *accessible* riches. He started with the shoes. His father's voice rang in his head: there was a lot you could tell about a man from what he wore on his feet—the quality of the leather, the thickness of the fur. The clothes too, of course. Silks and felts and richly dyed linen instead of rough-hewn wool. Broad and billowing versus skintight and threadbare. He watched people laugh. Tried to get a look at their teeth. Gold fillings or iron or no teeth at all. The polish of the buckles latching their belts. The number of jewels cresting their knuckles. Ribbons or combs. Hair washed or unwashed. Makeup or not. Women who wore makeup were wealthy. Men who wore it, doubly so.

He watched for other things. Gaits and stances. Did they walk slowly, determined, aware of their surroundings, or did they hustle, pushing through the crowd, oblivious to the people they bowled over? Did they keep their eyes on their feet or in the clouds? Were their hands empty, or were they burdened with packages and bags? The more distracted the better, he decided. Also, he had to be able to outrun them. He could already outrun seven of his sisters. Only Kale, with her unnaturally long legs, could best him. No matter how it went, the most important thing was not to get caught. There were punishments for pickpockets, much worse than a sting from an angry bee defending its hive. You could wind up short a finger. Or worse.

Colm looked for swords. Those he wanted to avoid most of all.

He saw one man with an ax slung across his back, standing at least twice Colm's size. The man held a whole roast chicken in one hand and was tearing into it, spitting out only the bones too big to chew. He looked completely out of place here, and for a moment Colm wondered if he wasn't one of *them*—one of the ones he'd heard about. Colm considered just walking behind this man with his clinking chain-mail shirt and steel-tipped boots and picking up the scraps that fell from his beard. But chicken bones wouldn't pay for a second bottle of medicine. He needed silver, or gold, better still. The contents of one lord's purse would be enough to feed him and his sisters for a week.

The minstrel finished his song to much applause, and passed his hat around. As the crowd started to disperse, Colm finally found what he was looking for.

The man's nose was thrust up so high, he couldn't see what was standing right in front of him. His clothes gave the impression of a gentleman; his bone-white complexion suggested he spent most days indoors, far from hard work. He wore a red tunic and white tights. It was impossible to keep anything white for long in Felhaven, not without constant laundering, and soap was expensive. From one side of the man's belt hung a dagger, blade barely longer than his own hooked nose, and it was almost enough to convince Colm to keep looking. Except this man didn't look like he could use the knife for anything other than buttering bread. And besides, on the opposite side from the knife hung the purse, weighty and awaiting.

Colm watched for another moment. Then he slipped into the throng.

The man was walking quickly, shouldering his way through clusters of people, headed, it seemed, to the edge of the square, where the crowd was thinner. Perhaps he had finished the business that brought him here, the business that had fattened the sack tied to his waist. Not too tightly, Colm hoped.

Colm circled around, dodging carts, positioning himself, calculating the distance, keeping a sideways eye on the man's bobbing head. He would have a second. Maybe two. Any longer, and the man would notice. Colm flexed his four fingers and looked down at his boots, trying not to think about the cobbler who had made them. Instead, he thought of his sisters. Of Seysha sick in bed. Of Celia, who wrote little poems in her head because there was no paper to copy them to. Two seconds. That's all it would take. Then it would be over, and he would leave.

The gentleman was right in front of him now. Colm listed to the side. He felt a shoulder press against his own.

"Watch it, you little whelp!" the man said, his face set in a sneer, looking down the length of his barbed nose.

"Sorry, sir," Colm choked. "My apologies. Please excuse me."

Colm stepped away, turning, his hands behind his back. He offered a short bow. The man huffed once, then resumed his quick pace, wedging his way through the crowd.

And forgive me, Colm thought, stuffing his hand into his pocket, feeling the sudden weight of it.

The purse hadn't been tied that tight, after all, coming free with a single tug. And the man shouldering his way bluntly through the crowd didn't seem to notice. Colm stood there in the center of Felhaven, amazed at how easy it had been, how effortless. He hadn't even thought about it, in the moment; had just acted on instinct. He imagined what it might be like to fill his pocket, both pockets. To be so leaden with coin that he couldn't lift his feet. Imagined the look on Celia's face when he showed her what he had done.

Colm flexed his nimble fingers. Then looked around for more fruit to pick.

It was near dark by the time he returned, his breeches sagging, his feet sore, his heart thumping rapidly from the excitement of the afternoon. The house was quiet. Everyone was preoccupied with something. He could hear his mother in the cellar. The kitchen, at least, was empty.

He left it on the table. All of it. Or almost all of it, anyway. He didn't take the time to stack it, just poured it all out into one giant, tinkling pile. He kept one silver piece himself. Finder's fee, he thought, tucking it into his pants, into a secret pocket he had sewn there himself to hide trinkets from his sisters.

He paused a moment and looked admiringly at the shape of

it, that mound of silver and gold, how it reflected the last glint of the fading sun that poured through the wide front window. He hadn't bothered to count it. He only had the coin. The purses of silk and calfskin had been tossed into the river on the way home; he wasn't sure how to explain them. Of course, he wasn't entirely sure how he would explain the money, either, but he figured it would be easier without the purses.

Colm heard heavy footsteps coming from the cellar and retreated before his mother could find him there. He stopped and listened from behind his closed bedroom door. Maybe she would take it for a miracle. Some divine intervention. The gods repaying the Candorly family for all of their honesty and hard work. Maybe she wouldn't even ask where it came from.

Through the crack in the door, Colm heard his mother shriek, then yell for one of Colm's sisters to go and get his father from the barn. Colm almost ran out to her, but then he heard the clomping step of his father, followed by the scuffle of his sisters' soles on the wood floor. He heard them whispering over one another, their voices impossible to distinguish as everyone shuffled into the kitchen at once.

"What is it? Is it Seysha? Is she worse?" Colm's father asked.

"Seysha's fine," he heard his mother say, her voice barely more than a whisper. "It's—"

"What is *that*?" Rove Candorly said. Colm imagined him, eyes wide with wonder, standing at the back door with his cobbler's hammer hanging by his side, blisters already broken, apron stinking of glue.

"It looks like money, Papa." Meera, the third youngest, said. Colm cracked open the door farther, peering out with one eye. They were all standing around the table, just staring at the pile of coin.

"I *know* it's money. What I want to know is, where did it *come* from? Is this any of your doing?" There was a long pause, long enough for seven sisters to shake their heads. "You?"

"I have no idea," Colm's mother said.

There was another moment. Then the rafters shook as Colm's father yelled his name.

Colm opened the door and stood in the frame, hands tucked into his empty pockets.

His father knew. Colm could tell just by looking at him. He knew exactly where the money had come from. At the very least, he knew that Colm was responsible. Everyone else's gaze was fixed on Colm as well, but only his father's mattered.

"Is this yours?"

Colm swallowed. It seemed like a thorny question. Or at least a matter of perspective. "It's ours," he muttered.

"Where did you get it?" Rove Candorly's voice was cold. Colm wasn't sure what he expected. He had hoped for joy. Gratitude. Or at the very least, relief. But all he could sense in his father's voice was anger. Colm didn't want to say. He had hoped the answer to that question wouldn't matter, but to someone like his father, it was probably all that mattered.

"Answer me, boy!"

Colm steeled himself, suddenly unsure of his footing. *Getting* the money had been so much easier than explaining *how* he got it. He looked over at his sisters. They were no help. Not against their father.

"I found it," Colm squeaked finally.

"You *found* it?" his father echoed. He pointed to the mountain of coin on the table. "You just *found* this much money? And *where*, exactly, did you find it?"

Colm ran through the possibilities, but there were none his father would believe. He had lied to his father only once before, and his backside had smarted for three days after.

"Where?" his father demanded.

"At the town square," Colm said.

"Town square?"

"In a purse," Colm added a little quieter.

"In a *purse*?" his mother said.

"Well, several purses, actually," Colm murmured. "And a couple pockets." Five purses and three pockets, to be exact, though one of the pockets turned out to be full of stones and not coins, so it didn't count. The purses were much easier, for obvious reasons, but over the course of the afternoon Colm had found that he had a knack for emptying a pocket, especially if the breeches were baggy and the gentleman wearing them was oblivious.

Mina Candorly suddenly turned to her daughters. "Why don't you take your little sister and go outside and make yourselves useful? Your father and I need to talk to Colm for a bit."

Colm stole a sharp sideways glance at Celia before she was shoved out the door. Like their sisters, she looked confused, her eyes searching him, asking him questions. But she was the only one in the room with the hint of a smile on her face.

Colm stood there as his sisters closed the door behind them. He tried looking everywhere but at his father, whose face was like a radish, purpling with anger. His mother's hands were wringing an imaginary cloth. Colm noticed that all the girls had crowded around the kitchen window, angling for a view—their idea of being useful.

Rove Candorly stood quivering, one hand on the back of a chair, clenching it so hard, Colm was certain it would snap in two.

"You mean to tell me that you robbed people in the middle of town in broad daylight?"

Said out loud, it sounded terrible—and perhaps just a little impressive. Colm tried to frown, to appear remorseful, but somehow a smile crept out instead. His father slammed his fists onto the table. His mother jumped, and Colm could see the O's of his sisters' lips through the window. Colm stopped smiling and looked down at his feet.

"Do you know what the magistrate does to pickpockets?" his father roared, reaching out with his cobbler's hands and snatching one of Colm's, the one with all of its fingers. "They take your hand. Right here!" He pinned Colm's fist to the table, made a chopping motion just above his wrist. It didn't hurt, but it startled him. Colm's father had never grabbed him quite like that before.

"Please, Ro," Colm's mother pleaded. "He was only trying to help."

Colm didn't speak. He knew anything he said now would only make it worse. Besides, his mother had just said the only thing he could think of. His father shook his head and let go. Then he started to gather up the pile of gold and silver, scraping it across the table toward him. Colm rubbed his wrist and tucked both hands under his arms. "We have to go back," his father said. "Return all this money. I hope you memorized the faces of the poor people you stole from."

"They weren't poor," Colm muttered. Half of the purses he had swiped were from the belts of ladies and gentlemen who wore twice that much gold on their necks and fingers.

"That's not the point!" his father yelled.

Colm couldn't look his father in the face. He certainly couldn't tell him that it was *exactly* the point, even though he wasn't sure about that anymore either. His eyes kept coming back to the pile of coins, then up to the window and his sisters, looking like the crowd at a funeral procession.

"Rove," Mina Candorly intruded. "It's already dark out. You're not going to find anyone tonight. Let it wait till morning, and we will think of what to do with the money."

Colm turned and stared at his mother. The way she said it. *What* to do with it. As if there was a choice?

His father's mouth worked back and forth, like he was chewing leather. Then he growled like a wild dog and pointed a raw, rough finger at Colm. "First thing tomorrow, we are going to take this to the magistrate and beg for leniency. Then we will spend all day, if we have to, tracking down every single person you stole from and returning their money, along with an apology and a promise to work off the debt you owe them for their forgiveness."

Colm stood silent.

"Do you understand?" his father yelled.

"Yes, sir," Colm mumbled.

"Go to your room. No supper. You probably stole something to eat already today."

Colm wanted to protest. As a point in fact, he *had* passed by a fruit seller and noticed that several apricots had fallen beneath the cart, and he had actually helped the man gather them—he'd had no intentions of stealing from a peddler. Should he say something about that? Should he mention Seysha's medicine or the empty pantry? Say something about how he had gathered in only a few hours what it would take his father months to earn?

And how easy it had been?

Instead he blurted out, "I didn't get caught. Nobody saw me."

But apparently that wasn't the right thing to say, either.

"*I* caught you," his father said. "*I* know. And even if I hadn't, I'd hope your conscience would catch up to you eventually."

"Dad, I . . . ," Colm started to say, but his father raised a hand.

"I don't want to hear it right now. Just go."

Colm looked to his mother, who nodded. He noticed his

sisters' eyes on him. Celia gave him a sympathetic shrug.

Colm walked to his room and quietly shut the door.

That night his stomach hurt. He sat and listened to the din-nertime conversation, what little of it there was. His father had demanded that no one speak of the money or of Colm, which, apparently, was all any of his sisters wanted to talk about, so nobody said much of anything. When Elmira asked where Colm was, his father said, "Hopefully on his knees in his room, praying for forgiveness," and left it at that. After supper, the sisters were sent to their own rooms to read.

Colm listened to the doors close, then heard his mother scraping the dishes. Even over the rumbling of his stomach, Colm could hear his parents whispering about him, his father's voice still gruff but at least quieted.

"What was he thinking?"

"He was thinking he could help," his mother replied. "He's a smart boy. And resourceful. And it's not as if you make any attempt to hide our troubles, always griping about how much everybody eats, how much it costs to fix things, how there's never enough to go around." Colm heard the clatter of dishes being stacked on one another.

"That's still no excuse," Rove Candorly hissed. "I won't have my son skulking about like a scoundrel or some petty thief, dipping his fingers into pockets, fishing for coins. Where'd he even learn to do something like that, anyways? I'm certain none of his sisters taught him. You *know* what the penalties for thieving are."

23

Colm looked at his right hand. He had gotten used to being short a finger. In truth, it hadn't been much of a hindrance—there were very few things five fingers could do that four couldn't—and today being short a finger almost seemed a blessing, his one hand slipping more easily in and out of pockets. But to lose the whole hand? Colm tucked them both under his chin for safekeeping.

"What does it matter where he learned it?" he heard his mother say. "He's obviously good at it."

"Mina!" His father's voice rose, then lowered again. "You can't be serious."

"I'm only saying that it's remarkable, if you think about it. To pickpocket that many people in broad daylight and *not* get caught."

"You're not suggesting it's *admirable*, what he did? He stole from people. Innocent, hardworking people."

"Well, as to that, I'm not sure how innocent or hardworking every person in town is, not to speak of those sleazy merchants from upriver who charge twice what they should for half of what you need. And you tell me if you've ever seen a nobleman lift a finger to help someone beneath him. And no, I'm not suggesting it's a *good* thing. I'm just saying it's . . . *astonishing*. It's a shame that he can't put that talent to better use."

"Now it's a *talent*? Our son is a criminal, and you are singing his praises? You're incorrigible, woman."

"Lucky for me you're too stubborn to leave."

Colm held his breath, waiting for one of them to speak again.

When they did, it was his father's voice, its edge blunted. Now resigned and thoughtful.

"It *is* a lot of coin," he mused. "I wonder how much is there."

And then his mother's voice, an even softer whisper, nearly impossible to make out through the crack beneath Colm's door.

"Let's count it. Just to see," she said.

A few hours later, after the table was cleared and all the candles had been snuffed, Colm heard his door open a crack and saw a wooden bowl of cold, congealed stew pushed inside, a hunk of bread sticking out of the top like a plume. He caught the flash of long strawberry curls before they disappeared, and he thought that there was more than one thief in the Candorly house that night.

2

EVEN FEWER FINGERS

Colm's father was gone the whole next day, leaving a small pile of shoes waiting by his bench to be repaired. He was gone, and so were all the coins Colm had taken. Colm's mother said that his father had decided to go to see the magistrate without him, afraid that Colm might do or say something to make it worse. The magistrate was the authority on most things in Felhaven, mediating disputes and enforcing the laws, elected by the villagers and nobles alike and serving as the chief official—though it was said those with deep coffers could persuade him to more consistently see their point of view. The plan was to see what the magistrate had in mind for punishment and then bring Colm before him afterward to have it meted out.

Colm tried to picture the magistrate. He had seen him on occasion, during festivals and funerals. A large figure with a plump, pink face and jowls that sagged like a bloodhound's. He didn't seem intimidating himself, but he no doubt had intimidating men who worked for him. At least his father and the magistrate were on good terms; Rove Candorly always fixed the man's shoes for free.

Colm spent the day on his chores, trying to hide behind his work, dodging his sisters whenever possible. Not because they were being mean. If anything, it was the opposite. It took an evening of whispers among themselves, he guessed, but they understood what he had done, and more important, why. Kale and Carmen, the other two triplets, managed to corner him behind the barn, where they proceeded to smother him in hugs.

"It was stupid," they said.

"You shouldn't have done it."

"I've never seen Father so angry."

But also, "It was very sweet."

And "How *did* you do it?"

And "Don't worry. He'll get over it eventually."

The elder twins, Cally and Nila, promised that they would not let the magistrate touch one hair on his body and vowed to fight tooth and nail if some armed guard showed up at the door. Elmira called him a "widdle feef," but in such an admiring way that he didn't take the slightest offense. They all brought him oatcakes and tried to distract him, and left him alone when he asked. Colm tried to focus on what he was doing—weeding or milking—but his eyes kept coming back to the road leading from the house to the center of Felhaven. A road that his father would be coming back on. Maybe trailing the magistrate. Or someone worse. Someone with a butcher's blade.

He would have to give the money back. That he understood. It wasn't his to take, though one could make the argument that once he had it, it might as well have been his family's to keep. He would have to apologize. He imagined there might even be some kind of public spectacle. Maybe they would put him in the stocks. He could stomach that. As long as he could keep both of his hands. If he saw someone with a blade—like that man yesterday, with the ax across his back—Colm had already made up his mind what he would do. He just wasn't sure where he would go.

By midafternoon, everyone was quiet, and nobody was hungry for once. Colm's father had been gone too long. The walk into town was only a couple miles. The magistrate was a busy man, of course, but even at that, Rove Candorly should have been home by now. Colm's mother paced the kitchen, holding a rolling pin, ready to club anyone who dared take her only son.

"Maybe they are finding out who the money belongs to and just giving it back," she said to nobody in particular. "Maybe they don't even need an apology from you." But even through her airy voice, Colm could tell she didn't believe it. He finished his chores and escaped to his room, rubbing his wrist.

He found Celia sitting on his bed.

"I thought we agreed that *I* was the problem child," she said. She was very astute for a ten-year-old. Sharper than her twin sister, though not quite as pretty. Not that Colm thought of them that way. If cornered, he would tell you that none of his sisters was the least bit good-looking.

"Nice to have Dad mad at someone else for a change?" he asked.

Celia shrugged. Colm sat beside her, and she leaned over and settled her head down, the butterfly pin lighting on his shoulder. They both looked out the window at the road.

"What was it like?" she said softly. "I mean, how did it feel, when you took it?"

Colm shook his head, chin rubbing against her hair. He liked it when she leaned on him. It made him feel stronger than he really was. He thought back to yesterday afternoon in the square, the purse strings unraveling, the weight of the coin in his hands. He felt frightened, of course. And nervous. And guilty, he supposed.

But that was all before and after. At the moment, at the very moment when his fingers slipped into the satin pocket or cinched around the silk strings, Colm had felt nothing, only the smooth fabric on the pads of his fingers, only the hollow sound of his own heart beating in his ears. No fear. No guilt. Just the exhilarating rush.

"I don't know," he said, looking at his hands again, as he had a hundred times today. "I guess you can't do the wrong thing, even for the right reasons."

"Hmph," Celia said, taking his hands in hers. "I do things just because I *want* to do them."

She turned and glanced out Colm's bedroom window again, and her face blanched. Colm looked to see two figures walking up the path to the house. His father had finally returned.

And he wasn't alone.

There was the sound of footsteps on the porch outside. Muffled voices. Then the door opened.

Rove Candorly stepped in, his hands chapped with cold. He looked haggard; his eyes were creased with worry. Behind him stepped the second figure. It was certainly not the magistrate. It was someone Colm had never seen before. He was tall and gaunt, the antithesis of Colm's father. Clean-shaven and hollow cheeked, wearing a long brown cloak that covered a tunic of studded leather and black pants caked in mud. Black leather gloves hugged both hands, and a hood covered the top half of his head, concealing even his eyes.

Colm's own eyes went instinctively to the man's belt. There was no coin purse hanging there, but there was a sword. An ivory handle polished smooth and a blade, long and thin, like its owner. *That's the sword that will take off my hand,* Colm thought to himself. *And this is the man who will take it.*

He turned and looked at his mother's face, her own hands cupped to her mouth to find an armed man in her house. Behind him, Colm's seven sisters—Seysha was still bedridden for the day—formed a united front. Elmira sat on Kale's

30

shoulders. Colm remembered what the twins had said to him—*tooth and nail*—but he didn't want any of them getting hurt. They hadn't done anything wrong. This was all on him. He wouldn't let them get in the way.

"Mina," Colm's father said, rubbing his hands together and nodding toward the stranger. "This is Mr. Finn Argos."

The stranger pulled back his hood, revealing a nest of tangled black hair and penetrating blue eyes. A ragged white scar etched a jagged path across one cheek. He looked young, maybe halfway between the ages of Colm and his father, and save for the one mark, his face was alabaster smooth. He gave Colm a look, a flash that shot straight down the boy's spine into his bowels, then turned to his mother. His voice purred.

"It's just Finn," he said. "And please excuse the intrusion, Mrs. Candorly. I apologize for bothering you at this hour." Colm realized all his sisters were just staring at the stranger—the older ones with eyes low, lashes up. The stranger noticed as well. "And what a lovely family you have. Seven daughters?"

"Eight," Mina Candorly corrected. "I'm afraid one isn't feeling well."

The stranger shook his head in admiration. "Eight daughters. And each just as beautiful as their mother." He smiled, revealing a fence of polished teeth, most of them pearl, but punctuated by one each of silver and gold. It was the smile of a man who always gets what he asks for, often without even

31

asking. Colm's mother blushed, as did two of three triplets. Colm didn't like this man already. He seemed . . . slippery, somehow. Rove Candorly cleared his throat.

"Mr. Argos . . ."

"Finn," the stranger corrected.

"Mr. Ar—*Finn* has come a long way," Colm's father said. "I'm sure he's thirsty."

"Some wine would be much appreciated, if you have it," the stranger said. "Water, if otherwise."

Mina Candorly didn't move, but the four oldest girls tripped over themselves to find a cup. The stranger turned abruptly. "And you must be Colm," he said, removing his gloves. "A pleasure to meet you."

The stranger held out his hand and Colm took it tentatively, afraid that this Finn Argos might grab it the way his father had, then reach for his sword with the other, doing the deed right there in the kitchen, making a puddle of blood on the floor. But instead he just took Colm's hand in his own. Colm noticed the man's hands were warm, his fingers long and callused.

All four of them.

He was missing one. The last one. The smallest one. Was missing them on both hands, in fact; though judging by the thick spiderweb of tissue, you could tell that he had had them once, unlike Colm.

"I have you beat," the stranger said, holding up both hands and wiggling eight fingers. Nila handed the man a cup of water—Colm didn't know the last time his parents had been able to afford wine.

"You say you've come a long way," Colm's mother pressed, making no attempt to hide her unease. The magistrate's house was close to the town center. An hour by foot, if you walked slow and tossed stones along the way. How far did you have to go to find someone who could cut off a hand? Weren't there at least half a dozen butchers in Felhaven? Something didn't seem right.

"Yes, I'm afraid it is quite a trek from the castle."

"Castle?" Cally said.

"Are you a prince?" ten-year-old Meera added. Celia slapped her twin's shoulder.

The stranger laughed. "A prince? Hardly."

"But you must be a prince, if you live in a castle," Meera insisted, slapping her sister back.

"I assure you, dear lady, there are many that live in castles who have no claim to a throne. Just ask the men hanging in their dungeons. No. Point of fact, I am neither prince nor king. I am only a humble teacher." He took a sip of his water and flung another sidelong look Colm's way. Colm took a step back, tucking his hands into his pockets, making them harder to get to.

Mina Candorly cast a similar squinted look in her husband's direction. "A teacher of what, exactly?"

"Do you mind if I sit?" the stranger asked, pointing to the long oak table that barely held the lot of them for supper, even with Elmira sitting on her mother's lap. "A bit of a trek, as I said."

Colm's mother nodded and found a seat of her own. Colm's father sat as well. Everyone else stood, including Colm. He wanted to be able to bolt for the door. *Always be sure you can outrun them.* But one look at this mysterious Mr. Argos was enough to convince Colm that he wouldn't be fast enough.

"I teach lots of things," the stranger said, adjusting the hilt of his sword. "History. Economy. Engineering."

"Engineering?" Mina Candorly said.

The man nodded. "I am well versed in the inner workings of certain mechanical contraptions."

"That's a lot," Kale remarked.

"It keeps me in demand," the stranger replied.

"And what . . ." Mina Candorly paused, as if gathering enough breath to speak again. "What function do you serve for the magistrate, exactly?" Colm knew what she was asking. She was asking if he was here to carry out Colm's sentence, whatever it was.

The confident smile surfaced again. "I do not work for the magistrate of Felhaven," Finn replied.

"Then why—" Mina started to say, but stopped when Colm's father put a hand on her shoulder. He and the stranger exchanged looks.

"Perhaps, Mr. Candorly, I could take my cup to your porch. The stars are just starting to peek, and it's a nice view out here near the countryside. That might give you and Mrs. Candorly some time to converse."

"That would be most appreciated," Colm's father said.

Then the stranger turned to Colm.

"Would you like to join me?"

Colm could think of very few things he would like less. Stepping into the near darkness with this man and his two metal teeth, sword at his side, and only four fingers on each hand. Colm glanced over at Celia, then looked at his father. His father nodded sternly. He didn't have a choice.

The stranger grabbed his cup and held open the door.

"After you," he said.

Colm waited for the shackles. For the sack to be thrown over his head. For the thick rope to be slipped around his neck. But nothing of the sort happened. Instead, the strange Mr. Argos with the blue eyes and the single scar found one of the wood stools that Colm had helped his father build and pulled it across from the other, motioning for Colm to have a seat. Colm noticed the man had another blade strapped above his boot, tucked away.

"Eight sisters." The man whistled, shaking his head. Colm sat. The stools were uncomfortable—Rove Candorly was an expert on shoes, but a terrible maker of furniture. Finn Argos didn't seem to mind. Colm got the impression he had been in much less comfortable places. "I only had two sisters myself, and it was enough to make me run away from home when I was a boy."

"You ran away from home?" Colm asked.

"Five or six times," Finn replied. "I had trouble sitting still.

35

An adventurous spirit. Always on the move. Wore out several pairs of boots—your father could help with that, I imagine. When I was about your age, I ran away for good. Not *from* something, exactly, more *to anything*. I had heard stories growing up, of men who made their fortunes out in the wilds." The stranger waved a four-fingered hand at the horizon. "Who ventured out with nothing but a sharp sword and fierce determination and who came back rich as kings. Men—and women—who banded together to descend into the darkness for the promise of a better life. And I was determined to be one of them."

The man laughed at some joke that he shared only with himself. Colm smiled politely. He wasn't sure what to say. Outside of their missing digits and some annoying siblings, he and this man didn't appear to have much in common. Colm had never run away from home. And he certainly had no scars like Finn's, which gave his smile a sort of lopside effect, somehow adding to its charm.

And there was the fact that he was obviously here to punish Colm for what he'd done. This man was dangerous, that much was plain. Colm decided it was better not to say anything.

"I suppose you want to know why I'm here."

There was no good answer to that question. It all depended on what the answer to *that* question was. The man took Colm's silence as invitation to continue. "It's no small feat, fleecing a sheep, though admittedly easier when there's a herd of them. Still, six or seven purses? And in the daylight. With no training." He shook his head and whistled. "Granted you have small hands, but it's still impressive."

"Impressive?" Colm croaked.

"And illegal," Finn added, almost as an afterthought. "Completely illegal. *And* morally reprehensible, I'm sure. But still . . . impressive. You turned it *all* over to your father, of course. The money you stole?"

"Of course," Colm said, swallowing hard. Then he remembered the one piece of silver. Tucked into these same pants, one of only two pairs he owned. He instinctively reached his right hand to the pocket. The secret pocket that nobody knew about.

He panicked.

The pocket was empty.

Finn Argos cleared his throat. "Looking for this?" The man held the silver coin pinched between two fingers.

"Hey, that's mine!" Colm reached out for it but was much too slow. The man closed his fist and made a tiny gesture, then opened his palm again. The coin was gone. "Wait. How did you?" Colm began to say.

"First off, it seems rude to say, 'Hey, that's mine!' when we have just established that you stole it from someone else. It is only yours while it is in your pocket. So it was. Now it's not. Such is the way of the world. Second, we will have to work on your lying. Not that I recommend it, of course. In most cases the truth is preferable, though keeping your fool mouth shut is always the best plan of action."

"Can I get my coin back?" Colm huffed, then corrected himself. "Excuse me. Can I get *the* coin back?"

"I don't know. Can you?" The stranger's tone was light-hearted, but the expression on his face held a note of challenge.

Colm took a deep breath. Obviously this man wasn't here to chop off his hand or to take him away in chains, or he would have done it already. He would have heard his mother wailing from the kitchen or seen his seven sisters come pouring out the door to his defense. So then what was Finn here for? And how had he managed to get that silver piece from Colm's pocket without him knowing? Was it when Colm passed by him to come outside? And what did he mean, he was from a castle? There were no castles within a hundred miles of here, just one small village after another. Felhaven was about as far from royalty or adventure as one could get, and yet this man looked like he had seen his fair share of the latter, at least.

"*You're* the one who's lying," Colm said. "How about you tell me who you really are?"

"I told you, I'm a teacher . . . or more of a mentor, really."

"Of history?"

"And geography. Though admittedly my focus is on economics."

"Economics?"

Finn nodded. "Namely the acquisition of resources, shiny or otherwise."

"And engineering. Mechanical contraptions. What, like waterwheels? Catapults? Weaving looms?" Colm asked.

"More like locks, traps, and . . . more *complicated* locks."

Colm leaned forward on his stool, catching the glint of moonlight in the man's eye. Suddenly it dawned on him. "You're a thief," he whispered.

Finn raised a finger. "I prefer the title of *rogue*, if you don't mind. If I were an out-and-out thief, I would be laughing my hindquarters off as I slipped into the darkness with all of your family's valuables . . . though in this particular case," he added, taking a long look at the cramped and boxy house, "I'd come away disappointed. No offense."

A thief. No matter what he wanted to be called, it was clear that's what he was. It explained the two missing fingers. And the disappearing coin. But he obviously wasn't just any thief. Traps? Castles? Though his clothes were shoddy, the sword by his side looked finer than anything Colm had ever seen. But why would his father bring a man like this back from the magistrate's? Was this stranger supposed to set Colm straight about the dangers and depravity of a life of stealing? If so, this Finn wasn't a terribly good example. He seemed quite comfortable with himself. "So then what *are* you doing here?"

"I'm looking for new apprentices, actually."

"Apprentices?"

"Apprenti? I'm not sure how you say it. Individuals with certain . . . proclivities. Talents that often escape the attention of a more *traditional* education."

Colm shook his head. "So you run a school for thieves . . . I mean, rogues," he corrected.

"*I* don't run it. I'm just a member in fine standing. And it's not a school. Schools are for learning to read and write, and I presume you already know how to do both of those."

Colm nodded.

"Excellent, because there's no time for learning your alphabet where I'm from. It's not a school so much as an organization. And it's not just for rogues. We train all kinds. Warriors. Clerics. Mages—"

"Mages?" Colm interrupted. "You mean *wizards*?"

"Wizards. Sorcerers. Spellcasters. Call them whatever you like. Personally I don't associate with them more than I have to, but even I admit they have a certain value."

Colm rubbed his eyes. At first he had thought this man was one of the magistrate's lackeys, here to torture him or drag him away. Now he realized that Finn Argos was simply out of his mind. "Next thing you are going to tell me that you and your . . . apprentices . . . venture into caverns, fighting off trolls and unearthing chests of gold," Colm scoffed. He waited for Finn to laugh along with him.

"Actually, most trolls don't live in caves," the man said thoughtfully. "They tend to dwell in swamps or forests. And nobody buries gold, really. It's too hard to remember where you've put it. Much simpler to stick it in a vault and guard it with a hundred screaming, ax-wielding goblins."

Colm took in the expression on the man's face. Not a trace of a smile. "You're serious?"

"Deadly so," Finn replied.

Colm shook his head, bewildered. "And what exactly do you teach them? These apprentices of yours?"

"The only thing worth learning: how to get rich." The rogue took the last swig from his cup, setting it on the porch beside him. "And how to share and work together and all that warm and fuzzy stuff. It's a joint enterprise. We have to work together. It's the only way any of us ever gets out alive."

Finn Argos leaned back on his stool and cracked his knuckles. "And now we get to the part where you ask what this has to do with you and your little venture in the village square yesterday. You see, I was fortunate enough to be at the magistrate's when your father arrived. I heard the conversation, and I offered a solution that seemed to satisfy all parties involved."

"A solution?"

"Yes. I offered to pay off your financial obligation to those you wronged, including additional compensation to the magistrate for his leniency, all in return for an opportunity."

"An opportunity?" Colm could do nothing but echo the man's words. Did this mean he wasn't in trouble? That he wasn't going to lose his hand? What had his father promised this man?

"A chance to get your coin back," Finn said, again holding the piece of silver between his two fingers as if it had been there all along. "You see, Master Thwodin is always on the

41

lookout for promising individuals, those he thinks might be a good fit for our program. Based on your performance yesterday, I'd say you have potential. Therefore, I propose we take a journey, you and I. Won't take more than a day. I've already discussed it with your father, and I assume he is in the process of clearing it with your mother. One day, during which I challenge you to get this piece of silver. If you don't, I will simply give it back to you and see you safely home."

"And if I do?"

The man named Finn flashed his silver and gold teeth again. "If you do . . . let's just say that someday there will probably be a story written about you."

He made a flickering motion with his four fingers, and the coin disappeared again.

There was more. So much more. There were papers to sign. Logistics to be arranged. But most of it would have to wait. It all hinged on what Colm decided. He could either accompany this Finn Argos on his journey back to this castle of his and learn what the man had to offer, or he could go face the magistrate and accept whatever punishment the governing head of Felhaven chose to mete out. If he went with Finn, then all charges of thievery would be dropped. Colm could keep both of his hands, and the Candorly name would not be smirched. If he didn't, Finn didn't know what would happen.

Colm wasn't sure what choice he had.

When Colm walked back into the house, he saw his mother

had been crying. She came up to him and crushed him in her arms, squeezing over and over as if she were kneading dough. His father stood behind her, frowning.

"Where's Mr. Argos?"

"He figured our quarters were a little cramped already. He said he would find a place to sleep for the night and then come back in the morning."

Colm's sisters huddled together in a bundle around the table. Celia was the first to look him in the eyes.

"What did he say?" she demanded. "What's happening? Is he going to take you away?"

Colm considered telling them everything. That the stranger who appeared at their door was a thief who was not a thief. That there really were goblins and trolls and dungeons filled with chests of gold and many other things that they had heard about but never seen before. And that this rogue had promised to teach Colm how to get that gold.

But he could see in the bite of her lip, the color drained from her cheeks, she was worried enough. So instead he told them only what they wanted to hear. That everything had been taken care of. That they had nothing to worry about.

And that he would come back soon.

3

THE BALLAD OF TRENDLE TREEBAND

The next morning Colm woke up before everyone, including Elmira, who usually beat the sun to the start of day. He washed as best he could in the premorning gloom and put on his cleaner pair of pants and less-tattered shirt. He double knotted his laces and tucked his spare pair of socks into his pocket. He had no idea how far he was going or what the journey entailed, but it never hurt to have a change of socks. Then he lay in bed and waited for the house to stir.

He wondered if it wasn't all a dream. The cloaked stranger coming to visit them last night, filling Colm's head with stories, insisting he could repair the damage Colm had done. Even better, that he might someday make Colm rich. It sounded too good to be true, which, Colm had learned, meant not only that it was, but that the reality might bite him where he sat.

But it wasn't a dream. There, right outside his window,

Colm saw that same man making his way up the road. He moved with a surprising swiftness, Colm noticed, tending to gravitate toward the shade—the shadow of a wagon, the canopy of a tree, the long silhouette of the house—as if he couldn't bear to be in the rising sun. Colm watched him slink up to the porch. Heard his knock on the door. Heard his mother's voice.

"Mr. Argos," she said, bright as polished steel. "You're just in time for breakfast."

Colm opened the door of his bedroom to find everyone seated at the table already. His father and all eight sisters. It was the first time he'd seen Seysha out of bed in two days. She looked better, though she still huddled in two layers of blankets and her plate was empty. Obviously she had insisted on coming downstairs to say good-bye. All the girls were glancing back and forth from Colm to the man standing in the doorway. Colm had never gotten such concerned looks from the whole lot of them before. He took a moment to revel in it.

The rogue smiled at Colm, then turned and gave a humble bow to his mother. "It smells divine, Mrs. Candorly, but I'm afraid Colm and I have a long journey ahead of us. It might be best if the boy takes his breakfast with him."

Colm's mother's face fell. "Oh," she said. "Very well, then," and she glanced at Colm before turning and rummaging through her cabinet for some food that might travel better. "I'll just pack a bag."

45

Rove Candorly rose from his seat at the head of the table and bent down to inspect Colm's boots. His mother with the pantry. His father with the boots. His sisters whispering and tittering to one another. They were all looking for comfort in the things they knew best.

Colm's father inspected the laces. Lifted one boot up and then the other, checking the heel, flicking the steel-tipped toes. "Seem all right to me," he said, straightening himself. "Yes. They're good," he said. "Quite good. They should hold up." He put his hands on Colm's arms as if making sure he was solid too: no holes or frayed ends, no parts needing to be nailed or glued together. "All good," Rove Candorly concluded, then turned to the girls, who instantly stopped their twitter. "Aren't you going to say good-bye to your brother?"

There was an uncomfortable silence, as if each of the sisters dared the others to speak first. Naturally it was Celia who said something, but it wasn't to Colm. It was to the man by the door.

"Mr. Argos," she began. She was only ten, but looking at her now, Colm might have guessed her to be the oldest of the eight. So calm and determined.

"Please, you can just call me Finn."

"Fine, Finn. I want to know, is it dangerous, this place you are taking our brother?"

The rogue pursed his lips, considering the question. He struck Colm as a man who carefully considered everything: Which table he took in a tavern. How much of his face to show in public. Which side of a cup to drink from.

Which pocket to keep a pilfered piece of silver in.

"I've found that, in most cases, it's not the places themselves that are dangerous, but the people who inhabit them. So no, the place we are going won't pose any threat to your brother."

"But there might be danger somewhere, maybe somewhere along the way, perhaps. After all, you carry a sword. Men who carry swords are obviously afraid of *something*."

Colm's father told Celia to hush, but Finn was laughing.

"Too true, Miss Candorly, and I would be lying if I said that I was fearless."

"You might be lying about everything," she snipped.

"Celia!" her father barked.

"Rove!" Mrs. Candorly scolded.

But in response, Finn took two steps toward Celia, knelt down before her, and took one of her hands between his gloves.

"You are wise beyond your years, Celia Candorly. But I make you this promise: I will look after your only brother with the same ferocious devotion that you would yourself."

Celia leaned in and whispered something in the rogue's ear that Colm strained to hear but couldn't. Finn nodded, then kissed her hand and stood up. He turned to Colm. "I will give you a moment," he said, looking over the full table. "Or maybe ten. When you've said your good-byes, I'll be right outside." Then he bowed to Colm's mother and father in turn and moved swiftly toward the front door, where he paused. "The difference between a good-bye and a bad one is in thinking there's a hello at the end."

Finn closed the door, and on cue, all of Colm's sisters rose from the table and swarmed him. Even Elmira, sensing the occasion, grabbed hold of one leg and latched on. There was a flurry of questions. Would they see him tomorrow or next month? (He didn't know.) Where exactly was this castle that Finn was taking him to? (Finn couldn't say.) Would he get a sword too? (Maybe; he hadn't really thought about it. Which was, in fact, a lie. He had thought about it all last night.)

There were a dozen more. But none of the answers really mattered, Colm knew, because he didn't really have a choice. He had to go. So he hugged them each in turn, spinning Elmira around twice for good measure. He had been smothered in his sisters' kisses before, but always as a form of torture. This time he didn't mind as much.

When he came at last to his mother, she handed him a thick wool hat and a small burlap sack full of food.

"Keep your cloak wrapped and stay out of the wind. Don't go stomping in puddles—you'll only dampen your socks. Be sure to eat, even if you're nervous. And no matter what happens, you let us know, somehow or other." Colm shrank under the weight of another crushing embrace.

His father held up his empty hands. "I wish I had something to give you. An heirloom or something. Maybe something to protect you." Colm thought of the hatchet they used to make kindling, thought of the dull knife his mother used to

48

slice potatoes. He imagined his father handing over the knife, reverently: "Your grandfather used this butter knife, and your grandfather's father, and his father before him. Wield it well, Colm Candorly, and may your bread never be eaten dry."

Instead, Rove Candorly leaned in close, whispering. "Watch out for that Finn fellow, understand? Be polite. Do what he asks. But at the first sign of trouble, you get away from him, you hear? You run as fast as you can and find your way back home. I don't care what the magistrate says."

Colm nodded, then clasped his father's hand. Behind him, Cally and Nila whimpered in unison. Colm made for the door before his mother could catch hold of him again. He heard his sisters telling him they loved him, probably even meaning it this time. Outside, he took a few faltering steps, as if imitating Elmira's wobbling gait. He looked back to see everyone standing in the door or the open window, watching.

Finn was preoccupied, staring at the pattern of veins along a leaf. He let it drift lazily to the ground when Colm approached. "They act like they'll never see you again," he said.

"I know," Colm said, faking a laugh. "Silly, isn't it?"

"There's nothing trivial about a family's devotion," Finn replied.

"Don't eat wild berries!" his mother shouted to him through the open door. "Watch out for wolves. Don't take food from strangers! And for gods' sakes, be careful!"

"She's a worrier," Colm muttered.

"She's a warrior," Finn corrected. "Anyone who can have

as many children as you have fingers is a force to be reckoned with." He turned and bowed to Colm's mother once more, then pushed Colm forward, giving him the momentum he needed to take the next step.

They walked to the dirt road, taking it the opposite way of the town square, which meant the opposite of every time Colm had ever traveled that road. He wasn't entirely sure what was out this way. More villages. Then woods. Mountains. And apparently, somewhere, castles. Colm didn't dare look back at that moment, afraid he would lose his nerve and run back into the house, so instead he looked at his new companion. The rogue was humming softly to himself.

"Mr. Argos?"

"Finn."

"All right. Finn. I don't mean to pry, but what did my sister whisper to you back there?" Colm thought of the deadly look on Celia's face.

Finn fingered the hilt of his sword and smiled. "She said if anything happened to you, she would hunt me down and kill me herself."

"I'm sure she meant it. My sisters can be vicious."

"One thing you should know about me, Colm Candorly. I never make a promise that I can't keep."

"There's a difference between *can't* and *won't*," Colm said.

Finn looked over at Colm and then laughed.

"Oh, yes. You are going to make a very good rogue."

★ ★ ★

They walked in silence for a ways, Colm nervously shifting his pack from one shoulder to the other, finding comfort in the fact that he could still make out the speck of his house on the horizon behind him, Finn continuing to hum quietly. He seemed to be a man perfectly at ease by himself, nearly oblivious to the fact he even had a companion. At one point Colm looked over and saw the rogue cutting an apple with the dagger from his boot. Finn licked the juice from the blade with a tongue nearly as pointed and popped the slice into his mouth.

"Want some? It's yours," he said, holding the half-eaten apple toward Colm. "Technically, it *was* yours."

Colm pulled open the bag around his shoulder. His mother had packed bread, figs, and a sizable hunk of cheese. There had been three apples. Now there were only two. "But how did you? I mean . . . it was on my back the whole time." Not that Colm minded sharing—it was more the audacity of the thing. And the skill. "You could have just asked, you know," he said.

"And I should have," Finn replied with a nod. "I've broken the very first rule."

"The first rule of what?"

"The first rule of being a rogue. Do not steal from your own kind unless it is absolutely necessary."

"From my own kind?"

"Men, of course . . . and women . . . and children, for that matter, though anyone who steals from children is less than human."

At least Finn didn't consider Colm to be a child. "Then who do you steal from?" he asked, but Finn put up one of eight fingers.

"Just listen; there will be plenty of time for questions later. Corollary to rule number one," he continued, pointing the tip of his knife at Colm. "You *may* steal from your own kind if the thing being stolen is rare or unique or cannot otherwise be acquired through more honest means, apples excluded."

"Rare or unique?"

Finn shushed him. "Subcorollary to corollary one. *Honest,* by definition, includes bartering, persuading, sweet-talking, swindling, and winning through games of chance or feats of strength and skill."

"Wait, how is swindling . . ."

"Ah ah ah! Rule number *two.* Never . . . ever . . . steal from your fellow adventurer. There is nothing worse than pilfering from a comrade or cheating him out of his fair share. Such an offense is tantamount to treason and punishable by death."

"Did you say *death*?"

"Unless, of course, your fellow adventurer is a jerk, at which point you can ignore rule number two . . . and rule number one, for that matter, and go straight to rule number three. If you are going to steal, steal from people who deserve it or who won't notice. Preferably both."

Colm shook his head, already lost. He wondered how long it had taken the townspeople he had pickpocketed to notice their purses were gone. He didn't think they deserved it, but he didn't think they'd be too put out, either. Did that mean it was all right to do what he had done, at least according to *this* man?

"Rule number four," Finn continued. "Always check for traps. Naturally, this requires some extensive training, but it usually falls to our profession to do the disarming. And believe me, you do *not* want to get an earful from a barbarian who's just had his face scorched by a fireball that he triggered because *you* weren't paying attention."

"*Our* profession . . ."

"Rule number five. Stay behind the big fellow. Of course, all parties are different, but indubitably there will be a shield of some sort, someone to soak up the brunt of the damage. Maybe it's a knight or a paladin or just some hulking mass of muscle with a peanut for a brain but a club the size of an oak tree—doesn't matter. Just stay behind him. Let him do most of the work. Help out where you can, but be stealthy. Dart in. Dart out. Stay in the shadows."

"What kind of work are you talking about?"

"Corollary to rule number five. If the situation calls for sneaking, skulking, or general skullduggery, never *ever* let the big guy do it. Most of them are dolts who think with their sticks, and if they aren't dolts, then they are self-righteous, chivalrous windbags who think they can solve all the world's problems with a lengthy speech and a sharp piece of metal. They simply aren't made for stealth."

"Skull digging what now?" Colm was feeling light-headed.

He wanted his apple back. And his coin.

"Rule number six—and this is more of my own personal rule. Give the mages some space. They are unpredictable at best, and a downright liability at worst. Sure, at a certain proficiency they can be quite powerful, but more often than not, you're going to find yourself caught in a stinking cloud of miasmatic fog that your own companion created, barely able to breathe."

"So asthmatic fog is bad . . ."

"Miasmatic. Please try to keep up. Rule number seven. Learn to share, even if you don't like it. Just because *you're* the one who disarmed the trap and sneaked past the guards, silenced the alarm, put the dragon to sleep with a draft, *and* broke through the locks on the chest, that does not give you the right to just take everything inside. You work as a team. And if you don't spread the loot, there will be consequences."

"Consequences?"

In answer Finn just held up his hands, spreading the fingers he had left. It looked like he was trying to wiggle the stubs. He smiled graciously.

"But how are you working as a team if you are just sneaking around doing your own thing all the time?"

Finn rubbed his chin thoughtfully. "We each have our part to play, Colm. We all bring something to the party. Like fingers," he said, splaying his own again. "You can hold a sword between thumb and fore, but you'll drop it with the first swing. It takes all five to clutch it tightly—or in your and my case, maybe just four."

Colm shook his head. This man, this rogue, seemed to talk *around* things more than *about* them, answering in riddles and leaving Colm more lost at the end than at the beginning. Colm stopped in the road and dug his fists into his hips. He wasn't going to take another step until he had some real answers.

"What are you even talking about?" he shouted. "Who even came up with these rules? And . . . what are you *talking* about?"

Finn looked taken aback. "I'm talking about your future, Mr. Candorly. I'm talking about becoming a dungeoneer."

Dungeoneer. Colm let the word sit on his tongue for a moment. He had never heard that particular name before, but he could guess at its meaning. What Finn called *dungeoneers* Colm had always called *adventurers* and his father had always called *fools.* He had never met anyone who actually did that sort of thing, only heard about them, read about them, fantasized about them. He didn't know they had a name. "You mean *you* . . ."

"Me." Finn smiled proudly. "And you too, provided you're interested." The rogue patted his side. "*And* you pass your test."

Colm's eyes went instinctively to the pockets on Finn's breeches.

"Still plenty of time to get that silver back, Colm Candorly. We aren't even out of Felhaven yet." He started down the road again, and Colm ran to catch up.

"I still don't understand," Colm said.

"Of course not. You've spent your entire life under a shoe cobbler's roof in a backwater village. You've only heard of people like me through tavern tales and candlelit ghost stories. You've probably never even seen a troll in your life."

Colm shook his head.

"Count your blessings—the pinnacle of ugliness, trolls. But you aren't the only one. We all had to start our education somewhere. Ever heard of Tye Thwodin?"

"Maybe," Colm said, though in truth he had never heard that name in his life. He just didn't want Finn calling him backwater again.

"Absolutely must work on the lying," Finn remarked. "Well, then, I suppose I should start at the beginning." Finn slowed his pace a step. Colm slowed to stay a step behind him. "The first thing to know about Tye Thwodin," Finn said, "is that he wasn't always rich. He started as a black-smith's apprentice, soot faced and thickheaded. When he wasn't bent over the anvil, he spent his hours wandering the woods outside his village of Stonewood, bordering on the Stormforge peaks."

Those, at least, Colm had heard of. His father had shown him a map once that stretched far beyond Felhaven and its neighboring villages, and Colm had traced the ragged path of the mountains and their inked-in caps. They seemed so much closer on the parchment, but Rove Candorly said he'd gone his whole life without ever once seeing them, and had no regrets.

"Those mountains are dangerous," Colm said, remembering something else he'd heard. Another story. Probably like the one Finn was just starting to tell.

"To be sure," Finn said. "There are tunnels coursing through their bellies, tunnels filled with all manner of things unseen by most of us. And unseen by young Tye Thwodin too, until he fell into a sinkhole and found himself surrounded by darkness, all alone.

"Armed only with his blacksmith's hammer, he groped his way along the passage until he came to a large, torchlit chamber littered with rotting wooden chests, each of them packed with precious, glittery gems. Being a poor blacksmith's apprentice, Tye followed his instincts, stuffing his pants as full as he could. He tucked jewels into his boots and hid them in his cheeks and under his tongue, wherever he could find a place to stash them.

"Then he grabbed a torch and turned back to the tunnel—to find his way blocked by an ogre. Full grown, ten feet tall, nothing but a giant stone in its hand, but more than enough to crack Tye's egg-shaped head. The ogre came for him, growling and swinging, and Tye did his best to ward him off, the torch in one hand and his hammer in the other, smashing the creature one solid blow across its boil-crusted jaw." Finn took a swing with his dagger in imitation, and Colm put another foot of space between the two of them. "But it wasn't enough. The ogre was too strong, and Tye was weighed down with all the loot he had taken. He tripped and fell and was just about to have his brains made into pudding when an arrow buried itself in the ogre's back.

"In the torchlight, young Tye could make out four figures, each of them armed, wearing everything from rune-etched robes to full plates of armor. And at the front of the pack stood a man in a sweeping black cloak holding a bow, a second arrow already nocked. The stranger asked for Tye's name and how he had happened upon this place. And if he was alone. Tye said yes, and all four of them laughed.

"'Then you are more thickskulled than that ogre,' the man with the bow said. 'Even a fool knows better than to venture beneath these mountains alone.' Then he asked if Tye had taken anything from the chests. The blacksmith's apprentice found it difficult to speak with all the emeralds in his mouth, which caused the stranger to laugh. He demanded that Tye empty his pockets, and his boots, and his cheeks. Then he gave over one spit-covered ruby, folding it into Tye's palm, saying that it was his first taste and that he'd never be rid of it. That it was in his blood now, and he would be haunted by the desire to descend for the rest of his life. Then the stranger with the bow pointed back down the tunnel, explaining which way to get to the surface, and warning Tye not to try and follow them.

"Tye learned two important lessons that day. One, there was more wealth to be had in a year of dungeoneering than a lifetime of smithing. And two, four blades were better than one. From that moment on," Finn said, "Tye Thwodin gave up being a blacksmith's apprentice and studied the art of dungeon delving, traveling the lands in search of treasure and of companions to aid him in his adventures. Eventually he took all the knowledge he acquired—and a good bit of the gold—and formed his own guild. The first of its kind. A place where those of a certain disposition could go to study, to learn the tricks of the trade. To become dungeoneers themselves."

"So let me get this straight, this school of yours—"

"It's not a school," Finn corrected.

"Fine, then. This guild. Whatever."

"And it's not mine," Finn interrupted.

"All right. This *guild* that you *work* for. They train people like me to venture into deep, dank, monster-infested dungeons—"

"And booby-trapped. Don't forget booby-trapped."

"Monster- *and* trap-infested dungeons in the hopes of stealing—"

"Retrieving," Finn amended.

"*Retrieving* buried treasure?"

Finn shook his head. "How many times must I tell you? Not buried. Locked away in vaults and guarded by huge, hulking, brutish, snot-covered creatures with necklaces of human bones and a stench that you can taste, wielding giant clubs studded with hollow iron spikes to let the blood flow easier. Or some such."

Colm pursed his lips. "Right. And these dungeoneers . . .

there are a lot of them? People like me?"

"Like you. Not like you. But most of the dungeoneers we train are young. Master Thwodin likes to get 'em started early."

"And you've actually *been* to one of these dungeons yourself?" Colm prodded.

Finn held up all the fingers on one hand, seemed to remember that it wasn't enough, then put up a finger on the other. "Five so far. But I've only officially been in the business for a short time. There are some at the guild who have explored ten times that many or more. Master Thwodin, of course . . . and some others. But it only takes one." The rogue licked his lips. "One moment when the door swings open and you bury your fingers in all that precious, gleaming good stuff, and just feel the weight of it, the cool electric tingle, the showering waterfall *clink* of it pouring down . . ." Finn's eyes seemed to glaze over.

Colm tried to picture it. All that gold. Enough so that his family would never have to worry about buying sugar again. Enough that they could build a bigger house. Enough that his father could quit his work as a cobbler, though Colm was sure he never would. It was in his blood, the same way that dungeoneering had somehow gotten into this Tye Thwodin's.

"There's plenty to be had, if you know where to look," Finn continued. "Though by the time Tye takes his share and you distribute the rest among your fellow adventurers, it never seems to last as long as you think it will."

Colm was about to ask another question when Finn's hand latched onto his arm. The rogue hissed for silence and cocked his head. Colm could hear it too.

Hoofbeats.

It was only a moment before the horses producing them appeared from around a bend of trees. Three men approaching. Colm didn't think much of it. There was only the one main road through Felhaven—not that there was much cause to go through Felhaven, but people sometimes did.

Finn had a different reaction. The man's face went white, and he quickly pulled up the hood of his cloak. "Don't say a word," he commanded.

"What?" Colm asked.

"Not even that one," Finn barked, then put a hand on Colm's elbow as they started walking slowly forward, staying to the side of the road, Finn ordering Colm to stare at his feet. Before looking down, Colm noticed that each of the approaching men wore bits and pieces of chain mail and leather—not quite armor, but enough to suggest that they had seen the business end of a blade before. Each rode with a sword on his hip as well. Colm wasn't sure what was happening, but he could tell by the grip Finn had on his elbow that it would be best if these three men passed without a word.

And for a moment, it looked like it might happen. Then the lead rider, a man with little hair save for a pointed flame-colored beard like a spearhead, pulled his gray stallion around.

"Trendle Treeband?" he asked, pointing a finger at Finn. "Is that you?"

Finn made as if he were going to keep walking, even hurried his step. Colm hurried alongside him. The man on the gray horse drew his sword.

"You there," he ordered. "A word."

Finn stopped, kept his hand around Colm's arm. "Let me do the talking," he whispered. Colm nodded eagerly as the horseman and his two fellow riders circled back around, all three facing Finn now, Colm standing behind him. The one in front rubbed his bald head with one gauntleted hand but kept the sword pointed at Finn.

"I'm afraid you have the wrong man," Finn said from beneath his cloak, his head hung low enough that the hood covered his face. It didn't stay there long, however, as the tip of the man's sword caught the front of the hood and peeled it back, revealing Finn's black coils and azure eyes. The eyes, Colm guessed, were a dead giveaway. Though giving away what, he wasn't sure.

"I *knew* it was you," the man with the orange beard said. "I saw that curly mop of hair and that little prancing step of yours from down the road, and I said to myself, 'Well, look what we have here. It's our old friend the tale teller.' How long has it been, Trendle? Three years?"

Colm stepped forward. He knew what Finn had said, but obviously there had been some mistake here. "Excuse me, sir. But you have the wrong man. This is F—*frwmrm fwmmwm.*"

62

Finn's hand clamped down tight over Colm's mouth. It tasted like salt and stolen apple.

"Trust me, boy." The bearded stranger laughed. "I wouldn't forget the face of the man who cheated me out of two hundred silver pieces."

"Technically, I didn't cheat you. You lost," Finn said.

"At a rigged game."

"There was still some small chance of you winning." Finn pinched two fingers together to indicate how small.

The man laughed. Finn did not. Colm saw the rogue's other hand inch a little closer to the ivory handle of his sword. Colm's stomach suddenly filled with worms.

"You know, they made up a song about you back in Stormgeld," the man with the sharp beard said. "'Be wary of Trendle Treeband. Only four fingers, but the quickest hands. He'll promise you silver and gold by the sack, then strip the shirt right off your back.'"

"That's not bad," Finn said, but found his words cut short by the edge of a sword balanced precariously on the tip of his nose. The other two horsemen drew their swords as well. Colm took another step back, then looked down the road, remembering what his father had said to do at the first sign of danger. This was definitely a sign, but there was no way he could outrun three men on horseback.

"I'd ask if you have the money you owe me, but I'm sure you've already spent it on wine or worse. Besides, at this point, I'd much rather have your head," Orange Beard said.

He didn't appear to be joking.

"The money would do you more good," Finn protested. "Severed heads have such limited utility, and a surprisingly short shelf life. Really, they are only good as conversation pieces for a day or two before the rot sets in—"

The sword pressed in tighter, shutting Finn up.

"You always were a talker, Trendle. Thankfully for you, I'm not a murderer, or a bloody thief like you. So I think instead I'll just tie some rope around those skinny wrists of yours and drag you to the magistrate at Felhaven and turn you in. Maybe there's a reward for you out there somewhere. You and your . . ." He looked at Colm and spit. "Accomplice."

Finn leaned back and shook his head, the man's sword still less than a finger from his face. "I'm afraid I can't let you do that," he said. "You see, I promised this boy's sister that I would take care of him. If anything should happen to him, she will hunt me down and strangle me with her bare hands, along with her sixteen other sisters." Colm flashed him a look, but Finn ignored it. "So instead I'm going to have to ask you to let bygones be bygones and allow this boy and me to pass."

Colm stared, slack-jawed, at his companion—with a sword at his throat, held by a very angry man with two more armed men behind him. The rogue didn't seem to be in any real position to make requests. And yet there he stood, polite but defiant.

"How about this?" the bearded man said. "How about I let

the boy go. We *skip* the trip to the magistrate. And you draw that pretty little sticker you have there, and we find out if it's half as sharp as your tongue?"

Finn looked at Colm. His casual smirk suggested he was bored by the whole exchange, but there was a spark in his eye, a suggestion.

"You'll want to duck," he hissed. Then he twisted sharply, bringing his left arm up against the bearded man's blade, striking it away with a dull, hollow ring. In the same motion, he freed his own sword, spinning and lashing out, parrying a blow from his attacker and making a lunge of his own that just missed the man's leg.

"Get him!" Orange Beard commanded.

The horses reeled. Colm heard a grunt, saw a blur of steel sweeping toward him, then felt his own feet kicked out from underneath him. He collapsed to the ground as the blade passed overhead, missing him by inches but catching Finn's forearm again, where it stopped cold. Finn was the one who had tripped him, he realized, bruising his back but saving his neck.

"I told you to duck!" Finn shouted, then spun and parried, blocking blows from all three riders now, who circled and slashed at him. Colm watched from the ground as the rogue bobbed and leaped and struck out with his ivory-handled blade, seeming to cut at the flank of the lead gray horse. The blow missed, however, only managing to split the leather that helped hold the saddle in place.

Or *maybe* it missed. Finn took a step back. The bearded man lunged, overreaching, swinging wildly, and his saddle, no longer secure, slipped off the animal's back. Orange Beard lost his balance and tumbled from his horse. In a flash, Finn was right on top of him, the dagger that he'd used to carve Colm's apple dimpling the hairy skin beneath the man's chin.

"Tell them to back away," Finn ordered.

The other two riders stood within striking distance, their swords extended. Colm was still on his back.

"Do as he says," the bearded man choked, finding it hard to talk with a knife at his throat.

"And swords on the ground."

"Swords on the ground," Orange Beard echoed.

"Mr. Black, if you would be so kind as to collect those blades."

It took a moment for Colm to realize Finn was talking to him. Obviously there was no rule about the number of names you could have. Colm scrambled up and collected three swords, holding them tight to his chest. He was surprised at how heavy they were. He could barely hold the lot of them.

"Excellent," Finn said, turning back to the man at his feet. "Now let's see about that rope you mentioned earlier."

By the time Finn and Colm were finished, it looked as if the three men were going to pass out from effort, struggling against the rope that bound them to the tree, but Finn was an expert on knots—securing and unsecuring things was a specialty of his, he said—and had managed to tie one that only got tighter the more they resisted. Their saddles and provisions had been stacked neatly in a pile next to them, and their horses left to graze freely in the fields along the road. The only added touch was the tunics—all three of them stolen from the men's backs, torn, and used as gags.

"I'd hate to disappoint whoever wrote that pretty song," Finn said, then knelt down and rubbed Orange Beard on his balding head and looked up at the sky. "I'm sure someone will be along eventually. Hopefully they will not mistake you for common thieves—an easy enough error. Otherwise you could be here awhile."

The man said something angry and incomprehensible through the sweaty shirt stuffed in his mouth. Finn stood and took a moment to inspect the sleeves of his own tunic. They had been torn in several places, revealing the steel vambraces he wore underneath, clamped tight to his forearms. He pulled up one sleeve and ran his finger along the new scratches and dents in the metal, then rolled it back down.

"Rule number eight," he whispered to Colm. "Remember the face of each and every man you've stolen from. Because they will no doubt remember you."

"But they were looking for Trendle Treeband," Colm whispered back.

"Faces are harder to change than names," Finn replied. The rogue straightened himself out, wiped his forehead with his sleeve, and tucked his knife back into his boot. He walked a few paces from the three bound men, and Colm hurried to catch up.

"Is it true?" Colm asked. "Did you really cheat those men?"

"It was a long time ago."

"He said it was only three years."

"A long time," Finn said, taking the three swords from Colm and adding them to the pile beside the tree. Colm looked at them, licking his lips. It couldn't hurt to ask, could it?

"I don't suppose, I could, you know . . ."

Finn followed his gaze and then shook his head. "These are broadswords. Heavy and cumbersome. You'd be stabbed six times before you even got it out of its scabbard. When the time comes—*if* the time comes—we will find a weapon suited to your stature. Now." He stretched, as if he had just woken up. "If this little detour is finished, we should be on our way. We still have a long road ahead of us."

Colm nodded, then looked at the three horses picking their way through the grass, loyal enough to their riders not to stray far. Colm pointed to them. "I've ridden horses before," he said. "We used to have one—two, in fact—but we had to sell them. It might be faster . . ."

"No doubt it would be faster," Finn agreed. "Except *that* would be stealing. Horses are neither rare nor unique, and they won't get us anywhere that our own feet can't. The penalty for horse thieving is almost always death, and I've already had one close encounter with *him* today. Besides, I think it best if we get off the road for a bit."

Colm shouldered his sack and followed Finn into the fields, glancing back with apprehension at the three half-naked men bound to the tree. Colm had witnessed fights before—a couple of men with too much ale in their bellies, tumbling through the dust in the village square—but he had never seen anything like that. Engineering and economics were his specialties, but it was clear that Finn Argos had spent some time mastering the blade hanging from his belt as well.

Colm ran to catch up to the rogue. He knew he should heed his father's advice and keep some distance, especially given what he'd just seen. Except this man with at least two names, and probably many more besides, had saved Colm's hand and his family's reputation. And now he had also saved Colm's life.

Not to mention he still had Colm's coin.

4

THE TEST THAT WASN'T
AND THE ONE THAT WAS

Thanks to Colm's eight sisters, most of the too-thin Candorly library was filled with fanciful tales of royal romances or tomes of flowery poetry, a few histories and several almanacs, a book of recipes, and the children's rhymes they had all learned to read by. But Colm did have one book, given to him on his tenth birthday, that told of several hair-raising adventures undertaken by half a dozen heroes. They were bard's tales, embellished beyond the point of believability, his father said, but Colm devoured them anyway. The stories were full of monsters and caverns and mazes punctuated with chests of gold, just the same as Finn had described. Except Colm had only *read* about them. Finn had *survived* them.

Or so he said.

"So if there are so many dungeons, and so much treasure

to be had from them," Colm asked, "how come there aren't more people like you?"

"It's not a profession for just anyone," Finn said, picking his way through the clinging brambles that multiplied with every step, the farther they strayed from the road; Colm's arms were already etched with tiny scratches. "Long hours. Cramped working conditions. Involuntary dismemberment." Finn picked a burr from his sleeve. "Bludgeoning, burning, magical transfiguration, the terror as you wake up in the middle of the night, drenched in your own cold sweat, memories of that giant spider scuttling across your paralyzed body, fangs hovering over your chest dripping with heart-stopping poison. It can start to wear on a man."

Colm's pace slowed. It was three steps before Finn even noticed.

"Don't worry," Finn said with a flash of teeth. "I'm making it sound worse than it is. Mostly it's just trudging through dark, empty tunnels, hoping to uncover a gem or two. Most of the time it's not that thrilling at all."

Colm nodded.

"Besides, in order to become a dungeoneer, you have to train. And in order to train, you have to be admitted to the program. And in order to be admitted into the program, you still have to pass your test. After all, if you can't get one measly little coin from me, there isn't much chance of you becoming a dungeoneer. Not to mention I'll have to come to Tye empty-handed when I promised him I'd find a worthy recruit."

"A worthy recruit?" Colm asked, feeling a slight flush of pride.

"Certainly," Finn said. "It was pure luck coming across you as I did. The girl I went looking for had already lost her hands before I could get to her. It's hard to find good rogue material these days." Finn looked up at the sun, then pointed to a patch of trees, one of them exploding with pears. "Looks like lunch," he said.

He led Colm to the spot of shade, then spread out his cloak as a makeshift blanket and propped himself against the tree trunk. Colm noticed the cloak had several little pockets sewn into the inside—he and the rogue shared a love of secret compartments, it seemed. They ate mostly in silence, splitting the cheese Colm's mother had packed and eating two pears apiece—though Colm had to be careful of the thorny branches when picking them, pricking his finger once.

"The guild has its own cook, of course, though he mostly just knows how to make stew," Finn remarked, licking the pear juice from his fingers with a deliberate smacking sound. Colm thought about the bowl of stew that Celia had secretly slipped him. He missed her already.

Colm finished his second pear, core and all, spitting the seeds into the grass, then studied his companion. "Who's Trendle Treeband?"

Finn smiled. "A charming scoundrel, dark and handsome. Uncannily lucky at cards and dice. A clever fellow. I think you'd like him. But I was only Trendle for a spell. I've been Finn for all my life."

"Is that how you got that scar? As Trendle Treeband?" Colm

pointed to the thick braid along Finn's cheek. Finn stroked it self-consciously.

"Alas, no. That's a different story altogether. And one that I promise to share, but not right now. Now, I think, we need some quiet time. The ground is comfier than it looks, and I don't sleep well at night. It's hard with one eye open."

"But—" Colm protested, a hundred more questions at the ready, but Finn stopped him with a warning look. Then the rogue dug into the largest pocket of his cloak and pulled out a roll of parchment and a rusty-looking padlock the size of an acorn. The lock was snapped tight.

"Here, these should keep you busy for a while. The first is the guild's contract. You can read it, but don't sign anything."

"And this?" Colm said, holding up the lock.

"That's practice," Finn said. "Your father mentioned that you had some small experience with picking locks."

"But I don't have anything to open it with," Colm protested.

"A good rogue makes do with what's around him. Use your imagination."

Colm wasn't sure how his imagination was supposed to help him open this tiny rusted lock, but Finn wasn't going to offer any helpful suggestions; his eyes were already half shut. "Wake me if you see or hear anything out of the ordinary. Like someone else who thinks I owe them money," the rogue said.

Colm wanted to protest again, but Finn turned his back to him. In a matter of seconds, it seemed, the man was snoring.

Colm put down the lock and picked up the parchment, unfurling it. It was printed on both sides. There were several words Colm didn't understand, but he managed to get the gist.

Be it henceforth known that _____
(hereafter referred to as THE APPRENTICE) is requesting admittance to Thwodin's Legion (hereafter referred to as THE GUILD) to be trained in the arts of dungeoneering, including, but not limited to, the study of dungeon navigation, warcraft, warding, archery, swordplay, brawling, breaching, healing, wizardry, monstrology, trap disarmament, and treasure retrieval. THE APPRENTICE enters into this agreement with THE GUILD in accordance with the following stipulations:

1. THE APPRENTICE exhibits promise in his or her chosen field (combat, thievery, mystical arts, etc.) and passes the entrance requirements as outlined by his or her recruiter.

2. THE APPRENTICE recognizes the potentially perilous nature of dungeoneering and accepts the risks inherent therein.

3. THE APPRENTICE agrees that any treasure acquired by THE APPRENTICE through his or her association with THE GUILD or utilizing any property associated with THE GUILD is subject to the following deductions:

Forty percent to THE GUILD to cover operating expenses.

Ten percent to TYE THWODIN, founder of THE GUILD, to use as he sees fit.

The remaining fifty percent to be split among the adventuring party in equal shares according to their rank: apprentice adventurers receiving a half share and masters receiving one full share.

In the event that not all party members return, their shares shall be split among remaining adventurers after the aforementioned expenses and deductions.

4. In the event that THE APPRENTICE wishes to terminate his or her association with THE GUILD, THE APPRENTICE may do so at a penalty of one third of the proceeds he or she has acquired through said association, to be used by THE GUILD to find a suitable replacement. In the event that THE APPRENTICE must quit the program due to life-altering injury such as loss of life or limb, THE APPRENTICE is not required to pay said penalty and all acquired assets shall be distributed to THE APPRENTICE and/or his or her next of kin.

5. THE APPRENTICE acknowledges that THE GUILD cannot be held liable for injuries or fatalities incurred by THE APPRENTICE while in training. This includes, but is not limited to, lacerations, fractures, bleeding, beheading, dismemberment, burning, scalding, drowning, electrocution, paralysis, implosion, curses, polymorphing or other transmogrification, zombification, mummification, reanimation following expiration, or any conditions caused by undue stress. Expenses for the treating of injuries, curses, diseases, and the like shall be incurred by THE GUILD at no cost to THE APPRENTICE so long as he or she is a member in good standing.

Signed on this day, _____,

by _____

Colm put down the parchment. He wasn't sure what *transmogrification* meant, though he guessed it wasn't good, and half of all treasure seemed excessive. He guessed this Tye Thwodin was probably a very rich man by now.

He looked at the blank reserved for his name, then looked behind him in the direction of the road that he could no longer see. He was already farther from home than he had ever been in his life. The woods were quiet, save for the crickets and the sound of Finn snoring; none of his sisters' incessant chatter. He wondered what Celia was doing right now. He imagined her tucked in his hammock, staring out his too-small window, waiting for him to come home.

Hoping for a distraction, Colm took the lock in his hands and gave the shackle a good tug. It didn't budge. The thing was probably rusted closed. If he had one of his mother's sewing needles, he might be able to undo it. Beside him, Finn Argos shifted so that he was on his back again, hands on his chest, both eyes closed.

"Make do with what's around you," Colm whispered to himself. He checked his pockets. There wasn't much chance of picking a lock with a spare pair of socks. He opened his sack. Figs. Apples. Bread. He needed something sharp and thin. He looked at the dot of already drying blood on his finger and then at the branches above him. Not all pear trees had thorns, he knew, but this one had them in abundance. "Worth a shot." He found the longest, thickest one he could and snapped it off at the base, then set to work, carefully feeling out the recesses of the keyhole, mindful not to break his makeshift lockpick. Not that he didn't have a thousand more where that came from, but he didn't want pieces lodged inside; no sense making the task even thornier, he thought with a smile.

Colm jumped as the padlock sprang open. It had taken very little to trigger it. It seemed even easier than the lock on the cellar at home. Or maybe Colm had just gotten lucky. He leaned forward, holding out the open padlock, about to say something, figuring it was a test of some kind Finn had given him, when another rumbling snore escaped the sleeping rogue.

The padlock was only an amusement. The real test was still hidden somewhere in that cloak. The one the rogue was sleeping on top of. Colm got to his knees and cleared his throat, softly, like a kitten's purr, then louder, like his father's grunt. Nothing. Not a flutter of lashes. Not a twitch of the nose. Colm put down the lock and whispered Finn's name. No response. The man was out.

Colm crept as close as he dared and gently reached across Finn's cloak to where three pockets were sewn in, each plenty big enough to hide a single piece of silver. He felt along the outside of each, then dipped in two fingers just to be sure. The top two were empty, but the bottom held a spool of bright yellow ribbon. Colm had no idea what Finn would need the ribbon for, but the sight of it reminded Colm of his sisters again. Colm peeled up the cloak and carefully checked the outside pocket, but all he found were the rogue's black leather gloves, the ones that hid the fact that he was two fingers short. There was no silver coin on this side.

Colm stood slowly, careful not to make a sound, and tiptoed around the tree to check the pockets on the other side, holding each breath as long as possible. He found a thimble and a small vial of ink and a carved wooden rune, but no coin.

It wasn't in the cloak. Too easy. Besides, hadn't Finn patted the pockets of his pants earlier that day when mentioning Colm's test? Colm inched closer, crouched on his haunches, one hand against the tree to steady himself. He was close enough to smell the rogue's pear-tinged breath, to see the intricate pattern that singular scar made along his cheek, jagging this way and that—clearly not a clean cut. Finn's hands were folded, fingers crossed, and Colm could see the stubs of the two smallest, the right slightly shorter than the left, the tip of it slightly pinker than its missing brother.

Colm studied the rogue's pants. They weren't the baggy silk breeches of the wealthy merchants who lined Felhaven square, so easy to dip into. They were sturdy and black, stitched tight and cinched with the rogue's thick leather belt. More leather was patched at the knees, and the cuffs were buried down into the scuffed black boots. There appeared to be only one pocket on each side, the opening barely large enough for Colm to slip in a hand. He looked for the silhouette of the coin, the marked outline of a circle, but the outside revealed nothing. Colm would just have to take a chance.

He held his breath again, keeping his eyes on Finn's face, looking for the slightest quiver as he wiggled one hand inside. A lip tremble, the flare of a nostril, his fingers digging, until . . .

Yes! That's it! Colm bit his lip, pinching the coin between two fingers, pulling it free with one swift motion. He suddenly felt every muscle tense as a hand shot up, securing him around the wrist, causing him to lose his balance and topple backward. Still, he held on to the coin, holding it out between him and Finn for the rogue to see.

"Aha! I got it! See? *See?*"

Finn smiled. Silver and gold flashing quickly, and then retreating back behind his lips.

"You got something," he said coolly.

Colm looked at the thing in his hand. It wasn't his silver at all. It was a piece of wood, carved in a perfect circle, sanded to an almost steely smoothness. Colm shook his head. "What the blazes is *this*?"

"It's a decoy. I whittled it myself last night while trying to fall asleep," Finn said. "Enough to fool a blind man, I suppose. Or a boy who thinks he's just discovered buried treasure." He let go of Colm's wrist with one hand and snatched the circle of wood from between Colm's fingers with the other, flipping it and catching it, closing his palm around it. When he opened his fingers, it was, of course, gone.

"You tricked me," Colm said bitterly.

"Said the pickpocket to his prey? 'I stole your purse and there was nothing in it!' Really, Colm, you cannot blame the man you pilfer from because he has nothing of value for you to steal."

"But you *do* have it. You stole it from *me!*"

"And who did *you* steal it from?" Finn asked, sitting upright. "Do you even know? Do you have a name? Do you remember which coin came from which pocket? Did you bother to say 'Thank you' or 'I'm sorry'? And who had it before that person? How many hands has that piece of silver known? Was it used to buy dinner from a hardworking fisherman on the pier? Did it trade hands at the mill for a bag of flour? Or did some pirate pry it from the hands of a dead seaman as his ship sank underneath him? I'm afraid you'll have to do better than that."

Finn looked around and saw the open padlock lying in the grass.

"I see you picked the lock, at least."

"*That* was easy," Colm huffed. He could still feel the coin between his thumb and forefinger. He'd been so certain he had succeeded.

"I imagine it was," Finn said, looking up at the sticky branches of the pear tree that shaded them. "Well, come on, then, and stop pouting. There's still several hours left in the day." He bent down and picked up his cloak, clasping it around his neck. He tucked the open lock into one of the outer pockets, then snatched up the parchment, handing it to Colm. "Save this for later." The rogue winked, then took off, heading in the same direction as before.

Colm rolled the contract and stuffed it into his own pants pocket, his hand brushing up against something smooth and round. He pulled out the little wooden token that, somehow, Finn had slipped in there.

"What's yours is yours," Finn said over his shoulder. Then he started humming again. Colm dropped the piece of wood in the grass.

The sun was exhausted, beginning its blushing descent, calling it quits. Finn had given him until the end of the day to get that piece of silver back. Time was running out.

"We are almost there," Finn said more than once, though Colm couldn't figure out where *there* was. They had tromped over hills, between stalks of wild wheat, past muddy creeks and mossy woods. At one point they crossed a decrepit stone bridge, Finn pausing, looking around, studying some imaginary map in his head, then nodding to himself before continuing.

They were walking along the edge of a forest now. Finn had said the name, but Colm didn't recognize it. He didn't recognize any of it. It wasn't within six miles of Felhaven, so it wasn't part of his world. He knew the names of some of the nearby hills and of the river that ran beside the town, knew the names of most of the neighboring villages—Blackhorn, Boughbridge, Wallford—but they didn't seem to be close to any of those. In fact, Colm hadn't seen a living soul since the encounter with the horsemen, unless he counted the mosquitoes that he mashed against his neck. If this castle of Finn's was nearby, it was very well hidden.

To make it worse, in addition to sore legs and feet, Colm had already failed three more times to get his coin back. Once, when they stopped by the riverbed for a drink, he attempted to reach into Finn's other pants pocket—but a swift move by the rogue caused Colm to lose his balance and fall into the water, soaking both pairs of socks. The other two attempts were equally sloppy: Colm pretending to stumble, claiming he was tired of walking (which was true) and bumping against Finn's side, hoping to make a quick grab. The first of those Finn sidestepped easily. The second he not only managed to keep Colm's hand from his pocket but also, somehow, got back into the bag slung across Colm's shoulder and stole another apple before Colm even knew he had done it.

It was looking hopeless. Even if he got to this castle of Finn's, it wouldn't matter. Even if he wanted to become a dungeoneer—and he wasn't at all certain—Finn wouldn't allow it. After all, how can you steal a trove of treasure from under an ogre's nose when you can't pinch one coin from a sleeping man's pocket? Colm would return home, empty-handed, an opportunity squandered, crawling back into his closet of a room to watch Celia restitch the seam of a dress worn a thousand times already.

Finn, for his part, hadn't given up, continuing to lecture Colm on what to expect when they arrived. "The guild's like a second family, I suppose," he said, "except your uncle's a barbarian and your second cousin summons lightning from the sky."

Colm had never seen anyone summon a lightning bolt from out of nowhere. Or summon anything, for that matter, unless you counted his mother's ability to summon them all to the table with the smell of bacon. "They must be very powerful," he said. "Those second cousins."

Finn shrugged. "I suppose. Though if you ask me, magic is worth no more than a quick wit and a sharp edge." He looked down at Colm's feet. "Or a good pair of boots to run in."

Colm couldn't imagine Finn Argos running from anything. Not after seeing what he'd done to those three men on horseback outside the village. But there was a lot about Finn that was a mystery.

"I've run from battles. From brawls. From giant boulders and balls of flame. From angry innkeepers and angry ladies and their angry fathers or husbands, or both, in one case. There's something to be said for running if it means you get to keep your head, especially if your pockets are full. Ah. Here we are."

The rogue walked up to a giant oak, easily three times the size of the elms that twisted for sunlight beneath its canopy. All manner of writing had been carved into it, strange letters in a language Colm couldn't read. He ran his finger along the carvings whittled deep into the bark. "What does it mean?" he asked.

"Nothing," Finn replied, walking past it toward a row of smaller trees. "It's gibberish. They're not even real words. The idea," he added, "is that most people look at *that* tree and assume it's hiding something, so they ignore this one." He stood beside an unassuming elm with a small hollow at its trunk and reached inside, pulling out a small pink shard. He held the crystal out for Colm to see. "Do you know what this is?"

Colm shook his head. Obviously it wasn't anything too special, or it wouldn't have been shoved inside the trunk of a tree in the middle of nowhere. "A pretty rock for marking nothing in particular?"

Finn snorted. "One of the things we will need to work on—in addition to your lying—is your assessment of value. This, Colm, is a key. A very special kind of key, in fact," he explained. "It opens a portal a long way from here, two more days' walking at least, and through somewhat treacherous territory. They are quite rare, these keys, their powers nearly impossible to harness. Tye Thwodin has spent most of his life collecting them, and I daresay we have more than our fair share. Most of them are used for dungeoneering, but we have a few scattered here and there to make our travels easier."

Colm stared at the crystal. It certainly didn't look magical. "How do they work?"

"I have no idea," the rogue replied. "I told you, the arcane arts aren't my forte. But I *can* tell you how you will feel when we use it." Judging by the look on Finn's face, Colm wasn't sure he wanted to know. "It's not *painful* . . . exactly. You might feel a stretch, and then your whole body may feel a little—how best to put this? *Unraveled.* But then, before you know it, *pop*, you are on the other side, good as new. Or at least good as you were when you started."

"The other side of what?" Colm asked.

Finn didn't answer. "Trust me. I've done it a fair dozen times myself. There is nothing to worry about."

Finn held out the crystal and instructed Colm to grab his hand. "Hold on tight, and don't let go." They were standing close together now, bodies nearly touching, and Colm realized this might be his last chance. Finn's other pants pocket, the one he hadn't checked yet, was only inches away. He had to move fast. But before he could get so much as one finger of his free hand in, he heard Finn whisper something.

Then Colm's head exploded.

Not literally, of course, but he understood what Finn meant by *unraveled*. He felt a tingling sensation and was suddenly aware of every particle of himself slowly coming unstitched. Blood and bones and skin and brains and muscle and sinew teased apart so that you could see how they were connected. *Disorienting* didn't begin to describe it, this sensation of separation, as if he were a piece of glass hitting a stone floor, shattering into a billion bits. Not painful, no, but uncomfortable, and nauseating, and just *strange*. Every memory seemed to flash before him at once, his thoughts strung out along a million threads that circled around him.

And then it was over. It had lasted only a moment. Two seconds, at most. And Colm found himself standing in the middle of a forest—much denser than the edge of the woods he had been skirting the moment before—staring at the mouth of a small cave, pitch-black, barely large enough for a man to squeeze into. Finn was standing right beside him, the crystal in his hand.

"We made it," he said, sounding relieved, which only made Colm more nervous. "See, I told you it wasn't so bad."

Colm didn't reply. His head was spinning. He patted himself down to make sure he was all accounted for, then looked around. The trees were so thick here, you couldn't see more than a half mile in front of you, their blanket of branches blocking out the sky and what was left of the pink horizon.

"What are you talking about?" Colm protested. "You said we were going to a castle. There's no castle here."

"Not that *you* can see," Finn replied enigmatically.

Colm looked around. Nothing but trees and the coal-black mouth of the cave, looking like a pocket sewn into the earth.

A pocket. Colm looked at the pockets of Finn's pants. They had arrived. The day was over. He had failed the test. Now he wasn't at all sure what was going to happen.

Finn seemed to read his mind. "Oh, that," he said. "Needn't worry about that." He pointed at Colm's side, at Colm's own pants pocket. Reluctantly Colm reached inside, past the rolled-up contract, where something cool stuck to his palm. He pulled the silver piece out and stared at it.

Finn held out both hands. "Always knew you had it in you," he said.

Colm shook his head, bewildered. "But it doesn't count. I didn't steal it," Colm protested, holding the coin out between them. "I mean, I didn't steal it *back*. You *gave* it to me. I didn't pass the test."

Finn smiled, though he had that look in his eye. That same look Colm had seen right before the rogue told him to duck. Right before he had drawn his sword and disarmed three men.

"The test?" the rogue said, putting an arm around Colm, holding him there at the edge of the cave. "The coin wasn't the test. *This* is the test."

Colm felt a shove. And the next thing he knew, he was falling.

5

THE BARBARIAN, THE MAGELING, AND THE GIRL WHO TALKS TO BUGS

It was more of a slide than a fall, though the rocky ground did little to slow Colm's progress, and the cold stone he eventually slammed his shoulder into jarred his teeth and sent a bolt of pain through his spine. Colm looked up, hoping that he hadn't slid as far as it seemed and there was an easy way to climb back up and out, but his heart sank. The cave entrance, a small circle of fading light, seemed as distant as a full moon. He looked for the shape of a figure in the halo. He called out Finn's name three times, though his echoes were the only response.

"This isn't funny," Colm called up. "I've decided I want to go back home. Stealing is bad. I've learned my lesson. Shoe cobbling is a very respectable profession. So if you could lower a rope or something . . ."

Still no response. Colm scrabbled up the slick surface of the stones, making it all of two feet before slipping back down to his knees. He called Finn's name one more time, then called Finn a name he usually reserved only for his sisters, and even then only behind their backs. Finally Colm turned and gazed down the length of the cave.

The first thing he realized was that it wasn't a cave. The floor was too smooth, the ceiling too uniform. It was more of a tunnel, the work of picks and shovels rather than nature and time. Someone had hollowed this space out of earth and stone on purpose, and someone else, maybe the same someone, had seen fit to leave a torch. Colm saw it fastened to the wall about fifty feet away, its light spreading along the cold, gray floor.

Colm looked around and then noticed a glimmer by his feet, peeking through a pile of loose rocks. He bent down and retrieved his silver coin, the one Finn had given back to him while he wasn't looking. He held it up to the flicker of light from the lonely torch.

This was the test. To get out of here. By himself. To conquer his very first dungeon. The realization hit Colm like a horse's hoof in the gut, but once it landed, there was no arguing with it. He didn't have a lot of options anyway. He couldn't climb back out, and even if Finn was up there, he obviously didn't intend to help. Colm needed to find his own way or be stuck here forever.

He walked slowly, keeping one hand on the wall for balance until he made it to the torch. It hadn't been burning for long, which meant someone must have lit it recently, which meant that there was another way out.

Unfortunately, it also meant that there was possibly someone else down here with him.

Colm removed the torch from its sconce and held it in front of him, stabbing at the darkness. He thought back to the pile of blades at the road and Finn's insistence that they weren't right for him. The dirty thief knew all along. He *intended* for Colm to come down here unarmed. If only Colm had had his father's hatchet. Even the butter knife would have been some consolation.

Colm stepped slowly, looking behind him constantly, trying not to jump at his own shadow. He had been in dark places before. He had spent hours in cabinets, corners, and crevices, hiding from his gaggle of scheming sisters. But this was a different kind of darkness. In the flicker of the torchlight, the shadow seemed to move, as if it were skulking around, sneaking up behind him. Looking down the black tunnel, he felt it could go on forever.

But it can't, he told himself. Every tunnel ends somewhere.

Colm paused as his tunnel crossed paths with another, the new one looking narrower and darker still. Now there were choices. That made it even worse. Now there was the possibility he might get lost, though in truth he already had no idea where he was.

Colm started to continue straight ahead, then froze, his ears perked. He was certain he heard something. A loose rock. A whisper.

Stop it, he told himself. *You're just imagining things.*

But he wasn't. He could distinctly hear the sound of feet shuffling along the stone. Except they weren't his feet.

Suddenly he felt something sharp and cold at his throat, followed by a voice.

"Go ahead," the voice said. "Give me an excuse."

It wasn't a knife or a sword. He could tell by the feel of it beneath his chin. It was a rock. A piece of shale or limestone, long and skinny enough to act as a makeshift dagger. It certainly felt sharp, though, nipping into his neck.

Colm felt his torch wrested from his grasp, the circle of light retreating behind him, leaving him staring into the darkness. He wanted to turn and see who it was who was holding him there. It obviously wasn't Finn. For starters, the person standing behind him had much smaller hands, with a full complement of fingers. And judging by the sound of the voice, it wasn't even a him. The person who spoke to Colm dared him in a voice that was confident and commanding but still distinctly female. It almost sounded like Celia, though of all of his sisters, Celia was the least likely to want to behead him.

"Who are you?" the female voice demanded, pressing the stone knife up and in.

"Colm. Colm Candorly," he choked, then realized his

91

mistake. He should have said Mr. Black. *Don't let someone who's about to kill you have your real name,* Finn would probably caution, *just in case he doesn't pull it off the first time and decides to track you down for another go.* But it was too late.

"What are you doing here?"

"Trying to keep my head about me," Colm replied.

There was a snort, something close to laughter, except it seemed to come off to Colm's right, and it didn't sound at all like the same person who had him at stone point, which meant that there were two figures there in the darkness. That didn't make Colm feel any better.

"I d-d-don't think he's any t-t-trouble," the new voice sputtered. "He c-c-could be one of us."

The sharp edge at Colm's neck slackened a bit, though not enough for him to safely turn around or slip free. "Why are you here?" the girl's voice demanded.

"I have no idea," Colm said honestly. "I was with this man. He said he was taking me to visit a guild of some kind. Then we grabbed hold of this magic crystal and I almost threw up, and the next thing I know he's pushing me down a hole and you're sticking a sharp rock under my chin."

"T-t-told you," came the other voice. A boy's voice. Suddenly the knife dropped, and Colm was free. He turned around slowly.

There, holding Colm's torch, was a boy close to his age, though shorter and even skinnier. (Colm wasn't sure how that was possible.) He wore a scarlet robe that fell well past his feet and dragged along the stone. His wrists were adorned with silver bracelets, and his underclothes were tattered and covered in grime. His face was pale, with giant globes for eyes and thin eyebrows that made the globes look even bigger. His hair, unlike Colm's, was long, falling over his shoulders in straw-colored strands. He looked frightened.

The girl standing next to him did not.

"My name is Lena," she said, putting one fist across her chest in a salute that Colm had never seen before. "Lena Proudmore. Sorry I almost decapitated you . . . Colm, was it?"

Colm just stared. In the flickering torchlight it was hard to make out all her features clearly, but he couldn't miss the sharp chisel of her chin, like a weapon itself. Her crimson hair was cropped short in back, falling across one eye in front, the other shining brown in the flicker of light. Her lips were pursed, pulled tight against her teeth in a determined smirk. Colm had never seen anyone with red hair and brown eyes before.

"You're kind of . . . ," Colm began.

"Intimidating. I know. Sorry. It's just that you can never be too careful."

Intimidating wasn't what he was thinking, but he couldn't deny it either.

"Um, p-p-pardon me," the boy in the robe said, inserting himself into the conversation and extending his free hand, his bracelets jangling. "I'm Quinn, but p-people sometimes c-c-call me N-nibbles, on account of how I'm always eating."

Then how come you're so skinny? Colm wondered to himself. "Nibbles," Colm said, taking the boy's hand but not taking his eyes off the girl, mostly because she had nearly slit his throat a second ago. Mostly.

"So what are *you*, then?" Lena said, her hands on her hips.

Colm wasn't sure he understood the question. "Um. Lost, I guess."

Quinn snorted again. Lena flashed him a dirty look, and he shut up.

"No. I mean, what *are* you? Are you a fighter? A wizard? You're certainly not dressed like much of anything. Oh, gods, please tell me you're not a bard."

Colm pointed to himself. "What? You mean like one of those guys who go around singing dopey songs all the time?" *Actually,* Colm thought, *maybe not such a bad life. Better than a shoe cobbler, at least.* He shook his head anyway.

"Well, then?" Lena pressed.

"I guess I'm a thie—" Colm stopped and corrected himself. "A rogue, I mean. Except not really. I was going to train to become one. Or I was going to *think* about it. Then I got thrown in this hole."

"A rogue," Lena whispered to herself. "Figures."

"Figures?"

She looked at him; even in the torchlight, he could see her rolling her eyes. "Haven't you ever studied Herm Hefflegeld's theories of proper party configuration? Didn't you ever read Stormfist's essay on the effects of class interdependency and dungeoneering efficacy?"

"Here we go," Quinn sighed, rubbing at his eyes.

"I'm sorry, I'm a little new to all of this," Colm said. "See, I come from Felhaven—you've probably never heard of it, it's, like, this little farm town ten miles and some freaky crystal teleportation jump away from here. And my family doesn't have a whole lot of money, and then my sister got sick, and I thought if I could help pay for the medicine, you know? So I went to the town square, and I—"

Lena put a hand in his face, actually smothering his still-moving lips. "We don't need your life story, farm boy," she said. "The important thing is that we finally have a rogue, so maybe we can get out of this place in one piece."

"One piece?" Colm said.

"You make sure we don't run into any traps, and Quinn and I will handle any monsters that come along."

"Monsters?"

"T-t-traps?" Quinn repeated.

"Please," Lena said. "You don't think they would throw us all down here and not give us *something* to do, do you?" She reached out and took the torch from Quinn's hand, then turned and continued along the same path that Colm had been taking. Colm watched her for a second, trying to decide if she was dangerous.

He was almost certain of it.

But she didn't seem like she posed any immediate threat to him, at least, and obviously she and this other boy had agreed to work together, even seemed to know each other somehow. Colm had no idea what Herm Hefflegeld's theories of proper party configuration had to do with anything, but he did understand that three people were better than one, and was thankful not to be alone any longer. Still, he walked behind her as he had walked behind Finn at the start. The boy named Quinn shuffled beside him, nearly tripping over his oversized robe.

"So y-you're a ruh-rogue?" he mumbled.

Actually, Colm thought, *I'm just a pickpocket. And only recently one of those.* "More or less," he said, then nodded at the boy's strange attire. "And what are you, exactly?" Quinn looked like a kid who had decided to try on his father's bathing gown.

"Oh, m-me? I'm a m-m-m-m-mageling," the boy said.

"It's like a mage. Only clumsier," Lena explained from over her shoulder, and Quinn nodded. He didn't seem to take offense.

Colm instinctively stepped away, remembering what Finn had said about mages. Except Quinn didn't look like he could call lightning from the sky or produce fireballs from his fingers. Colm had expected the first wizard he met to be more in keeping with the descriptions from his book—white-bearded and billowing and larger than life. Quinn looked barely big enough to summon his own shadow. Colm nodded toward Lena and whispered to Quinn, "So, then, what is she?"

Whatever she was, she obviously had good hearing, because she stopped and spun. "I am a barbarian," she responded curtly. "At least, I hope to be someday."

Colm shook his head. From what little he'd read, barbarians were loud, long-haired, half-naked men who spoke in bellows and ate their meat raw. "Really? A barbarian? You? Are you sure about that?"

"Uh-oh," Quinn whispered.

The girl suddenly advanced on Colm, her eyes slits, teeth bared. She looked terrifying in the torchlight. "Are you suggesting I *can't* be a barbarian?" Colm threw up his hands, shaking his head, but she started jabbing a finger into his chest. "Because there is absolutely no law that says women can't be barbarians. In fact, I'll have you know there are several famous female barbarians in dungeoneering lore."

"No. I believe you, honestly," Colm said. He had never met a barbarian before. Not even the half-naked, raw-meat-eating male variety.

"Just because I don't wear the hide of some dead animal across my shoulders and I have all my teeth does not mean that I'm *not* a barbarian."

"I . . . I never . . . you are . . . absolutely . . . so *completely* a barbarian," Colm stumbled.

Lena huffed, then spun back around and started walking faster down the dark hall.

"She really is nice, once you get to know her," Quinn said, gathering his robe about him as he and Colm each quickened his pace to catch up.

Once you get to know her? Colm thought. "Wait a minute. How long have you two been *down* here?"

"We were friends before," Quinn explained as they came to

another fork. "We come from the same town. We are pretty much in this together. And now so are you." The boy smiled brightly.

Lena made the choice on which direction to take. She made all the choices as the forks multiplied. She led them right. Then left. Then right again. The idea, she said, was to avoid going in a circle.

"The idea," Colm said, "is to find the way out."

"The idea," Quinn added, "is to stay alive. And m-m-maybe f-find something to eat. I'm starving."

Colm fished in his sack for his last apple and handed it over. Quinn took it eagerly.

"I wouldn't worry," Lena said. "We've been down here for some time now and haven't seen anything remotely danger-ous. I'm guessing the place is deserted."

Quinn reached out and clutched Colm's arm as a shrill screech, like the sound a wounded animal might make, came from their left.

"That doesn't sound deserted," Colm said. "Maybe we should go right this time."

Lena looked like she *wanted* to disagree, but instead she nod-ded and turned right, Colm following behind her. *Stay behind the big guy,* he thought to himself. That was Finn's advice. He just hadn't said that the big guy might be a girl. Or that the girl would have such brilliant red hair.

They continued deeper, away from the screeching, Colm walking on tiptoe. He listened for sounds. He watched for traps.

He inspected the walls for levers or pulleys or anything vaguely mechanical, something that might trigger a secret door or a falling rock. He wasn't sure why he was doing these things or what, exactly, he was even looking for, but his instincts—honed by so many years of sibling torture—had kicked in. Quinn held on to Colm's belt strap the way Colm used to do with his father when he was three. He had finished the apple.

"So you say you're a mage," Colm whispered behind him. "That means you cast spells and stuff?"

"I'm n-n-not qu-qu-quite a mage yet. I'm only a m-m-m-m—"

"Mageling. Yes. But even a mageling must know *some* magic, right? I mean, you could maybe fill these tunnels with light or see through the walls or even maybe teleport us all out of here," Colm suggested.

Quinn shook his head emphatically, eyes somehow growing even wider. "Oh, you don't want me to do that," he said.

"No, you really don't," Lena seconded from up ahead.

"I t-t-tried t-teleporting my cat once. Poor F-F-F-Friskers. All that was left was her t-t-t— her t-t-t— her—"

"Tail?" Colm guessed.

"Toes," Quinn said. "Four little sets of toes. C-c-claws and all. And all the rest . . . *p-p-poof.*"

Quinn let go of Colm's belt long enough to make an imitation of a cat exploding, then latched back on. Colm decided that was enough talk of spells. He focused his attention forward and then ran smack into Lena's backside.

"Sshhh!" she hissed. "Hear that?"

Colm listened. He *could* hear something coming from up the hall. It sounded like someone singing. Soft and melodic. Much better than the screeching they had left behind. Colm thought of Finn humming on their way out of Felhaven. Maybe it was him. "Maybe this is the end," he said.

"Or maybe it's a trap," Lena countered, but even as she said it, she smiled, as if a trap were preferable to an exit. Beside Colm, the mageling started to shiver, but Lena Proudmore was already moving in the direction of the sound, torch in one hand, her makeshift stone dagger in the other. The three of them turned the corner.

They found themselves staring into a small chamber, lit with another torch. There was no ogre, but there was something. Another girl, her features sharper and even more angled than Lena's. She had skin the color of tree bark and short black tufts of hair that were cinched with all manner of thread and twine, making little horns jutting out in all directions. She wore a cloak, much the same as Finn's, save hers was brown and spilled out behind her as she sat cross-legged on the floor, humming and admiring something in her hand.

"Is that a spider?" Lena whispered, but the girl in the room heard her and turned. Startled, she threw up her hands, and the spider she'd been holding somersaulted in the air. It hit the ground, then gathered its legs back underneath it and scurried off into the shadows.

"Now look what you've done," the stranger said. "You

scared Mr. Tickletoes."

The girl with the spiky hair turned and crawled after the spider on her hands and knees, refusing to say another word until she found him, despite Lena's repeatedly asking her who she was and how she had gotten down there. Finally, when the spider had been coaxed back into her open palm, the girl stood up and addressed them.

"Greetings. My name is Serene. I am a child of the woods."

"Oh, great. A squirrel hugger," Quinn mumbled. Colm couldn't tell why the boy stuttered sometimes and not others, and he didn't know what "squirrel hugger" meant, but judging by Quinn's tone, it wasn't necessarily something to be proud of.

Lena stepped forward, bathing the girl in torchlight. She didn't appear to be armed in any way. Her shoes, Colm noticed, were barely more than a single plank of wood strapped with twine (his father wouldn't approve). Her underclothes were threadbare, lacking ornamentation of any kind. She did, however, have tattoos scrawled down the length of her forearms. They looked like tree roots weaving up toward her elbows.

"You're a druid?" Lena asked.

"No," the girl said. "I mean, yes, I suppose, theoretically, but not *technically*, no. I haven't passed the ritual yet. I was *supposed* to, except I couldn't because . . . well . . . it was just so big, and with those teeth and everything . . . and why'd you have to go and scare Mr. Tickletoes like that?"

"Mr. Tickletoes?"

101

Serene ran a finger along the back of the spider crouched in her hand. "It's all right, Mr. Tickletoes," she cooed to it. "I won't let these people hurt you."

"She's crazy," Quinn muttered beneath his breath. Colm nodded. Last he checked, spiders didn't even *have* toes.

"She's a natureling," Lena corrected. "She can talk to animals. Plants too, probably."

The other girl, Serene, continued to whisper to the arachnid curled up in her palm. The druid turned and cocked her head. "Mr. Tickletoes wants to know if you intend to squash him."

Lena shook her head. "I am Lena Proudmore. This is Quinn Frostfoot and Colm . . . something or other. We were all three thrown into this dungeon, probably just like you. I promise we are not here to squash Mr. . . ."

"Tickletoes," Colm whispered.

"Right. Whatever," Lena said. "Honestly, we are just looking for the way out."

"How fortuitous," Serene sang, her green eyes sparkling. "Mr. Tickletoes and I were just talking about that before you showed up. He says he knows the way out. He can show us, can't you, Mr. Tickletoes?"

In response, the spider crawled to the edge of the dark-skinned girl's fingers and lowered itself to the ground with its silky cord. Then it scurried across the floor and out into the hall, passing too close to Quinn, who jumped back instinctively. Serene leaped up and brushed right past them as well, pausing only to look behind her.

"Well, come on, then! Hurry!"

Colm looked at Lena, who shrugged. "What are you wait-ing for?" she asked. "Follow the spider."

Colm did. Technically he followed the barbarian, who fol-lowed the druid, who followed the spider . . . though, in truth, apparently, Lena wasn't really a barbarian yet, and Serene wasn't really a druid yet, and Quinn, who still hung on to Colm's belt strap, wasn't really a mage. But it hardly mattered, as Colm was still little more than the son of a shoe cobbler. The important thing, he reminded himself, was that he wasn't alone. Besides, the newest addition to their party seemed friendly. She was certainly talkative.

"I should have expected it. You can't fail your druidic rites twice and not face some sort of consequence. But I had no idea how truly horrible it would be in a dungeon without grass or trees or light. There isn't even any moss down here. If it weren't for Mr. Tickletoes, I would have gone crazy. But he told me not to worry. That I wasn't the first person to be stuck down in these tunnels, and that it was always nice for him to have someone to talk to as well. Did you know he recently became a father? Three hundred beautiful babies."

Colm shuddered. He thought eight sisters was a lot.

"I *should* have passed the trial. It's not that I didn't *want* to talk to the bear," Serene continued. "I understand how important it is. After all, what good is being a druid if you can't commune with *all* of nature? But let's face it, Nature can

103

be downright frightening sometimes. Have you seen a bear's claws? They're as long as my fingers!"

"She doesn't take a breath," Quinn whispered in Colm's ear.

"Probably comes from talking to trees," Colm whispered back. "She's used to having to keep up both sides of a conversation."

"It's mostly about the size, I think. And the teeth. I told Mr. Tickletoes how much I enjoyed *his* company and that he was much easier to talk to than wolves or panthers or anything, and that, honestly, I see no point in trying to converse with anything bigger than a bunny. Regular chatterboxes, rabbits. Hard to get a word in."

"I c–c–can't imagine," Quinn remarked.

Colm looked down at the floor, where the spider was moving as fast as its spindly legs would carry it. The darkness was overbearing, and the chill bit into his skin, and there was still this lingering feeling that they weren't alone. Yet there was something about being down here, underneath the surface, ferreting out the exit, that made him tingle. It was exciting *and* terrifying, and for a moment he imagined what Tye Thwodin, the young blacksmith's apprentice, had felt when he fell into a sinkhole and came face-to-face with his first ogre so many years ago. He thought about the pockets full of jewels. What if there was some kind of treasure down here as well? Maybe they should take a look around. "You don't think . . . ," Colm started to say, but stopped as Serene bent down to pick up their eight-legged guide. She brought it up to her ear and frowned.

The spider whisperer turned to Colm and the others. "Mr. Tickletoes says we should hurry. He says the Overseer is coming."

Maybe looking around wasn't a good idea.

"The Overseer?" Lena repeated. Colm didn't like the sound of it either. It wasn't as bad as, say, the Intestine Ripper or the Blood Guzzler, but it had an ominous weight to it.

"He says the overseer always comes when you're near the end," Serene said.

"So we *are* close, then," Lena confirmed. Colm felt a nervous tug on his belt and put a hand on Quinn's shoulder. Lena started spinning in circles, torch in hand. "I knew it was too easy. I *knew* there'd be a butt to kick."

"Mr. Tickletoes says we can still get away if we hurry."

"Get away?" Lena scoffed, holding out her rock. "The Proudmores don't shy from a fight."

Colm put a finger up. "Yes, well, the Candorlys are naturally shy, so I recommend taking the spider's advice and getting out of here." Quinn and Serene nodded emphatically.

Lena scowled. "Fine. But if this overseer confronts us, I get to kill it."

No one argued. Serene scooped up the spider, holding him in her palm and whispering to him. To Colm's surprise, the spider lifted its two front legs and pointed with the toes it didn't have to one of the six tunnels branching outward. From behind them came the grating screech they'd heard before. Except this time, it was much louder.

Which meant it was a lot closer.

They quickened their pace, Serene in the lead with Colm on her heels, dragging Quinn. At one point the tunnel narrowed, and Colm slammed his head once as they stooped down to crawl through a small opening in the rock. He heard Lena behind him do the same thing and then let out a hiss.

"Are you all right?"

"Just a nick," she said. "I'm fine."

They pushed through the rock into another tunnel, this one wider, leading to an archway and an open chamber beyond, lit by several more torches. Colm could make out an iron door on the far side of the room. The way out, he hoped.

He turned back to see Lena propped against the wall, eyes closed, stretching out her hand. There was a small cut on the palm, less than a coin's width across, little prickles of blood beading up. Quinn quickly wiped them away with a corner of his sleeve and whispered something to her.

"You sure you're all right?" Colm asked. Lena didn't seem to be in any pain, but she refused to open her eyes until Quinn was finished cleaning her hand.

"I told you, I'm fine," she snapped.

Colm looked at Serene, who shrugged. Then all four of them stood in the archway and stared across the room.

"You think it's really the exit?" Lena asked, keeping her hand closed.

"Mr. Tickletoes says so," Serene offered.

"He *is* a spider," Quinn reminded them. "They trap things for a living."

Lena took a deep breath. "Only one way to find out." She started across the room and toward the door, Serene behind her. Colm followed, casting backward glances, sometimes looking at his feet or the wall, still not sure what he was looking for, but looking just the same. Something on the floor caught his eye, and he paused to get a closer look, squinting in the light offered by the torches lining the chamber.

It was a stone, like all the others. Nothing remarkable except for how polished it was, and how round. The ones surrounding it were irregular and jagged, but this one was almost as perfect as a pearl.

He spotted another one just a ways up, almost identical to its brother. In fact, looking closely now, he could see the whole floor was littered with them, spread out at wide intervals, but plentiful enough that you would almost certainly step on one if you weren't watching.

"Stop!"

Colm's cry rebounded off the walls. Everyone froze. Lena turned, a look of annoyance on her face. She was nearly to the door.

Colm pointed at the floor. "Those stones, the round ones. They don't look right to me." He looked over at the wall. There, next to one of the torches, was a small crack, except it too was unnatural, carefully carved. The wall was studded with them, just as the floor was covered in the stones, all running parallel to one another.

"Watch your step," he warned.

Lena and Serene looked around them, pointing out the stones that they had barely missed and the ones that lay between them and the exit. They would be easy to avoid, once you knew what you were looking for.

"Um. C-C-C-Colm?"

Colm turned around to see Quinn staring at his feet. At his right foot in particular. And the smooth round stone that right foot pressed flush to the floor.

"Ooooh-kay," Colm said. Serene gasped, and Lena made a move to come toward them, but Colm waved her off. "It's all right. Just stay there. We've got this," he said, then turned to Quinn. "Just don't move, okay?"

Colm took a cautious step toward the mageling, careful to watch where his own boots landed. He could see Quinn trembling in the torchlight, even underneath his giant folds of robe. Colm moved carefully, Finn's words ringing in his head. *Your face scorched by a fireball.* Colm looked at the cracks in the wall, one lined up evenly with Quinn's head. He had no idea what might come out of it.

"Mr. Tickletoes says be careful!" Serene cried.

Colm nodded and wiped his forehead. Picking a padlock with a pear thorn was one thing. He had no idea how to disarm a trap. When he was young, his sisters would hold him down, pin his arms to his back, and tickle him until he peed his pants. He had never even learned how to get out of *that*. He studied the smooth stone Quinn's foot pressed against. There was clearly no way he could keep this thing from triggering;

something was going to shoot out of that hole in the wall as soon as Quinn took a step.

But maybe Colm could make sure it missed.

Colm stood right in front of Quinn now, the boy's blue eyes big as pumpkins. Colm checked to make sure the space behind him was clear of triggers.

"All right, Nibbles, listen to me. When I say three, I want you to jump, all right?"

"J-j-jump?"

"Yes. Jump as high as you can. Got it?"

Quinn looked at the wall, panicked. "B-b-but I d-don't see how . . ."

"Just trust me on this one." Colm got down on his knees, held out both hands. He could sense the boy tensing. This would only work if Quinn was taken completely by surprise. The same way Colm had been, back on the road with that sword aimed straight for his head. Colm put both of his hands right by Quinn's feet. He saw Lena and Serene huddled together.

"All right. Here we go. One."

Colm positioned his hands right above the boy's ankles, calculating the angle. He really hoped that whatever shot out of the wall came out straight.

"Two!"

Colm grabbed hold of Quinn's feet and yanked hard. Quinn fell backward, feet slipping from beneath him just as a sizzling bolt of blue electricity burst from the crevice, frying the space where his head had just been. Colm could hear it cackle as it passed. The bolt splashed against the opposite wall and dissipated into nothing. The trap missed.

Quinn hit the floor hard, and his curse filled the chamber. "Fergin flagnaggats!" he said, rubbing the back of his skull.

Colm took a deep breath and looked at the mageling struggling up to his elbows. *"Flagnaggats?"*

Then they both started laughing. Colm couldn't think of anything terribly funny about seeing Quinn nearly electrocuted, but there must have been, because he couldn't stop himself. They huddled together there on the dungeon floor, arms crossed on their knees, rocking back and forth.

"You swept me off my f-f-feet," Quinn said through heaving snorts.

"Bzzzzzzttttt!" Colm said, pretending to be zapped by lightning, which was easy because the laughter was making him shake uncontrollably.

"Um, guys . . ."

Colm somehow managed to get control of himself, then glanced over at Lena, who was pointing to the hallway they had come from. The torches cast enough light that they could see their own shadows on the far wall. And one shadow that wasn't theirs, growing larger by the second.

Without another word, Colm bent down and pulled Quinn up, the two of them quickly but carefully picking their way across the booby-trapped floor to the iron door at the opposite end of the chamber. They could hear footsteps coming from the hall now, and an awful sound, like claws scraped along stone. Lena reached for the door, but it wouldn't budge.

"Locked!"

From the hallway, the scraping grew louder. Whatever was coming was right outside the entryway now. Colm saw Mr. Tickletoes suddenly leap from Serene's hand, land on the floor, and head straight for the darkest corner. Lena slammed her chain-mailed shoulder into the door. Nothing.

"Here, let me try." Colm pushed her out of the way and bent down to inspect the lock. It didn't look complicated. In fact, it looked like the one on his own front door in Felhaven. He could pick it . . . maybe . . . *if* he had one of his sisters' hairpins. He turned to Lena and asked if she had one.

"Do I look like the kind of girl who does her hair?" she snapped.

He turned to Serene, who shook her head. "Druids aren't allowed to wear metal," she said.

Colm sighed, but then Quinn said, "I have this," and handed Colm a feathered quill produced from his robe, the feather white and brown and frayed along the edges. It was thin enough, but Colm wasn't sure it would hold; it wasn't even as strong as a pear-tree thorn. It could easily snap, but he didn't have any other options. Colm took the feather and inserted it into the lock, putting his ear against the iron door. He thought he knew what to listen for, but it was a little hard with Lena shouting at him.

"Hurry!"

"I am hurrying!"

"Hurry *faster!*"

Colm glared at Lena, who glared back. Then he felt Serene tap him on the shoulder. He was too late.

Standing in the entryway, across the chamber floor, was the Overseer.

"*That's* the Overseer?" Lena exclaimed.

Colm looked across the room at the figure standing in the entryway.

"He's just a goblin," Lena said dismissively.

Colm had never seen a goblin before. He had read about them. Had heard about them, but he had never laid eyes on one in the leathery flesh. The Overseer was a wiry-looking thing, mostly bones with a little muscle to hold them in place, and flat ears the color of cabbage poking out on either side of a bald, sloping, greenish head. Its hooked nose hung well over its upper lip. It might have been comical if it weren't for the very nasty-looking axes the goblin held in each hand. Hatchets with curved blades that glinted in the torchlight. He looked to be even smaller than Quinn.

"I'll handle this," Lena said, brushing her bangs from her eye with one hand and adjusting her grip on her stone dagger with the other. Colm knew he should turn his attention back to the lock, try to get them out of there, but he couldn't help himself. He had never seen a would-be barbarian battle a goblin in the middle of a trap-filled dungeon before either.

112

From across the chamber, the goblin spoke. "Behold. It is I. The overseer. Lord of the Labyrinth. Keeper of the Keys. You have trespassed. Prepare to meet your doom."

Colm expected a voice terrible and menacing, the kind of voice that puts ice in your veins. Instead the goblin sounded bored, slurring the words as if it couldn't get them out fast enough.

Lena was menacing enough for both of them. "I am Lena Proudmore, warrior and barbarian, and my heart is as steel as my . . ." She looked down at the rock she was holding, licked her lips, then continued. "Erm, my resolve is as unyielding as the stone in my hand. Surrender now, and I may see fit to spare your life. Or take another step, and forfeit it altogether." She held her makeshift dagger before her, pointing it at the creature.

The goblin nodded as if he'd actually heard this speech before and was just waiting for it to end so he could deliver his next line, which he did with the same apathetic monotone as before. "Then I shall make gravy of your blood and pick my teeth with your finger bones as I feast upon your skewered flesh."

Then, with what looked like a sigh, though it was hard to tell from all the way across the room, the goblin charged—or at least began to hobble quickly. Lena held her ground, eyebrows cinched. Serene looked around wildly for Mr. Tickletoes. Beside Colm, Quinn was stuttering through half a dozen words that Colm didn't recognize. Colm frantically turned back to the lock, working the tip of the quill around, desperately trying to get the tumbler to fall. If he could just get it open before the raging goblin made it across the room. The raging goblin who seemed to dodge the traps with ease, as if he had the route memorized. The raging goblin who was only ten feet away now, both axes raised, ready to take off Lena's head.

The raging goblin whose legs were suddenly on fire.

Who cursed and dropped both of his axes, dancing around before curling up and rolling on the cold stone floor to smother the flames, triggering traps that caused more bolts of electricity to zap across the room, making the whole place buzz, just as Colm felt the last tumbler drop and the lock give way.

The goblin screamed.

The door swung open.

Revealing a grin of silver and gold.

6

OUT OF THE DUNGEON, INTO DUNGEONEERS

The rogue smiled at them.

They tumbled through the door and into an immense chamber, falling at Finn's feet, a bundle of limbs entwined. Colm untangled his legs from Serene's robe and managed to pull himself up.

He was immediately dumbstruck by what he saw.

In contrast to the dreary tunnel behind them, the great hall before them was filled with light. Huge chandeliers hung from chains of gold, the flicker of a thousand candles casting fiery halos against the ceiling. Giant marble pillars anchored the four corners of the room, and a huge winding staircase with gold railings led both up and down in its center like a vortex. The floors were polished marble as well, dark green and buffed to a mirror sheen. A strange clock with twenty-four separate hourglasses hung over a set of huge double doors, and

Colm noted that most of the sand had sifted to the bottoms.

Lush tapestries draped each wall, interspersed with paintings depicting all manner of brutal but courageous confrontations. In one, a band of armored knights was surrounded by a horde of wolves. In another, a figure in a black cloak was dueling a towering demon. In yet another, a wizard was calling down the stars from the sky.

At least two dozen doors and arches led to more rooms besides. This one hall was five times as large as the magistrate's house in Felhaven (which made it fifty times the size of Colm's house). Colm looked over at Quinn, whose face held a similar expression of awe. Even Lena looked impressed, and she didn't strike Colm as the kind to be impressed easily.

Suddenly Colm felt a shove in his side as something small blustered by, trailing tendrils of smoke. It was the Overseer, his pants scorched, marching up to Finn, who seemed to be stifling a laugh.

"You didn't tell me the bloody mageling was a blaster!" the goblin shouted, indicating his burned pants with both hands. Here, in all this light, the goblin looked much uglier than he had in the dungeon. You could really make out the crusted warts on his nose.

"I didn't know." Finn shrugged. "I didn't recruit him."

"Well, someone could have given me a warning," the goblin shrieked. "He could have killed me!"

"I hardly think a pair of smoking breeches counts as attempted murder," Finn quipped. "Besides, you're the Overseer.

It's your dungeon. One would think you'd be a little better prepared for a pack of first timers such as these."

Colm felt another push as Lena jostled her way to the front, stone still in hand. She pointed the tip of it at Finn and the goblin in turn.

"Wait a minute, what's going on? Who are you? What's the meaning of all of this? Where is the woman who brought us here? Master Stormbow? And why are you speaking with that vile creature?"

"Ah, Miss Lena Proudmore," the rogue said with the same bow he'd used on Colm's mother. "Allow me to introduce myself. My name is Finn Argos. I am one of the masters of the guild. And this is my associate, Herren Bloodclaw."

"Your *associate*?" Lena squawked.

"B-but he's a g-g—"

"Spit it out, will ya?" Herren Bloodclaw snapped, glaring at Quinn with beady orange eyes. "I'm a goblin. And a right ticked one at that. Didn't anyone teach you not to fling fire at your elders?" Quinn looked like he might be sick.

Finn put a hand on Herren's shoulder. "Renny here is no ordinary goblin," he explained. "He is a valuable member of our staff and has worked at the guild much longer than I have. He is also the primary architect of our practice dungeon, which you conquered with aplomb, by the way. Congratulations."

Colm blushed. He couldn't help it. Lena, on the other hand, seemed to grow even more irritated.

"Congratulations?" she pressed.

"On passing your test," Finn explained. "Not only did you make it out unharmed, you each exhibited courage and poise and used your natural talents when it mattered. Talking to animals, discovering traps, picking locks, singeing Herren's backside. A joint effort." He looked at each of them in turn.

The goblin grunted. Apparently he didn't think being set on fire was commendable at all.

Lena shook her head. "But what about me? I didn't do any of those things. I was going to slay him with my dagger, but Nibbles beat me to it."

"Excuse me?" the goblin interjected. "I am no thing to be slain. I am a true-blooded cave goblin of the Black Hills clan!"

Lena wasn't deterred. "Oh, please let me fight it," she pleaded with Finn. "Just to show you how I *would have* killed it." She turned to the goblin and half whispered. "Don't worry, I won't really slay you."

"You're flamblasted right you won't!" Herren Bloodclaw shouted, reaching out for her with both hands, but Finn held him back.

"That won't be necessary, Miss Proudmore," the rogue said. "Your courage was never in doubt, and we are thankful that a well-timed spell from Mr. Frostfoot here probably spared the overseer's life. Aren't we, Ren?" Finn looked at the goblin, who huffed but didn't say otherwise.

"What matters is that you are here at last." The rogue indicated the great gleaming hall with both hands. "Normally there would be a warmer welcome, but I'm afraid the other masters are preoccupied at the moment, and your fellow apprentices are all asleep."

"Fellow apprentices? Does that mean we've been accepted?" Serene asked in her reticent whisper, peeking over Colm's shoulder.

"It means you passed," Finn repeated. "Though nothing is official, not without Master Thwodin's approval. You still have some time to think it over. Tomorrow we will give you a proper introduction, give you a feel for what we do here, what you can hope to accomplish as a member of our guild. Then you can decide whether this line of work is right for you."

He was speaking to everyone, but Finn was looking dead at Colm. Colm took in the vast chamber, thinking of how much it must have cost to build. Just one of those paintings was probably worth more than his father made in a month, or even a year. Not to speak of the gold chandeliers or the marble pedestals that lined both sides of the room.

He looked back at the hole they had just crawled out of. This was it. This was the treasure at the end.

Finn Argos pointed up at the bottom-heavy hourglasses. "No doubt you have hundreds of questions, but as you can see, it's late, and I'm sure we are all tired from the long roads we took to get here. I'm afraid sleeping space is limited, so you will have to share a room. Master Bloodclaw, if you could please escort Miss Proudmore and Miss Willowtree to the ladies' hall . . ."

"I'm not goin' anyplace with her," the goblin spit, pointing a crooked green finger at Lena.

"Then if you could take Mr. Candorly and Mr. Frost-foot . . ."

The goblin looked at Quinn and cringed, even though the mageling was still tucked behind Lena, just as scared of the goblin as the goblin was of him.

"Fine. I'll take the girls," Herren grumbled. "But if the red one so much as touches me, I'm going to bite her head off."

"Good luck trying, with my fist crammed down your throat," Lena muttered. Colm watched as Quinn whispered something to Lena. "It will be all right," she said to him. "Colm will be with you." She gave Colm a lingering look; then the goblin escorted the girls to the stairs.

Colm felt a tug on his belt, saw the question in Quinn's eyes as they darted back and forth from him to Finn. After what they'd just been through, it made sense that the mageling would be a little wary.

"It's all right. I know this guy," Colm said. "He's the one who brought me here." *And pushed me down the hole,* he thought—but at least now he had an explanation for that.

"But he only has *four fingers*," Quinn whispered.

Colm held up his right hand.

"Oh."

Colm grabbed Quinn's hand as the rogue led them through the great hall, through one of its many oaken doors into a well-lit corridor lined with even more rooms. Colm heard

120

noises coming from most of them. Conversations. Laughter. Snoring. The sound of a blade being sharpened. Someone moaning in his sleep about not wanting to be turned into a pig again. None of his sisters ever complained about *that* in their sleep, at least.

"Here we are, then."

The room Colm and Quinn found themselves in was sparsely decorated—especially compared to the great hall—but it was still an improvement over Colm's closet at home. Each bed was twice the size of his hammock and came furnished with an actual pillow, so he wouldn't have to make one out of his pack. A dresser separated the two beds, and another stood against the far wall, candles burning on each. Two desks sat next to each other, with hard wooden chairs to match. They didn't have a window, but they did have a mirror—a precious commodity in a house full of girls, and not something Colm was used to having pretty much to himself.

One look in the mirror confirmed what Colm suspected: he was a mess. Hair matted. Pants wet and ripped. Knees bloody. Face caked brown and gray, eyes red, nails broken from scrabbling along stone. No wonder Lena had mistaken him for some kind of monster down in the dungeon. He could use a thorough scrubbing. He hadn't thought to bring spare clothes, save for the extra pair of socks, still damp in his pocket.

As if reading his thoughts, Finn pointed to the dressers. "You'll find basins by your bedsides to wash up, and there are clean clothes in the drawers. You can find parchment and quill in the desk. All letters go out the very next day. I would stay and chat, but you need your rest for tomorrow."

As if on cue, Quinn yawned and collapsed onto one of the beds. Finn took Colm by the shoulder as they walked back to the door, leaning in close. "You did it. I knew you would. I had a hunch about you, Colm Candorly, and my instincts are seldom wrong."

"So this is it, then?" Colm asked. "This is where people like us come to get rich?"

Finn shook his head. "This is where people like us learn how not to get killed. The getting rich comes after."

Colm nodded. Not getting killed sounded like a good first step. He must have looked worried, though, because Finn immediately tried to reassure him. "I'm not saying you have to stay. If you wake up tomorrow and decide you want to go back, I will take you. I am a man of my word, and you are a long way from home. I know how important your family is to you."

Which is exactly why I need to stay, Colm thought to himself, but he didn't say it.

"Most of us are born below," Finn whispered. "Closed in. Locked out. Few of us ever get a chance to rise above our station, to claw our way up. A rogue is always aware when an opportunity presents itself. He knows which doors to open."

"Thank you," Colm said. "For the opportunity."

Finn shook his head. "Don't thank me yet. You've only had a taste of what lies ahead."

And with that, the rogue bade them both good night and shut the door.

Colm sat on the corner of his bed and kicked off his boots. As well as they fit—and they fit perfectly—it was still a relief to finally have them off, along with the soaked and stinking socks. The day caught up to him in a rush, and Colm was suddenly overcome with exhaustion. His whole body ached, and he lay there paralyzed, barely able to lift a finger, let alone nine, recalling everything that had happened over the course of that one day. The duel on the road out of Felhaven. The failed attempts to get his coin back. Being pushed into the dungeon, saving Quinn from that trap, seeing Serene with that spider. And the goblin—Colm had never seen anything quite like him before.

And Lena. She was something. What, he wasn't sure yet, but definitely something.

Colm turned to ask Quinn what he thought of it, this place, but he was too late. The mageling had already fallen asleep, fully dressed, without even bothering to get under his covers.

It would all still be here in the morning, Colm told himself. He crawled beneath his blanket, this one plenty large enough to reach his feet, and nestled his head on his new pillow, relishing the suppleness of it. It seemed so extravagant, having a soft spot for your head.

He considered snuffing the candle beside him, but then he remembered the darkness of the dungeon when he had first descended, how *close* it was, as if it could attach itself to you and follow you everywhere. How it made it hard just to breathe.

Colm let the candle burn. A little light wasn't going to hurt anyone.

He woke to the sound of Quinn nibbling.

The mageling was sitting on the edge of Colm's bed with a sweet roll in his hand.

"Good morning," Quinn said between bites. "You are a heavy sleeper."

He said it without a single stumble, confirming at least one suspicion: that the boy's stutter was mostly a matter of nerves. He could speak just fine, Colm noticed, as long as he wasn't being attacked or electrocuted. "There's some for you too," Quinn said, pointing to the plate by Colm's bed. Colm sat up and rubbed his eyes, getting his bearings. He thought at first he wasn't hungry, but then the smell hit him.

"They're really good," Quinn mumbled through a mouthful. Colm didn't argue, devouring his own roll in four bites. Obviously Tye Thwodin didn't have to skimp on butter or sugar. They sat together on Colm's bed, polishing their plates, licking their fingers to get to the crumbs. Colm stopped once to pinch himself, just to make sure that he really was in a castle in the middle of nowhere with a boy named Frostfoot who could shoot fire from his fingers.

"You eat fast too," Quinn remarked.

"I have eight sisters," Colm reasoned. "The faster you eat, the more you get."

"Wow. Eight sisters. Your parents must be crazy."

Colm nodded. It was as good an explanation as any.

"I have two sisters," Quinn continued. "At least, I used to. When I was four, my parents disowned me."

"Disowned you?"

"Abandoned me. They knew I was different and it scared them, so they bundled me in a wagon and took me on a long ride, then left me in the woods outside another town, far away."

"That's horrible," Colm said. Of course, his own father had threatened to do the same thing to each of them at least a dozen times, but Colm knew it was only in jest. He had never met anyone who'd actually been abandoned.

"My father—the man who raised me, I mean—he says my first parents were horrible people. It might have been worse, though. In some places they consider mages to be demons, so they bind them with rope, stuff them into baskets, and throw them in the river."

"Well, at least *that* didn't happen," Colm remarked.

"Lucky, right? Mum and Dad found me in the woods and took me in. They didn't even kick me out when I accidentally set Dad's beard on fire. That's how come I'm here, you know. They thought it might help me get better control of my power, some more formal training."

"So, then, you actually *knew* about this place?" Colm wondered how Tye Thwodin went about finding new recruits. Finn had made it sound as if he had discovered Colm by accident. Maybe he had. Then again, Finn didn't strike Colm as the kind of man who did anything accidentally.

"Actually, they came to recruit Lena. We are both from Kingsfort. My father works for the Proudmores, so I've known her most of my life. When Master Stormbow heard what I could do, she told me I should come along too. A long wagon ride later, Lena and I found ourselves stuck in that gloomy dungeon. Then we met you. And then Serene. And now we are here."

That at least explained their constant whispers and the way Quinn always looked to Lena for confirmation. "So you and she are just friends, then?" Not that it mattered. Just a curiosity.

Quinn shrugged. "She needs me. She doesn't have that many friends. She's not so easy to get along with sometimes, in case you haven't noticed."

"Not at all," Colm lied.

"She's an only child, and she comes from a long line of warriors, so she kind of has a lot to live up to, I guess. She thinks becoming a dungeoneer is the best way to earn her name."

Earn her name. Colm had to stop and think about that one. He figured the whole reason people became dungeoneers was for the treasure. He hadn't considered that there might be other reasons.

"Don't get me wrong," Quinn added. "She can be nice when she wants to be. She just seldom ever wants to be."

As Colm got dressed, Quinn told more stories about him and Lena growing up in Kingsfort. Unlike Colm's backwater, edge-of-the-map hamlet, Kingsfort sounded like a sprawling city, where warriors and wizards were not unusual, even if they were still uncommon. He was about to ask Quinn what it was like using magic—how it worked, how it felt, what the most powerful spell he'd ever cast was—when someone knocked on their door.

"Morning, gentleman," Finn chirped, peeking his head in the door and eyeing the empty plates on Colm's bed. "I see you've already taken care of breakfast, which is good, though I believe, Mr. Frostfoot, that you already had one breakfast this morning."

Quinn blushed and looked down at his feet. Colm wondered how someone with such a large appetite could be so bone skinny.

"You two should hurry and get outside," Finn said. "It's a big day. You're going to miss the tour, and believe me, you don't want Master Fimbly to have to repeat himself."

"Welcome to Thwodin Castle, home of Thwodin's Legion, the most accomplished dungeoneering guild this side of the Stormforge Mountains, built by one of the greatest dungeon divers who has ever lived."

Colm rubbed the gooseflesh on his arms. They were standing outside, and for the first time, Colm got a good look at where Finn had brought him. It wasn't the chill that prickled his hair but the view: the enormous castle sitting in the center of a clearing, ringed by a forest; the forest encapsulated by a halo of snowcapped mountains, blue-gray mounds iced over. The castle was equally stunning, looming four stories tall, its crenellated battlements boasting an even better view of the neighboring range, its seven towers and accompanying smaller balustrades of whitewashed stone stretching skyward and casting their long shadows behind them. The center tower stood tallest, topped, as it was, with a tarnished silver pinnacle that still sparkled in the sun. Colm stood and marveled at it, this hidden jewel, tucked here on its field of emerald grass glossed with dew.

"Wow."

Quinn stood next to him, gape mouthed. He was dressed in new robes that he'd found in his drawers, red with bright blue sunbursts stitched along the sleeves, actually his size. Both of them had discovered several pairs of pants and shirts and even new boots, though Colm preferred to keep his old ones. Still, the new clothes were in much better condition than the ones he'd brought, and he felt invigorated with a full stomach and dry socks on his feet.

They weren't the only ones cleaned up. Serene had on an emerald cloak that came past her knees. Her hair had been plaited into several glossy black rows that fell to her shoulders and curtained her eyes. She held a dark wooden staff, sanded and polished, and looked almost regal. And Lena . . . Colm tried not to look at Lena, because the glint from the sun striking her new shirt of chain mail blinded him. Still, he noticed she no longer had a rock for a weapon. Instead, a broadsword bounced against her leg. Colm wondered why she got a sword and he didn't, but he didn't say anything. She was a barbarian in training, after all. He still wasn't quite sure what he was.

"As you probably know, Thwodin's Legion was founded twenty-three years ago by the great warrior Tye Thwodin himself. And I am proud to say that I have been here for every one of those years."

By the look of him, Colm would guess that the old man addressing them had been around for every one of everybody's years. He had been introduced as Carrol Fimbly, expert in history and tactics and the oldest living member of the guild. Master Fimbly was, by his own admission, the foremost repository of knowledge on the history of dungeons, and thus the most suited for giving a formal introduction to the practice of treasure hunting. It was in his wrinkled hands that Colm and the others had been placed for the morning, with a promise from Finn that they would be retrieved after lunch, by which point they would be "more than ready to do almost anything else."

Master Fimbly, Colm noticed, talked so loud you couldn't hear your own thoughts. Colm couldn't imagine this old man ever venturing into a dungeon, though. He'd probably break a hip trying to squeeze through the entrance.

"As you may be aware," Master Fimbly yelled, "Tye Thwodin founded the guild with the express purpose of training aspiring young dungeoneers, much like yourselves, to share in the bountiful treasure that is ripe for the taking. And as you can see by the beautiful structure behind me, his hopes were well founded."

The old man coughed up a phlegm-filled laugh. Colm thought about the contract Finn had given him, the one that was sitting on his new desk in his new room inside said beautiful structure. The contract that said fifty percent of earnings came right back to Tye Thwodin and the guild. That, at least, explained the fancy chandeliers.

"Castle Thwodin," Fimbly continued, "is a vast estate, comprising some one hundred eighty-six rooms, including laboratories, libraries, training halls, kitchens, dining areas, dungeons, armories, and one of the largest treasuries known to man. We have our own smithy, our own indoor archery range, and our very own hot springs. The whole estate is supplied to withstand a siege of several months, though I have yet to meet any army that would dare attack it. The castle cannot be found on a map, and save for a few individuals in Master Thwodin's confidence, it cannot be accessed by anyone who isn't a member of the guild."

"Unless you've got one of those magic crystals," Serene whispered, and Colm realized she must have gotten here the same way he did: turned inside out and upside down and then thrown down a hole.

"As a member of this guild, you will undergo a rigorous training regimen. You will progress according to your ability and your aptitude. When we feel you have acquired all the skills necessary to be successful in your chosen vocation, you will be granted the rank of master. This may take several years . . . and assumes you don't die in the process." The old man smiled.

No one smiled back.

"Now, before we continue our tour, let me address some frequently asked questions." The old man pulled a scroll from his robe and unfurled it. It nearly reached his feet. "Question one. 'What is dungeoneering?' Well, you all know what dungeoneering is, don't you? I don't have to get into that. Ahem. Question two. 'Is dungeoneering dangerous?' What kind of nonsense is this? Anyone who's ever stared into the eye of a beholder and felt his legs turn to stone beneath him knows the answer to that one. Stupid question, moving on . . ."

Quinn shot Colm a concerned look. "I'm not sure I like that old man," he said. Colm nodded in agreement.

"Let's find a good one," Master Fimbly continued. "Ah. Here we are. Question seventeen. 'How many guildsmen have perished while in training?' Now that's an interesting one, let me see. . . ." He began to tick off his fingers, "Him, and her, and those four, and then there was that whole debacle with the gorgon. Oh, and then there was the poisonous fog—still not sure how *that* happened . . . twenty-four, twenty-five . . . plus seven—eight if you count her, though she's technically still *alive*. My land. You know? I'll have to get back to you on that one." The old man began to furl his scroll even though he had only answered one question and didn't really give an adequate answer to it. "Let's head indoors, shall we? Still so much to see."

Master Fimbly turned and started to make his way inside. Serene grabbed hold of Colm's arm. "He wasn't serious, was he? I mean, you can't really *die* here. . . ."

"Only if you're not good enough," Lena said, marching past them with one hand on the hilt of her new sword.

The four of them followed Master Fimbly through the wide double doors and into the great hall. During the day, the castle was a vastly different place. Last night, when they had emerged from the dungeon, the hall had been deserted. Today it was packed. Most everyone was Seysha's age or younger, though Colm spotted a few grown men and women bustling through. Colm remembered what Finn had said about Master Thwodin liking to start them young.

They made their way down to the dining area, where several recruits were finishing a meal. Colm noticed most of the trainees stared at him for a moment before returning to their bowls. It's all right, he told himself. You're new. A little staring is to be expected.

"And here," Master Fimbly said, pushing open a huge iron door, "is where the magic happens." Quinn rubbed his hands together.

Colm entered the room and immediately felt a blast of heat. He expected to find himself in some arcane laboratory where potions were brewing and newts were having their eyes poked out, but it was only the kitchen. At least a half dozen fires were raging beneath giant pots. In the center of these stood an intimidating figure. He wore an apron stained several shades of smeared green and red. His shaggy mop of silver hair hung down into his eyes, one of which only seemed to stare at the tip of his onion-bulb nose. He was at least as big as a horse. And almost as hairy.

"This is Fungus," Master Fimbly said. "Fungus, these are the new recruits." Fungus sniffed at them, stuck a finger in his ear, considered what he found there, then wiped it on his shirt, adding it to the mix. "What's for lunch, Fungus?" Fimbly inquired.

"Stew," Fungus grunted.

"And dinner?"

"Stew," Fungus grunted again.

Fimbly turned to them and spoke in a low voice, which was somehow still loud. "As you can see, Fungus isn't the most creative cook you'll ever meet, but the food is always hot and you seldom find anything in your bowl that you can't identify."

Master Fimbly ushered them out the door and down another set of stairs. From behind him, Colm heard Lena say something about Fungus being an unfortunate name for a cook. They passed several training halls and a large room where, it appeared, guild members were busy weighing gold and silver coins, learning to tell the real from the counterfeit, or maybe just helping to count the contents of Tye Thwodin's coffers. Master Fimbly showed them the stables and the henhouse and the dungeons—"Not the exploring kind," he explained.

"The keeping-prisoners-in kind. Though we currently have no residents." He showed them a dozen more rooms where people were busy casting spells, swinging axes, or shooting arrows, and all the while the old man recited statistics about how much gold the guild took in per annum and how many famous dungeoneers had served in its hallowed halls. None of them were names Colm had heard of, but at the mention of several, Lena's face lit like a full moon.

"Of course, there are some rooms you aren't allowed to see yet, but it won't hurt to show you one more."

Master Fimbly stopped at another large iron door and inserted a key, swinging it open to reveal a chamber nearly as large as the great hall itself.

Lena's eyes suddenly seemed to catch fire, and Colm could actually trace the shiver that made its way along her body. She reached out and steadied herself against Quinn's shoulder.

"Breathe, Lena. Just breathe," she told herself.

"Behold . . . the armory," Master Fimbly said.

Colm had to admit it was impressive. At least a hundred racks and tables dripping with wood and metal, all of it polished and gleaming, the edges so sharp it hurt to look at them. There was a wall of axes, some of them as tall as Colm himself, and another full of swords. Maces. Morning stars. Slings. Bows. Halberds. There were weapons Colm didn't know the name of, multibladed staffs that looked impossible to hold. Clubs with so many spikes that they looked like brush bristles. There were enough pointy things in this one room to impale a thousand men ten thousand times over. Lena and Quinn rushed to the first weapon they saw, *ooh*ing and *aah*ing to each other. Serene waited by the door. Colm politely stood beside her.

"It's fine," she said. "Go ahead."

Colm walked in and stood in front of the wall of swords, taking in one that was longer than his leg by half, its grip crested with a round blue stone, its blade etched with unknown symbols. It didn't look that heavy. He could probably lift it. Could maybe even give it a good, solid swing. Then Finn's voice whispered inside his head. *"You'd be stabbed six times before you even got it out of its scabbard."* He let his eyes gravitate down to the smaller, thinner blades. The ones like Finn's. He was reaching out for one when he heard Quinn calling him.

He and Lena were standing at a glass case at the back of the room, just staring at it.

"Um. It's a hammer," Colm said, coming over. And it was. Just a simple smith's hammer, plain wooden handle, black iron head, notched and dented from use.

"It's not *just* a hammer," Lena chided him. "This is *the* hammer. Tye Thwodin's hammer. The one he used to attack his very first ogre."

So Finn hadn't made that story up, at least.

"I see you've found Smashy," Professor Fimbly said, sauntering up to join them. "Not a terribly creative name, but then again, Master Thwodin never was much of a poet."

"Does he still use it?" Lena asked.

"Excuse me, dear?"

"I said, DOES HE STILL USE IT?" Master Fimbly seemed to be terribly hard of hearing. Could explain why he was always yelling.

"That? Heavens, no. He uses *that* one now."

The old man pointed to the wall behind the case and a war hammer that hung there, its gleaming head easily ten times the size of its diminutive brother. It was five feet long from tip to tip, about as long as Quinn.

"Its head is triple-folded steel, fused by both fire and magic to a handle of cold iron. It's been known to bash in armor so badly that parts of the person inside were squeezed out between the slats. It can shatter a dragon's scale or turn a diamond to dust. And it's said that the very sight of it causes an ogre's heart to explode in its very chest."

"Wow," Quinn said. Lena reached out and touched the handle.

"Does it have a name?" Colm wanted to know.

The old man nodded. "Smashy Two," he said reverently.

Not much of a poet was an understatement.

"Well, then. Come along now. Tour's almost over, and I'm afraid Miss Proudmore's drool might rust the metal." Fimbly led the way out and Colm followed, pausing to help Quinn drag Lena away. They made it to the door and then got some help from Serene.

"But I don't *want* to go," Lena pleaded. "Just look at them. They're all so pretty. Aren't they beautiful?"

Serene shook her head. "My culture forbids me to carry

weapons forged of iron or steel. They're an affront to Mother Nature."

"So what do you cut your meat with?" Quinn asked, but Serene took a step away, grimacing.

"I don't think she eats meat," Colm whispered.

"I guess it would be harder if you could talk to your food," Quinn surmised.

"And it could talk back," Colm said.

On the way out of the armory, they were all intercepted by Finn.

"Professor Fimbly, I do hate to interrupt, but I have to borrow your four charges for a moment," the rogue said. "The founder has managed to find some time in his otherwise busy schedule to meet his new recruits."

Carrol Fimbly nodded. "They are all yours, Master Finn," he said. Colm looked at the old man, wondering how it was he managed to hear Finn just fine when the four of them had to shout to get his attention. Finn seemed to read his thoughts.

"Master Fimbly only has trouble hearing *young* voices," he explained. "Come on. There are some very important people you need to meet."

Finn escorted the four of them through a series of twisting hallways and up three flights of stairs, passing a handful of trainees who greeted the rogue with nods of deference but seemed to ignore Colm and the others. One of them looked at Lena and rolled her eyes. Lena stuck out her tongue. Finn noticed, of course. Colm had a feeling there was little that escaped the man.

"I would like to say that we're one happy family here, everyone getting along with everyone else, but even I'm not that good a liar," he said. "No family is happy all the time. We try to discourage infighting, boasting, and taunting as much as possible, but it is the nature of the business. It gets a little competitive."

Colm was no stranger to taunting. Serene looked appalled, though. This was the same girl who apologized to the grass as she stepped on it.

"Of course, once you are down in the depths running from a nest of ogres bent on your untimely demise, you find a way to work out your differences," the rogue added.

Finn led them around another corner and paused outside a set of wooden doors trimmed in gold. He smoothed out the wrinkles in his tunic and stood up straight. He looked more nervous than he had when the man outside Felhaven had a sword to his neck. "Listen carefully: The people on the other side of this door have slain six dragons between them. They have journeyed to the ends of the world. They have fought rampaging hordes of undead warriors. They have, in short, seen more between blinks of their eyes than the four of you have seen in a lifetime, so don't expect them to be too terribly impressed by anything you have to say. Just be respectful, speak only when spoken to, and be sure to address everyone as master." Finn went to open the door, then stopped himself.

"Oh. And don't say anything about Master Velmoth's ears."

"Wait, what?" Colm said, but Finn had already thrown open the doors.

Colm expected some fancy hall complete with gilded thrones and bleating trumpets, but he walked into a small room with a single fireplace and one long crescent-shaped table that stretched halfway across it. There were nine chairs at the table, but only four of them were occupied. On the left end sat a tall, raven-haired woman with eyes like ponds and a plum-colored cape draped across her shoulders. Her almost coal-black skin shone in the firelight. Next to her sat Herren Bloodclaw, the goblin responsible for scaring Colm half to death last night. He was busy scribbling something on a piece of parchment and didn't even bother to look up when Finn escorted them in. To the far right sat another man Colm had never seen before. Spindly, pale, and anemic-looking, he had a beakish nose, a bald head, and two solid black eyes that shone like marbles.

And bunny ears.

Not the perky ovals of the white rabbits Colm would sometimes catch in Felhaven, but two sad, droopy, flopping brown flaps like fallen oak leaves hanging down over his cheeks.

Master Velmoth, Colm presumed.

In the center sat a hulking, armor-clad behemoth with a sun-colored bush of a beard and feet as big as ship's hulls. The only man in the room who could probably even lift Smashy Two, let alone swing it. It gave Colm pause just looking at

139

him, sitting in a chair at least twice the size of the others, his huge fists like iron anvils, stacked one upon the other.

He looked bored to death.

It was obvious that they had walked in on an argument, though it seemed to be only between the two masters sitting on the ends.

"I'm telling you, you have to try a reverse transfiguration spell."

"And I'm telling you that I already tried one," Master Velmoth spit.

"Not using my incantation, you haven't."

"I can't use your incantation, Merribell. You're a bloody cleric. If I let you try to reverse it, you'll end up cleansing my soul or some such nonsense, and then where will I be?"

"At peace with the world?" the woman suggested.

"Exactly! When all I really want is my old ears back!"

"Shut your traps," Master Thwodin commanded, pointing with one meaty finger at Colm and the rest. "Master Argos has brought our guests."

The woman named Merribell and the man with the floppy ears instantly shut up. Herren Bloodclaw looked up, sighed, and then went back to his scribbling.

"Our newest recruits," Finn said, pushing Colm and the others forward a step, like he was corralling sheep. "May I introduce you to Lena Proudmore from Kingsfort. A fighter by nature, but hoping someday to become"—Finn coughed, cleared his throat—"a barbarian."

140

Lena bowed, then stood at attention, one hand across her chest in that same gesture Colm had seen her make before. "My sword is yours, masters," she said gravely.

"Then tell it to stay the bloody hell away from me," the goblin sniped without looking up. Tye Thwodin chuckled. He waved his hand, indicating that Finn should move along.

"Ahem. Yes," Finn continued, nudging Lena out of the way. "Next we have Quinn Frostfoot. A mageling with much untapped talent, also from Kingsfort."

"Um. At your s-s-service, if it pl-pl-please you, masters."

"You stay away from me too, Tremble Tongue." The goblin snorted.

"Please, Renny. I don't think your commentary is called for," Master Merribell, the woman at the far end of the table, chided. "The poor lad is obviously nervous enough."

"All the more reason!" the goblin snapped. On the far other side of the table, Master Velmoth shook his head, ears slapping against his cheeks.

"Serene Willowtree of the Eve," Finn said, interrupting by pushing the reluctant girl forward. "A druid with an innate ability to commune with the natural world. Up to a point."

Serene held her staff in front of her and bowed reverently. "I am here to learn," she said softly. Colm noticed Master Merribell's smile. He had a good guess who had brought Serene into the fold.

"And finally, may I present Colm Candorly of Felhaven."

Colm felt a nudge from Finn's boot and took a step forward.

141

He didn't know what to do with his hands, so he shoved them into his pockets, feeling the silver coin that was his again and clutching it fiercely in his palm.

"Um. Hello . . . I mean, I'm honored, your . . . master-full-ness . . . sir."

"And what exactly are you supposed to be?" Master Velmoth asked, his voice cold and stern. Colm looked at his enormous ears and felt like he could ask the man the very same question.

"I'm a thief," Colm said.

"A rogue," Finn corrected quickly.

"He's a thief," Tye Thwodin fired back. "And he will be a thief until you train him to be otherwise. Tell me, Colm Candorly, how much coin have you collected in your life?"

"I don't know, sir," Colm answered, wondering why, of all of them, he was the only one being questioned. Was it simply because he was last? Or was it because he didn't have a fancy salute or a sword? Was it because he didn't have untapped magical talent or couldn't talk to birds? Did that mean he didn't belong here with the rest of them? Colm thought of the coins spread out over his table at home. "I had a pretty big pile," he said.

Tye Thwodin laughed. "A pretty big pile? Could it fill this room three times over?"

"No, sir."

"Well, then, you have a lot of catching up to do."

Master Velmoth of the floppy ears laughed. Colm was about to respond when Finn stepped forward.

142

"Mr. Candorly is an expert pickpocket, Master Thwodin, snatching a piece of silver from my very boot while I wasn't looking."

"Is that so?" Tye Thwodin said, narrowing his eyes at Finn and then turning them on Colm. He felt Finn's arm draped across his shoulder, four fingers giving his arm the slightest squeeze.

"Yes, sir," Colm said. "It was part of my test. That, and the dungeon."

"Yes, the dungeon," Master Thwodin said dismissively. "A level one, standard grid, only one trap, tumble lock, no real monsters to speak of."

The goblin grunted.

"Excuse me, Ren. No *dangerous* monsters to speak of. And yet one of you nearly got his head zapped by a bolt of lightning," Tye Thwodin grumbled.

Colm sensed that this wasn't going well. Or maybe this is how it always went. Maybe that was the point of this meeting, for Tye Thwodin, the founder, the man with dungeon diving dripping in his veins, to size up his prospective recruits, to weed through them before they even got started.

Finn quickly came to their defense. "They made it through in record time, I believe. I submitted all the paperwork to you this morning."

"Yes. Yes. The report." Master Thwodin reached inside his tunic and removed a pair of glasses that were too small for his mountainside face, then snatched a piece of parchment from the table. "Here we are. A thief with nine fingers

143

who's never held a sword in his life."

"I picked one up just yesterday," Colm started to say, but another squeeze of his shoulder told him to be quiet. Tye Thwodin continued.

"A would-be druid who can't seem to pass her trials because she's afraid of talking to bears and mountain lions."

"It's the teeth." Serene sighed. "Mostly."

"Mm. A mageling who stutters when he's casting spells, often causing them to misfire."

"Only when I'm n-n-nervous," Quinn explained.

"And a warrior who can't bear the sight of blood."

Colm looked over at Lena, who was blushing fiercely, squeezing the handle of her sword so tight that her fingertips were white.

"Just my own blood," she protested through clenched teeth. "I have no problem with anyone else's."

"Well, then, you had better be the greatest warrior in all the land." Master Velmoth smirked.

"I plan to be," Lena responded coolly. Velmoth's grin instantly reversed itself.

But Tye Thwodin was smiling now, at least. He leaned back in his chair, the wood creaking at the effort of holding him up. "She's a fiery one," he said.

"I told you," Herren Bloodclaw added.

"Though if she falls down and skins her knee, she's done for." Tye Thwodin wound his massive fingers into his thicket of beard, twisting it this way and that. "So this is what an

144

adventuring party looks like nowadays," he said, staring at them in turn. "Do you know what our guild's motto is?"

Colm had no idea. He hadn't seen it written on any statues in the numerous gardens. It hadn't been emblazoned on any banners hanging from the stone walls. And he wasn't alone. Even Lena didn't know, and he thought she knew everything about this stuff.

"'We descend so we may rise,'" Tye Thwodin answered.

"I thought it was 'One for you. Two for me,'" the goblin remarked, earning a reproachful look from the armored giant and quickly shutting up.

"It means," Thwodin growled, "that even in the deepest, dankest, most decrepit dungeons can be found the most priceless treasure. It means that there are ways to make it in this world without being born with a silver spoon shoved in your gullet. It means that no matter where you start from, you can claw your way to the surface and feel that golden sun shining on your face. Now I'm not sure how a stuttering mage, a swooning barbarian, a timid druid, and a fledgling rogue will play out in the bards' songs, but I've shaped the most brittle iron into a blade so strong it can cut through a behemoth's hide. So as long as you are members of this guild, we will turn you into dungeoneers, or my name's not Tye Thwodin." He pounded on the table, causing the other three sitting at it to jump. Then he spread his giant arms.

"Welcome to my Legion."

7

GETTING A SCRATCH

That could have gone worse," Finn said as he escorted them back toward the great hall.

"It could have?" Quinn questioned.

Finn nodded emphatically. "I've seen Master Thwodin reduce fresh recruits to sniveling puddles of snot, making them quit before they even got started. I think he was impressed. In his own way."

Colm couldn't imagine why. Tye Thwodin had spent most of the time pointing out their faults. It didn't seem like it had gone well at all. But at least it was over.

They entered the great hall, and Finn informed them that they would be spending the rest of the afternoon with their mentors—the masters who would be primarily responsible for helping each of them hone his or her respective talent. For Lena, it meant an afternoon with Sasha Stormbow, the swordswoman who had recruited her. Serene would spend it with Evelan Merribell, the cleric, which made Serene smile.

Quinn, on the other hand, was shaking in his robes.

"M-master V-v-v . . . Master V-v-v . . ." He couldn't spit out the name.

"I assure you Master Velmoth is a very capable mage, bunny ears aside," Finn said. "And he's the only spellcaster here who specializes in offensive magic, so he's really an ideal fit for you."

"B-b-b-but I've heard s-s-stories . . ."

Finn shook his head, putting a hand reassuringly on Quinn's shoulder. "We all have stories," he said. "And I assure you that in Master Velmoth's case, only half of them are true."

Quinn nodded, uneasy.

Colm, of course, would spend the afternoon with Finn.

"It's a matter of necessity, really," the rogue explained as they left the other three in the hall to await their mentors. "As it happens, I am the only rogue in residence, so most of your training will be my responsibility. There used to be three of us, but Master Passel retired recently with a bad case of nerves—shaky hands make disarming traps a touchy business—and Master Belm tripped his trigger a few moons ago, exploring Orc's Pass."

"Tripped his trigger?" Colm asked, looking back at his friends, then thinking about how strange it was for him to use that word already. *Friends.* He had known them for less than a day. And yet he felt connected to them. Something about thinking

you are all going to die in a smelly old dungeon together does that to you, he guessed.

"That's rogue-speak for met his makers," Finn explained. "There's also 'picked the wrong pocket,' 'unlocked his own door,' 'stopped the dagger with his back,' 'paid his debts,' 'lost his wager,' 'slipped into the shadow,' and 'cut the wrong rope.' There's more. Would you like to hear them?"

"No. Thank you," Colm said. He followed Finn through a series of twists and turns. He had no idea where in the castle they were. Or where they were headed.

"Of course, anyone else—a warrior, a wizard, a ranger, you name it—they just *die*, plain and simple. But we rogues are much too clever for that. Here, I want you to see something."

Finn led Colm down a set of stairs and along a hall. He took several turns and opened several more doors, using a set of keys produced from his cloak, before stopping in front of a rather unassuming iron portal with no window and only one keyhole. The keyhole was set into a complicated-looking mechanism made entirely of silver. A gold placard by the door said PROPERTY OF TYE THWODIN. KEEP OUT.

"Do you know what this is?" he asked, knocking on the door, which responded with a hollow echo.

Colm had seen dozens of rooms already. He couldn't remember which door led where. For all he knew, they were at the back door of the kitchen, though he would have at least smelled Fungus's stew simmering. "Storage closet?" he guessed.

Finn shook his head. "*This* is the most important room in the whole castle."

It didn't look like the most important room in the castle. Aside from its fancy lock, it looked completely ordinary. "What's inside?"

Finn's eyes grew big. "Half," he said.

"Half?"

"Half. Half of everything. Every bag of silver. Every cache of jewels. Every chest. You've read the contract. The guild gets half, and Tye Thwodin sticks it down here."

Colm moved to put his hand on the door, but Finn caught him around the wrist. He shook his head. "Better not." Colm pulled his hand back.

"How much is half?" he wondered.

Finn Argos shrugged and leaned against the wall. "Enough to make a hundred kings weep. Enough to buy a dozen castles . . . or maybe not. Truth be told, I've never been inside. No one has, save for Tye Thwodin himself."

Colm had a hard time believing that. It was just a door. With only the one lock. Surely someone would have gotten inside eventually, if only out of curiosity, just to take a look. "You'd think someone would have tried to open it," Colm ventured.

"Many have," Finn replied. He pointed to the silver lock. "Except that single lock is the most complicated combination of magic and mechanization that has ever been invented. Failed attempts to pick it can result in death by half a dozen means. Incineration. Disintegration. Decapitation. Currently I believe it's a stone-turning spell, which is a nasty enough way to go. The only way to get past it is with the key, and the only known key stays close to Master Thwodin's heart, tied to an unbreakable cord around his neck."

Colm shook his head. "So if we can't even look inside, what's the point? Why even bring me down here?"

"To show you that treasure does exist for people like us. That if you decide to stay and learn and be part of our guild, you can become rich—rich enough to feed your whole family yourself. Rich enough to build a bigger house, or kick the magistrate out of his. Rich enough that all of them will be looking up at *you*."

Colm didn't say anything. He imagined what his parents would say if they were standing here beside him. Would they tell him to stay? To learn to become a dungeoneer on the chance that he might one day share in Tye Thwodin's wealth? Or would they beg him to just come home already? To go help his father fixing shoes in the barn?

"You miss them, your family," Finn said. "But this is what you were made for, Colm. You have a gift. Maybe it's not highly thought of by all, but I can teach you how to use it. If you'll let me. Then, one day, maybe, we can sit and count our coin together."

He put a hand on Colm's shoulder, and Colm let it linger. He still felt as if there were too many things he didn't know about Finn Argos, but at least the rogue was looking after him. He clearly wanted Colm to stay.

Colm wanted to stay.

"Enough daydreaming." The rogue sighed. "Did Fimbly get around to showing you the back gardens? They are rather pretty, if you like that sort of thing." Colm shook his head, and Finn said, "Let's go."

"All right," Colm said. But he didn't move.

He simply couldn't take his eyes off the door.

Colm spent the rest of the afternoon viewing the gardens and the springs and the waterfall where, Finn said, most everyone but Fungus took their weekly bath. Finn showed him more training rooms where dungeoneers practiced their combat skills, avoiding the charmed ones where the mages practiced theirs—rule number six. On the way, they ran into Lena and Master Stormbow, who were already hard at work dueling with wooden swords and shields. The castle's resident weapons master looked hawkishly graceful and just as deadly, and was clearly the superior in every possible way, but Lena held her own, doing her best to parry each thrust. Colm just hoped she wouldn't get a splinter.

"It looks like *she* decided to stay," Colm said, watching Lena spin and whirl like a maple seed caught in the wind.

Finn nodded. "Miss Proudmore signed her contract before we even dumped her in the dungeon," he replied.

"And the others?" Colm asked.

"Both Quinn and Serene have signed on as well," Finn said

with a smile. "But no party is complete without a rogue."

Colm looked back at Lena. That sounded like something she would say.

They finished the afternoon back at the armory. Even though Colm told him that Master Fimbly had already taken them there, Finn insisted they visit again.

"A thousand different weapons," Finn pondered as they entered, "but none as sharp as that one between your ears."

Colm noticed him rubbing at his scar, the one that charted a course from cheek to chin. "You never told me how you got it," he said, pointing. "The scar, I mean. The fingers I know, but not that."

Actually, Finn hadn't told Colm the full story of how he'd lost his fingers either, except that they had been taken from him as punishment for acts of thievery, back before he joined the guild and became, in his words, "somewhat respectable."

"Oh, this little thing?" Finn said, tracing the white stitching with his fingertip. "This was the work of goblins. A goblin executioner, to be precise. A burly, red-skinned fellow, almost orc sized, if you can believe it. Had a gut that you could rest your feet on and an ax that could take them off in one stroke. I had been captured trying to nip some of their knickknacks, and they had me tied to a rock to keep my handsome head in place so they could part it from my shoulders." The rogue drew his finger beneath his chin.

"You were about to unlock your own door," Colm said.

"So to speak. Lucky for me, goblins aren't terribly good at

tying knots. When the ax came down, I shifted just enough—and yet not quite enough. The ax tore through the hemp that held me as I had hoped, but it left this reminder. I kicked Red Face in his prodigious gut and sent him bowling into his friends, then freed my hands, scooped some gold, and took the first tunnel I could find to safety, running so fast my feet hardly touched ground."

Colm looked at Finn, making no attempt to hide his awe.

"You can pick up your chin, Mr. Candorly. There are many here with even better stories than that one. Now let's see." The rogue strolled over to the wall of swords, a finger to his lips. Finally he nodded, then pulled a short, thin one from its hooks and held it in both hands, feeling the balance. It was less than three feet long, with a razor-thin blade that looked like it might snap if bent over a man's knee. But it had a beautiful silver hilt, and a pommel fashioned in the likeness of a cat's paw. The point of it was so fine, Colm was sure he could clean under his nails with it.

"It's called Scratch," Finn said. "Don't let the kitty fool you. It's incredibly light, and the steel is quite strong . . . and," he said, holding the hilt out for Colm to see, "it has a surprise." He flipped a tiny latch, and the cat's paw flipped open, revealing a hollow space in the handle. "Perfect for storing a pick or a pinch of poison or even a scroll, if it's rolled tight enough. It's a rogue's weapon if I've ever seen one." He held it out to Colm, who took it reluctantly, almost as if he were afraid it would bite him.

"Scratch," he whispered to himself.

As a young boy back in Felhaven, Colm had been the scourge of the nearby woods. At least ten thousand leaves had perished at his hand. Untold dandelions had lost their heads as he gamboled through, swinging tree branches, felling giants and slaying dragons by the score. But this wasn't a stripped tree branch. Colm held Scratch in his five-fingered hand and gave it a tentative thrust. Apparently he looked like a fool doing it, because Finn laughed. Determined, or just irritated, Colm turned and slashed out with greater force, managing to knock over a rack of spears, which clattered to the ground, making an enormous racket.

"Sorry," he said, setting the sword down on the floor.

"Yes, well. Maybe we should find a safe place to stick that thing for now," and the rogue began searching for a scabbard while Colm cleaned up his mess.

By the time they were finished at the armory, Colm not only had a Scratch on his leg—he also had a new bag complete with everything he would need to start his training as a rogue. "All the tools of the trade," Finn said, cinching the sack closed and handing it over.

Colm had to admit he felt different, decked out as he was, armed for the first time in his life. He could start to imagine himself as someone with a story. And for the first time since arriving at the castle, he didn't feel completely out of place. He glanced in his bag. It held a set of lockpicks, a small dagger—good mostly for carving your initials in things, Finn said—and a small gem that Finn called a sunstone. Amber colored and barely the size of a coin, it would glow in the dark if allowed to charge first in daylight, Finn insisted. A handy thing when the last torch dies. As they walked back to the great hall together, Colm stayed back a pace, admiring his new sword. Finn stopped beside the archway. The room was nearly full, Colm saw. Fungus was busy dishing up supper.

"I believe your friends are waiting for you," Finn said, pointing to a table in the back corner where Serene, Lena, and Quinn looked up. "I trust you don't need me to show you how to eat?"

Colm shook his head. "So what happens next?"

"Well, if you're lucky, there's dessert. Fungus makes a passable cobbler."

"No. I mean, what's next for me?"

Finn turned and looked up at the hourglass clock hanging above the huge front doors. "You have until midnight to decide. If you want to stay and learn to be a dungeoneer, simply sign your contract and slip it under your door. Somebody will come and retrieve it."

"And if I decide to go back home?"

"Then more gold for me, I suppose," Finn said with smirk.

Colm looked over the rogue's shoulder at the complicated clock, nineteen of its hourglasses empty, only five remaining. "I don't suppose they'd let me keep the sword."

Finn shook his head. "Property of the guild. Taking it without joining would be an act of thievery, and you know how thieves are punished." Finn waggled his fingers. "But you don't need a sword like that back in Felhaven anyways, now do you?"

Colm traced his finger along Scratch's silver paw. The rogue nodded toward the corner where Serene was standing, waving Colm over.

"Rule number forty-seven. Never keep a woman waiting,"

"You skipped a few," Colm said. He was pretty sure the last rule he'd learned was number eight.

"Another reason for you to stay," Finn fired back. "You still have a lot to learn."

Colm entered the dining hall and made his way to the back. He sat next to Quinn, who had his chin in his stew. As soon as Colm sat, Serene pounced on him, grabbing his arm with both hands.

"You'll never guess what *I* got to do today!" she said; then she did a double take. "Did you cut your hair? There's something different about you."

"He got a sword," Lena said, pointing to Colm's side with her spoon. Naturally she would be the first to notice.

"Oh. One of *those*," Serene muttered. "You people and your love for pointy things."

"Your hair is pointy," Quinn said, nodding toward Serene's braided tufts.

"Yes, but I can't *stab* anyone with it."

"I doubt Colm can either," Lena said from across the table.

Her hair, which normally draped over one eye, had been pinned back, and he could see both of those eyes sparkling from across the table.

"How hard can it be?" he said, pointing to the hilt of Scratch. "Just hold it out and wait for something to run into it."

Lena grunted. "You'll be short another finger by the end of the week," she said. She was teasing him, Colm knew. He just wasn't sure what that meant, that they knew each other so short a time and she already felt like she could mock him without him getting mad. And what it meant that she was right.

"Anyways," Serene interrupted. "As *I* was saying. Today Master Merribell took me out to the forest around the castle, and we came across a lame doe. One of her front legs was broken. And Master Merribell actually let me help her mend it. Isn't that *amazing*?"

Colm smiled and congratulated her. It was more than he'd accomplished today, walking along the stream and gawking with Finn at Tye Thwodin's treasury door.

"That's great, Serene," Lena said, though she didn't sound too enthused. Lena had probably grown up skinning deer, not healing them. "I learned how to perform a spinning tri-parry back thrust."

"Oh. Well. Wow," Colm said.

"You have no idea what that is, do you?"

"Not the slightest." Colm looked over at Quinn, who seemed as if he was about to dunk his whole face into his bowl, which would be unfortunate, as the thick brown stuff inside was still steaming. "What did *you* do this afternoon, Quinn?"

The mageling looked up finally and shook his head. He was pale as morning frost.

"Maybe shouldn't ask," Lena whispered across the table. "There was an *incident*."

"It's no big deal," Quinn said.

"He almost killed someone."

"It wasn't *that* bad," Quinn retorted. "I just caught his robes on fire, is all."

Colm wasn't sure he had heard right. "*What?* Whose robes?"

"Master Velmoth's," Quinn muttered. "He said to show him my best spell, which is the one where I shoot blue flames out of my fingers." He looked imploringly at Lena.

"It's true. It's very impressive," she confirmed.

"Except I didn't quite get the words out right, and the flames shot out of my ears instead."

Colm quickly clamped a hand over his mouth. He didn't want to laugh. Not at Quinn, who looked so forlorn. It was obvious the boy felt terrible about what had happened. But the image of Quinn with flame spurting out of his ears was too much. Colm saw he wasn't the only one holding back. Lena also had that look in her eye, her lower lip trembling.

"He was standing right beside me," Quinn continued plaintively, still staring at his stew. "There wasn't a lot I could do. I tried blowing out the flames, but that only made it worse. He kept running away from me, those big ears of his flapping up and down like he was trying to fly."

That did it. The image of bunny-eared Master Velmoth running around with his robes on fire and poor Quinn chasing after him, blowing on the flames, making them bigger—Colm snorted once, and then Lena lost it. They both looked at each other and exploded.

"I'm so sorry, Quinn," he said. "Really. It's just . . ."

The mageling tried to look angry, but even he started to chuckle. "It really was horrible."

"I'm just glad you both are okay," Serene said, frowning at the lot of them, clearly not amused. "It could have been much worse. You could have really hurt him. Or yourself."

"You might have caught *his* ears on fire," Lena said, holding her hands to either side of her head and flapping them, then laughing all over again. Colm nearly knocked over his stew.

Serene continued to scold. "That's why you shouldn't dabble in that kind of destructive magic. Magic should be used to heal, to bring a little more light to the world."

"I'd say he brought light to the world," Colm said, which caused Quinn to laugh harder.

"You know what I mean," Serene said, doing her best not to smile.

"I just hope he doesn't hold it against me," Quinn said after everyone had caught their breath. "It was embarrassing. My whole face turned red."

This set them off all over again. Other trainees were starting to look at them. They quickly tried to regain their composure. After several deep breaths, Lena wiped her eyes. "It's not that big a deal. I'm sure it happens all the time. It's nothing they would kick you out over," she assured him. "Besides, you are still more powerful than half of the mages here."

She looked at Colm for backup. He nodded, though he honestly had no clue. He knew even less about casting spells than he did about spinning tri-parry back thrusts."Yeah. Absolutely," he said. "A little training and you'll be the scourge of goblins and bunny-eared wizards alike."

Colm looked around the vast dining hall, with its thirty-foot ceilings and scalloped marble pillars. At the heaping silver plates of hot bread and the endless river of stew that seemed to flow from Fungus's kitchen. It sure wasn't home. He thought of the others at his table. Quinn was younger than he was, by a year at least, and he could cast spells, albeit inconsistently. Lena and Serene were both his age, but one could talk to animals and the other could probably best him in a duel using only the spoon in her hand. If he stayed, he would have just as much to learn as anyone.

He wondered what would happen to the rest of them if he left now. If he would even see them again.

"Are you all right?" Serene was fixing him with those cat-yellow eyes of hers.

"Yeah." Colm nodded. "Just thinking about how incredible it is, just being here."

"We still have a couple of hours before we have to be back

in our rooms. Thought maybe we'd take another look around outside. Want to come?"

Colm nodded again and stood up with the others as they made their way through the busy hall. Lena walked beside him. "So a spinning tri-parry back thrust is when you twist your body like this, and hold your sword first over your head, then swing like so . . . ," she started to explain. They passed a group of obviously older trainees just coming in. One of them, the larger of two boys, brushed up against Quinn, nearly knocking him over.

"Watch it."

"I'm s-s-sorry," Quinn said, making a move to squeeze by, but the boy grabbed Quinn's robe, spinning him around so that they were facing each other.

Colm stopped with the others, forming a half circle behind Quinn. There were three in the other group, two boys and a girl, and Colm wondered if the three of them hadn't all been thrown down the same pit together some time ago. The one who had ahold of Quinn's robe was dressed much the same as Lena: chain-mail shirt, leather everywhere else, a long sword with a curve hung at his hip—obviously a warrior of some kind. His goatee was shaped into a point. The other boy was taller and thinner than his companion, with a gray cloak and an ax slung across his back, another brawler probably, a criss-cross of scars on his chin. The girl had straight blond hair down to her waist and a mischievous grin spanning sunken cheeks. Judging by her dress, she was probably a mage. A necklace of runes circled her throat.

The boy with the sword squinted at Quinn. His nose, Colm noticed, was crooked. "I know you," he said. "You're the kid that blows fire out of his arse." This earned a laugh from his companions. Colm didn't crack a smile. He watched Quinn's face flush.

"It was his ears, actually," Serene corrected, but this just caused the other three to laugh again.

"You must be the new arrivals," the boy with the crooked nose said, taking them all in. "In that case I should introduce myself. I'm Tyren. This is Minx and she's Vala."

"Greetings," the girl named Vala said, her voice like a cat's purr. Minx nodded.

"So let me see, we know Flame Ears already. And you," Tyren said, pointing a finger at Serene. "You must be the bug whisperer."

"Her name is Serene," Lena said, stepping forward so that she stood between Quinn and Tyren, who instinctively took a step back, rubbing his fuzzy chin.

"Right. And you are?"

"Lena Proudmore. And if that's too hard, I can give you something to help you remember." Lena's hand went to the pommel of her sword. Just resting it there. Tyren put up his hands in mock surrender.

"That's okay, Red. I think it would be hard to forget a face like yours." He looked at Colm, who resisted the temptation to look down at his boots. "We heard you four made it

162

through Renny's maze in record time."

"We did all right," Colm said. He found it was a whole lot easier to say something so long as he was standing next to Lena, who still had her hand on her sword.

"Of course, that's about as easy as they come," Tyren mused. "We'll have to wait and see how you do later, when it actually *means* something. When there's something of value at stake. Until then," he added, looking specifically at Quinn, "try not to sneeze or anything. I'd hate for you to hurt someone." He patted the mageling once on the shoulder—a gesture that seemed in no way friendly—then nodded coolly at Lena before pulling his two companions along. Vala bumped into Colm's shoulder on her way past, though admittedly he might have blocked her path a little. It looked for a moment like Lena would follow them, say something else, or maybe, knowing her, challenge them to a duel there in the middle of the dining hall. But she got control of herself.

"What was that all about?" Serene asked.

"Welcoming committee," Quinn said.

"He's a nobleman's son," Colm said. "Or at least he comes from wealth—you can tell by the boots." Tyren's steel-toed boots were lined with fox fur, Colm noticed, with a studded cuff. Too fancy for a layman's kid. "He's probably used to being the center of attention."

Lena looked down at her own boots, then quickly turned to Quinn. "Come on. Let's take our walk."

Just as they were about to pass beneath the archway leading

163

out of the dining hall, they heard a shriek. Colm turned with the others to see Vala reaching for her neck, for the string of runes that had been there moments before.

Colm calmly dropped the necklace into a bowl full of stew, then followed his friends out into the great hall.

Colm had seen most of the grounds already, and Serene had spent most of her afternoon outdoors, so the two of them acted as guides for Quinn and Lena as they circled the castle and walked to the edge of the woods. The would-be barbarian walked with her arm still draped around the younger boy's shoulder, the way Colm sometimes walked with Celia. Quinn seemed to forget all about his rough day when Serene convinced a wild hare to sit in his lap. "See," she said, "most things with floppy ears aren't scary at all."

Colm found a nearby log to serve as a bench, still struggling with how to sit without jabbing his ribs on the paw of his sword. He wasn't used to carrying something so long and awkward at his side. It had a fitting name, at least; he had three scratches on his side already. He was a little surprised when Lena came to sit next to him, the moonlight adding a certain luster to the chinks of her shirt, glittering like fish scales.

"I saw that, you know," she said.

Colm shook his head. "Saw what?"

"Vala's necklace. I didn't see you *take* it, but I saw you dump it in the stew. You're pretty sneaky."

"Thanks," Colm said, not sure whether to feel embarrassed, guilty, or proud. He settled for proud. "Kind of childish, I guess."

"She deserved it. You can just tell about some people. The sense of superiority. And in a place like this, it's inevitable. Everyone wants to be the best."

"I don't," Colm said matter-of-factly. "I'm perfectly content being slightly above average."

Lena rolled her eyes. "I'm not sure I believe that." She unsheathed her sword and laid it across her lap, catching her reflection in the steel. "My father was a dungeoneer, you know? He wasn't part of a guild or anything. He did it the old-fashioned way. Spent his youth as a soldier. Learned how to handle an ax and sword. He and his friends would get to telling stories at a tavern. Then he'd come home and grab his armor and take off for the hills. Wouldn't even say where he was going or when he'd be back. Sometimes days, sometimes weeks. One month. Two. He'd come back with a chest of gold. Or maybe just a sack. Or maybe just a broken arm. One time he came back draped over his horse, barely breathing. That was the last time my mother let him go. But even then, he said it was still worth the trip."

"My father makes shoes," Colm said.

Lena looked at him, seemingly confused, as if he were making a joke and she were waiting for the funny part. He just stared back at her. Finally she nodded.

"Shoes are good," she said.

"Keep your feet warm," he said.

They watched as the hare leaped over Quinn's shoulder, causing him to lose his balance and fall backward. Serene pulled him up, the two of them giggling. Lena rubbed her hands together, looked up at the stars just starting to materialize. "That's why I'm here, you know? He wants me to follow in his footsteps. He says I was made for this kind of thing. But it's hard. Being everything they expect you to be."

Colm wanted to tell her not to worry. That he had only spent a day with her, had only been through one little dungeon with her, that he hadn't even really seen her fight, and yet he still thought she was amazing. He was trying to think of the best way to say all that without sounding like an idiot when he heard a rustle in the grass behind them. He turned to see a figure dressed in black, hood over his face, hands in his sleeves.

Colm slipped and fell off the log, but Lena was instantly on her feet, sword in hand pointed at the figure's chin. Serene and Quinn stood up behind her.

"Please, Miss Proudmore, I hardly think that's any way to greet a fellow dungeoneer. Especially not one as handsome as me."

Colm instantly recognized the voice. He reached up and put a hand on Lena's arm, lowering her sword as Finn Argos pulled back his hood to reveal his sparkling smile.

"Nice to see such sound reflexes, though. And marvelous tumbling skills, Mr. Candorly. That will come in handy

166

anytime you have to strategically fall off something." Colm stood and brushed the leaves from his pants.

"Sorry, Master Argos," Lena said, sheathing her sword and bowing with a blush.

"Don't apologize for being on your guard. And don't call me Master Argos. I'm just Finn. I'm also afraid it's time to head back, however. It's getting late, and there are a few creatures in these woods that might not make for good conversation, even for someone like you, Miss Willowtree."

Serene nodded, perhaps thinking of mountain lions and bears again, and the four of them gathered their things and followed the rogue back to the huge oaken doors of the castle. Once inside, Finn pointed them toward their chambers and bade each of them get a good night's rest in preparation for their first full day of training. Lena whispered something in Quinn's ear again, then snatched Serene's hand and pulled her toward the stairs. Colm had started to follow Quinn to their room when Finn drew him aside. The day was almost over. Colm was exhausted. Quinn turned around, but Colm motioned for him to go ahead.

Finn's eyes followed Lena up the stairs.

"She needs you, Colm," Finn said. "It may not seem like it, but it's true. They all do. Master Thwodin's always looking for talent, and I certainly wouldn't mind having another rogue around to teach me a thing or two, but they . . ." He looked back at the stairs, then at the retreating figure of Quinn just turning down the hall. "They might not succeed without you. You four were put together for a reason. You each have your hang-ups, but together you can compensate. That's how it works."

"Balance," Colm said, remembering what Lena had told him in the dungeon, about proper party configuration and whatnot, but Finn shook his head.

"Family," he said.

Colm took his time making it back to the room, wandering the castle's torchlit halls until it seemed every other door had been closed. When he did make it in, he found Quinn already sleeping, still fully dressed again, one leg hanging off the end of his bed, his head burrowed between two pillows. Colm tiptoed across the room and sat at the edge of his own bed, carefully taking off his boots. He stared at them for a while. Outstanding works of craftsmanship. Nearly perfect.

It's important to be good at something, Colm thought. Did it matter what the thing was? Or just how well you did it? Boot maker? Dungeoneer? Thief? Colm reached over and opened the desk drawer, pulling out the sheet of parchment that he had put there earlier that morning.

Be it henceforth known that _____
(hereafter referred to as THE APPRENTICE) is requesting admittance to Thwodin's Legion (hereafter referred to as THE GUILD) to be trained in the arts of dungeoneering . . .

Colm looked over at Quinn. Thought about Serene and Lena, sleeping in some room above them. Thought about the look on Finn's face when he had shown Colm the treasury. Enough gold to make a hundred kings weep . . .

Then he thought about Felhaven and his father's callused hands and his mother's tired smile. And the horses they'd had to sell to make it through the winter. And Celia, with only a silver butterfly pin to hoard as a treasure.

Imagine if she could see him now, sitting in this castle, surrounded by swordsmen and mages and healers and *goblins*. Colm looked at Scratch resting beside him, admired the intricate engraving on the handle. He had never owned anything like it before. It looked nice, riding at his hip; it made him walk a little straighter. But Lena was right; he had no idea what to do with it. He could learn, though. He could keep it if he stayed.

Colm opened the drawer and removed the ink and quill, as well as a blank sheet of parchment. He wasn't a great writer—his sisters all had a much better knack for it—and he usually struggled over each word whenever his mother made him practice. But once he started, he found he couldn't stop. He told them almost everything. About where he was and what he'd seen. About Lena and Serene and Quinn and how they'd made it through the dungeon, leaving out the part where poor Quinn nearly got sizzled—no need to worry them too much. He told them about the masters, Finn especially, and Tye Thwodin, who looked strong enough to pull a tree out of the earth, roots and all.

And he told them how much he missed them all already. And how he would see them soon.

When he was finished, he read it over and blew on the ink to dry it.

Then he signed his name in the space left over.

8

A THOUSAND WAYS
TO DIE

For breakfast there was stew.

It wasn't the same stew as the night before, Colm noted. It was mostly potatoes and ham, with a rogue carrot surfacing every now and again. The bread that accompanied it was glazed in honey, at least, but that didn't make it *not* stew for breakfast.

"I'm thinking I could get tired of this," Lena said, staring at her spoon.

"Not me," Quinn said through a slurpful. "My mother is a terrible cook. You *know* she's a terrible cook."

"Yes, but at least she's not named after something you find under your toenails," Lena fired back.

Colm smiled. He could get tired of it too, he supposed—the stew at least—but he owed it to himself, and to his family, to see just how long it would take. He had made his decision, and any minute now he expected to see Finn's hawkish nose appearing in the archway, ready to congratulate him.

Serene was trying to pick around the ham, but eventually she gave up and pushed her bowl toward Quinn, who traded his roll for it. She muttered something about the need for more nature-sensitive options.

"Fungus doesn't look like the kind of guy who takes requests," Colm said, glancing back toward the kitchen, where the gruff giant of a man had a cleaver in one hand, hacking away at something that would surely find its way into lunch.

Colm had spent the entire night last night wondering what he was getting himself into, and had awakened this morning with a sense of unease, a feeling that he was out of place, pretending to be something he wasn't. But when he showed up for breakfast, Lena simply said, "Nice of you to join us," and offered him the seat beside her. He took it without hesitation.

"We got our training itineraries," Quinn said, handing a piece of parchment to Colm; on it was listed a breakdown of where they needed to be when. "We spend the mornings together and then meet with our mentors for individualized instruction in the afternoon."

Colm looked at the sheet. History of Dungeoneering with Master Fimbly. Dungeon Ecology with Master Bloodclaw. Basic Survival Skills with Master Argos.

"Master Wolfe was supposed to lead that last one," Quinn said, "but he's still away."

Colm didn't know who Master Wolfe was. He hadn't been

one of the four sitting at the long oak table yesterday—presumably one of the empty seats. Colm was glad to be spending more time with Finn, though. Master Fimbly was obviously very knowledgeable, but you couldn't ask him any questions without shouting, and the goblin was still unnerving.

"What a waste of time," Lena moaned, slumping in her chair. "Basic Survival Skills? What's he going to teach us? How to rub sticks together? If you ask me, I think all that time would be much better spent in combat training."

"I don't know," Serene chimed in. "Maybe we'll get to identify different kinds of edible moss." She sounded sincere. Then again, Serene always sounded sincere.

Colm had to side with Lena on this one: If it came down to eating moss or learning how to use Scratch without hurting himself, he would pass on the moss.

"I'm sure it's all important," Quinn said. "Master Thwodin wants us fit for delving as soon as possible. He wouldn't have us wasting time on anything pointless."

"You're just glad you don't have to spend all day with Flopsy," Lena chided. Quinn turned red and went back to Serene's stew.

Colm looked around for the three older members who had bumped into them yesterday but couldn't spot them. Maybe they had already eaten. Or maybe Tye Thwodin had sent them into a dungeon, and they were eaten *by* something.

Quinn pointed to the last two bites of Colm's roll, sitting beside his empty bowl. "Are you going to eat that?"

From the apex of the castle came the chime of the bell.

Colm pushed the half-chewed remainders of his breakfast across the table. It was his first official day as a dungeoneer, and all of a sudden he didn't have much of an appetite.

The training regimen at the guild, Master Fimbly had explained the day before, consisted of two parts: theoretical knowledge and practical application. The theoretical portion was taught in the castle's western wing, in a series of mostly windowless chambers that were little more than rows of splintered tables and blankets of dust. The practical application took place in a variety of locations: the training rooms, for example, or in Master Bloodclaw's labyrinthine playground beneath the castle, or—eventually—in real dungeons with actual treasure, though Colm was certain that those would come much later. In the beginning, Fimbly told them, they could expect to spend a good deal more time in an old chair than an orc's lair.

And so it was that Colm and his companions squeezed into a set of uncomfortable wooden seats in a musty room. They weren't alone. There were five other would-be dungeoneers in the room, clustered into a group on the other side. Judging by the style of dress and weaponry, Colm guessed they probably satisfied Herm Hefflegeld's requirements for proper party configuration. He had only been here one day, but he had already gotten fairly adept at identifying who was what. Shirt made of metal, heavy sharp things dangling off you like icicles? Probably a warrior of some kind. More into black leather and short, pokey weapons that can be tucked up shirt-sleeves or hidden in boots? A rogue. Elaborate, multicolored bathrobe and occasional nose piercing? A wizard of some sort. Talking to every buzzing, crawling, squawking thing you see? Must be a druid. Colm had overheard talk of others—paladins and healers and clerics and such—but it seemed like his crew covered all the most popular bases.

The five sitting across from them ran the gamut, and they obviously knew each other, but unlike Tyren and his two cronies at dinner last night, these five didn't scowl at Colm as soon as he walked in the door. If anything, they looked just as nervous as he was. Colm smiled and waved, and one of the five, a girl, waved meekly back.

Master Fimbly stumbled in, dressed in the same robes as the day before, whispering to himself. On his desk he set a tottering stack of leather tomes that nearly reached the ceiling, threatening to topple and crush the old man as he bustled by. "Please take your seats," Fimbly said, even though everyone already had. The old man rifled through several sheets of parchment before finding the one he wanted. Then he began calling names, checking them off with a quill. "Candorly?"

"Here," Colm said, his voice still gravelly from morning.

"Candorly?"

"Yes, sir," he said a little more clearly.

"COLM CANDORLY?" the old man repeated.

"HERE, SIR!" Colm yelled.

Fimbly looked up and smiled. "Ah good. Thought maybe you decided not to join us after all," he said with a wink. Master Fimbly proceeded to call the other names. "Crowfriend? Dagnor? Golen? Johaggen? Tobbs?" When he got to the end, he looked over the class, took a deep breath, and said, quite matter-of-factly: "One of you will be dead within a year."

Colm shook his head, wondering if the old man's hearing problems had rubbed off on him.

"Actually, it's more like one and a half of you," Fimbly explained, "though I'm not sure you can be half dead. That is, unless you are transformed into a zombie, which is entirely possible."

"*Complete* waste of time," Lena muttered to herself, rolling her eyes.

"Excuse me, MASTER FIMBLY?" called out Johaggen, the girl who had waved at Colm. She was dressed the same as Master Merribell—white cloth with gold and silver embroidery and swatches with arcane symbols sewn into them, bits of armor across the legs and shoulders, and a mace that looked just right for caving skulls in by her side. "How exactly do you *know* that one of us will die before the year is over? I mean, is there a prophecy or something?"

Master Fimbly shook his head. "No prophecy, dear. Just the law of averages. It is dangerous work, dungeoneering; has the second highest on-the-job mortality rate in the land, next to lumberjacks. Terrible business, lumberjacking."

"I agree completely," Serene said.

Fimbly began fumbling at the stack of books, handing out one for each of the nine trainees, who were still staring at each other, no doubt thinking the same thing Colm was: *Which one of us does he have in mind?*

"Make no mistake," Fimbly continued, "the history of dungeoneering is full of acts of tremendous valor and cunning, with gifted and masterful young men and women, many of them not much older than yourselves, bravely descending into the deepest, darkest corners of the world, armed with wits, weaponry, and wizardry, chasing after the promise of untold riches and unbridled distinction . . . and often ending in an untimely and gruesome death."

Serene passed back a copy of the book, and Colm looked at the cover. It showed a gleaming knight standing tall against a rearing dragon, its ragged black wings spread, smoke pouring from its nostrils, ready to confront the stalwart dungeoneer. A promising start. He flipped it over to the back to find the same dragon, curled up asleep around its treasure, the hollowed, smoking remains of a suit of armor on the ground beside it. So much for happy endings.

Colm held up the back of the book to show Lena.

"That would never happen to us," she whispered.

"Over the course of the next several weeks," Fimbly continued, "we will study the chronology of dungeoneering, from the early days of the barbarian hordes to the present-day bards' songs you are all probably familiar with. Along the way, we will consider the implications such history has on our own endeavors, namely, what we can learn from the successes—and failures—of the dungeoneers who have come before us."

"Bor-ring," Lena groaned, blowing her bangs out of her face. Quinn was busy gawking at the smoking remains of the knight on the back cover of the book.

Master Fimbly reached behind his podium and produced a drawing, a sketch in black and white showing a giant head perched upon an equally bloated body, all of which was about to be punctured by what looked to be a wall of thorns. Serene brought a hand to her mouth.

"Case study number one," Fimbly said. "The Wolf Pack. Cal Steelheart, warrior. Chloe Silverfoot, cleric. Fern Fiddlehorn, mage. Darren D'Arlen, rogue. Ventured into Thorn's Hollow in search of the lost treasure of the famous orc raider Vergo Bloodringer. Things went well until Darren failed to disarm a class five spiked wall trap, Chloe's globe of protection fizzled, and Fern accidentally reversed his shrinking spell, making the party of four even larger as the walls closed in."

"Oooh." Serene winced, mirroring the look of terror on the face of the giant-headed man about to be pincushioned in the picture.

"Goes to show that even the most well-balanced party can fall apart sometimes," Fimbly added.

Colm didn't know a lot about magic, but he guessed an enlarging spell and a spiked wall trap weren't an ideal combo. Professor Fimbly put the sketch on his desk and pulled up another drawing. This one showed four knights, dressed to the hilt in plate armor, riding astride equally well-armored steeds. Everything about them radiated courage and righteousness.

"The Brothers of the Four Swords. Sworn paladins. Twice blessed with every manner of protection you could think of. Protection from fire. From lightning. From cold, charm, disintegration, poison, lava, you name it. Descended into the underbelly of Bloodtooth Gorge but forgot to bring a rogue along with them, or maybe just thought they were too good for one. Triggered a simple level one pit trap just inside the entrance and fell to their deaths, impaling themselves on their own swords."

The Brothers of the Four Swords disappeared, dropping facedown onto the desk much the same way they had dropped into that pit. Fimbly's next drawing was a landscape, showing a peaceful wood and a river coursing through it. There was no sign of dragons or orcs or collapsing walls or fireballs anywhere. No geysers of blood or circling vultures. Colm could see the mountains swelling in the background, but that was about it.

"The infamous Imon Invale. A gifted adventurer with a knack for both thievery and spellcasting. Considered by many to be the greatest solo adventurer of his time. One night, on a bet, Invale descended into Fang's Hollow. He supposedly fought off three packs of goblins, a skeleton warlord, and a giant wyrm, all by his lonesome. Filled his purses and pockets with gold and made it back to the surface without a scratch. There he tripped on a branch, lost his balance, tumbled into a

river, and drowned. You can see his hand sticking out right . . .
here." Fimbly pointed to a splotch in the drawing that looked
like it was just the current of the river moving.

"Why didn't he swim back to shore?" Lena asked.

"The gold in his pockets probably weighed him down,"
Quinn guessed.

Fimbly set down the picture of Imon Invale's unfortunate
last step, then reached under his podium and pulled out a huge
stack, each of them an artist's rendering of a dungeoneer who
had met an unfortunate demise. He started holding them up
one by one, rattling them off—not the names any longer, just
how they'd perished, slapping them emphatically on the desk.
"Impaled, drowned, burned, impaled, cursed, exploded,
slashed, imploded, frozen, poisoned, turned to stone, turned
to ash, turned into a chicken, impaled, crushed, smashed,
stepped on, disintegrated, turned into stone and *then* smashed,
turned into a chicken and then *eaten,* burned, squished, suf-
focated, swallowed whole, and *mostly* turned into a chicken."

The last drawing showed a man—at least, it might have been
a man, except he was covered in feathers and had wings instead
of arms, and spindly stalks for legs ending in clawed toes. He
had a beak for a nose. It was the most grotesque thing Colm had
ever seen, and he had changed Elmira's soiled linens. Twice.

"Of course, no reward comes without some risk," Master
Fimbly concluded.

"I think I'm going to pass out," said the girl with the long
braids on the opposite side of the room. Serene had stopped

looking long ago, her hands cupped over her eyes. Lena doodled on a piece of parchment. Colm was fascinated.

Master Fimbly put his gory sketches away and took a deep breath. "The history of dungeoneering is essentially the history of retribution. Ever since the first goblin raiding parties decided to venture out of their caves and steal our sheep and torch our crops, our kind has sought to settle the debt. Only we can't very well steal our livestock back after the filthy, bloodthirsty creatures have devoured them raw, can we? So instead we take their gold. You might say that it is the orcs and trolls and goblins and all the other shadow-loving, vile denizens of the deep who brought it on themselves. We're just taking back what's ours."

Colm thought of the silver coin. It was still in his pocket. He had put it there this morning when he changed. There was nothing to spend it on here—everything he could want was provided for him—but he thought it might be good luck.

"Dungeoneering," Fimbly continued, "is about a group of people coming together, using their various skills and talents to face untold dangers in the hopes of sharing the bounty bought by their courage. It is brothers and sisters standing back to back amid the crash of blades, the sizzle of spells, and the snarl of hideous beasts. It is the snap of the lock and the creak of the lid as the chest opens to reveal a sea of sparkling coin that blinds you if you stare too long.

"But mostly it is about revenge."

★ ★ ★

181

"Dungeoneering is little more than armed robbery."

Those were the first words out of Herren Bloodclaw's mouth the moment Colm and his companions shuffled in and took their seats. At first he hadn't actually even seen the goblin, standing behind the podium in the front of the room, his head barely tall enough to crest it. Only when the bell chimed did Master Bloodclaw get their attention, scrambling on top of the podium so that he was finally taller than they were—provided they stayed seated.

"Let's get one thing straight!" the goblin shouted. "I don't like you. In fact, deep down, I detest each and every one of you. It's in my blood. I'm a goblin, and that's just how it goes. The truth is, none of them like you. Not the trolls or the orcs or the ogres or the crawlers or the kobolds or the wyverns. Not the basilisks or the brownies or the lichs or the wraiths or the wights or the gorgons or the gargoyles. To them, you are nothing more than a bunch of gold-grubbing thieves with pasty faces and sticky fingers."

Lena and Colm looked at each other. She shrugged.

"Unfortunately for me," Herren continued, "my parents didn't like me either. Kicked me out of my clan when I was a wee gob because I forgot to set one little trap and a buncha bloody chest snatchers like yourselves took everything we had. Now, as a result, here I am, teaching *you* all about *them* just to earn my keep."

Herren Bloodclaw hopped down from the desk and proceeded to walk up and down between the rows, giving a glare to each young dungeoneer in turn, sometimes pointing with his crooked green finger for emphasis. "I don't like you. Or you. Or you. Especially not fond of you," he said to Quinn. "You. You. You. You. Or you." He turned around and ambled back down the center aisle and resumed his spot at the front of the room.

"But we all agree on one thing. We all like . . . *this.*"

The goblin reached into one of the pouches hanging from his belt and produced a single gold coin, holding it up so it caught the light from the window.

"Over the course of your training, I will tell you everything I know about dungeoneering from the perspective of those who inhabit the dungeons themselves. By the time I'm finished, you will know how to slay every creature you're likely to run across, though knowing and doing are vastly different things."

"I know how to slay goblins," whispered one of the other trainees, a sinewy, sword-wielding boy with bronze skin and black hair. He must have forgotten he wasn't in Fimbly's class anymore. The goblin could hear just fine.

"And I know how long to roast a human over a spit to keep his juices in, Mr. Dagnor, so maybe you should shut your trap." The boy huddled, browbeaten, in his seat. "Let's start with the basic, fundamental question: Why do monsters build dungeons?"

The goblin looked around the room for an answer. Serene timidly raised her hand.

"Because they like the dark?"

The goblin took a deep breath, then threw the gold coin at Serene, just missing her. The coin clattered across the floor and landed next to her. "We build dungeons to hide from people like *you*. My ancestors used to live on the surface in large, sprawling villages, till *your* ancestors forced us into caves and tunnels, sent us into mountains and the thick hearts of dark forests. And even then you followed us."

"But Master Fimbly said—" Serene began.

"I know what that old coot said, something about stealing goats and burning cows and the bonds of brotherhood or some ballyhoo, but make no mistake. Your kind started it. Waited for us to do all the dirty work, mining the mountains and caves for metals and gems, then came and snatched it out from under our noses. So we had to get creative. We started designing ways to keep you out. We added locks to our doors. We added traps to the locks. We put traps on the traps. Then, when all else failed, we hired help."

The goblin got on his knees and crawled under a table, pulling out a metal box and pushing it toward the center of the room. From his chair, Colm could see that the box contained a clay jar of some kind, nearly twice as big as his head.

"Gather around, now. Come on. Don't be shy. You there, pickpocket." He pointed to Colm. "Give me a hand with this thing." As everyone else formed a circle, Colm helped the goblin lift the jar out of the chest. He noticed the lid was sealed tight, but he could feel the weight of it shifting. There was something heavy inside. And it was moving.

"Now spread out a little bit, give us some space," Herren Bloodclaw said, motioning for Colm to set the jar on its side. Colm stepped back between Lena and Quinn as the goblin straddled his mysterious treasure, his yellow-clawed fingers grasping at the lid.

"Whatever you do, don't panic. Some of you are green as a lily and will likely not have seen anything quite like this before, but you are in no real danger." He started to twist the lid, then stopped, looking back at the class. "Not mortal danger, anyways."

Herren Bloodclaw twisted and pulled, popping the seal, and then leaped aside. Colm instinctively took another step back, as did everyone else, including Lena. They all watched the mouth of the jar.

Nothing happened.

The goblin stood behind it, arms crossed, waiting.

Colm angled to get a better look inside, but the opening was too narrow to see anything.

"There's nothing in there," the boy named Dagnor said, taking a step forward and then kneeling down, pressing his face into the hole. Herren Bloodclaw shook his head.

"I don't think that's such a good—" Serene started to say, but it was too late. A handful of green slime shot out of the opening, latching onto the boy's cheek like a leech. Dagnor screamed and staggered to his feet, spinning wildly and grabbing the goo with both hands, flinging it against the wall, where it hit with a slurping, sucking sound. The boy brought one hand to his face and drew his sword with the other, holding it in front of him, ready to strike. Colm watched in horror as the rest of what was in the jar slowly slithered out.

"*Jellus ooziferos*, also known as a slime. Sometimes called ogre's jelly, dragon snot, vile pudding, or simply a bloblin. It comes in over a dozen known varieties, each with varying chemical properties and resistances, some of them quite nasty. This one is known as the common green and is the least dangerous of its kind." The goblin grinned mischievously.

The pool of slime inched over the lid of its jar with a sickening *shlurp*. It didn't appear to have eyes or a nose or any sensory organ of any kind, yet it seemed to feel its way around regardless. As it moved, it spread and then contracted, leaving a gluey trail behind it.

"The green slime is not lethal," Herren Bloodclaw said. "It is, however, toxic to the touch and will cause a man's skin to blister or break into boils on contact." He pointed to Dagnor. Colm noticed that the boy's left cheek had turned a sickly shade of yellow and that several large, round pustules had started bubbling up from the skin. The goblin was no longer the owner of the ugliest face in the room.

Dagnor raised his hand to his cheek, a look of anger on his face. Then he shouted, raised his sword, and attacked the blob in a flurry, hacking away at it with ferocious strokes. Everyone instinctively stepped back even farther, including Master Bloodclaw, as the slime was split into a half dozen pieces and those same pieces split again. Colm noticed that Lena was the

186

only one in the room with a weapon who wasn't cupping its hilt, as if she knew something Dagnor didn't. The boy stopped to catch his breath, standing over his vanquished foe, now diced into a dozen quivering chunks.

"There are, as I said, lots of different varieties," the goblin continued over the sound of Dagnor's grunting. "But all slimes have three things in common. First off, they are notoriously slow, which makes them easy to avoid. They also feel absolutely no pain, so far as we can tell. And finally," he said, pointing to the various puddles of goo that were now crawling back toward each other, inching along the stone floor, "they are all fully capable of reassembling themselves."

Colm watched, fascinated, as the slime fused all its parts back together, including the one that Dagnor had thrown against the wall, regaining its original size. Dagnor dropped his slimy sword in disbelief.

"For that reason, blades and arrows are quite useless against it. However, each slime is highly susceptible to a certain element that can be reproduced through either chemical or magical means. The common green, for example, is particularly vulnerable to fire. Mister Frostfoot, if you don't mind?" The goblin pointed to the blob, which was very slowly inching its way toward the outer ring of trainees.

"Me?" Quinn pointed. "I really d-d-don't think that's a g-g-good—"

"Stop your stammering, boy, and give us some flames. You certainly didn't have any trouble scorching *me* a couple days back."

"B-b-but Master Velmoth said . . ."

"That cantankerous old rat put you on his leash already? Bah." The goblin turned to a boy with a purple cloak that clashed considerably with his orange hair. "Mister Tobbs . . . you're not Velmoth's lapdog yet, are you?" The boy shook his head. "Good. Then toast this jelly before it makes Dagnor any uglier, will you?"

The boy took a step forward and rolled up his sleeves. Beside Colm, Serene gave a little whimper. Colm looked at the seeping gelatinous mass wobbling on the floor, the same one that had just attacked poor Dagnor, leaving one side of his face a weepy mess. Tobbs clasped his hands together and began chanting under his breath, and a jet of flame burst forth, orange to match his hair, slamming straight into the creature. The slime writhed for a moment, then began to melt, forming a slick green smudge on the floor. Dagnor, the right side of his face now fully erupted in a rolling sea of boils, said, "Good riddance." Lena noted that it smelled a little like Fungus's kitchen. Colm just stared at the puddle.

"Well, now," Master Bloodclaw announced, rubbing his hooked nose. "That's probably enough hands-on experience for one day. Miss Johaggen, if you would please escort your overzealous companion to Master Merribell to have his face tended to, I'm sure she has some kind of ointment that will clear that up nicely. The rest of you gather your things and be careful of the floor. I'd hate for one of you to slip and hurt yourself.

"All except for you, Mr. Frostfoot."

Quinn pointed to himself.

"Yes. You haven't proven yourself to be much of a spell-caster today, I'm afraid, so let's see how you handle a mop."

"That was . . . so wrong," Quinn said when he finally joined the others out in the hall. His entire body was shaking.

"I don't know," Lena countered. "At least Master Blood-claw let us get our hands dirty. Or your hands, anyways," she added. She still sounded disappointed. Colm saw the look in her eyes. He had only known Lena Proudmore a day, yet he already knew what she was thinking.

"How badly did you want to take a swing at it?" he asked.

Lena bounced on her toes. "*So* badly," she said. "Good thing I didn't, though." She turned to Serene. "Let me guess. You wanted to rescue it, didn't you?"

"What? No! Of course not."

They all looked at her.

"Well. Maybe a little. It was kind of cute, the way it just inched along like that."

"That's because you didn't have to mop it up," Quinn remarked. "Or what was left of it."

Finn was waiting for them out in the hall when they made it to their last training session of the morning. The room was the same as the others, except, Colm noted, there was no tower of books on the desk and no mysterious chest under-neath it. As they took their seats—Colm making it a point

189

to sit next to Lena again—the girl named Johaggen with the long woven hair returned, assuring her own companions that Dagnor would be okay.

"I'm glad," Colm said from across his table, but the girl just gave him a dismissive look, as if he had been the one who'd tried to suck the boy's face off. He began to wonder if he was automatically limited to having only three good friends in this place, if that was just the way it had to be. He knew everyone had their group—whoever they were matched up with at the start—but did that mean that the groups themselves couldn't get along? Obviously Tyren's group didn't think so. Maybe none of them did.

"All right, adventurers, take your seats." Finn sighed. "Welcome to Basic Survival. Here we will cover a cornucopia of skills that you will need to be a successful dungeoneer. For as we all know, the history of dungeoneering is the history of survival."

Colm felt the impulse to raise his hand and ask how that fit in with revenge and armed robbery, but he resisted. After all, if it came down to following the advice of an ancient, hard-of-hearing has-been, a bitter, excommunicated goblin, or Finn Argos, Colm knew whom he would side with.

"As many of you know, this topic is often covered by Master Wolfe, but as is frequently the case, Master Wolfe is away at the moment, so I will be training you in his stead. . . . Yes, Mister Tobbs?"

The mageling who had vanquished the slime put down his hand. "Is it true Master Wolfe once escaped an enchanted tower fifty stories tall by killing a giant spider and then weaving a rope out of its silk?"

Finn nodded slowly. "That *is* the story, yes, though no one was actually there to confirm it. Now, the purpose of our meeting is . . . Yes, Miss Golen?"

"Is it true that Master Wolfe once survived being stranded in a snowstorm by killing a bear with his bare hands, skinning it with his teeth, and then using its hide as a tent?" the girl with the braided hair asked.

Finn sighed. "I think that might be a slight exaggeration. I'm fairly certain he had a dagger with him at the time, which would have made both killing and skinning the bear considerably easier. However, this story, though embellished, does yield interesting implica— Yes, Miss Proudmore?"

Lena lowered her spastically waving hand and leaned across her desk. "I heard that Master Wolfe once slew a dozen dragon hatchlings with a sword he'd whittled from an orc's leg bone."

"Yes. I've heard that too," Finn said, clearly exasperated. "And were he *here*, I'm sure Master Wolfe could regale you with that and a hundred other fantastic tales of how he narrowly escaped death, killing giants with a piece of tree bark and snaring goblins using nets made out of his own plucked chest hairs. But since he is *not* here, you will have to make do with me."

"Can you even do that?" Quinn whispered to Colm. "Make a net out of chest hair?"

"I don't think so," Colm said. He didn't have any chest hair yet to say for certain.

"Now," Finn said with a huff of impatience, "if there are no more questions—" Four trainees raised their hands. "Not including any about Master Wolfe." The same four lowered them again. "Then who here can tell me what the key to surviving any dungeon is?"

Colm quickly ran through the list of rules Finn had already taught him. Stay behind the big guy. Give the mage some space. Don't steal from your friends. Most of it seemed practical enough, but none of it screamed most-important-rule-ever.

Lena raised her hand. "Kill it before it kills you?" she offered.

Finn scrunched his nose. "A good policy, provided you are certain it is going to kill you, but there are numerous ways to die in a dungeon, and many of them don't come at the hands of anything you can stab with a sword. Yes, Mr. Frostfoot?"

"Enunciate," he said, clear as a bell.

Colm chuckled. Even Finn smiled. "I can see where that might be good counsel for some, but I doubt Miss Proudmore's battle cry requires careful elocution." He looked around the room for another response. Colm thought about two nights ago and the four of them in the dungeon and the only time they were really in any danger. He raised his hand.

"Watch your step?" he said.

Finn nodded, eyes bright and beaming. "Master Fimbly told you about the four brothers, did he? Did you know that the first dungeon ever built was nothing more than a cave with a hole in the middle of it, covered with tree branches? That's how an ogre chose to protect his treasure. So simple, and yet no fewer than seven adventurers perished trying to get at that ogre's gold. The treasure was ultimately snagged by the blind bard Bartholomew Plink, who walked *around* the hole simply because he had to keep his hand against the wall of the cave to get there.

"From that hole in the ground, the art and science of dungeon making has evolved, from the humble simplicity of the Straight Hall of Singular Death to the majesty of the Lich Lord's Labyrinth of Lost Souls, a nearly impenetrable maze crawling with all manner of traps and beasts that managed to exist unmolested for two hundred years."

Colm had never heard of either of these, but everyone around him seemed to be nodding in appreciation. Serene was even taking notes, scribbling them all over a cloth-bound book that she'd brought seemingly for that purpose.

"And yet half of all dungeon-related deaths could be prevented if people would only keep their eyes open and look where they are going."

"Keep your eyes open," Serene whispered as she wrote.

"And what," Finn continued, "is the single most important asset you need to have when tackling a dungeon?"

"A sword. Der," Lena said.

"A positive attitude?" Serene suggested.

"Food," Quinn offered.

To each of these, Finn Argos shook his head. The others threw out more suggestions.

"My spell book?"

"Some heavy rope."

"A torch. No . . . wait . . . lots of torches."

A good pair of shoes, Colm thought to himself, but that was just his father talking. He considered all the items in his bag: the lockpicks, the dagger, the sunstone. All useful, but was any of them really more important than the other? Were any of them more valuable than Scratch or even the cloak on his back? Finn continued to shake his head, continued to let them guess, his smile fading.

"A sword *and* a crossbow . . ."

"A map. Definitely a map."

". . . with poison-tipped bolts . . ."

"A potion of invisibility? No. In*vuln*erability. Wait, *is* there such a thing?"

"I'm still thinking food. . . ."

Colm racked his brain. He knew they were missing the point. He could tell by the look on Finn's face. Finally it came to him. Of course. What was the one thing you absolutely needed more than anything else? He raised his hand. "A way out," he said.

Behind him, Lena cursed as if she had been about to say the same thing and he'd beaten her to it. Colm waited for the smile to return, but Finn just shook his head again.

"No, I'm afraid. The answer is *each other.*" It was the first time Colm had ever seen the rogue look disappointed—in him, at least. "You will need each other if you are to stand any chance of surviving a dungeon. And until you realize that, none of you has any business setting foot in one."

Colm felt Finn's eyes on him and looked away. Beside him, Lena leaned over. "I thought your answer was better." He looked at her and smiled.

"Though I'd still rather just have my sword," she added.

Colm chanced to look back at Finn, who had moved on and was outlining the various survival skills they would learn over the next several weeks, including, believe it or not, the identification of various edible berries, roots, grasses, and mosses. Serene clapped her hands in anticipation. Quinn said he knew it would come back to food eventually.

Colm just shut his mouth and leaned back in his seat, feeling uneasy again. Over the course of the entire morning, he felt like he had learned only one thing for sure.

That he knew almost nothing.

9

THE RANGER'S RETURN

After Finn let them go, Quinn sat in front of his four bowls of stew, a dense, dark broth with chunks of pink meat congealed by means of gluey fat to overcooked beets. Colm and Serene both took one look at lunch and declared themselves not hungry. Even Lena said she had to pass. Maybe it was the slime. Or maybe it was the sketches of all those doomed dungeoneers. Or maybe it was Finn's description of exactly what an acid trap would do to you if you triggered it. Something had squelched their appetites, leaving a feast for Quinn. *That boy's stomach will be the subject of bards' songs someday,* Colm thought.

"That was depressing," Serene concluded as they discussed everything they'd done that morning. "It's like they're trying to spook us. Like they want us to quit before we even get started."

Lena wasn't convinced.

"Believe me. If they wanted us to quit, the goblin would have unleashed something more menacing than a pile of green goo," she said. Colm agreed. Though it certainly had done a number on Dagnor's face, a little fire and a mop had been all that was required to vanquish it. Hardly the stuff of legends.

"I'll just be happy to spend the afternoon with Master Merribell," Serene said. "She's promised to teach me how to conjure butterflies from flower petals."

"Terrific," Lena countered. "Can't imagine how *that* won't be useful."

"You don't have to be snotty about it," Serene said. "I suppose you'll just spend the afternoon hacking away at something."

"If I'm lucky," Lena replied.

Colm put a hand on Scratch's paw, then caught sight of Tyren and his two friends taking seats four tables away, laughing and making faces. They weren't alone. There was another girl with them this time, one Colm hadn't seen before. She had hair so black it looked almost blue, pulled back into a single braid that fell across one shoulder like a sash. Unlike the other three, who were busy throwing food or pounding on the table, her narrow face was shoved into a book big enough to be ammunition for catapults. She had bronze skin and long, thin fingers—the usual number—and looked like she might have come from somewhere far away. Far from Felhaven, at least. Maybe across the seas. She wasn't particularly beautiful, but there was something about her absolute stillness, her total disregard for what was happening around her, that captured Colm's attention.

"Who's she?"

Lena twisted around to get a look, then shook her head.

"Don't know," she said. "She's no warrior, though. A warrior would never be caught dead in leather armor that thin."

"Her name's Ravena Heartfall," Quinn said, moving on to his third bowl, though he seemed to be slowing a little. "She's a talent."

Colm gave Quinn his don't-forget-I'm-just-the-poor-son-of-a-shoe-cobbler look. He had perfected it over the course of the morning, whenever one of them took something for granted as common knowledge.

"You know, a talent? A person with a wide variety of natural abilities. Like Imon Invale. Spellcasting, fencing, disarmament . . . she was working by herself when I was practicing with Master Velmoth yesterday. She can summon a sword out of thin air, and swing it pretty well too."

Colm nodded, impressed.

"Big deal," Lena snipped.

Quinn gave her a surprised look. "Rumor has it that she conquered Bloodclaw's little maze by herself. She's like a whole dungeoneering party wrapped into one."

"Why is she hanging out with those three, then?" Serene asked. Like Colm, she was studying the strange figure of Ravena Heartfall intensely.

"Yeah," Lena seconded, reaching out and snatching her bowl of stew back from Quinn, stabbing forcefully at a carrot. "If she's so amazing, how come she needs that ogre Tyren?" She stuffed a hunk of meat into her mouth, determined to chew it to oblivion.

Quinn shrugged. "You heard what Master Argos said. None of us can do everything all the time."

Colm tried not to keep staring. Quinn was right. Finn had made that perfectly clear. In fact, they all had. Fimbly with his sketches. Herren with his slime. If Colm had to take any *other* lesson from this morning—outside of his being so ignorant of things—it was that anyone, even a talented anyone, would be a fool to try to make it through a dungeon by himself.

Still, he thought, taking one last glance at Ravena Heartfall, *it wouldn't hurt to have someone like that on your side.*

"Whatever," Lena said dismissively. "There's nothing she can do that we can't do better."

"But there's lots of things she can do that I can't do at all," Quinn said. Then he tried to steal Lena's stew back from her, but she wrapped both hands about it and growled at him. He wasn't a very good thief.

Odds were, Ravena Heartfall was a better one.

After lunch, Serene and Lena marched off eagerly to meet their mentors and do pretty much the opposite of each other, the druid learning to heal the wounds that the warrior was learning to make. Quinn moped glumly toward the spellcasters' hall to face one of two masters he'd *already* set fire to. "And I've only been here a day," he complained. Finn came to collect Colm, seeming to melt right out of the walls.

"Ready to get your hands dirty?" he asked. Colm thought about the ogre's jelly that had nearly sucked poor Dagnor's face off. Finn flashed his confident smile. "Don't worry," he said. "This is more in your direct line of work."

They walked along the western corridor, passing by rooms where other dungeoneers were in the middle of their training. Colm peeked, hoping to catch another glimpse of Ravena the Talent, but the only one he recognized was Tyren, hacking away at a practice dummy with a battle-ax. Tyren turned to see Colm spying on him, then gave the dummy one more solid *thwack*, splitting it down the middle. Colm quickly caught back up to Finn.

"I mailed your letter this morning," the rogue said. "Though I should tell you, it might take a while. The hawks seldom fly to Felhaven. It's not exactly the hub of commerce and adventure."

Colm didn't need Finn to tell him that. "Can they write back?"

Finn nodded. "You will hear from them soon, I'm sure. I wouldn't worry. I doubt your sister Celia would let anything happen in your absence."

Colm nodded appreciatively, though the thought of his sister made his insides ache. "Can I ask you something?"

"If this is about the scar, I told you, I got it in a knife fight with a pirate lord off the coast of Mardoon."

"You said it was a goblin executioner," Colm corrected.

"Who just happened to be a pirate lord," Finn replied wryly. "What was your question?"

"I was thinking about the test. To get into the guild. Not the dungeon. That I understand. But the coin. I mean, what was the point, if you were just going to give it to me regardless? Why even make me try to get it? Was it just a trick? Or did you just want to see me make a fool out of myself?"

Finn stopped in front of a door, the last one at the end of the hall.

"No trick, Colm Candorly. I just wanted to make it clear which of us was the master."

"As if that was ever in doubt," Colm muttered. Finn shook his head.

"Rule number twenty-three. Be the best there is at what you do, and always be aware that someone does it better." Finn opened the door and ushered Colm inside. "Welcome," he said, "to my workshop."

Colm looked around the room. It didn't look anything like his father's workshop back home. Of course, Rove Candorly's shop wasn't much more than a table and a barrel of tools in one corner of their warped wooden barn. Finn's workshop was much more elaborate, overflowing with cabinets and chests, shelves nearly collapsing under the weight of books, the floor littered with all manner of gadgets that Colm couldn't identify. One wall was covered in maps, most of them ancient-looking and torn. Another was covered in keys of varying lengths and designs, each hanging from its own ring. A skull sat on the corner of a large walnut desk, its top sawed off to make a morbid candleholder.

"Wow," Colm said.

"It's nothing like Tye Thwodin's, I can tell you that, but it serves its purpose."

Colm walked over to the wall of keys and started touching them. They made a kind of forlorn music when they fell against one another. "Do you know what they all go to?"

Finn shrugged. "I did at one time, I suppose, but there are a lot of doors that, once opened, are never shut again, making half of those keys superfluous. Besides," he added, "rule number thirty-nine. Most of the doors worth opening don't have a key—at least not one you can easily get your hands on. That's why there are people like us."

Colm turned from the keys to the maps, running his fingers along the borders of mountains, tracing the snaking trails of rivers. He didn't recognize most of the names of the places he read. He found Felhaven on one of them and was surprised at just how small it was. Barely a dot, with its name scrawled in scrunched letters.

Then he turned to the far wall, and the most unusual door he had ever seen.

"What's that?"

"That," Finn said, beaming proudly, "is my own personal

invention. My pride and joy." He pursed his lips. "Well, it's not exactly *my* invention. I had some help from Renny . . . and Velmoth . . . and some of the other masters. But it was still my idea. I needed an easy way to teach the craft that we rogues are so well known for, so I created . . ." Finn paused for dramatic effect, then thrust both hands toward it. "The Door of a Hundred Locks."

Colm stood at the door, which had been set into the wall. Sure enough, it was practically covered in intricate plates of copper, iron, and silver, each with a keyhole, some big enough to shove in a dagger, others barely large enough for a horse's hair. "Where does it lead?"

"Where do you think? To a mystical land teeming with nymphs and sirens and sprites that tumble playfully through the eaves of dancing trees and feed you sweet nectar from a crystal bowl," Finn said, his eyes wide.

Colm raised an eyebrow, put a hand on the door. "Sure. But where does it really lead?" he asked.

"It's actually just the closet where I keep my spare shoes. But it's not what's behind the door that matters. Not in this case, anyways. It's the getting it open. After all, we are rogues. We are counted on to get into places and things we otherwise shouldn't. That requires tremendous skill."

Colm nodded. "And there are really a hundred different locks?" Colm had only counted the top row.

"Not exactly." Finn coughed. "But the Door of Sixty-Seven Locks didn't have quite the same ring to it."

Still, sixty-seven locks was impressive. Colm wondered what you would have to be hiding to need so many different locks. Certainly something more valuable than Finn's spare boots. "And you know how to pick every single one of them?"

Finn nodded. "Though I admit some of them still pose a challenge for me. This one, for example"—he pointed to a lock along the top with a golden face no larger than Colm's thumbnail and a hole no bigger than a freckle—"is called the Twitch. The tumbler inside requires only the most infinitesimal movement, barely a nudge. Less than a nudge. A breath. Force it too much one way or the other, and it triggers its fail-safe mechanism, usually a trap of some kind leading to your—"

"Untimely demise," Colm finished. The lessons of the morning weren't lost on him.

"Right. And this row," Finn continued, pointing to a column of locks marching down the door's right side, "is made up entirely of enchanted locks, which means that they are protected by magic of some sort or another. Even the most skilled rogue in history couldn't get past them without some means of countering that magic."

"Like a counterspell?" Colm wondered.

"A counterspell, certainly. Though you know how I feel about letting mages handle anything as sensitive as picking locks. There are other things that rogues can use. Scrolls. Talismans. Magic Dan's Antimagic Paste."

"Magic Dan?" He was sure Finn was teasing him again.

204

"Of course you haven't heard of Magic Dan's. They probably don't carry it in any of the stores in Felhaven. Fantastic stuff, though. Comes in a little jar. Rub a little on the outside, and it eats away at the enchantment. Not good for really high-level magic, mind, but it can nullify a goblin shaman's ward in minutes."

"How come you didn't put any of it in my bag, then?"

"Oh. It's terribly expensive," Finn explained. "We don't go handing it out to just anybody. Now look here." He pointed to a series of ten locks on the left. They were not particularly ornate, though they seemed to grow more complex as they descended. "These are the starters. This first one"—pointing to the top—"is just like the one you picked to get out of Renny's dungeon. We begin with these, doing them over and over again until you can unlock them in your sleep; then we move on to the next ten and the next ten and so on, until finally you tackle *that* one." Finn turned and pointed to the corner of the room, to a small chest made of iron, sealed with a silver plate. "Pick that, and you'll be my hero."

"You'll have to show me how," Colm said, staring at the lock, thinking it looked like many of the others already set into the door and wondering what was so special about it.

"I wish I could." Finn shrugged.

"You mean you've never even opened it?"

Finn shook his head.

"You don't even know what's inside?"

The corners of Finn's mouth twitched. "Nobody knows,"

he said. "Maybe all the treasure in the world. Maybe a pile of dust. Maybe my missing fingers." The glint in the rogue's eye soon faded as he turned back to the door of a hundred locks—rounded up. "But as in all things, the best place to start is the beginning."

Colm fished in his sack for his lockpick set, the one Finn had given him, but found only the dagger and the jewel. He dug through the sack again, then looked up.

Finn dangled the picks over his head.

"Even I have to stay in practice," he said.

Colm snatched them back, then turned toward what had to be the best-protected pair of old boots in history.

He picked until he had blisters. Then he picked until they burst. It was excruciating. The picks were finicky, and he found he had to hold them in a variety of awkward positions depending on what lock he was working on.

In addition, he had several different picks to choose from, some with diamond tips or circles, some shaped like a saw blade or a pair of fangs or a rake. At first Finn wouldn't tell him which pick to use for which lock, just let him fumble around for a bit, experimenting. Only when Colm's sighs grew sufficiently exasperated did the rogue stop to explain, pointing to the proper pick and describing the mechanism inside the lock, how the tumblers worked and how many pins each one contained. He taught Colm the difference between a wafer lock and a disk lock, when to rake and when to push, how much tension to apply to get everything lined up just right. He taught Colm how to listen, putting his ear to the door, waiting for the characteristic *click* that Finn said was "the sound of gold in your pocket." He held Colm's hands and moved them around, like a puppeteer, but with such minute gestures it hardly seemed like either of them was moving at all. After each lock, Colm would open the door to reveal one pair of dusty boots. Then Finn would set the next one and close the door again.

Colm conquered the first two locks with little trouble. The third took most of an hour.

"Patience," Finn would say, and Colm would relax for a moment, take a deep breath, and flex his fingers to get the blood back in them. Then, two minutes later, Finn would scream "Troll!" or "Spider!" or "Flaming skull!" and beg Colm to hurry lest they both perish by the claw of whatever imaginary creature was stalking them, causing Colm to get nervous and fumble with the lock, dropping his picks and losing any progress he had made.

"Stop *doing* that!" Colm protested.

"Working under pressure is the rogue's hallmark. One slip, and your whole party is doomed. Your craft requires the utmost concentration and mental agility. Now hurry up before this imaginary ogre eats me."

By the time the afternoon was over, Colm had managed to undo the third lock and the fourth. He was just starting on the fifth when Finn told him his time was up, reminding Colm that he wasn't the only member of the guild who needed training.

Colm nodded. He had hoped to make it further. He had had a notion, when he first saw the door, that he would make it through the first ten locks in a day. After the first lock, Finn had called Colm "a natural." But Colm couldn't help but feel disappointed.

"You know," Finn said, stopping him on the way out, "lock number three is the same one the magistrate of Felhaven uses for the town's treasury. I know. I've seen it."

Colm wasn't sure why Finn was telling him this. He didn't respond.

"Which means you already know enough to be as rich as him." The rogue offered Colm a wink and then shooed him out the door.

Colm left the workshop, picturing himself breaking into the Felhaven treasury in the middle of the night. Imagine the look on the magistrate's face when he woke up to find his coffers empty. But as soon as the thought sneaked in, Colm felt guilty for having it. He had no intentions of robbing the magistrate. Rule number one. He gently rubbed his three sore fingers with his other hand and made his way to the dining hall.

The evening stew was whitish, with beans and bacon, a smell that reminded Colm of home—on the rare occasions when his family could afford bacon. An afternoon of listening for dropping tumblers and fidgeting with picks had given him an appetite, at least.

Serene noticed him in the archway and waved him over. She looked to be her normally cheery self, and Quinn also seemed pleased, which was nice; Colm had hoped the mageling would have a better afternoon. This time it was Lena who was scowling. One look at her finger told Colm most of what he needed to know. He sat across from her, pulling the basket of bread away from Quinn, who appeared to be hoarding it like a dragon, and pointed to the bandage on Lena's finger.

"I don't want to talk about it," she snapped, slowly bending her iron spoon in half. Colm looked to Quinn, who raised his eyebrows sympathetically.

"She lost," he said.

Colm nodded solemnly. She lost. It didn't even matter what she had lost at. Lena was the kind of girl who could take a bad coin flip personally. But this was much more serious.

"She was bested in single combat," Quinn explained. "By him." The mageling pointed across the room with his spoon at the table in the corner where Tyren was attempting to eat an entire loaf of bread in one mouthful. Lena twisted the spoon some more, apparently trying to tie it into a knot.

"Oh," Colm said. That was serious.

Quinn and Serene both nodded. "Only wooden swords, but apparently he caught her knuckle just right. There was a little . . . you know." Across the table, Lena shuddered and closed her eyes. "She didn't faint—but she did get a little woozy and lost her balance. Tyren disarmed her in two moves."

"It was a cheap shot," Lena said. "He *tried* to draw blood."

Colm considered telling her that that was generally what sword fighting was all about, but thought better of it. The spoon was a mangled loop of twisted metal already, and he thought she might just throw it at him.

"On the plus side," Quinn remarked, "I learned how to boil water today. Watch."

The mageling pointed at his bowl of stew and began chanting under his breath. A moment later, you could see the first bubble start to surface, and soon the bowl of bacon and beans was bubbling and popping like it was still over the coals. "You want yours warmed up?"

Colm shook his head. Better not to risk it.

"I learned how to speak dog," Serene said, beaming. "I mean, I knew already, but I was a little rusty. We don't have wild dogs in the glade. Most of the elders prefer owls for pets. Or wolves." She shivered in her seat.

"Wolves are just big dogs," Colm suggested.

"And panthers are just big cats too, but you wouldn't just go up and pet one."

Colm was about to tell them about the door of not nearly a hundred locks and how he had managed to get through the first four already when the normally boisterous dining hall fell silent. A familiar figure stood in the archway, practically filling it. He peered out from behind his lion's mane of hair, his bulk barely contained in his golden armor.

"Don't be quiet on my account," Tye Thwodin said. "Roar!

Boast! Shout! We are adventurers! We are meant to be loud!" There was a pause, and then slowly conversation returned as Master Thwodin stomped through the room.

"What's he doing here?" Colm wondered.

"He does this, I hear," Lena offered, snapped out of her funk by the presence of the guild's founder mingling with his charges. "To get to know his new dungeoneers better."

Colm watched the legendary warrior work his way down the tables, clapping his recruits so hard on the back that it made them choke, sometimes reaching over and stealing some of their food or swigs from their cups. Nobody dared tell him no. It was his castle, after all. Finally he made his way to Colm's table and peered down at the lot of them.

"Aha. Here's some fresh faces," he bellowed. "How was your first full day as official dungeoneers in training?"

Quinn nodded eagerly, probably too nervous to try and speak. Serene said it was excellent, thank you. Colm smiled.

"And you, Miss . . . Proudmore, is it? Got your first war wound, I see." He pointed to her knuckle.

"Just a scrape, sir," she said, not looking up. So there was at least *somebody* she didn't have the nerve to stare down.

"Just a scrape? Judging by the size of that bandage, I'd say you nearly lost the finger! You might know something about that, though, wouldn't you?" Tye added, staring at Colm. Colm was about to explain how he had actually been born that way when a young man Colm didn't recognize walked briskly through the dining hall, snapping to attention in front of the head of the legion.

"Master Thwodin, there's a matter requiring your attention, sir," the young man whispered.

"Can't you see I'm mingling?" Tye Thwodin barked.

"Yes, sir. But it's kind of urgent," the messenger insisted. "It's Master Wolfe, sir. He has returned."

Colm noticed that everyone within earshot suddenly froze, mouths shut, ears perked, eyes wide.

Tye Thwodin simply shrugged. "And what? He wants me to fetch his slippers for him? I assure you, Grahm Wolfe can find the front door by himself. He's a bloody ranger who killed his first orc when you were still sucking on your own toes. Let's just leave the poor man alone."

"That's the thing, sir," the messenger said. "He's *not* alone. He has . . . *company.*"

There was a heavy pause as Master Thwodin considered the implications. Then he gave the young man a penetrating stare. "Well, in that case, call the other masters. And then run down to the armory and grab my hammer. You know which one."

The messenger spun around and ran back through the archway at twice the speed he had come in. Master Thwodin turned back to Colm's table. "Sorry to cut the conversation short," he said. "But it appears we have guests."

It didn't take long for the dining hall to clear out. Once Tye Thwodin gave the command for the other masters to arm themselves and meet him at the front gates, the younger dungeoneers collectively determined that dinner was over. Even

Colm got a little chill when the gilded giant of a man stomped out of the dining hall, bellowing commands. There was a huge commotion as the surge of trainees funneled through the archway into the great hall to the front doors, but they were quickly stopped by Master Merribell, who had both hands raised, commanding them to halt.

"Where do you think you're going?" she demanded.

"To watch," Lena said eagerly.

"I'm afraid not. The castle is on lockdown. You should return to the dining hall until the lookout rings the all clear."

Master Thwodin, Smashy Two now slung across one shoulder, heard the collective groan and turned around. "It's all right, Bell. It's just a little raiding party. Let them watch from up top. It will be educational." Then he turned and strode toward the giant double doors beneath the hourglasses, Masters Velmoth and Stormbow in tow, along with the goblin. Colm noticed that Finn was not among them. Apparently rogues weren't called upon to defend the castle from invaders.

"Come on!" Quinn said, tugging on Colm shoulder. "I don't want to miss this!"

Colm turned and followed Quinn up the stairs, catching Lena and Serene and the rest of the crowd as they made their way through the halls to the doors leading out to the battlements. Colm had been on the roof to visit the rookery on his first day, but this time they moved toward the front of the castle, looking down over the courtyard and the field beyond, edged by the emerald forest all around.

Colm froze. There, racing across the wet grass, leaning hard

213

into his horse's mane, was a figure dressed in black. Both hands clutched the reins as the steed's hooves kicked up clods of mud behind him, the pair making straight for the castle gate.

This, apparently, was Master Wolfe. And the messenger was right: he wasn't alone.

Along the edge of the forest, pouring out from between the trees, was a wave of orcs—Colm recognized them from the book Herren Bloodclaw had insisted they read. In person, they looked much more vicious than their black-and-white engravings: clubs and axes brandished, ugly green-and-brown faces contorted in snarls. The monsters were mounted on what looked to be giant boars with tusks the size of tree branches, two to a back, careening down the sloping plain that led to the castle's outer wall. You could hear the thunder of their hoofbeats.

"Didn't he say *little* raiding party?" Serene asked. There had to be at least fifty of them.

The boars were fast—faster than Colm had ever imagined they could be—but the black-clad figure's horse was faster. There was no way they would catch him. All around him, he heard the other young dungeoneers cheering Master Wolfe on. Colm had to admit, it was more exciting than sitting in Finn's office blistering his fingers.

"He's going to make it," Quinn said.

Colm agreed. The ranger would have, certainly. That is, if he hadn't stopped, his mottled gray mare reeling back and wheeling around to face the horde bearing down on him.

"What's he doing?"

A girl standing behind them, tall enough to look over the top of Colm's sandy mop of hair, laughed. "It's Master Wolfe. What do you think he's doing?"

The figure on the horse crossed both arms, reaching down to either side of his belt and drawing the two swords he found there. Colm thought he could almost hear, from all the way up the castle walls, the *zing* of the metal pulled from the scabbards.

"Anywhere and Anytime," Lena cooed, her voice steeped in pure awe. "The twin blades of one of the most feared swordsmen ever." Colm looked down at Scratch by his side.

"Wait a minute. He's not actually going to attack them, is he?" Quinn croaked.

Colm wondered what Finn would say, outnumbered fifty to one. Run. Run and hide and live to fight again. But the man with a sword in each hand charged instead—the clop of the horse's hooves mixed with the rolling drums of two dozen barreling boars, destined for a collision in the middle of the field. Colm figured the ranger might take down four of them. Ten, if he was as legendary as everyone around here seemed to think he was. But that still left forty clubs, axes, and scimitars to deal with, not to mention all those gouging tusks. It looked like suicide.

The ground swelled. The loose stones on the battlements quivered. Beside Colm, Serene covered her eyes. Lena let go of the edge of the stone wall she'd been gripping and took a step backward. They were only twenty yards apart now. Ten. Five.

Suddenly there was a booming *crack*, loud enough to make Colm cover his ears. The steed and her rider skidded to a halt just as the ground trembled and split right in front of him, a huge wall of stone erupting from the earth in the middle of the field, towering up toward the clouds in an instant. The first row of boars crashed into the spontaneously erected rock wall, careening into one another, spilling their riders. The stone wall was so tall, Colm could barely see over it, even from four stories up, and it caught nearly half of the orcs in the pileup. But the half behind split like a stream and circled around the wall toward the ranger, who had taken several steps back, swords in hands.

Then there was another shout. One young girl pointed down over the ramparts, and everyone surged to see the other masters galloping forth on horses of their own, Tye Thwodin in the lead, riding a warhorse as big as a barge, his giant hammer incomprehensibly held upright in just one hand. The crowd let out another cheer. Colm cheered right alongside them.

The two armies met in the middle of the field.

What followed was pure chaos—a little like watching all of his sisters try and get ready for the town festival. A flurry of motion and squealing and squabbling with limbs flying, clothes ripped and torn, spit and sweat and even a little blood. Colm tried to take it all in at once, realized that was impossible, then simply let his eyes dance from one spectacle to another.

He saw one orc take an arrow to the leg and fall from his mount. Saw another zapped by a jolt of lightning brought down from the clouds. He saw Smashy Two literally send a boar and its two riders airborne, somersaulting twice before hitting the ground. But for all there was to see—Master Stormbow crunching skulls with her mace; Master Velmoth, his rabbit ears somewhat shrunken but still bouncing, summoning balls of blue energy in his palms and tossing them at incoming riders; Master Thwodin smashing orcs from their mounts as if it were a carnival game—Colm's eyes kept coming back to the ranger, Wolfe, who fought with the same ferocity as Master Thwodin but with twice as much grace, striking and thrusting, feinting and parrying as if it had all been rehearsed, a dance he'd performed a thousand times. Colm could hardly catch his breath.

It was over almost as soon as it began. Though well over half the orcs still stood, they knew they were beaten. Gathering their wounded and remounting as best they were able, they sounded a plaintive howl of retreat and thundered back toward the edge of the forest, the chorus of shouts from the roof of the castle and Tye Thwodin following after them.

"Did you *see* that?" Quinn asked, jumping up and down. Serene shook her head emphatically, only now peering through slits between her fingers. Colm looked around, casually at first, then with a stone dropping in his stomach.

"Lena?"

She was gone.

"Where did she go?"

"I don't know. She was j-j-just here," Quinn stammered, instantly panicked.

Colm searched the crowd. Quinn called her name. There was no response, though it was nearly impossible to hear anything through all the cheering. She should have been at the front, angling for a better view. She would have wanted to be as close to the action as possible. That was her way.

"Oh, no," Colm groaned to himself. Just then they heard some shouts coming from the corner of the parapet. Several trainees were pointing over the ledge. "Oh no," he repeated.

Colm, Quinn, and Serene shouldered their way to the front.

"So typical," Serene said.

There, down below, far from the center of the battle that had already come to a close, stood a trio of orcs that had split off from their war band, looking for an easier way into the castle. Either they hadn't heard the call to retreat or they were too brave or too stupid to follow it.

Lena stood in front of them, sword in hand, just as brave and stupid.

How she had sneaked past Master Merribell, Colm didn't know, but it was definitely her. Grunting and snarling, the three orcs surrounded her, their black blades held high, ready to cleave her in two. Lena spun in place, trying to keep an eye on all of them at once. Colm glanced back toward the front of the castle. In the courtyard, Tye Thwodin was busy cursing the fleeing orcs, imploring them to come back and meet the end of his hammer. The masters didn't know that one of their young dungeoneers was about to be skewered.

"Quinn, do something! Shoot a fireball or something," Serene pleaded, but the mageling just shook his head.

"I have j-j-just as g-g-good a chance of hitting her!" he said. "Or you!"

Colm looked around frantically and found a loose stone that had come free from the wall. It was pear sized, hardly big enough to do any damage, but with the right throw . . . Colm closed one eye and launched the rock over the side of the rampart, catching one of the three orcs in the shoulder, causing it to look up.

It was just the distraction Lena needed. The moment the orc took its eyes off her, she spun and lunged, striking a blow that caused it to stumble backward. The other two swung for her, but she somehow managed to turn in time to deflect them. With cries of rage, the creatures advanced, lashing out, forcing her to the defensive. There was nothing subtle about their movements, and Lena managed to meet each stroke easily, but the force of their blows knocked her sword back every time, giving her no chance to recover. The orcs' furious assault had her backed against the castle's outer wall.

Colm knew he had to act. It would take too long to get down there using the stairs; she wouldn't last ten more seconds. The castle roof was four stories from the ground. A fall from this height would break several bones, but maybe he could use the stones to climb down somehow. He had one foot over the ledge when Serene's hand stopped him. She pointed toward the courtyard, to a blur of black and gray bearing down on Lena and her two assailants, a blade in each of the rider's hands.

Anywhere and Anytime struck once apiece, and it was over. Two orcs hit the ground, and the third scurried away with a shriek. Grahm Wolfe circled around, leaned over, and with one hand pulled Lena up to his horse. The crowd around Colm loosed another cheer. Serene leaned over the castle wall, head in her hands.

"She's safe," Quinn said.

"She's *something*," Colm said.

Down below, Lena wrapped her arms around the ranger newly returned, burying her head in his cloak.

As quickly as they had galloped up the stairs to the roof to watch the battle, the wave of young dungeoneers washed back down to the great hall to see the victorious masters parade through the doors. The entry was instantly filled with the hulking frame of the guild's shining founder, Smashy Two sitting atop his shoulder, a look of satisfaction emblazoned on his face. There was a round of huzzahs as the rest of the masters filed in, chins in full jut, eyes burning with blood lust and pride.

Bringing up the rear was Master Wolfe.

For the first time, Colm got a good look at his face. It was depressingly handsome. Thin scruff of black beard and cold gray eyes like thunderclouds. Not a scar to be seen. Finn had a certain charm, a disarming smile, but his face was too sharp. Master Wolfe looked positively princely.

Beside him, armor covered in mud, Lena walked with her chin dug into her chest. Neither of them seemed to pay any heed to the cheering, even though Master Wolfe had been responsible for taking out seven orcs himself—and that was only what Colm had seen.

"Well, that was a romp," Tye Thwodin bellowed. "Who did they think they were, taking on Thwodin's Legion, hm? And on our own home turf, no less. Now, who wants dessert?"

The crowd of dungeoneers cheered in affirmation, then followed the boisterous master back toward the dining hall, the founder calling for Fungus to serve up something rich for a change. Colm, Quinn, and Serene held back. Master Wolfe had drawn Lena aside and was talking to her in whispers. He wasn't pointing fingers, and his expression never changed. If it was a lecture, it was a mild one. Finally she nodded and he touched her lightly on the shoulder, then turned away. Colm watched the ranger quickly catch up to Master Thwodin and pull him over to the spiral staircase, their heads pressed close together, quickly immersed in quiet conversation.

Lena shuffled over to them. She had a strange look on her face. Colm quickly considered what to say. He *should* tell her just how foolish she had been, to sneak off like that and run blindly into a battle all by herself. A speech on the nature of teamwork and patience and knowing one's limitations seemed called for. He also wanted to mention that it was he who had thrown the stone that distracted the orcs, just in case she didn't know. He cleared his throat. "That was . . . ," he began.

"I know," she said. She looked at him briefly, but then her eyes gravitated toward the stairs and the ranger who had rescued her. "Amazing," she finished. "Did you see him? Did you see what he can *do*?"

"Not quite what I was going to say," Colm mumbled, but he had lost his chance to say what he really thought. Over by the stairs, Tye Thwodin nodded gravely at something Master Wolfe was saying. Colm watched Lena stare a moment more. Then he turned away and looked around the now-empty hall.

He spotted Finn, standing on the far side, underneath the clocks, hands tucked into his pockets.

Staring intently at the returned ranger as well.

10

WHY WIZARDS SHOULDN'T CARRY SWORDS

The next morning brought both stew and conversation left over from the night before. The dining hall hummed with accounts of the attack on the castle, each version a revision of the last. In the latest telling, there were at least three hundred orcs, the wall of stone was twice the size of the castle, and Tye Thwodin had actually bested two orcs by smothering them beneath his armpits. And yet every conversation eventually circled around to Grahm Wolfe.

"I heard he was on a quest to find the entrance to the fabled mines of D'al Mordain."

"No, you idiot; he was scouting out prospects along the Gray Hills."

"Everyone knows he's been hunting the lair of the Spider King."

Nobody could stop talking about him. Even at Colm's own

table. Quinn, as it turned out, was quite an expert on the mysterious ranger.

"Haven't you spent any time in the library?" he said, explaining how he had nearly finished both Master Fimbly's *A Brief History of Dungeoneering* and Rolf Timlinsire's *Who's Who of Adventurers* in the short time they'd been here.

"I've been busy picking locks," Colm said.

"Making butterflies," Serene added.

Lena didn't comment. She was staring dreamily at her knob of bread.

"So you're saying you hadn't even *heard* of him?"

"Is it that surprising that I never heard of one guy?" Colm said defensively.

Quinn actually stopped eating, spoon hovering over his bowl. "One guy? Are you kidding? Grahm Wolfe is probably the most feared ranger in all the land, not to mention he's Tye Thwodin's closest companion. Without him, there probably wouldn't even be a legion."

"Right," Colm said, then shook his head. "Why is that again?"

"Rangers are scouts," Serene explained. "They are responsible for finding the dungeons and lairs and vaults where treasure might be held. And because they venture into these places alone, it is often considered the most dangerous class of adventurer to aspire to."

Quinn nodded in affirmation. "Once a ranger discovers a dungeon, he marks it and then reports back so a full-fledged exploration party can go tackle it and take its treasure."

Colm hadn't really thought about it before—how dungeons

were discovered. He just kind of assumed you fell into them, like Master Thwodin had so many years ago—or were pushed into them, like he had been. He didn't know somebody actually went out and *searched* for them.

"Grahm Wolfe is as close to family as Master Thwodin has left," Quinn said. "He's practically Tye's son." The mageling took another bite of roll and then launched into a tale of how a ten-year-old Grahm had been found sneaking around this very same castle one night, back before the guild was even founded. Tye Thwodin captured the boy, gave his ears a good boxing, and demanded to know if he was looking for treasure. Supposedly the response from the boy was "Food, but treasure will do." In return for a hot meal, the boy explained that his parents had been killed by ogres, and that he had been traveling from town to town, begging, borrowing, stealing, and fighting for his livelihood.

"So Tye Thwodin took him in, and when he formed the guild three years later, Wolfe was his first and best trainee," Quinn concluded. "He's the reason Master Thwodin is so successful."

"And you really believe all of that?" Colm questioned, remembering what Finn had said about the ranger—chest-hair nets and tree-bark swords.

"There are *lots* of stories about Master Wolfe," Serene said. "They can't all be true."

"Exactly," Colm said.

"Then why was he being chased by a hundred orcs?" Quinn prodded.

"It was only fifty," Colm countered. *Though that's easy to say when you are watching from the rooftops.*

"Whatever. I'm telling you, there are plenty of nasty things out there that would love to have Grahm Wolfe's head on a pike. He must have found something out there," Quinn said. "Something worth drawing that kind of attention."

"Remind me never to get that famous, then," Colm said, earning him nods of agreement from Serene.

Across the table, Lena sighed.

Despite the excitement of the previous evening, the morning schedule was the same as the day before. A painful lecture on the continued failed exploits of pioneering dungeoneers from Master Fimbly, followed by a torturous lecture on the dangers of regenerating mushroom monsters by Master Bloodclaw, followed by a marginally useful demonstration on knots by a seemingly distant and more reserved Finn. By the end of the morning, Colm had learned that no amount of armor can protect you from a vorpal blade, that mushroom monsters are, in proven fact, inedible (even if you could catch one to eat it), and that it's almost always easier to cut a rope than to try to untie it. All useful information, of course, but Colm found he was learning almost as much just by listening to the conversations of the dungeoneers he passed in the hall. Finn was teaching him to keep his ears pricked.

"Information is often more valuable than gold," Finn told him. "You'd be surprised how much you can learn just by standing in the shadows and keeping your mouth shut."

So in between training, Colm practiced eavesdropping on conversations. By the end of the morning, he had learned that Master Velmoth had finally broken down and guzzled one of Master Merribell's elixirs, effectively ridding him of his bunny ears but giving him terrible indigestion. He learned that Phoebe Flaxfire, a guild member for three years, was accidentally hexed by one of her own party during a combat exercise and was slowly turning into a dandelion. He even learned that Master Fimbly was taking herbal supplements to try and grow his hair back, though it seemed to be going straight to the stuff in his ears rather than on his crown.

He didn't learn anything more about Grahm Wolfe, however, except that nearly every female trainee in the castle was jealous of Lena because she actually got to ride on his horse with him. Nothing about why the orcs were chasing him or where he had been or what he and Tye Thwodin had been whispering about by the stairs. Whatever it was, it clearly was none of anybody else's business.

Colm did learn one thing that turned his ears red, though: that Herren Bloodclaw, goblin expatriate and master of the dungeon beneath the castle, was already busy planning the next round of trials.

Colm didn't even make it inside Finn's workshop before sharing what he'd overheard.

"Trials!" Colm blurted out.

The rogue grinned. "Oh, *those*. I'm surprised your friends

didn't say anything about them, though I suppose you are all a little fresh still. Yes, the trials are a tradition here. They're a lot like your initial test," Finn explained. "Only harder. And with more chances to hurt yourself. But they are nothing to worry about."

Colm thought about the bolt of lightning that had nearly fried half the hair off Quinn's skull during that initial test. It seemed worth worrying about. "They are called trials," he said. "They are not called trivial-little-things-you-shouldn't-concern-yourself-over."

Finn shrugged. "They happen a few times each year. Renny reconfigures his maze a little, then we toss you and your friends in and watch the clocks. The party that makes it through the fastest gets the prize."

"The prize?" Colm repeated, his interest finally overcoming his initial unease.

"Treasure, of course," Finn replied. "Of some kind or another."

"Is it dangerous?"

"Well, of course it's dangerous," the rogue scoffed. "But in all the time the guild has been around, we've had very few fatalities."

Colm still stood in the doorway, propping himself up. "Wait a minute. You're telling me I could *die* taking this test?"

"You could die falling out of bed," Finn said, reaching over and pulling Colm inside. "Trip over a stone and impale yourself on a tree root. Choke on a piece of rancid meat. Every step through life is a tenuous one. But *you* won't," Finn concluded. "Because you're smarter than that. And because you have me to train you." He pushed Colm toward the Door of a Hundred Locks and then sat down at his desk. "Now, where were we? Ah, yes, lock number five. Be careful with this one. Last time I picked one of these, a swinging scythe nearly took off my head."

Colm quietly unpacked his picks and laid them all out in front of him, but he wasn't ready to concentrate on the door quite yet. "So it's a competition?" he asked over his shoulder.

"It's a chance for you to put your newfound skills to use. To see how well your party works together. To get a taste for what the real thing is like."

"So there will be traps?" Colm asked.

"Yes."

"And monsters?"

Finn gave Colm a thoughtful look. "It won't do you any good to worry over it," he said. "It's still a few weeks away. By then you will know everything necessary to get out of Renny's dungeon in one piece. I promise."

Colm nodded and tried to focus on what he was doing, tried *not* to think about all the things that devious little goblin might think of to test them with. He flexed three fingers and took a deep breath, then inserted his diamond pick into lock number five, feeling for the pins, trying to push them into place. Traps and monsters. Whatever it was, it would likely be quite a bit more intimidating than the Overseer and his scorched pants. Colm gave his attention to the lock.

After several attempts, Colm stopped and sucked on his fingertips. A new set of blisters was crowding out the old ones. His head throbbed. His knees cracked from stiffness. His right ear was sweaty and numb from being pressed against the door's steel frame. Finn must have noticed him rubbing it.

"Listening is all well and good," he said. "Some rogues *have* to hear it; it's the only way they work. But sometimes that's not possible. Ever hear a gorgon scream? Terrible sound. Deafens you for hours. Makes you tear your hair out. You can't always count on sound. No way can you hear a pin drop when there're swords clashing and warriors shouting all around you."

There was no way Colm could hear anything with Finn constantly jabbering at him, either. But he guessed that was probably the point. He slumped against the door.

"The man who taught me how to pick . . . his name was Narl. Crazy old man. Deaf in both ears. Couldn't hear his own name if you or I were shouting it in his face. But he could blaze through nearly every lock on this door like he was picking his teeth. Did it all by touch, see? He had the most sensitive fingers. He could feel a fly's fart on those fingertips."

Colm laughed. He hadn't ever stopped to think about Finn having somebody like Finn in his life. He had kind of assumed that the rogue was self-taught, that it all just came to him, like intuition, like divine inspiration. But even mentors must have mentors.

"They have their own memory, fingers," Finn continued. "It's funny, but you'll come across a lock and the moment you touch it, you get that sense. You say, 'Hey, don't I know you from somewhere?' And you don't even have to think. It just all falls into place. You feel it in the ridges, in the joints and the bones and the little hairs that stand on your knuckles. You feel it on the surface and it tingles and travels down your fingers and the length of your arm into your chest and to the very core of you. It's electric. And it's instantaneous. And it's fleeting. But you will come to recognize it, the feel of each lock, the sensation of release. That old man . . . he said he felt closer to some locks than he ever did to a living soul."

Colm closed his eyes and turned back to the door. He didn't put his head against it anymore, operating solely on touch this time. Sensing the vibrations in the pads of his fingers, the subtle shifts, the slightest resistance. Until, finally, something clicked. Colm reached out and tried the handle. The door opened, revealing Finn's musty old boots for the fifth time in two days.

"Excellent," the rogue said, beaming. "See. Told you. Those trials will be as easy as picking a nobleman's purse."

Colm flushed with a momentary burst of pride, then turned back to the door. He could feel Finn smiling behind him.

He finagled his way through locks six and then seven before Finn said he could stop. Seven was an especially tricky tumbler series, with eight separate levers requiring the use of three separate picks, each set at a particular angle and all at the same time. The slightest slip caused the whole thing to reset. Having one more finger wouldn't have helped, Colm thought, but having another hand would have been incredibly useful. He said as much to Finn. That they could have done it so much faster working together.

"In case you haven't noticed, good rogues are hard to come by these days. Most people would rather be a warrior or a knight than one of our kind. More honor in it, I suppose, though less brains."

Colm thought about Lena. She seemed smart. Except when she was running off to fight those orcs last night. That was a little thoughtless. And today at breakfast. And at lunch. And in their last training together—sitting and staring mindlessly out the window. More than once today, he had caught her doodling in a notebook, seen the sketch. A figure in a cloak on horseback, a blade in each hand. Anywhere and Anytime.

Finn shut the door on his spare boots and handed Colm a canteen—the reward for all his efforts: a swig of lukewarm water. "What do you know about Master Wolfe?" Colm asked after a swallow.

Finn's features darkened. It was the same look Colm's father got when a nail split straight through a heel he was trying to repair. The same look Celia got when his mother asked her to do something around the house. Finn Argos was the only person who reacted to the ranger that way, Colm noticed, and the reaction was instantaneous.

"What do I *know* about him?" Finn began. "Not much.

I know he spends most of his days wandering through the wilderness sniffing out goblins and ogres and harpies and such, venturing into dark places that no man in his right mind would ever dare venture alone. I know he's probably single-handedly responsible for the discovery of half of the dungeons in the guild's archives and that he's planted more crystal keys than all the other masters combined. I know his horse is named Trample, his bow is named Eyesoar, and his swords have names too. Probably his underwear has a name, though I hope to never learn it."

Colm laughed again, trying to imagine what the ranger's famous underwear would be called. Rosebottom, maybe. Or Fancypants.

"Truth is," Finn continued, "Grahm Wolfe spends most of his days out there, digging up secrets. Following paw prints and goblin trails. Always on the lookout for it."

"It?" Colm asked.

"It," Finn repeated, spreading his hands. "The big score. Some fabled trove that they've all heard about in prophecies and bards' songs and are foolish enough to believe exists, even though there is plenty of treasure right here under these floors." Finn stamped on the cold stone for emphasis. "Not surprising. It's hard *not* to believe in legends when you do what we do. Everything and everyone around here is an exaggeration. Master Velmoth supposedly once conjured a demon from the netherworld, yet he can't seem to shrink his own ears. Master Stormbow supposedly slew a giant by strangling it with its own ponytail, but she once was bested in single combat by a one-armed man. Master Merribell is a skilled healer and can bless you eight times over, but she's actually never stepped foot in a dungeon, as far as I know. And Tye Thwodin . . ." Finn stopped and stroked his chin, touching the very edge of his scar. "Tye Thwodin knows what he wants and knows just how to get it."

"You make that sound like a bad thing," Colm prodded.

"Certainly not. You have to admire what he's accomplished here. With this place. I'm only saying that nobody is without failings. We all have a weak spot."

"Including Master Wolfe?"

"Wolfe," Finn repeated, passing one hand over the candle flame flickering inside the skull, nearly snuffing it. "Grahm Wolfe is the one person who's probably as dangerous as everybody thinks he is. Trying to get a handle on him is like trying to wrestle your own shadow. And yet he's the one person around here Master Thwodin trusts above everyone else. He's earned it, I'm sure, but it's hard to tell who he counts on, if anyone. I don't believe anybody makes it in this world alone."

"So *you* don't trust him?" Colm questioned.

"I didn't say that," Finn replied, then stood abruptly, pulling his cloak tight about him. "I think that's enough for today," he said. "Outstanding work. I think even old Narl would be impressed."

Colm gathered his things and stuffed them back in his bag, slinging it over his shoulder, and stood in the doorway, one hand resting on Scratch. "I can feel it, you know," he said. "The lock. I can sense when it's about to give. Just like you said."

Finn nodded, face full of satisfaction.

"I hoped you might," he said.

The stew was especially thick that night, so thick you had to scrape it from the edge of your spoon with your front teeth like furrowing a field. Quinn likened it to eating masonry paste, even as he finished his second bowl. Colm fashioned his into a little mountain and then buried his spoon on top as a flag. "Behold . . . Mount Fungus," he said.

The others laughed, even Lena, who seemed to have broken out of her ranger-induced trance. Colm wasn't sure what had changed but figured he should just let it go.

Serene didn't. "So did you get to see your knight in shining armor again today?"

Lena blushed. "For your information, Master Wolfe doesn't wear armor. Like most rangers, he finds it cumbersome to fight in all that restrictive gear. And since you asked, no, I didn't see him. Master Stormbow said he had to leave again."

"Leave? But he just got here," Quinn said.

"He apparently only came to tell Master Thwodin some important news and resupply," Lena explained. *And change into a new pair of Fancypants,* Colm thought to himself. Still, he wondered what the important news might be. Wondered what passed for whispered conversation between those two men in particular. No doubt that would be information worth knowing. "I'm sure he's out there finding more work for the rest of us," Lena continued. "The sooner we get into a real dungeon, the better. My father already sent a letter asking if I've slain anything yet. I told him I'm working on it."

"You may get a chance sooner than you think," Colm said. Then he mentioned what he had overheard about the upcoming trials. He waited for looks of surprise but instead got knowing nods and an eye roll from the wannabe barbarian, clearly unperturbed.

"There's absolutely nothing that stunted little leathery turncoat can cook up that we can't handle. Am I right?" Lena looked around the table.

Colm nodded. She was right. Provided she didn't bleed and Quinn didn't open his mouth and Colm didn't have to Scratch anything.

"Still," Lena added thoughtfully, "it might not hurt to get in a *little* extra training before then."

Colm was about to ask her what kind of training she had in mind when they were cut off by three familiar faces leering over them.

"If it isn't the freckled fainter."

Colm tensed. It was Tyren again, flanked by Vala and Minx. Colm noticed that Vala had her necklace back and wondered if she'd dug it out herself or if someone had given it back to her. They weren't alone this time, either. Standing back a few paces, as if she were tethered to them by an invisible cord, was

Ravena Heartfall, her face firmly planted in another book. She didn't look up.

Tyren practically radiated smugness. "Just wanted to say I'm sorry about yesterday. I didn't mean to make you swoon like that."

Lena cocked her head, looked at him with disbelief. "Tyren Troge, you should know by now that just *looking* at you puts butterflies in my stomach."

Tyren blinked repeatedly, cheeks pinking.

"Completely making me want to throw up," she finished.

Vala twittered and covered her mouth. Tyren's face turned full-out red. He took a moment to gather himself before turning to his companions. "She's just jealous because she knows a guy like me has a ten times better chance of making his name as a barbarian."

"Uh-oh," Quinn mumbled.

Lena was up out of her seat in an instant, her nose inches away from Tyren's, who at least had the sense to take a step back.

"Are you suggesting that I can't be a barbarian because I'm a girl?"

"We should get somebody," Quinn said anxiously, looking around the room for one of the masters.

"I'm saying," Tyren shot back, "that anyone who faints at the sight of a parchment cut has no chance against a real warrior."

"Well, if you ever see a real warrior, you point her out to me, all right?"

"What's that supposed to mean?"

"It means you should shut your stew hole before I cram my foot down it."

"I'd like to see you try!"

Lena looked at Tyren. Then at her foot. Then back at Tyren. She was going to try.

Colm stood up beside her and was reaching out to grab her arm when a deep, steady voice told them, "Enough."

Ravena Heartfall closed her book softly and glared, not at Lena, but at Tyren. "You're acting like a toddler with a tree branch, standing on top of a pile of cow dung pretending to be king. Go sit down." It wasn't a suggestion, it was a command. Colm waited for Tyren to blow her off, push her away, but to his surprise, Tyren snorted, then turned and left without a word, the other two following him, leaving Ravena standing in front of Colm and Lena, her thick leather tome pressed close to her chest, her black braid falling down her back.

"I apologize," she said. "Tyren can be a little brusque sometimes. I'll have a talk with him." Then, without another word, she turned and followed the others to the back of the dining hall, leaving Colm just standing there, staring after her.

"Guess we know who wears the breeches in that party," Quinn whispered, clearly impressed.

Lena crossed her arms gruffly, blowing her bangs from her eyes. "That big mouth. I could have shoved *both* feet in there if I'd wanted to."

"If you ask me, I'd say he probably likes you," Serene said.

Lena turned and glared.

"But you didn't ask me," Serene mumbled.

"He just better hope that girl keeps him on a short leash. Right, Colm? Colm?" Lena tapped Colm on the shoulder, but he didn't really notice.

He was busy watching the long, black braid pendulum back and forth across Ravena's back.

"Yeah," he said. "One can only hope."

They woke the next morning to a special announcement. All morning sessions would be suspended to accommodate special combat training, led by Master Thwodin. All junior guildsmen were expected to attend.

"Combat training?" Quinn mumbled for the seventeenth time under his breath. "I've only held a sword once in my life, and I dropped it on my foot."

Colm had done more than that, at least. After Quinn had fallen asleep, Colm had practiced, lunging and twisting, imagining he was battling one of the orcs that had cornered Lena. Imagining, in fact, that he had swung down from the ramparts on a rope just in time to parry the blow that would surely have killed her, then picturing the two of them fighting, back to back, as the three orcs multiplied to six and then to a dozen, each one of them falling to his stroke or hers. Then Quinn stirred in his sheets and mumbled something about his ears burning, and Colm self-consciously put Scratch away and crawled into bed.

Fighting imaginary orcs in your room at night dressed only

in your underwear probably didn't count as combat training, though. Colm wished Finn had spent a little less time making him pick locks and a little more time teaching him how to use Scratch. Serene didn't make things better, stating smugly that she was surely exempt from the training because she was not permitted to wield weapons of iron or steel.

"They're expressly forbidden by my druidic order," she said, smiling.

Then Master Merribell came by the table to remind Serene to bring her nice, new wooden staff. Serene's face fell.

"Come on. It will be fun," Lena said. Then Quinn pointed out that she was the only one of them wearing armor, including a set of gauntlets that covered all but the tips of her fingers. Almost no hope of anyone drawing blood from her today.

They gathered in the largest training room in the castle. Several different areas had been roped off, providing stages for two or more combatants to have at each other with blunt weapons designed to do little more than raise welts. The masters had all lined up at the back of the room next to the weapon racks, Tye Thwodin in the middle, wearing his suit of golden armor to match his beard. Colm noticed Finn standing off to the side, looking distracted. Thwodin cleared his throat.

"In the wake of the recent attack, and with the trials looming, I've decided that we all need to spend a little more time trying to beat the snot out of one another."

Beside Master Thwodin, Herren Bloodclaw frowned. Colm wondered how many of the goblin's ancestors' heads Tye

Thwodin had bashed over the course of his career. "To that end," Tye continued, "I'm going to teach you all a move or two. I will, of course, need a partner."

Tye Thwodin combed his thick beard, then turned to the row of masters standing beside him. Colm fully expected him to pick Master Stormbow. She seemed the most qualified as resident weapons master, at least with Grahm Wolfe back in the wilderness hunting for who knows what, but instead the headmaster looked to the end of the line.

"Master Argos, would you mind?"

The rogue flashed Colm a look, then bowed graciously and stepped into the center ring, now walled by trainees. Finn carefully undid his cloak and handed it to Master Merribell. Then he and Master Thwodin each selected a blunted sword and a wooden shield from the rack.

"Go easy on me, Argos. I'm twice as old as you," Master Thwodin grunted. *And twice as big,* Colm thought to himself.

"I'll do my best," Finn replied, then instantly took to his guard as the head of the guild barreled toward him. The hall was instantly filled with the repeated clash of dulled steel as the two masters danced around the circle. Rather, Finn danced; Tye Thwodin moved like an avalanche. As they fought, Master Thwodin bellowed instructions, grunting out his moves: "Downward thrust!" "Cross slash!" "Reverse parry!" Finn, on the other hand, stayed silent, seeming to retreat across the arena under the bigger man's advances, taking measured steps, every move precise.

Colm watched wordlessly. It was exciting to see the two of them have at each other—but something seemed off. No doubt Master Thwodin was strong, every swing carrying enough force to send splinters of Finn's shield flying. But he was also slow, often overswinging, revealing weak spots that the more nimble rogue should have easily exploited. Colm thought back to the riders who had confronted them on the road out of Felhaven. Finn had managed to fend off three attackers at once, and all on horseback, no less. Here he seemed reticent, offering only weak thrusts and slashes that just barely missed their mark, yet missed it every time. It wasn't long before a blow shattered his wooden shield completely. The next one sent the rogue's sword clattering to the ground. Finn dropped to his knees, bested.

The masses cheered as Tye Thwodin raised his fists into the air, then turned and helped Finn to his feet. "Well fought, Master Argos."

"Thank you," Finn replied. "I'm afraid I'm just no match for you." Then the rogue glanced Colm's way once more, offering a hint of a smile, before retrieving his cloak and taking his place back in line.

"All right, dungeoneers. Let's see if you learned anything!" Tye Thwodin bellowed. Then he clapped his hands and all the trainees were separated by class: fighters versus fighters, rogues versus rogues, and so on, breaking into small groups and heading to their designated lines. Colm tried to comfort Quinn, who was handed a short iron sword so blunt it could barely cut water.

"You hold *this* end," Colm reminded him. Quinn just shook in place.

Soon the whole hall was filled with ringing metal and split wood. Occasionally you would hear a grunt instead and see one of two dungeoneers lying on the stone floor. The victor would cheer, the loser would slouch off; then whichever master was watching would say, "Next!" and the next two adventurers in line would enter the arena.

Colm gripped his practice sword uneasily; it was bigger than Scratch, with a thicker blade and a leather-strapped handle that was somehow harder to get a grip on. His only hope was that he would face off against somebody who knew even less about sword fighting than he did.

"Candorly!"

Colm turned to see Master Bloodclaw glaring at him, handing him a shield, the wood already cracked halfway down its center. "Do you have anything that's not already broken?" Colm asked, but the goblin just snorted and pushed him into the roped-off area. *It's all right,* he told himself, giving his blunt sword a few practice swings. *What's the worst that could happen? A skinned knuckle or a bruised shoulder.* Who knows, he might even win. He turned to see who he would be fighting, hoping for another fresh-faced pickpocket like himself.

He felt his legs nearly give out beneath him.

Ravena Heartfall spun her sword and took a couple of practice lunges. Her hair had escaped from its characteristic braid, cresting her shoulders and cascading down both sides. Before,

243

she had always looked so closed off. Wound tight. Now she looked almost feral. Beautiful . . . but in an alarming, I-think-I'm-about-to-devour-you sort of way.

"Good luck," Herren Bloodclaw said, then motioned for the match to start. Across the floor, Ravena bowed, then brought her sword up.

"Wait, how do I—" Colm began, but he didn't have time to finish the thought; Ravena was upon him, closing the space that separated them in a single breath. He felt her sword strike once, saw his own sword fly from his hand, then felt the blunt tip of her weapon pressed against his chest. The match lasted three seconds.

Ravena didn't say a word. She wasn't even breathing heavy.

"That doesn't count," Herren Bloodclaw spit. "Pick up your sword, boy, and try again."

Colm stood and retrieved his sword and looked again at the girl, who had retreated back to her side of the ring. At the goblin's command, she charged again, unblinking. Colm tried to remember what he had just seen Master Thwodin do—cross thrust or reverse-downward-parry-spin-something-or-other. But watching wasn't the same as doing, and while he managed to somehow deflect two of Ravena's blows, a swift kick to his gut sent him sprawling across the floor. Again, he felt the tip of her sword in his chest as he tried to catch his breath.

The goblin shook his head.

"That's the best you can do?" he grumbled. "My blind

244

grandmother could beat ya with her legs tied together. Now stand up and fight!"

Colm gathered himself, rubbing his gut where she had planted her foot. Quinn had said that Ravena Heartfall was a talent, good at everything. Obviously that included kicking Colm's butt. "How is this teaching me anything?" he pleaded with the goblin.

"It should be teachin' ya to stay out of her way, at least. Though it looks like you still need another lesson."

The goblin raised his hand and Ravena charged again, spinning her sword effortlessly, dancing toward him, except this time Colm didn't wait for her. He leaped backward, once, twice, avoiding the kinds of blows that had disarmed him before. He kept his shield in front of him—blocking the strikes that he couldn't dodge, simply trying to stay on his feet. He thought about what Finn might say, about being patient, watching, anticipating, waiting for just the right moment.

Except there didn't seem to be a right moment. Ravena was relentless, doubling her attack, spinning and thrusting, until she was practically chasing Colm around in a circle. He spun and ducked and scrambled, but he didn't get hit. He could see the frustration in her face as she swung wildly, overreaching. She lashed out, seeming to want to take his head off. Colm ducked and gave a halfhearted thrust with his sword.

Ravena's hands dropped to her sides. She stood there, the blunted tip of Colm's sword pressed to the tea-colored skin of her neck. She smiled. Colm had never seen her smile before.

Her already-narrowed eyes narrowed further.

Then he felt his sword knocked out of one hand and his shield knocked out of the other. In a blink, she had him on the ground. Again.

"Rule number one," she said, leaning in, whispering to him. "Never let your guard down."

"That's not rule number one," Colm grunted.

Ravena stood up, letting Colm breathe again. Then she reached down and took his hand. "We don't all play by the same rules," she said, pulling him up. Beside him, Herren Bloodclaw simply shook his head.

From behind, Colm heard a familiar voice shouting in triumph. He turned and craned his neck to see Lena standing over the prone body of Tyren Troge, who was rolling around on the floor, clutching his ear. It appeared to be bleeding, but Lena clearly had no problem with that, judging by her smile. Colm waved to her, trying to get her attention, but he couldn't see if she waved back. He couldn't see anything anymore.

The whole room was suddenly filled with shouting and smoke.

It was a miscalculation, Tye Thwodin said afterward. We weren't all created equal. Every dungeoneer was blessed with certain abilities, and it was, perhaps, better to nurture those naturally inborn talents than to try and impose others.

In other words, Quinn shouldn't have been asked to hold a sword.

Not that the sword itself had anything to do with it. Only that, in his frustration at trying to *use* it, the mageling had lost control. His nerves got the better of him. He panicked, said a few things he didn't mean to, and didn't say any of *them* quite clearly enough. The result was a sudden end to Thwodin's Legion's impromptu combat training.

The clothes, of course, could be replaced. The injuries were minor, easily treated by Master Merribell, who had plenty of remedies for basic burns. The scorch marks along the floor, however, were probably permanent, an indelible tribute to the unbridled power of a mageling with a nervous disposition.

The fire, apparently, shot out from practically everywhere. Ears. Nose. Throat. Fingers. *Everywhere.*

Afterward, as they were all making their way through the great hall, Quinn couldn't hide his embarrassment, blushing at everyone who passed. "I mean, what did they expect? Isn't that why we work together? They didn't stick a spell book in *your* hand and ask you to shoot fire out your ears, did they?"

Colm couldn't argue, though if it had just been the ears, it might not have been so bad.

"It's common sense," Quinn continued. "Rule number one. Leave the fighting to the big lugs with the swords." Quinn suddenly stopped and looked up at Lena with her sword strapped to her side. "Sorry. I didn't mean to suggest . . . you know . . . it's just something Master Velmoth told me."

Lena just smiled. "That's okay. Rule number seven. Never let one of those crazy, unpredictable mages cast a spell unless you're hiding behind a very thick wall."

"Rule number four," Serene echoed. "Always pack extra healing potions for when those thick-headed warriors and masochistic mages go insane and get themselves hurt."

They all looked at Colm.

"Rule number fifteen," he said. "Don't share your rules with others." He had just made that one up, though he imagined Finn would appreciate it.

"That's a good rule," Serene said.

"Well, the morning wasn't a total waste." Quinn sighed, leaning up against Lena. "I got a new set of robes, and I bet Tyren Troge thinks twice before he teases you again. You nearly took off his ear."

Lena shrugged. "I was swinging for his teeth. I need to work on my aim, I guess. And you," she said, looking over at Colm, "need to work on just about everything. Can't very well tackle those trials with you fighting like *that*. I can't kill everything for you. I mean . . . I probably can . . . but just in case."

Colm couldn't argue. He had about as much business carrying a sword as Quinn did.

Lena wasn't the only one who thought he needed to work on his swordplay. When he arrived at Finn's workshop for his afternoon training, the rogue was waiting for him outside.

"Did you lock yourself out?" Colm asked.

"That's funny," Finn said. "Almost as funny as watching you run in circles from Ravena Heartfall this morning. Granted, it was a poor pairing—there are few apprentices at this guild who could have bested her—but it showed me how lopsided our focus of instruction has been. After all, as good as a rogue's wits and his picks are, they can't get him out of *every* situation."

Finn led Colm back through the halls and out into the courtyard, finding a patch of grass out of sight of anyone. "All right then," Finn began. "Pull that toothpick out of its sleeve and let's see what we can do to keep pretty girls from beating you up again."

"At least they're pretty," Colm said, earning him a smile from the rogue.

For the next three hours, Colm didn't pick a single lock. Instead, Finn taught him the most basic elements of combat. It was all in slow motion, thankfully, Finn taking the time to correct every little move, standing behind Colm and moving along with him, hands on elbows, striking together. Scratch felt much more comfortable in his hand than the blunt steel stick he had been wielding that morning, and by the time they were finished, Colm was able to counter the majority of Finn's slower strikes with ease.

"You're going easy on me," Colm said as they sat down to rest afterward. Finn had a blushing peach and was carefully cutting pieces for them to share. Colm wondered who he had taken the peach from.

"You're just starting out," Finn explained. "You'll get better."

"And Master Thwodin?" Colm prodded. "Was he just starting out too?"

Finn paused, then traced a pattern along the skin of the peach with the tip of his knife. He looked sideways at Colm. "Tye Thwodin is a gifted warrior. It's only natural that he would best me in single combat."

"Oh," Colm said. "Because it looked to me like you were letting him win."

Finn smiled wryly. "We show only what we want others to see, and see what others wish we hadn't."

"Is that another rule?"

"Just an observation," the rogue said. He held the last of the peach to Colm, then wiped his hands on his cloak. "There is so much more I have to teach you, Colm Candorly, so much we still have to accomplish. I want you to be ready."

"For the trials, you mean," Colm said.

"For anything," Finn replied. "Impossible to know what life has destined for you, what choices you will be forced to make. You need to be prepared, not just to fight for what's yours, but to seize the opportunities when they present themselves. Unfortunately, we are all out of time for today. Be sure to practice what we went over. Maybe even corner that redheaded barbarian friend of yours and have her show you a thing or two. Poor Tyren's ear looks worse than Master Velmoth's ever did."

Colm stuffed Scratch back into its scabbard and grabbed his sack. As he turned back toward the castle, Finn stopped him, reaching into his gray cloak and removing a scroll, wound tight and tied with a white satin ribbon.

"Nearly forgot. This arrived for you earlier this morning," he said. "From Felhaven."

Colm took the rolled parchment and held it nervously. He started to open it, but Finn stopped him. "Certain things should be read in private, just in case they contain information that you wouldn't want to share with others."

Colm felt his stomach sink. "Did something happen? Is my family all right?" What if Seysha's illness had worsened and the medicine wasn't enough? Or what if the magistrate had gone back on his word and punished his father in his place for stealing all that coin? Colm had only been gone a few short days, but there were so many things that could have gone wrong. Things that he was powerless to do anything about.

"It's addressed to Colm Candorly," the rogue said, "not to Finn Argos. It's none of my business."

But even as he said it, he smiled.

By the time he made it back to his room, Colm already had the scroll unfurled. He shut the door and sat on the edge of his bed, holding the parchment between trembling fingers.

Dear Colm,

The girls all wanted to write separately, but we feared the bird couldn't carry them all, so we all sat down and wrote this together. We hope that you are happy and, above all, safe. We want you to know that we miss you terribly, but that we understand and appreciate what you are doing. Your father

says everything is cleared with the magistrate and that you are
welcome to come home whenever you like. Rest assured we
are all well, though lonely without you. Seysha is back to full
health, and despite their entreaties, your father and I haven't
let any of the girls take over your room. We hope that you will
return to us soon. Never forget how much we love you.

At the bottom they had all scrawled their names, including Elmira, though hers was more of a smudge.

Everyone, Colm noticed, but Celia. Colm felt a pang in his gut. Maybe she was mad at him for not coming home. She felt betrayed, and probably a little bit jealous. Here he was having an adventure without her, abandoning her. He guessed he couldn't blame her for being angry.

Colm flipped the parchment over. There, on the back, was another message, this one hastily written in half-smeared ink.

I miss you. Be careful.
Come home soon.
> *Celia*

And beneath the message, fastened with a bit of wax, was her hairpin. The long silver one no thicker than a sewing needle, with the emblem of the butterfly molded to its head, handed down from one great-grandmother on Mina Candorly's side. Each of the girls had a treasure—something special that they could call their own, that they wouldn't be forced to share with the others. Colm knew because he had stolen quite a few of them, out of revenge for various pranks they had pulled on him. This hairpin was Celia's.

Now it was his.

Come home soon.

It was a trap. He knew he couldn't keep it forever. She *knew* he knew. It meant he would have to come home, eventually, just to give it back.

Colm placed the parchment beneath his pillow after reading it three more times, then tucked the hairpin into his bag for luck. With the trials not far away, and whatever challenges awaited him after that, he figured he would need it.

His thoughts were still on Celia when he was startled by a knock on the door. It wasn't Quinn. Quinn would just barge right in. Colm opened it to reveal Lena standing in the hall, hands on her hips.

"A little bird whispered that there's a rogue with a sword on his hip and no clue how to use it."

A little bird. *With eight fingers and a penchant for whispering things,* Colm thought.

"I suppose you're here to teach me," he said.

"If you're going to learn," she said smugly, "you might as well learn from the best."

Colm looked at the pillow and the treasure he had stowed underneath. Come home soon, they said. Understandable. He missed them too.

But he wasn't going home empty-handed.

11

ALL OUT OF ORDER

Master Fimbly hadn't lied about the menu. When he had shown them the kitchen that first day, the old man had said that it was where the magic happened. The real magic, Colm decided, was that they all managed to eat the same thing day in and day out without jumping out of the castle's highest tower.

Outside of the menu, however, life at Thwodin's Legion was anything but dull. Master Fimbly had exhausted his supply of horrifying anecdotes about dungeoneers who had lost life or limb and was introducing some success stories—parties returning with limbs not only intact, but hefting huge sacks of gold. Master Bloodclaw was proving to be an expert in all things monstrous (takes one to know one) and had introduced Colm and the others to the carrion wyrm, the choke beetle, and the screeching harpy—which shattered the glass windows the moment Herren let her out of her box.

There were other forms of instruction as well: Colm learned how to identify medicinal herbs with Master Merribell and how to throw an ax with Master Stormbow, though he only managed to stick it in a tree once. There was even a quick overview of wilderness cuisine presented by Fungus himself, though that only amounted to a list of things you could put in a stew and things you couldn't. (Squirrel innards were, unfortunately, a "could.") After the first two weeks, Colm knew more about dungeoneering than he had ever cared to know about cobbling shoes.

He especially looked forward to his afternoons with Finn. The rogue had quickly expanded the breadth of Colm's training, teaching him more than just picking locks, though they still spent most of their time standing before that closet door. There were further lessons in swordplay and subterfuge. He taught Colm how to write and decipher several kinds of code and how to blend in with his surroundings. They spent an afternoon learning how to shadow someone, keeping to the corners and out of sight. That particular afternoon had culminated in Colm successfully stalking Lena for nearly thirty minutes, until she finally caught on and tackled him, threatening to beat his face in until she realized who he was. Even when she did, she still kept him pinned to the ground for a moment longer than necessary.

And there was more than one afternoon already spent on the delicate art of finding and disarming traps. These sessions

255

were often held outdoors or down in a special section of Renny's dungeon. And they almost always ended with Colm nursing fresh bruises.

"It is the rogue's responsibility to do all the disarming, even if it means you are dis-armed in the process," Finn told him.

Or deboned, disfigured, or decapitated. It was the main hazard of the occupation, Finn explained as they walked along the rows of flowers: that for every hundred doors you open, only one will be trapped, but you can be sure *that's* where the treasure is.

"Take this," Finn said, handing Colm a leatherbound book small enough to fit in the pocket of his cloak. *The Rogue's Encyclopedia*, Volume Two: *Traps and Contraptions*. Colm asked about Volume One. It seemed, once again, that Finn was getting ahead of himself.

"Volume One is remedial stuff. Hardly worth the time of innately gifted individuals such as ourselves. But *this* book is a lifesaver. In time you will come to memorize every word."

Colm flipped through the three-hundred-some pages. He hoped Finn was exaggerating.

"For now, you should know that most traps fall into a few major categories. You have your droppers—things falling on you. Your fallers—you falling in things. Your slicers. Your scorchers. Your snatchers. Your drowners. Your crushers. Your poisoners, and worst of all, your too-short good-byes."

"Too-short good-byes?" Colm echoed.

Finn snapped his fingers. "You'll barely have time to wave

farewell to your fellow party members before you are decorating the dungeon walls with your brains. But the most common kind of trap is the faller—usually into a pit. Often filled with something."

"Water?" Colm guessed hopefully.

Finn shrugged. "If it's boiling. More likely spikes. Snakes. Giant rats. Acidic slime. Molten lava . . . It's really best not to test it. And that requires an ever-watchful eye."

Then Finn gave Colm a little nudge, and he felt the ground give out beneath him, grass and dirt collapsing as he slid to the bottom of a hole barely as high as himself. There was nothing at the bottom but dirt, but Colm's pride was immediately bruised. The rogue crouched at the edge of the pit and smiled.

"If you had looked closely, you would have seen the grass thatched together, would have noted the bits of loose dirt along the edge. Of course, skilled trap makers won't leave such clues. Their work is almost seamless."

"Is Master Bloodclaw a skilled trap maker?" Colm asked, brushing himself off and thinking of the looming trials.

"He's a goblin. They make the best traps of all," Finn replied. "Of course, they say the mad sorcerer Azanab once conjured a never-ending pit and then accidentally tripped over his own robes and fell into it. That was over a hundred years ago, and he is presumably still falling."

Colm took Finn's extended hand and scrabbled up the edge. "And your point is . . ."

"At least *you* can crawl back out."

Though Colm actually couldn't. Not without a little help.

Colm's days belonged to Finn Argos and the other masters of the guild, but his evenings were spent with his party, the four of them lounging in the archives, listening to Quinn expound on some bit of arcane knowledge he'd discovered (never once stuttering) or soaking their feet in the steaming water of the hot springs, listening to a lecture from Serene on the importance of communing with nature ("Can't you hear the grass whispering?").

Every night, for an hourglass of time at least, Lena would drag Colm to one of the practice rooms for a friendly duel, two words that Colm didn't think mixed in her vocabulary. The other two would follow along and cheer Colm on, figuring Lena didn't need the encouragement. She never let him win, of course, but she did say he was at least losing more gracefully.

"So did you hear?" Lena said as she removed her gauntlets after their latest bout, offering that suggestive smile of hers that Colm had learned meant she was going to say something that only she would think was good news. "Master Thwodin has announced there will be a *special* prize for whichever party completes the next trial the fastest."

"Chests full of gold?" Colm wondered.

"A pet dragon?" Serene said.

"Something besides stew for dinner?" Quinn pondered.

"I thought you liked the stew," Colm questioned.

"I do," Quinn answered. "I just could go for a nice roasted

pheasant every now and then."

"Um. Hello? Pet *dra*-gon?"

"You can't even talk to bears. What makes you think you can talk to dragons?" Lena prodded.

Serene looked hurt. "I could if it was a *baby* dragon. Anything is cute when it's little."

"I have a younger sister who proves otherwise," Colm said.

"Well, whatever it is, it's ours," Lena said emphatically. "I mean, we have just as good a chance at winning as any other party here, right?" She looked at the other three in turn.

"Of course we do," Colm said, with more confidence than he actually felt. Finn had been coaching him on how to be a more convincing liar.

"I don't know," Quinn countered. "There are groups here that have been around a lot longer than we have."

"Then we will just have to spend even *more* time training together," Lena said.

The other three let out a groan, but it was just to give her a hard time. Truth was, Colm couldn't think of anywhere else he'd rather be.

By the end of the week, the trials were all anyone could talk about. There were wagers about who would win Tye Thwodin's coveted prize. Colm heard the names of several groups mentioned as having a chance, but by far one was whispered more than any others: Tyren Troge's. Not because of Tyren, who many considered to be far more boast than blade, or his flunkies Minx and Vala. By all accounts, Ravena Heartfall was the dungeoneer to beat. The other three would just be tagging along to hold doors open.

Of course, there were also bets concerning who *wouldn't* make it through the goblin's dungeon at all—those who would have to be rescued, carried out unconscious or worse. Colm heard his name mentioned more than once. It didn't help that the masters were making almost as big a deal of it as the trainees. A day after Finn introduced Colm to the joy of swinging scythe traps, Master Fimbly spent half a morning lecturing them about the importance of the upcoming trials.

"The whole point is to see if you can put the knowledge you've gained to practical use. After all, if you can't actually make it through a dungeon and score some coin, what use are you to us?" It was Fimbly speaking, but it sounded like something Tye Thwodin might say.

"WILL THERE BE MONSTERS?" Lena shouted.

"I cannot divulge what manner of difficulties you will face," Fimbly continued. "But I can tell you that the trials are designed to develop each of your talents, individually and as a—"

"BUT THERE *WILL* BE MONSTERS," she interrupted again.

"As I said, I am not at liberty to discuss the nature of your impediments or aid you in any way—it would be entirely unfair to the other parties—but rest assured it wouldn't be much of a challenge if there wasn't something standing in your way. Now, if you would please—"

"AND IF THERE ARE MONSTERS, WILL WE GET A CHANCE TO SLAY THEM, I MEAN, FOR REAL THIS TIME?"

Fimbly sighed. "You are permitted to do what is necessary in order to survive the dungeon and accomplish your task, though if you have learned anything from me in the past week, it is that fighting is only *one* of the many keys to survival, and that oftentimes . . . yes?"

"ARE WE ALLOWED TO BRING AS MANY WEAPONS AS WE WANT?"

"And just how many weapons would you intend to carry, Miss Proudmore?"

Lena actually stopped to count on her fingers. "SEVEN," she announced.

"Seven?" Quinn said.

"So barbaric." Serene sighed, which brought an instant smile to Lena's face. Colm thought of Master Wolfe, a blade in each hand. Anywhere and Anytime. If Colm were to have two more swords, he might call them In Broad Daylight and Only When Necessary.

"You will each be outfitted appropriately for your particular challenge," the old man said. "Though I would remind you that good friends are the best weapons of all."

"Provided *they're* not dull," Dagnor remarked. After more than a week, his face was finally boil-free.

"I'm sorry," Lena said, turning in her seat. "Did you say something, blob lover?"

Dagnor sat up straighter. "I said maybe seven isn't such a great idea. It only increases your chances of pricking your finger and slipping into a coma." He pretended to accidentally cut his thumb and swoon out of his chair in dramatic fashion. The other members of his party started laughing. The trials were bringing out the competitive spirit in everyone.

Lena was unperturbed. "Maybe," she said. "Or maybe Herren Bloodclaw will let his pet slime loose, and it can make out with the other half of your face." Lena took her right hand and attached it to her cheek in imitation of the common green jelly latching on, then made a strange slurping sound.

Quinn snickered. Dagnor's eyes narrowed. Master Fimbly simply looked confused. It looked as if the other members of Dagnor's party were about to add insults of their own when a shout from the corner of the room made them all freeze.

"Stop it!"

Colm turned to see Serene standing with her hands on her hips, her brown eyes narrowed to knife edges. She started to say something else but then gave up, grabbed her staff, and hurried out of the room.

Dagnor pulled himself back into his chair, all the laughter suddenly stifled. Lena started to get up, but Colm stopped her. "It's all right," he said. "I'll go."

She wasn't hard to find. Colm went straight to the back garden and spotted her slouched beneath one of the cherry

262

trees. Even though none of the other trees had bloomed yet, this one was bursting with vibrant pink petals, as if it had gotten its seasons crossed. He assumed it was her doing; probably she had coaxed it into blossoming early. When she saw him, Serene looked away and drew her knees close to her chest, scrunching into a knot. Colm sat beside her anyways. If his sisters had taught him anything, it was how *not* to leave someone alone.

He didn't say anything, though. Finn had taught him that most of the time, if you just stay quiet, the other person will start talking, even if it's just to fill the space. Eventually they will get around to telling you what you want to know. After a while, Serene finally loosed an exasperated sigh.

"She brings it on herself, you know?"

Lena, he assumed. And the teasing. He couldn't disagree. It seemed as if she was always looking for a fight. "She can't help it," he said. "It's her nature. And it's this place. Just look at all the paintings on the walls. It's the warrior mentality. Swing first, ask questions later."

"But it shouldn't be that way. We shouldn't be competing with each other. We should all be working together."

That would be fine, Colm thought, *if there was always enough to go around. If there was plenty to share and everyone shared equally.* "Like one big, happy party, traipsing through dungeons, holding hands and singing songs?" he suggested. He tried to imagine it. What would the ogres think?

"I'm not saying that. I'm just saying that sometimes, I think

263

we lose sight of what's important. Where I come from, in the Grove, living among the order, there's none of this bragging about who's better. There is just nature, so vast, so encompassing. And you learn to be in harmony with it, to appreciate how delicately balanced it is. And it's humbling, to realize your place. To know that one day you will be food for birds and trees and worms. That you will be energy and growth. You don't think about prizes and treasures and trinkets and all of that, because you realize, in the end, it doesn't matter. All that matters are the connections you make to what lives and breathes around you." Serene closed her eyes and took a deep breath.

"Huh." Colm said. He hadn't given it much thought, the whole delicate-balancing-act-of-nature thing. "But if you don't care at *all* about the treasure, what's the point? Why even come here?"

Serene stroked the grass beside her. At each stroke, the blades quivered beneath her touch, as though they were laughing. "Druids are not supposed to be afraid. Not of anything. Not even death. And there are still so many things out there that scare me." Serene turned and looked at Colm. "That's why I'm here. To learn how not to be afraid anymore."

Colm touched the grass. It kind of prickled. "Finn says fear is a good thing. Makes you cautious. Aware. Sometimes fear's the only thing that keeps a rogue alive."

"Maybe I should be a rogue, then."

"You would never make it as a rogue," Colm said. "We

264

spend our days lurking in the shadows, scheming and stuff. You have to be devious and underhanded."

"If that's the case, you're never going to make it as one either," Serene said with a smile. He knew what she meant. At least he thought he did. "Of course, if we *did* win . . . ," she pondered.

Colm recognized the look in her eye. He had seen the look before. On his mother's face after he'd stolen the money. On Quinn's face when he'd first stumbled into the great hall, with its grand pillars. On Finn's face when he described the wealth buried in the castle's treasury. They all got that look sometimes. That was *human* nature.

Serene took a long, deep breath. "It's going to storm soon," she said. Then she stood up, and Colm stood with her. She touched him lightly on his sleeve. "Hold on. I want to show you something."

Colm stood by and watched as Serene approached the blossoming cherry tree. She placed one hand against its bark, the two seeming to blend together, and whispered to it gently, her eyes closed, her body swaying.

Then, suddenly, it *was* raining. Not fat droplets, but petals. A shower of pink flowers falling free from their branches. Hundreds of them at first. Then thousands. Until all he could see was this cascade of pink petals, soft as satin, lighting on his shoulders, in his hair, covering his boots, piling to his ankles. The gardens vanished. The castle too. Even Serene was gone. Just this blooming curtain enveloping him, tickling his bare arms, getting stuck to his cloak, and the gentle patter of them hitting the ground.

Until finally the storm of cherry blossoms trickled to a stop, and Colm could see Serene again, standing beside the trunk of the now-barren tree, its branches naked, a skeleton of brown against the full green stature of its cousins beside it. And Colm suddenly felt guilty for having stood there while the tree shed the full weight of its beauty on him, leaving him with the memory and it with nothing.

Serene stepped over and took his hand.

"What is it? Didn't you like it?"

"I did," he said. "It was amazing. But . . ." Colm pointed to the empty boughs. "It's not pretty anymore."

Serene shook her head, gazing up at the tree's bones.

"I disagree completely," she said.

"I think we should skip ahead a little and work on lock twenty-four."

Colm was in Finn's workshop for the afternoon. Morning classes were over. Lena and Serene had made amends, apologizing though neither of them was quite sure what they were apologizing for. For being so different, Colm supposed.

At lunch, Colm tried to steer the topic of conversation away from the coming trials by asking Lena who she thought the greatest dungeoneer in history was, a topic that produced no end of discussion between her and Quinn. Quinn argued for Imon Invale, despite his unfortunate end. Lena went, predictably, with Grahm Wolfe. They looked to Colm to decide the champion. He sided with Quinn. There was something about Master Wolfe that Colm didn't like. Probably the fact that everyone else adored him. Everyone except Finn.

Finn, who told Colm to try lock twenty-four. Colm found himself staring blankly at the door while Finn hunched over his desk, pounding what looked to be sunflower seeds with a mortar and pestle. The whole room smelled different today, much like the cure-all's cart back in Felhaven—an earthy, almost rancid stench that Colm attributed to the new collection of powders and liquids lining Finn's shelves. Or maybe part of it was him. Colm hadn't bathed in a while.

"But I'm only on lock fourteen," Colm protested. It was true. He was making excellent progress, had worked his way down the first column and started in on the second. His father had a cobbler's hands—thick fingered and rougher than the steel wool he used to sand the soles of boots. Colm's hands, it seemed, were custom-made for the act of picking locks. Thin and nimble, the skin smooth and ticklish, responsive to a feather's touch.

"And normally we would take them in order," Finn explained. "But twenty-four is the first one on that door of the magical variety. It won't hurt you to get some experience with those before the trials."

Colm reached out, tentatively touching lock twenty-four. It hummed at his touch with a kind of magnetic resonance. "I can sense it," he said.

Finn nodded. "Most magic has its own aura, though you often don't notice unless you are looking for it." Finn opened the center drawer of his desk and removed a small silver container, tossing it to Colm.

"Is this . . . ?"

Finn nodded. "'Don't trust your locks to any man; for magic locks, use Magic Dan's,'" he sang. "Magic locks require disenchantment before they can be picked, otherwise you are likely to find yourself on fire or transformed into a frog or simply blinked out of existence. Most of the time that responsibility falls to a mage or a cleric; they can usually dispel a magical ward on a lock in a finger snap. But there are times when a rogue finds himself forced to tackle one on his own. There are trinkets out there that will also do the trick. Magic amulets and the like. Legend has it that the rogue Andres Kyn had a skeleton key with a disenchantment blessing built right in. But for most of us humble practitioners of the pilfering arts, Magic Dan's is the way to go."

Colm unscrewed the lid. Magic Dan's Antimagic Paste was thick and pale, like the buttercream frosting his sister Cally would sometimes top her oatcakes with—when she could afford to.

"Just rub a little along the edges of the lock. And don't swallow any," Finn warned.

Colm paused, a huge dollop of the stuff balanced precariously on one finger. "Why? Is it poisonous?"

"Not poisonous, exactly. Most likely it will do absolutely

nothing to *you*. I just don't want you to waste it. The stuff is incredibly expensive."

Colm gave it a sniff. It smelled vaguely sweet, with maybe a hint of wintergreen. He shrugged and turned to the door, carefully working the paste around the edges of the lock. At his desk, Finn started measuring powders into cylinders and vials, constantly consulting various pieces of parchment that were strewn about. "Of course, if you were a mage, it would be different," he continued. "Renny slipped some Magic Dan's into Velmoth's stew once, as a joke. Velmo couldn't cast spells for a week."

Colm watched the paste seep into the cracks along the edge of the lock. He wondered if that meant it was working, or if the magic it was supposed to counter had countered it instead. He turned to Finn, who seemed to be involved in his mashing and grinding again. "Just give it a moment," the rogue said.

Then Colm felt the humming stop. He guessed that meant it was ready. He retrieved the lockpicks from his bag, his hand brushing against Celia's hairpin, then proceeded to undo lock number twenty-four. It took a little extra courage to insert the pick—if the paste hadn't really worked, there was a chance he was going to trigger a spell of some sort. And though he didn't think Finn would be so callous as to have the door enchanted with anything terribly painful, Colm got a picture of himself sitting at dinner with a pair of huge bunny ears flopping across his shoulders. But the pin slid in easily, and Colm's ears—and the rest of him—remained the same.

"You don't want to dally," Finn said. "For all its merits, Magic Dan's antimagic magic is only temporary. The enchantment will return if you don't get the lock picked in time."

"How will I know when it's coming back?"

"Usually just about the time the whole thing erupts in blue flame," Finn said helpfully.

But there were no flames. Magic Dan's paste held, and Colm managed to pick lock twenty-four not once, but three times, getting a feel for exactly which motions to make, how to angle the pick, how much torque to give, how far it had to turn to catch each lever. Finn was right—the more you practiced picking a lock, the stronger the memory of it held in your fingers. Without its magic to protect it, lock twenty-four wasn't much harder than the others he'd undone.

When he finished, Finn made Colm go back and run through locks one through ten again as review. Colm could pick lock number one with one hand in his pocket and both eyes closed. It was easier than tying his boots.

"That's enough for now," Finn said when lock number ten clicked free. Colm stretched his legs, massaged the calluses on his fingers, and rubbed out the cramp in his hand. The rogue was still seated at his desk, though he had moved on from his grinding and was now busy remixing the contents of his many vials drop by steady drop, producing seemingly no end of small, billowing black and green clouds that hovered over the desk for a moment and then disappeared. The whole workshop was starting to smell like burned wood and rotten eggs.

"Is that supposed to happen?" Colm asked, pinching his nose.

Finn shook his head. "Not at all." He poured some purplish liquid into a larger vial of green liquid, producing another noxious brown cloud.

"Why are you doing it?" Colm meant to ask, "What are you doing?" but somehow the *why* seemed more important. After all, potions and elixirs were the domain of Master Merribell. They were the province of healers and druids and old women who lived in huts on the edge of town and polished their glass eyes on tattered gowns. Not to mention it looked as if Finn hadn't the slightest clue what he was up to. He looked to be haphazardly stirring things together as the whim caught him.

"Witches and warlocks aren't the only ones who use potions," Finn answered. "You'd be surprised how often we rogues are called upon to slip a little something into a goblet of wine."

Colm took a step back. "You mean poison?"

"No," Finn scoffed, waving the cloud away. "Well. Not *just* poison. Sometimes it's a little something to numb your senses. Or to make you more agreeable to things you otherwise might not be open to. *This* one, for example, is a sleeping draft. Lights out to anyone who takes so much as a sip."

"Oh," Colm said, leaning over the desk to get a better look, still careful to hold his nose. "What do you need it for?" Colm thought of the rogue sleeping with one eye open. Finn did look tired.

"I don't *need* it for anything. I just want to know that I can make it, should the time come when I might. Which reminds me . . ."

The rogue opened another drawer of his desk and removed a small package wrapped in thick brown paper and tied with cord. He handed it to Colm. At first Colm thought it might be something from home. Another letter, perhaps. Or one of Cally's treats. Except there didn't appear to be any writing. Colm peeled back one corner of the paper and saw a thick green leaf with red veins etched across it.

"It's called stimsickle," Finn said, turning back to his experiment. "A plant with a wide variety of medicinal properties. I was out in the woods this morning, gathering the ingredients for this foul-smelling concoction, when I spied it and thought it might come in handy. Remember the rogues' motto."

He turned back to look at Colm, no doubt waiting for a recitation. Except Finn had never taught him the rogues' motto. He didn't even know they had a motto.

"Don't get killed?" Colm guessed.

Finn laughed. "That's more of a daily affirmation. The rogue's motto is 'Ready for everything, guilty of nothing.'"

Colm raised an eyebrow. "Really?"

Finn smiled. "No. Not really. There really is no motto. But it's good advice regardless. Let's say we quit for the day.

There's an increasingly likely chance that I'm going to blow myself up here, and I would feel a little guilty taking you with me."

"You just said rogues weren't guilty of anything."

"That's only because they don't get caught." Finn smiled.

As Colm walked out the door, Finn asked him if he'd had the chance to read the book he'd given him. Colm shook his head. He'd been busy in the evenings training with Lena, trying to get a handle on Scratch.

"Well, it's probably worth a look, if you can find the time," Finn said, then cursed as another cloud the color and smell of pea soup billowed around him. Colm left before the smell seeped into his clothes.

That night Colm retired to his room with Quinn yawning beside him. The mageling collapsed into a drooling heap as always, and Colm carefully pulled off the boy's boots and set them beside his bed, then brought the thick wool blanket to his dimpled chin.

With Quinn tucked in, Colm sat at his desk and pulled out *The Rogue's Encyclopedia*, Volume Two. It appeared to be hurriedly copied and heavily marked, with writing going up and down and diagonally, and hand-drawn figures stuffed into corners and spaces or sometimes just drawn right over the words themselves. Whole sentences were crossed out or amended, and at least three pages were torn out completely. It was clear that this was somebody's well-worn copy, maybe

Finn's, and that it had seen more adventure than Colm had probably dreamed of (though maybe not—Colm had dreamed an awful lot). Colm flipped through the pages, most of them elaborate diagrams and illustrations of traps. He paused at a dog-eared page, the only one in the book. It was the start of a chapter, and it began with a story of a goblin.

His name, Colm read, was Gall Gorebones, and he was one of the most gifted dungeon designers in goblin history. But he was also absentminded, concocting some diabolical new device in his head when he should have been watching his step. One day, Gall was inspecting a dungeon when he accidentally triggered his own trap, losing his left eye to a spike.

From that moment on, Gall "Cyclops" Gorebones began to fashion all of his traps with fail-safe mechanisms—tiny, well-concealed levers that would disarm the trap and allow for free passage. Of course, only he and the lord of the dungeon would know what the fail-safe was, but it made the goblin feel better, knowing that he wouldn't be killed by his own handiwork again.

The point, the encyclopedia explained, was that many traps—especially those of goblin design—include such a fail-safe mechanism, though they could be notoriously tricky to find and should not be counted on as a means of escape. Much better to disarm a trap, or to avoid it altogether.

Colm flipped through several more pages, marveling at the sheer number of ways creatures of all kinds had developed for keeping their treasure safe. Ingenious mechanical contraptions so sensitive they could be triggered by a breath or the flutter of a moth's wings. Gears and levers and pulleys combining to form such intricate engines of death that even the masters of dungeons would marvel at their elaborate workings. So many clever and diabolical ways to ward off would-be thieves.

And to think, all Tye Thwodin had to keep people from his mountains of gold was a lock on the door.

And a castle full of dungeoneers.

12

THE ICING ON THE ROLL

Over the next five days, Lena insisted they ramp up their training, spending the entirety of every evening in a secluded corner of the library debating team dynamics or out on the castle grounds running mock engagements with all manner of imagined creatures. They battled pretend monsters and fell to imaginary wounds so that Serene could treat them with invisible elixirs. Quinn spent long hours casting minor spells while the others did their best to distract him, screaming for him to hurry or sneaking up behind him (though admittedly they only tried that once). When Serene and Quinn broke off to practice blessings and curses, Lena made Colm draw Scratch and defend himself against her ever-more-fervent onslaught. The results were often more scratches, and some bruises the size of Fungus's biscuits, not to mention stiff fingers from gripping the handle so hard that it made it almost impossible to pick locks the next day.

Nor were they the only ones. Everywhere he looked, Colm saw clusters of dungeoneers huddled together, whispering and plotting. He could hear them behind the closed doors of training rooms after hours, bellowing commands and beating on one another. Fellow trainees who used to at least nod in acknowledgment when Colm passed in the halls now cast their eyes downward and kept their distance. They were all part of Tye Thwodin's grand enterprise, members of the same glorious legion—but for the days leading up to the trials, at least, every party was on its own.

The only group Colm *didn't* see squeezing in extra practice was Tyren's. While Colm and Lena dueled and Serene identified herbs and Quinn practiced his elocution, Tyren's party simply sat on the side and laughed or walked by shaking their heads. Perhaps they didn't need to train. They had the most talent, after all; the only talent, though more often than not, Ravena wasn't even with them, and if she was, she usually hid behind one of her books.

"Why is she even with them, do you think?" Colm wondered.

It was the evening before the trials, and they were all seated around one of the circular wooden tables in the creature archives of the library, going over the literally thousands of possible monstrosities Herren Bloodclaw might throw into his dungeon to torment them. It was well known that the goblin kept a wide array of pets to be used in the trials, only a few of which they'd been formally introduced to.

"It's like your family. You don't get to choose," Lena said. "Quinn and I didn't choose you. Or Serene. Not that *we're* complaining. Ravena must have gotten tossed in with them."

"Not that she even needs them," Quinn mumbled.

"One person who is good at *everything* still can't compete with four people who are each great at *their* thing, whatever their thing is," Serene said.

"I'm pretty fantastic at eating," Quinn concluded.

"See," Lena said. "If we ever get trapped in a dungeon made of pastries, we will be set."

"I'm not sure dessert monsters are what Renny has in mind," Colm said. Then he opened the book in front of him—*Blandburg's Bestiary,* Volume Three: *Denizens of the Deep*—and began quizzing the others on how they would best subdue any number of horrible creatures. "Poisonous pus bug!"

"Fireball," Quinn said.

"Paralyzing potion," Serene suggested.

"Stab it," Lena answered.

Colm flipped to another random page, pressed down with his finger. "Raging flame troll?"

"Frost ray?" Quinn offered.

"Blessing of fire resistance."

"Stab it," Lena said.

"Wandering behemoth."

"Oh gods, I don't know, death fog? Forget it. I don't know

how to cast death fog. How about Balustrade's magic bullet?"

"Protection from stone turning. Or stone form. Or form turning," Serene fumbled.

"Stab it," Lena concluded.

Colm found a good one. "Gigantic plated dungeon maggot."

"What the heck is that?" Quinn asked. "Is there a picture? You know what? Don't show me."

Serene shuddered. "Protection from disgusting things?" she ventured.

"Flip it over," Lena said. "Then stab it."

"All right," Colm said. "How about this: three . . . headed . . . dragon."

They all looked at him.

"Run," Lena said.

That night, after running through seventy more possible creatures they might encounter (Lena's solutions ranging from "stab it" to "knock it unconscious and *then* stab it") and an exchange of nervous see-you-in-the-mornings, Colm carefully unpacked and repacked his bag, making sure he had everything he needed for the trials and some things he probably didn't. He had to remind himself that he wasn't going down there alone. He had Lena to protect him. And Serene to bless and heal him. And Quinn to catch them all on fire and to eat anything suspicious. He looked over at the mageling, contentedly snoring.

The trouble with counting on people wasn't trusting them

to do what was necessary, Colm thought. It was knowing they were trusting you to do the same.

He lay in bed and thought of Felhaven. Right now his sisters would all be asleep. All except for Celia, who might have slipped out into the kitchen to read by the last embers of the fire. Perhaps his father was still in the barn, mending a split heel or trimming a wolf pelt to line the cuff of a boot for some noblewoman who insisted on showing off. Maybe his mother was looking out the window at the only road out of town, waiting for Colm to just appear from nowhere. But thoughts of home only made him more nervous, so instead he tried to remember all the different kinds of bats he was likely to encounter—brown, screeching, vampire, giant, spear-nosed, giant vampire, hammerhead, skeletal, giant screeching vampire—and how each one might go about killing him and he likewise.

In most cases, "stab it" seemed to work just fine.

The morning that the trials were to begin, the dining hall was gravely quiet. Parties sat at separate tables, as usual, but now each group was huddled together in confidence, speaking just above a whisper. Quinn was already demolishing his breakfast when Colm entered. Fungus had outdone himself for once. While the stew looked to be little more than sausage soaked in water, it was accompanied by heaping platefuls of sticky rolls, powdered in cinnamon and then topped with hills of icing. His talents as a baker far surpassed his abilities as a cook.

"That looks good," Colm said, pointing to the roll on

Quinn's plate, which was easily the largest at the table and had icing piled twice as high as any of the others.

"I know. It was just sitting there. Calling to me. I call it the Roll of Destiny." The mageling's eyes grew large as he sank his teeth into it. He grunted in ecstasy.

Colm smiled and grabbed a pastry of his own as he took the seat next to Serene. There was still one empty seat. "Training hall?" he asked, nodding toward the Lena-less space.

"Training hall," the other two answered, then Serene added, "She said to eat without her."

"Mission accomplished," Quinn remarked, his face smeared with icing. Colm noticed quite a bit of it had dripped onto his robes and the collar of his tunic.

"Aren't you the least bit nervous?" Colm asked.

"I eat when I'm nervous," Quinn muttered through crumbs. "Could explain why I'm always hungry."

Colm was reaching for a second roll to keep in reserve when a fat, brown, hairy spider scurried across his plate. Colm jerked his hand back, nearly smashing the creature with his palm before remembering. He turned and gave Serene a dirty look.

"Mr. Tickletoes is hungry too," she said. But Colm was pretty sure spiders didn't eat cinnamon buns.

"Let me guess. He's coming with us."

"He's just as much a dungeoneer as you or me," Serene said. "Plus he can see in the dark." Colm was about to say something about getting easily squished under bootheels when he noticed several dozen heads turning to the entry.

There, standing beneath the archway leading to the great hall, was a walking armory.

Lena Proudmore strode into the dining hall, clanking with every step, the links in her silver armor singing to one another. What parts of her weren't covered in steel were garnished with weapons. Her sword rode at her left hip, of course, but a shorter version of it sat astride the right. Two throwing axes hung from her waist in front, and a dagger was somehow clipped to the gauntlet on each hand. The only part of her that wasn't armored or edged was her head. Helmets were for scaredy knights and milksops, she always insisted. She was a barbarian—and the look in her eye was pointed enough to impale everyone in the room three times over. She made her way to the table and awkwardly managed to squeeze into her seat. Serene scooted to give her some space. Lena looked them all over, pausing, assessing. She pointed to Scratch at Colm's side.

"That's it?"

Colm nodded. "I've also got a knife in my bag," he added. "And a hairpin." Compared to her, he felt naked. She could probably slay creatures with a hug. "You planning on using all of those at once?"

Lena gave him a condescending look. "It's important to have a backup plan."

"It's the same plan," Colm said. "Just a slightly different way of carrying it out."

"So I was thinking," Serene interrupted. "We should have a name. Nothing official, of course, just something for us."

Lena slammed a gauntleted fist on the table. "That's a great idea. We could call ourselves Lena's Legion. You know, like Thwodin's Legion. Only better."

Quinn dropped his last bite of roll, getting even more frosting on his sleeve.

"How about Quinn's Questors?" he countered.

"Or Serene's Soldiers? No. I don't like the sound of that. Serene's Saints. That's better."

Colm watched as Serene's pet spider skittered back across the table and up her arm.

He suddenly had an idea.

"What about Team Tickletoes?" he said.

Serene clapped her hands. Quinn shrugged. Lena said that it was the stupidest thing she'd ever heard.

"Tickletoes? How are you supposed to make somebody's blood curdle with a name like that? Why not the Blood Guzzlers? Or the Orc Slayers, or the Ferocious Foursome?"

"All in favor of Team Tickletoes?" Colm said. He, Serene, and Quinn raised their hands.

"Fine—just don't tell anyone else. I'll never live it down."

"Tell anyone else what?"

Colm turned to see Tyren, Minx, and Vala in full smirk. He looked around for Ravena but couldn't find her. Probably in the training hall too. Or already in the dungeon, tackling it without the rest of her party. He wouldn't blame her.

Lena spun around. "How's the ear? CAN YOU HEAR ME OKAY?" she shouted.

Tyren reached self-consciously to his scabbed-over ear, then

283

looked at Quinn, robes covered in crumbs. "Enjoying your breakfast? You're going to need your energy if you hope to come in second."

"I don't care how we do, just so long as we don't have to go down after you," Lena fired back. "That dungeon smells bad enough as it is." The two locked eyes, seeming to size each other up, deciding how far to push it. Then Tyren broke it off and turned to go, but not before pointing at Quinn and touching his own chin.

"You missed some," he said.

Quinn wiped the frosting from his chin on his sleeve. "I don't care if we win, so long as we beat those guys," he said, glaring after them.

The bells up in the tower rang, and everyone in the dining hall froze.

It was time.

Colm followed the others into the great hall, where a small stage had been set up at one end. A thickly woven black-and-red carpet covered half of the stage, the masters covering the other half. Herren Bloodclaw stood next to Tye Thwodin, on a wooden pedestal so that he could easily be seen, though the founder still dwarfed him. Colm saw Finn standing on the end, as usual. The rogue was cleaning his nails with his knife.

"I don't feel so good," Quinn mumbled, one hand clutched over his stomach.

"It's just nerves," Colm told him.

"No. Seriously. I think I ate too much."

"You'll be fine."

Quinn nodded meekly as they pushed themselves toward the front of the crowd of close to a hundred young dungeoneers, all clustered in their respective parties, each one waiting for the chance to win Tye Thwodin's mystery prize. As the hall filled, Master Thwodin rubbed his stomach appreciatively.

"First off, I'd like to thank Fungus for that delicious breakfast. I could almost identify the meat in the stew this morning. But today poses an even greater challenge—one that will help us see who is most prepared for this noble profession. To explain the rules, let me turn this over to the keeper of the dungeon himself."

Beside Colm, Quinn groaned again. "It's not even a real dungeon," Colm whispered to him. "It's only a test. There's nothing to worry about."

The goblin stomped on his stool to get everyone's attention.

"Listen up, you pox-livered, pale-faced goblin killers. As far as you're concerned, this is a real dungeon. It's got traps. It's got monsters. It's got dead ends and drops and locks and everything else you're likely to find out there. And somewhere in this dungeon is a chest. Find the chest, grab the treasure, and get out. Returning without what's inside the chest results in failure. Each team has two glasses' worth of sand to complete the dungeon. And don't think I'm going to go easy on you just because half of you are greener than your own snot. There's still goblin blood in these veins, and nothing gives me quite such a thrill as watching one of you lose a finger to a trap I devised."

Colm looked at his own hands, then over at Finn.

"Thank you, Renny—" Master Thwodin said, but the goblin wasn't finished.

"And don't come whining to me when it's over saying that it was too hard or it was unfair, because there's nothing fair about any of it. It's not fair your kind going in and stealing our gold in the first place, and it's not fair me getting kicked out of my clan and having to come work for you meat sacks. And it's certainly not fair how much taller you are, or how I have to put up with the smell of your—"

Master Thwodin placed a hand over the goblin's face, shutting him up, then looked over the crowd of dungeoneers. "Do we have any volunteers?"

As soon as he said it, Colm knew what was coming. He quickly reached across Quinn and tried to pull her arm down, but it was too late. Lena's hand was already dancing above her.

"Very well, Miss Proudmore. Bring your team up."

"Seriously, I d-d-don't feel right at all," Quinn whispered. Colm gave Lena a dirty look, but she ignored him, striding toward the makeshift stage, pausing only to glare mockingly at Tyren. Colm followed her up the stairs and onto the velvet rug, facing the masters.

"Since you were brave enough to volunteer to go first," Master Thwodin said, "I'm going to give you all a piece of advice. . . ."

Colm stole a glance at Finn, who nodded. Or maybe he looked down at the floor. Colm instinctively reached out and took Lena's hand. It was cold and half covered in metal, but it comforted him anyway.

"Watch the first step. It's a doozy."

Master Thwodin gave a short tug on his beard. Herren Bloodclaw stepped off his stool.

And Colm felt the rug give out beneath them.

The velvet carpet careened down an angled slab of smooth stone, with the four of them clutching it with white-knuckled ferocity. In between Quinn's screams, Colm could hear some of Lena's armor scraping against the rock as they plummeted into the darkness, though it did little to slow her down. They weren't *going* to slow down, Colm thought. They were only going to stop. Abruptly. At the end.

The ground came up quickly to meet them, and all four of them tumbled over one another, somehow getting tangled up in the rug. Colm felt something jabbing him in the side and assumed it was one of Lena's pointier parts. He pulled something out of his mouth, realized it was Serene's hair, and then noticed Quinn's face was squished under his armpit.

"*Wffff wrrf frf fwff.*"

Colm managed to untangle himself and stand up, then pulled Quinn to his feet.

"I said, when's the last t-time you had a b-b-bath?"

Colm didn't answer; he was too busy watching Lena roll

around on the cold stone floor of the dungeon, her armor and weapons making it impossible for her to stand on her own. She looked like a flipped beetle.

"Are you just going to stand there and watch?" she sniped. The three of them worked together to pull her to her feet. "I hadn't planned on getting knocked down," she explained.

"Always the optimist," Colm said. He looked around. The guild's practice dungeon seemed much the same as it had the first time they were all there. The air still carried the tang of moss and mold, and prickled with cold. They stood in a gray hallway stretching off in four different directions leading into four interminable shadows, except this time the only light came from the dim circle above them, illuminating the long stone slide that had led them here—a dim circle that slowly disappeared as the trapdoor above closed, leaving them in almost total darkness. Colm could barely see his four fingers held in front of him.

"I don't suppose anyone thought to bring a torch," Lena remarked.

"No, but we do have more *weapons* than we could possibly hope to hold," Serene said.

"Hang on, g-g-guys. I g-g-got this," Quinn said. The mageling took a deep breath and rubbed his hands together. Colm instinctively took a step away from the sound of Quinn's voice. He trusted Quinn, but a rogue's got rules. Quinn muttered something under his breath.

Nothing happened.

He said it again, speaking louder this time. It was a chant Colm had heard from Quinn a dozen times in training before. It usually resulted in ample amount of light, a bright yellow globe like a miniature sun sitting in the palm of the mageling's hand. This time, all it produced was a single spark that disappeared the instant it came into being, like a firefly's flash.

"Fizzled," Quinn said, perplexed.

"It's all right," Lena said. "It happens to everyone." She reached out for Quinn.

"That's me," Colm said.

"Oh."

Colm couldn't see Quinn, but he could hear the frustration in his voice. "I d-d-don't know what's happening. It's not hard. It's really a s-s-simple sp-sp-spell."

He tried twice more to no effect, then groaned, his frustration echoing off the walls. Less than a minute into their first real test, and already their mageling had lost his magic. Colm put his hand out to comfort him. "Don't worry about it."

"That's me," Serene snipped.

"Oh. Right."

"Well, we need to think of something. There's no way I am wandering through here in pitch-black darkness," Lena said. Then Colm remembered. Reaching into his bag, he dug around until he found it, nestled beneath his picks. He had even thought to charge it yesterday, keeping it on his windowsill all afternoon.

Colm rubbed the sunstone and held it in his palm, watching

its inner glow seep out, growing stronger, until he could see the faces of his friends in its amber light. Quinn's, he saw, was beet red. The light barely provided a pool for them all to stand in, but it was enough that they could continue. Lena drew her longest sword and held it out in front of her.

"All right, then," she said. "Which way? I don't suppose that little pet of yours has any thoughts?" Lena asked, but Serene shook her head.

"Mr. Tickletoes says he's never been to this part of the dungeon before."

"And to think we chose him as our mascot," Lena scoffed. "Straight then," pointing with her sword. "Until we have cause to go otherwise." Serene dug into her robes for a chunk of white rock, then went over to the wall and scrawled the number one.

"To mark our path," she said.

"That's smart," Quinn said. Even in the poor light, Colm could see the druid's smile.

"Keep your eyes peeled, people. I'm pretty sure that twerpy little goblin's got it out for me," Lena said. She ventured into the darkness with uncharacteristic caution, and Colm followed right behind, holding the stone out over her shoulder to light their path. They came to a T, and Lena turned right, still leading them by sword point, it seemed, as if the blade was making the decisions. Serene marked the intersection with a two.

"So what do you think is down here?" Serene said. "You

don't think it's wolves, do you? I really can't deal with wolves today."

"I hope it is a dragon," Lena said. "You can't be a proper barbarian without a dragon fang hanging around your neck."

"I think we probably would have noticed if Tye Thwodin owned a dragon," Colm remarked.

At the rear of the line, Quinn was still mumbling chants to himself and grunting with disappointment. Apparently *none* of his spells were working, even the simplest ones. It was probably just nerves, Colm thought, except even when he was nervous, Quinn's magic did *something*. He only hoped Quinn got over it, whatever it was, before they encountered anything more dangerous than darkness and dead ends. They made several more turns, passing through curtains of cobwebs—Mr. Tickletoes insisted they were for decorative purposes—Serene marking their path, Colm's eyes darting left and right for any sign of traps. Lena led them around another corner and stopped.

"Look."

Colm peered down the corridor and saw two flickering torches set into the walls on either side of a metal door. The light seemed to beckon them.

"You think that's where the treasure is?" Lena asked.

Colm shrugged. The torches were probably marking *something*. Knowing Master Bloodclaw, they were deliberately set there to lure them, like moths. Probably so they could perish. Like moths. Colm grabbed Lena's arm, pulling her back.

"Let me go first," he said. "It could be trapped."

It was the right thing to say, of course, even though he knew she would refuse. She was a barbarian, after all. She was the wall. The shield. The one you stood behind. Rule number five. She would insist on taking the lead.

"Okay," Lena said.

"Okay?" Colm repeated.

Lena stepped aside and gave him a little nudge forward.

"Okay. Go for it."

So much for rule number five.

"Rule number twelve," Lena whispered to Serene. "Always let the rogue go first."

Serene nodded. "Number nine for me."

"Fourteen," Quinn added.

"Right," Colm said, swallowing hard. He stepped in front of Lena, walking slowly, scanning the walls and the floor for the slightest irregularities, trying to remember everything Finn had taught him. Checking for thin strands of wire, no bigger than spider's silk, looking for circles of dust or small engravings in the stone, trusting his other senses even as the corridor got brighter, listening for strange sounds, taking ginger steps, pretending he was trying to sneak past his sisters at night, until he stood before the door with the torches bracketing it.

It appeared to be one thick sheet of solid iron with a single latch. No keyhole or contraption. No runes or inscriptions. Completely smooth. Colm took one of the torches from its mooring and examined the door from top to bottom. It was odd, this door with no lock. *It must be warded somehow,* he thought. Or maybe the lock mechanism was embedded in the surrounding wall somewhere. Or even up in the ceiling. Colm shook his head. This was impossible. How was he expected to unlock it if he couldn't even find the lock?

Lena reached over his shoulder and gave the door a push. It swung open easily.

"Ta-da," she whispered.

"Seriously?" Colm hissed.

Lena bowed, then waved her arm. "After you, O talented rogue."

"It could have been trapped, you know," Colm said. "You might have just gotten us all killed."

"Or we might still be standing there, waiting for you to figure out whether to push or pull," she said. "Sometimes a door is just a door."

Colm took a deep breath and then handed his torch to Serene. He grabbed the other one from the wall and stepped into a large, airy room. A round chamber of gray stone, much like the training halls in the castle above them. In the glow of his torch, Colm could make out two other doors on the opposite side. There was more than one way to get here, which meant that this probably was *the* place to get to, which meant it could be where the treasure was.

Which *meant* that they should all be especially careful.

Colm took a step into the chamber, moving cautiously, trying to look up and down at the same time. "Watch your step," he said. "Look for any loose stones." They circled around the chamber slowly, heading toward the doors on the far side, both of them open already. Colm noted that one was much larger than the other.

To his right, Serene started to dance. At first Colm thought that she had stepped onto a shock trap and was being electrocuted, the way she wriggled. "You all right?" he asked.

"I don't know," the druid said. "It's Mr. Tickletoes. He just ran up my sleeve!" Serene brought the hem of the sleeve to her lips and whispered into it, then brought the sleeve up to her ear. Her eyes narrowed, then flew open again.

"What'd he say?" Lena asked.

"He's says something's coming. An old enemy. Something about claws and a tail and poison. He's talking so fast, I can barely understand him."

Colm tried to think, running through the list of creatures they'd been quizzing each other on the last few days. Which one had claws and a tail and would be a natural enemy to a spider? He snapped his fingers. "A scorpion!" he said.

"Oh, I hate scorpions," Quinn mumbled.

Lena sheathed her sword and rested both hands defiantly on her hips. "No offense, Serene, but I think if Mr. Tickletoes can fight it, we really don't need to worry." She turned to Colm. "Do you want to step on it or should I?"

Colm looked at his boots. Outstanding boots. Perfect for squashing things.

Serene was still trying to calm the frantic spider buried in her sleeve. "He says it's not the same as last time. He says . . . he says it's *bigger.*"

"How much bigger?" Colm asked. Then he saw the look of terror on Serene's face; she pointed with a trembling finger.

Colm turned and reached instinctively for Scratch's paw with one hand and grabbed Lena with the other.

"I think you're going to need a bigger boot," he said.

Even at regular size, scorpions are hideous creatures. But this one had been magnified, enlarged through some arcane means, probably Master Velmoth's doing. It was easily the size of a horse. Its pincers snapped open and shut with a sickening clicking *clack* as it advanced. The creature's whole body was lined with spiky hairs, its brown armor plating crusted with ridges and horns. But the worst was its tail, arcing up over its back in scrunched segments, the hooked stinger already dripping with some noxious yellow liquid.

Colm drew Scratch and held it in front of him unsteadily. Up till now, he had used it only in practice duels with Lena or Finn. He had yet to win any of those. Lena already had her sword back out and a second blade in her other hand, circling around to the opposite side of the gruesome beast. "On second thought, let's make this a joint effort," she said.

Quinn had backed against the far wall and was mumbling to himself, still trying to get his magic to cooperate. The giant scorpion scuttled forward, its terrifying spidery legs quivering. It struck out with one claw, knocking Lena backward. She slashed out with both swords, but they only bounced off the creature's thick hide. Colm saw her back up next to Serene, the druid clutching her torch with both hands, feet stuck to the stone beneath her, it seemed.

"Maybe you could try talking to it," Lena grunted. "It's just another one of nature's beautiful creatures, after all."

The druid shook her head emphatically. "Oh, I don't think so," she said.

"You talk to *spiders!*"

"Size matters! That thing is terrifying!"

"Just pretend it's a kitten!" Lena shouted, then turned just in time to dodge a strike from the scorpion's tail, slashing at it and nearly taking off its tip. She advanced toward the beast, swinging at it with each grunted word. "An evil . . . ugly . . . oversized . . . armor-plated . . . bug-eyed . . . lobster-clawed . . . poison-dripping kitten!"

The last blow clanged off the monster's thick plating. The scorpion scampered sideways and caught Lena in one pincer, squeezing her tight.

"Lena!" Colm rolled sideways as the other claw swept over his head, and he made an ineffectual jab with Scratch. He could see chinks in the monster's armor, soft fleshy parts that would invite a more effective blow. He dodged another swipe and then lunged—the way Finn had taught him—aiming for the spot where the claw attached to the body. He felt Scratch sink in, saw the scorpion arch backward, then felt a blow to his side.

Colm spun and hit the stone floor, turning to see the creature's mandibles working angrily above his face, dripping with scorpion drool, which, for all Colm knew, was probably designed to dissolve his skin and melt his bones. He tried to swing Scratch, but one of the monster's pincers had him pinned to the floor. Colm turned his head—he couldn't bear to look at those dripping jaws opening and closing, reaching down for him. Then he felt a flash of heat, everything exploding in a burst of orange and red. The weight lifted, the scorpion retreating a step, its grip on Lena loosening just enough for her to wriggle free as well.

He looked up to see Quinn standing over him, torch in hand.

"You make do," he said. Then the mageling shrieked and fell backward as the scorpion jabbed again with its stinger, just missing but causing Quinn to drop his torch. Colm shouted to get the monster's attention, giving Quinn a chance to escape.

The scorpion turned and advanced, causing Colm to scrabble backward on feet and elbows. The creature was right on top of him again. For a split second, Colm thought about home. He could almost see Celia waiting for him at the door. He thought of Finn's promise.

There was a flash of silver as Lena leaped over Colm, sword in hand. Colm watched the scorpion's tail strike, jabbing her in the shoulder, in the chink of her own armor, as she lunged. He heard a horrible sound as her blade found its mark between

297

the creature's eyes. It reeled in pain, tail thrashing, legs wavering, then turned and scurried back through the archway and into the shadows.

Lena stood there for a moment, sword in hand. Then she looked at her shoulder and the spot of red blossoming between the plates of steel.

Colm saw her eyes roll into the back of her head just before she hit the floor.

It wasn't a lot of blood. But it didn't take much. The scorpion's stinger had caught her just above the armpit, finding her weak spot the same way she had found its—a small puncture, as if she had been jabbed with a quill. Except it was quickly turning black.

"What's happening?" Quinn asked as the three of them huddled over Lena's stiffening body.

"What do you think? She fainted," Colm said. Lena was still breathing, but he could tell there was something else wrong. He looked over at Serene, who had removed the pauldron that hadn't covered enough of Lena's shoulder and was now bent over, studying the wound. She wiped away the spot of blood and touched it gingerly. Lena's eyes shot open.

"I'll kill them! I'll tackle them all!" Her eyeballs danced back and forth from Colm to Serene to Quinn; then they shot down to her feet. "Wait. Why can't I move my legs?"

"That's what I was afraid of," Serene said, giving the wound another prod. "Scorpion venom varies by type. Some are poisons meant to kill, others to cause pain. Some are just meant to paralyze."

"Well, I guess it could be worse," Colm said.

It got worse.

"I can't move my arms either." Lena shouted. Her eyes flew wide with panic. "How am I supposed to slay anything if I can't move my *mrrfm frrfermrrfer*. . . ."

Colm kept his hand over Lena's mouth, then turned back to Serene. "You're up," he said.

The druid tugged on her braids, her face full of worry. "I know, I know," she hissed. "Don't rush me! It's not magic, it's poison, so blessings or countercurses won't work. You need a natural remedy." She slipped her bag off her shoulder and frantically started digging through the jars she kept there, pulling out little vials of ground-up powders and multicolored pastes. "Stupid! I brought all of this stuff, but I don't have anything that specifically counteracts paralyzing scorpion venom."

"All that and you've got nothing?" Quinn remarked.

"I don't see you doing anything to help!" Serene snapped.

Colm tried to get her to focus. "Counteracts? Like what?"

"I don't know," Serene said. "Like . . . telarium root, or stimsickle juice, or even if I just had some ballum balm."

"Wait, what was that middle part again?" Colm said.

"Stimsickle?"

Colm smiled and held up a finger, then fished in his own bag for the package, still tied with twine. He handed it to Serene.

"Where did you—" she started to ask, but Colm shook his head.

"Rogues' motto," he said. He grabbed Lena's hand and watched as Serene frantically tore the stimsickle leaf to bits, dropping those into a vial of clear liquid from her own pack. It instantly turned yellow and gave off a rankled smell as the leaf dissolved—something like pickled onions. The concoction fizzed for a moment, then settled. Serene handed it to Colm, who brought it to Lena's nose.

Lena shook her head vehemently, clamping her lips as tight as scorpion pincers.

"You have to drink it," Colm insisted.

"Mm-mm!" Lena insisted right back. Serene put a finger to Lena's lips.

"You need to trust me," she said. "This is *my* thing."

Lena took a deep breath, then nodded. "This better work."

"If it doesn't, it's not like you'll be able to do much about it," Colm pointed out. Lena shut her eyes and he tipped the vial, emptying the reeking contents down her throat. She choked once but managed to swallow most of it.

"How long will it take to work, do you think?" Quinn asked, but before Serene could even answer, Lena's eyes shot back open and she bolted upright. Then she turned and gave Colm a shove, knocking him backward.

"Hey! What was that for?"

"Just testing," she said.

She kicked with both legs and wiggled her fingers. "That

was, by far, the nastiest stuff I have ever tasted," she concluded. "Makes squirrel innard stew sound appealing."

"You could just say thanks, you know," Serene said.

"Guys," Quinn said, holding one of the torches and pointing it at the smaller of the two entries on the far wall. "You're not going to believe this."

Colm helped Lena to her feet, and they all walked to where Quinn was standing. It was another room, much smaller than the chamber they stood in now. The only light came from the torches they carried. Colm glanced up, but the ceiling was too high and shrouded in darkness. The back wall, on the other hand, was clearly visible. As was what sat against it.

"We found it," Lena said.

A chest. Solid oak, by the look of it, with gold hasps and bracings and black iron chain handles. It looked huge, large enough to hold all of Lena's weapons, and much too heavy for even two of them to lift together. An elaborate-looking lock was set into its center, like a solitary eye staring at Colm, almost mocking him. All four of them stepped gingerly into the close chamber.

"There's no way we are going to be able to carry that thing," Serene said.

"We don't have to," Lena said. "We just need what's inside."

Three pairs of eyes turned and looked at Colm.

"Right," he said. He knelt down in front of the chest, gingerly running his hand along its smooth top and then placing it on the lock itself. He immediately got a chill, a tingle that worked its way up the length of his arm and down his spine. He had felt it before.

In fact, this lock looked almost identical to lock twenty-four. Colm slumped backward, hands on his knees.

"Is there a problem?" Lena prodded.

"Well . . . yes and no," he said. "I know how to pick it. Not too hard, really. It's just that this particular lock happens to be . . . enchanted."

"So?"

"So . . . enchanted locks need to be disenchanted. Which is usually the mage's responsibility." He looked at Quinn.

"Oh." The mageling sighed. "Well, I c-c-could give it a tr-tr-try, I g-g-guess."

Colm thought about Master Velmoth's flaming robes, about the training hall going up in smoke. He was pretty sure Lena and Serene were thinking the same thing.

"Are there no other ways around it?" Lena asked.

"Sure. There are other ways. There are special keys, scrolls, Magic Dan's Antimagic Paste . . ."

"Magic who?"

"You know," Colm said, humming the tune. "'Don't trust your locks to any man; for magic locks, use Magic Dan's.' It's this white stuff. Comes in a jar. Smells sweet. Looks like . . ."

Colm looked at Quinn. The boy was a mess. Eyes bloodshot. Face flushed. Little bits of frosting from breakfast still in the corners of his mouth. And on his chin. And his sleeve.

Colm leaned over and sniffed the boy's chin, the boy who had no magic today.

It smelled like wintergreen.

"Renny slipped some into Velmoth's stew once, as a joke. Velmo couldn't cast spells for a week."

"That jerk," Colm whispered to himself.

"Why are you sn-sniffing me?" Quinn wanted to know.

Colm shook his head. "Tyren was right. You missed some," he said. Then he reached over and scraped the dollop of white paste that was stuck to the mageling's sleeve.

"Just out of curiosity," Lena began, "what the heck are you doing?"

"New rule," Colm said. "Never choose the roll with the most frosting." He rounded back on the chest and spread the white paste around the edges of the lock.

"Do you expect Quinn to eat his way through the lock?" Serene asked.

"It's not frosting," Colm replied. "We have to wait for the enchantment to dissolve." Quinn still looked confused, scraping at another bit of frosting still sitting on his sleeve. Colm pressed his hand to the lock, felt the magical aura dissolve; then he reached in his bag for his picks, choosing the one that had worked before. The other three hunched around him.

"This is exciting," Serene said, sounding a little surprised.

Colm licked his lips and felt each lever give in turn. With the enchantment gone, it was a matter of memory, his fingertips tracing over all the movements he'd made before. The lock sprang free. Colm hesitated, then felt Lena's elbow in his ribs.

"What are you waiting for? *Open* it."

Colm gingerly lifted the lid, lips pursed, eyes slit against what he assumed would be the blinding intensity of a pile of gold or a cache of glittering gemstones. He held his breath. This was the moment he had been training so hard for.

The chest was empty. Or almost empty. There was a single coin sitting at the bottom.

Silver.

Colm picked it up, reached for his pocket, then shook his head. He couldn't help it. He started laughing, his laughter echoing off the stone walls.

"What is this? Some kind of joke?" Lena remarked, staring at the huge, hollow treasure chest that contained no treasure. Colm spun the silver coin in his palm.

"Inside joke," he said. He looked again and noticed the small scrap of parchment sitting at the bottom of the chest. He dug it out and held it up to the torchlight to read. "It's from Master Bloodclaw." Colm read the message out loud: "'You groped and moped and found your way around my little maze. You ducked the claw and dodged the tail and drove the beast away.'"

"That doesn't even rhyme," Lena said.

Colm continued: "'You found the chest and broke the lock and think your task is done. But we still have a little time to have a lot of fun. So be proud of what you've done here, and hold your head up high. But if you dare, you should beware of the falling sky.'"

"What p-p-part of this was f-fun?" Quinn wanted to know.

"Whatever. Let's just take the stupid coin and get out of here." Lena slammed the lid of the treasure chest shut, the sound of it rebounding off the walls of the small chamber, causing Colm to jump.

"Careful!" Colm hissed, bringing his finger to his lips. There was another sound. One he recognized from his recent afternoons with Finn. The mechanical *click* of something being set in motion, sliding into place. Levers and gears suddenly animated, working in rhythm.

The sound of a trap.

Colm spun just in time to see a giant slab of stone sliding into place out of nowhere, sealing them inside the small chamber. They all rushed for the door, but too late. The mechanical sound didn't stop, though. If anything, it intensified, transforming into a grinding, the sound of stone scraping against stone.

"Is that the ceiling?" Serene asked, pointing upward.

"And what are those tiny black bristles?" Quinn wanted to know.

Colm looked up. In the flicker of the torch, he could just make out the curved ceiling, slowly descending. He heard Quinn moan. He let the goblin's terrible poem drop to the floor.

The sky was falling. And it was covered in spikes.

★ ★ ★

Colm's first thought was of the Wolf Pack, the ones they had learned about from Master Fimbly. They were professionals, and they still fell victim to a trap just like this. At least Quinn was currently incapable of accidentally casting an enlarging spell on them. If they were going to get skewered, they would be their regular size.

His second thought was that it must have been the chest. When Lena closed it, she tripped a hidden lever, activating the trap. It wasn't her fault. He should have looked. He should have been more careful.

His third thought—and the most pressing—was getting out of the room before the ceiling made pincushions of them all. All four of them started pounding on the stone slab door.

"Open it!"

"I can't!"

"Then unlock it!"

"There's no lock!" Colm ran his hands along the edges of the stone, feeling for something, anything. A notch. A release. A lever. There was nothing. He felt Lena shove him to the side.

"Then I'll bust it down," she said, driving her shoulder into it and rebounding off ineffectually. She reached to her belt and removed one of her hatchets, striking the door over and over until the handle of the hatchet splintered in her hand, its iron head clunking to the floor. She had only scratched the surface. Colm looked back at the dropping ceiling. There must be a hundred spikes jutting out of it. Lena kicked at the door with one steel-toed boot. "I swear when I get out of here, I'm going to grab that goblin and throw him down here, poke *him* full of little holes, and see how *he* likes it."

Right, Colm thought. *I'm sure Herren Bloodclaw would just love a taste of his own medicine. A goblin falling for his own trap.*

Colm froze. "Lena, you're a genius!"

"What does that have to do with anything?" she shouted.

"The fail-safe? Don't you see? It's a goblin trap, which means there's probably an escape mechanism!" Colm snatched the torch out of Quinn's hand and held it up to get a better look at the ceiling of pointy death. "Goblins who design traps like this usually put in a release in case they accidentally wander into them. A lever or a button or something. Look around the walls or on the floor. Anything out of the ordinary. A loose stone or a knob or latch of some kind." Lena and the others turned away from the door and started looking frantically around the room.

"There's nothing here!" Serene shouted, angling her torch to illuminate the wall.

She was right. The walls were smooth. The stones were all even. The only thing that stuck out were the spikes in the ceiling, now only a spear's length above them. At least a hundred barbs of black iron, each coming to a keen point that could easily bite through leather, skin, and metal alike. Colm was hunchbacked now. Serene and Quinn had both dropped to their knees, frantically feeling around, shaking their heads. Lena was trying to wedge her sword in between the ceiling and the wall.

"All right, Quinn. If ever there was a time to get your magic on and cast a spell of getting-us-the-heck-out-of-here, now is it!" Lena barked. Only four feet separated floor from spikes.

"He can't cast spells," Colm shouted. "He's had too much to eat."

"Well, then you do something!" Lena said. "I can't fight a *ceiling*!"

Colm took a focusing breath and held it, tried to summon Finn's voice in his head. *"It's all about the little things. The way the grass bends when you walk on it. The whistle of the wind changing direction. The way the light flashes off the surface of polished stone."*

The light.

More specifically, the torchlight. It didn't reflect off any of the spikes; the coal-black iron was too dull to offer a shine.

Except for one.

Crawling on all fours now, Colm scrambled across the floor like Mr. Tickletoes. He reached out and touched the spike, the only one with a glossy reflection. The one that was simply *painted* black to match the others but was made of an entirely different material. He gave it a sharp tug, and it snapped off in his hands, wooden and hollow.

The ceiling suddenly ground to a stop.

Everyone froze, not even daring to breathe. There was a hesitation, pure silence, and then the spikes began to retreat, crawling back up the walls into the darkness.

Colm felt something lasso around his neck, nearly strangling him to death—Serene's dark, thin, tattooed arm choking him in relief. Quinn lay on the floor, panting. "P-please t-t-tell me it w-would've stopped anyway," he said.

"It would have stopped," Colm said. *The floor would have stopped it, at least. After it ground our bones.*

"Look," Lena shouted, pointing to the back of the room, to a dark tunnel that had appeared behind the treasure chest with its meager bounty—a secret door that had revealed itself only after the trap was disarmed.

"Do you think it's an exit?" Serene asked.

"If so, it's even b-better than a chest full of g-g-gold," Quinn muttered.

Colm wasn't sure he agreed, but he took the torch and inspected the new entry, a short hallway leading to a set of stone stairs. He felt Lena's hand on his shoulder.

"Could be more scorpions," Lena suggested. She turned to Serene. "What does the spider think?"

"Mr. Tickletoes says we are bad for his health and that as soon as he gets out of here he is going back home to his wife and his three hundred children," Serene said with a pout.

Colm palmed the silver coin and cautiously stepped into the corridor, scanning every cranny and crevice. He had already missed the trap on the chest and hadn't noticed the secret door recessed into the wall. He couldn't afford to make any more mistakes. He made it to the foot of the stairs and looked up. It could still be a dead end. Worse still, it could just be another trap. The stairs could collapse about halfway up. A giant boulder might come rolling down. There was really no telling what possible horrors awaited them at the top.

A door creaked open, flooding the staircase with dull white light, revealing another monster with yellow eyes and even yellower teeth, staring down at them menacingly.

"Well. What are you waiting for? Come up and have a gloat," the goblin said.

When he stepped out into the great hall, through an entrance that had been concealed by one of Tye Thwodin's giant paintings, the crowd of dungeoneers in training erupted with applause. Colm's eyes instantly darted over to the hourglasses along the wall, hunting for the one that had turned the moment the carpet slipped out from beneath them. There was still a little sand at the top. That meant that Team Tickletoes had made it through the dungeon in less than half the allotted time.

Colm felt Lena's gauntleted fist punch him in the shoulder, much harder than he would have liked. Behind him, Serene and Quinn were dancing in circles. Colm felt a strange sensation work its way through him, warming him from the inside.

Tye Thwodin stepped up to them, face deadly serious, the other masters in tow. His grunt silenced the room. The warm sensation vanished.

"You have the treasure, I presume." He held out his hand, large enough, it seemed, to crush Colm's skull with one squeeze. Colm opened his own hand to reveal the silver coin.

Tye Thwodin turned to Herren and Finn. "I thought it was

supposed to be gold? Are you skimping on me, Argos?"

"Wouldn't dream of it, Master Thwodin," Finn explained. "It's just a little joke among us rogues. I can fully attest that that is the very coin I put in the chest this morning. This team has successfully retrieved the treasure."

Master Thwodin nodded, satisfied. "Then to the victors go the spoils." He flipped the silver coin back to Colm, who caught it against his chest. Then the guild's founder proceeded to pound Quinn on the back, nearly knocking him over before turning to the room full of recruits. "And as for the rest of you—mark this time. It is the one to beat."

There was a murmur in the crowd. Colm caught sight of Ravena standing at the edge of it, away from her own party, away from everyone. He couldn't be sure, but he thought maybe, just maybe, she looked concerned. He smiled in her direction and offered a shrug. She turned her back on him.

"Time to beat indeed," Herren Bloodclaw spit. "No way a bunch of green cave crawlers like you could make it through so fast. Not without cheating somehow."

Colm's smile disappeared. He instantly thought of the stimsickle leaves. The earmarked book. Lock twenty-four. Colm looked at Finn, but the rogue didn't return his glance.

"Or maybe you're just getting soft in your old age," Finn said to the goblin instead.

"No sense getting all bent out of shape over it, Renny," Tye Thwodin boomed. "Obviously this just shows what outstanding mentors you both are. Now go reset the dungeon so we can throw someone else down there. I'm getting hungry already."

As Tye Thwodin and the other masters turned back to the stage, Finn grabbed Colm's arm and leaned in close, whispering in his ear.

"Remember our motto," he said. "Ready for anything . . ."

Guilty of nothing, Colm finished in his own head as the rogue turned to follow the others. Colm watched him go, then flinched as Lena put her face in his, eyes bright and beaming. "See. I told you. Nothing the four of us can't handle." She reached out and took his four-fingered hand, squeezing tight. "You were almost as awesome as I was down there."

"Yeah," Colm said.

In his other hand he squeezed the silver coin even tighter.

13

THE FOOT RUB OF
VENGEANCE

Well, at least nobody died.

That was what the masters kept saying to one another as the last party was rescued from Renny's dungeon after a full day of trials that stretched well into the night. Nobody died and, somewhat surprisingly, only a few young dungeoneers were injured. It was a splendid success.

Precautions had been taken, of course. The scorpions Master Bloodclaw had used had been handpicked for the nonfatal toxin in their stingers before being enlarged through magical means. And the spiked floor was engineered to stop with two feet to spare so that trapped dungeoneers could lie down and await rescue if they couldn't trigger the escape. The magic-imbued lock gave a nasty shock to anyone who tried to pick it without disenchanting it first, causing one young dungeoneer to smoke from the ears and experience some short-term memory loss. Another had a leg broken by the scorpion's claw, and a third tripped while climbing the stairs at the end, knocking himself unconscious and earning his party a penalty for having to carry him out, causing Tye Thwodin to joke that stairs were "the worst."

The other surprise, besides the dearth of injuries, was that the odds-on favorite, the party of Tyren Troge, didn't break the record as anticipated. They might have, if it hadn't been for the chest. While she broke through the enchantment with ease, using a counterspell of her own devising, Ravena Heartfall struggled with the lock itself, taking a full ten minutes to pick it. She emerged from the dungeon scowling, clearly disappointed, slapping the gold coin—everyone else got gold—into Master Thwodin's hands and then disappearing to her chambers without a word while Tyren raged and attacked the floor, resulting only in a scratched floor and a bent sword. It was an excellent run, Tye Thwodin said in consolation, and one that they should be proud of.

It just wasn't the best.

Colm wasn't sure what to expect.

He woke to the splatter of fat raindrops, set loose by a dark gray sky, bursting against his window. Not necessarily a good sign, but he wasn't going to let a little rain dampen his spirits. Not today. Not after what had happened. Nervous hands fumbled at his bootlaces as he quickly got dressed and made his way down to breakfast. Working his way through the halls, he noticed strange things happening.

"Hi, Colm."

"Hey, Colm."

"Nice run, rogue."

People talking to him. Trainees of all ages. He knew their faces and maybe could guess at some of their names, but he didn't know them well enough yet to call them out, to speak to them. And yet here they were, slapping him on the back or giving him sly winks, as if they shared some secret. By the time he made it to breakfast, he was sure it was a trap. They were all up to something. His sisters always smiled and said "Hi" in a sweet voice before they gang-tackled him too. He worked his way past the greetings and entered the dining hall, looking for his friends.

He spotted Lena instantly. She was surrounded by no fewer than ten other apprentices, encasing her like a second set of armor. She waved him over.

"Naturally I was the one responsible for defeating the scorpion. It wasn't that difficult, really. I considered wrestling it to the ground and flipping it over to expose its underbelly to the death knell of my sword, which would have been noticeably more barbaric, but time counts in a dungeon, and there are no points given for style."

The crowd of trainees beamed at Lena with doe-eyed wonder—the same look *she* got whenever someone mentioned Master Wolfe. The older girl who had had her leg broken by another scorpion's pincer begged Lena to sign her cast. Lena pulled Colm toward her.

"Of course, we wouldn't have made it without this guy," she said. "The best rogue in Thwodin's Legion. Heck, the best rogue in all the land. Isn't that right?"

Colm smiled nervously, waved to the gawkers. They all waved back with three fingers and a thumb. He couldn't tell if they were mocking him or saluting him. The girl with the cast smiled politely at Colm, then turned back to Lena.

"But how did it feel, you know, when you were stung? Did you think you were going to die?"

"Are you kidding?" Lena scoffed. "I hardly felt a thing. If it hadn't been for a structural flaw in my armor, the beast never would have touched me. I plan on writing a note to the blacksmith who manufactured it, recommending several improvements to the design. . . ."

Colm had heard enough. He slipped away—it wasn't difficult—and found Serene and Quinn hiding at their table. Maybe it was the incident with the frosted roll, or maybe it was their newfound fame, but Quinn had hardly touched his food for once.

"To the victor go the spoils indeed," Colm said, glancing back over his shoulder at the radiant barbarian and her new-found groupies.

"That's always the way," Serene said with a smirk. "The warriors get all the attention. It's the shiny armor, I think. And the swagger. She definitely has the swagger."

"You mean you two don't have little mobs following you around?" Colm asked, thinking about all the people who had at least greeted him on the way down. Serene shook her head.

"I'm the Girl Who Whispers into Her Robes a Lot and he's . . ." She looked at Quinn, who scowled.

"I'm What's His Face . . . You Know, the Short One," he said.

Apparently word had already gotten out that Quinn hadn't done much down in Renny's dungeon. Not that he could be blamed. It wasn't his fault he had ingested three full servings of Magic Dan's Anti-Magic Paste. "At least that's better than Smoke for Brains," Colm said, using one of the names whispered about Quinn after the whole fire-out-the-ears incident.

"Who called me Smoke for Brains?" Quinn whined. Colm tried to change the subject as Lena finally pulled herself away from her admirers.

"You sure they don't want to join us?" Colm asked when she sat down, all flushed, fanning herself.

Lena shook her head. "What? No. They just wanted to hear how I slew that giant, disgusting, deadly monster, is all."

"Did they want to hear about your fainting too?" Quinn asked.

"Or how I cured your paralysis?" Serene added.

"Or how you started freaking out and hacking away at the ceiling while the rest of us were looking for the release on the trap?" Colm said.

Lena's shoulders slouched, the buzz of her celebrity crashing. "I told them all about you guys," she said quickly. "I swear. It's just . . . you know . . . whoever kills the dragon gets the glory."

"It was a bug," Quinn muttered.

"Technically, it was an arachnid," Serene corrected.

"Technically, it was ugly and freakish and terrifying and I'm glad you stabbed it," Colm said. Truth was, he would rather Lena be the one in the torchlight. He was quickly discovering how much he preferred to be in the shadows. Quinn still looked sour, though.

"Let's be honest," Lena whispered, leaning across the table. "We all know I wouldn't have made it half a step down there without you guys." She reached over and touched Quinn's hand, and he softened instantly. "And speaking of ugly and freakish," she added, looking around, "where are Tyren and his crew? We still need to get him back for that little icing stunt of his."

Colm looked around with her, but apparently Tyren Troge's party had decided to skip breakfast, Ravena included. *Off somewhere sulking,* Colm thought with some satisfaction. He wondered if Tyren even knew what he had done, if he somehow learned that his prank had been the key to Colm getting past the enchanted lock. Of course, given how much of the icing Quinn had eaten, it could still be several days before he would cast a spell again. Maybe Lena was right. Maybe a little more justice was called for.

"I'm not so sure revenge is the answer," Serene said.

"Don't think of it as revenge," Lena said. "Think of it as reciprocation."

That sounded like something Finn would say.

Quinn smiled. Then his smile instantly disappeared as an

obnoxious blast filled the dining hall. Colm turned to the archway to see Tye Thwodin with a copper cornet to his lips, face somehow even redder than usual as he blurted out the last of his breath, then handed the horn to the goblin standing beside him.

"Attention, please." He coughed. "Where's the party of the hour?" The guild's founder scanned the crowd, his eyes finally alighting on Colm's table. He strode toward them, Herren Bloodclaw ambling behind, motioning behind Tye Thwodin's back for them all to stand. The whole room was watching, silent, enthralled by the massive figure. Tye Thwodin's hand shot out and grabbed Lena's, swallowing it whole, dragging her to her feet. His voice easily carried throughout the hall. "Miss Proudmore, Mr. Candorly, Ms. Willowtree, and Mr. . . ."

"Frostfoot," the goblin whispered.

"Frostfoot, yes. It is my pleasure, as head of this guild, to present you with your reward."

Colm looked at Lena expectantly. Her face was serious, but he could see her bouncing on the balls of her feet. Tye Thwodin snapped his fingers, and Herren Bloodclaw reluctantly unfurled a scroll. The goblin cleared his throat. "As winners of the most recent dungeon trials, slaying the monster and retrieving the treasure in record time, the party of Proudmore et al. is hereby entitled to the following reward—"

Colm felt Lena's arm around him, pulling him close. The

room was suddenly so quiet you could hear Fungus snoring in the kitchen.

"All the treasure they can carry from the . . ."

The goblin stopped reading and looked up—way up—at Tye Thwodin, who stood with his arms across his chest, beaming at the lot of them like a proud father. "You can't be serious," Herren Bloodclaw said. "These four?"

"Just read it, Renny," Master Thwodin commanded.

The goblin shook his head. "Ahem, all the treasure they can carry from the . . . very *real* dungeon into which they will accompany Master Thwodin in five days' time."

Everyone froze. From the kitchen came another sonorous rumble. Then Tye Thwodin's face exploded into an even bigger grin, his giant arms stretched wide. "So what d'ya think? Get to dive with the big boys, eh? How's *that* for a reward?"

"Oh, my leaves and branches," Serene whispered.

"You're j-j-joking," Quinn said. "A real dungeon?"

Colm glanced at Lena. She looked like she was going to soak her armor. She was practically vibrating, biting her lip. A hundred pairs of eyes seemed to be staring directly at Colm. He wasn't sure what he saw in their faces, jealousy or sympathy, envy or relief. Maybe all of it.

"A real dungeon? With real treasure? And we can take as much as we want?" Lena asked.

"Minus the guild's cut, of course, and split according to your rank as outlined in our agreement. But yes—we're not talking about some little goblin playground tucked in a basement.

And best of all, *I'm* coming with you . . . and some of the other masters, of course."

Quinn's mouth was working, his lips were moving, but he wasn't producing any sound anymore, just indecipherable grunts. Tye Thwodin took them as groans of appreciation, though Colm was fairly certain they weren't.

"Don't bother thanking me. It wasn't my idea. It was Master Argos's. He came up with it a while ago, said that whoever makes it through the trials should get a chance at the real deal—with chaperones, of course. In fact, I believe he already has a dungeon in mind."

"B-but what if we're n-n-not ready?" Quinn finally managed to blurt out.

Tye Thwodin cocked his head sideways, as if he didn't hear quite right. "Not ready? Well, then I suppose we could offer the reward to the second-place party. Who was that, Renny?"

"That would be Tyren Troge's party," the goblin said. Tye Thwodin started to look around the room, but he didn't get very far.

"Don't you dare!" Lena said defiantly, stepping in front of Quinn.

Colm stared at her. He couldn't imagine talking to Tye Thwodin that way, but the head of the guild bellowed laughter.

"By gods, she reminds me of me," he said. "I wouldn't dream of it, lass." Master Thwodin turned to address the whole crowd of budding dungeoneers. "Now why don't all of you take the morning off, as a reward for your efforts yesterday? It won't be long before you're *all* diving into dungeons and raking in coin!" The guild's founder rubbed his hands together in anticipation. "Won't be long," he repeated.

After Master Thwodin left, goblin in tow, Colm and the others stared at their food for all of six seconds, then decided they were finished eating. Colm followed his comrades out into the great hall, with its whitewashed walls and its glittering chandeliers, listening to Quinn, who was no longer stuttering, though he talked without taking a breath.

"Why couldn't it have been gemstones? Or a new set of robes? Everybody likes new clothes! I'm not ready to go into another dungeon. I'm still recovering from the last one."

"This is an honor," Lena insisted. "Most apprentices don't even step foot in a real dungeon until they've been here a year or more. We are fortunate."

"I don't feel fortunate," Quinn said. "I feel like I might be sick."

Colm decided to follow rule number six a little bit, taking a step away from Quinn.

"Don't get me wrong," Quinn continued. "I want to go eventually. But in *five days*? I'm not even sure my magic will be *back* by then."

Serene snapped her fingers. "Since we've got the morning off, we should go see Master Merribell," she suggested. "I once watched one of her elixirs bring a dead frog back to life. Of course, the next day she cut out its tongue and ground up its liver to make another potion—but that's beside the point.

She's bound to have something to help get that Magic Dan's stuff out of your system."

"She did help shrink Master Velmoth's ears," Colm added.

Quinn nodded. "What will you two do?"

"Are you kidding?" Lena said. "In less than five days, we will be deep in the festering putrid bowels of our very first bona fide, monster-infested dungeon. I've got to get sharpening." She turned to Colm. "You want to come? I can make sure Scratch has a good edge."

Colm glanced around the great hall at the paintings, the stalwart portraits of heroes standing boot to claw with terrifying creatures. Suddenly the immense castle, with its giant marble pillars and its constant reminders of mortal danger, felt strangely claustrophobic, especially with all the sidelong glances from the other dungeoneers. He felt like everyone was watching him, waiting to see what he would say, what he would do. His eyes darted to the massive front entrance.

"I'll catch up with you later," he said. "I think I need some fresh air."

Master Velmoth's giant slab of rock, produced during the orcs' assault, still protruded from the center of the field edging the castle's front courtyard. Colm touched it, marveling at how cool it stayed, even soaked in sunlight. He pressed his back against it and stared out across the sea of grass into the wall of woods beyond, from which, not too long ago, had poured dozens of screaming orcs—the first monsters Colm had ever seen, unless you counted Renny, of course, which Colm no longer did. Colm could still make out the hoofprints in the soft earth, punctuated by a scrap of armor or a broken arrow shaft, reminders of a battle that he had watched from a distance. He pictured Master Wolfe, sword in each hand, charging to meet the horde head-on. Lena called it bravery. Finn called it foolishness. Colm had sided with Finn at the time, though he supposed he could see it both ways.

The trees seemed to stretch on forever. Somewhere beyond that interminable horizon lay roads and villages and homes where men mended shoes and sisters braided one another's hair. There were also mountains and bogs and caves, and tucked somewhere beneath those, there were dungeons. Hundreds of them. And one in particular, picked out already. Colm reached into his bag and found his sister's silver hairpin. He rubbed the butterfly's shimmering wings with his thumb and wondered how far it was to Felhaven, if you were to just walk it, not travel by crystal or other magical means. Wondered whether, if he left here, he could ever find his way back.

"Thinking about running away?"

Colm spun, hand leaping to the hilt of Scratch—no doubt Lena rubbing off on him. He figured it was probably her, following him out here to ask what was wrong. Or maybe Finn. The rogue had a knack for appearing out of nowhere. But this was one of the last people he would have expected.

Ravena stood just behind him, dressed in a black tunic and billowing black pants to match her hair. She looked to be more rogue herself today, though Colm knew she could be lots of things at once. "You shouldn't sneak up on people like that," he said.

"For your information, that was *exactly* how you should sneak up on people," she replied. "But I shouldn't have to tell you that." Her long braid of black hair hung like a chain down her back. "You didn't answer my question."

"I'm just catching my breath," Colm said. "What are you doing out here? Where's your book? I'm not used to being able to see your whole face." Though now that he could, he had trouble looking into her eyes for too long. It made him anxious. Not the nervousness that came from staring down one of Finn's locks, but a different kind of nerves. A sort of clammy, clumsy giddiness that he didn't really understand or have any control over. It wasn't just because she was older or more talented than he was, though that was certainly part of it. It was something else.

"Actually, I saw you slip out the door and came out to apologize. I know all about Tyren's little stunt with the paste."

"It worked out okay," Colm said, thinking about the look on Quinn's face when Colm had scraped the icing from his chin to disable the lock. "It only slowed us down a little."

"Obviously not enough," Ravena replied. "Though if we had ended up beating you, I would have said something to Master Thwodin about it."

"That's nice of you."

"It's not nice. It's fair. We didn't deserve to win. Not after

325

that. Even if I hadn't fumbled with that lock, even if we had beaten your time, I could never have accepted it."

"It was a tricky lock."

"Number twenty-four. Not that tricky," she said.

Colm stared at her.

"Don't look so dumbfounded. I've been working with Master Argos longer than you have. Surely you didn't think you were the only one around here learning how to disarm traps and pick pockets?"

"No. Of course not," Colm said.

"He did tell me that you are one of the most talented rogues he's ever seen, though," she added offhandedly.

"Really? He said that?" Colm couldn't help but sound surprised. Finn had said that directly to him at least a half dozen times, but it was different coming secondhand, knowing he said the same thing to others. Not just others. Ravena Heartfall.

She rolled her eyes. She was standing over him now. Shadowing him. "Of course, you can't believe *everything* Master Argos says. Did he ever tell you how he got that scar of his?"

"Pirates," Colm said. "Or goblins."

"Fishing accident," Ravena countered. "Or a failed assassination attempt. I've heard them all. They all have their stories, each one bigger than the last. Just like the rest of us." Ravena knelt down and put her hand to the grass, just brushing the surface. Colm wondered if she didn't have a little druid in her too. She glanced back at Colm, spied the butterfly in his hand. "That's beautiful. Who did you steal it from?"

Colm knelt beside her and held up the hairpin. "I didn't steal it. It's my sister's."

"So you have a sister."

"Eight of them, actually." He held the pin out so she could get a better look.

Ravena took the pin, spinning it slowly in her own hand, pretending to make it fly. "I wish I had a sister."

"One, maybe. Eight is a little much. No brothers either?"

"No sisters. No brothers. No mother. I grew up in a quiet house. I've learned to make do by myself."

"That explains some things," Colm said, though he instantly wished he hadn't.

"Like what, exactly?" she asked, pinning him with her eyes.

"Well . . . like how even though you are with Tyren and them, you aren't really *with* them. I mean, you don't really seem to fit, is all," Colm managed.

"They're not as bad as they seem," she said, handing Celia's pin back. "Like all your warrior friend's shiny weapons, most of it is for show. Tyren Troge would probably risk his life to save mine, if it came to it."

"I picture it the other way around," Colm countered.

"Maybe," she said. Then she stood back up and looked behind her at the castle gates. "Though it looks like you'll get a chance to go diving before I will. Do me a favor and tell Frostfoot I'm sorry, and pass along the apology to the rest of your party. And congratulations for winning the trials. You deserved it."

Colm wasn't exactly sure about that, but he told her thanks anyways. She turned to go.

"What's yours?" he blurted out, stopping her.

"What's my what?"

"Your story. You said everyone has one."

Ravena shrugged. "Still working on it," she said. Then she vanished back beneath the castle gates as quietly as she had appeared.

Colm arrived at Finn's workshop later than usual, though the rogue barely seemed to notice. He was still surrounded by his flasks. The room smelled much better than it had on previous afternoons. Maybe that meant he was making progress.

"Ah. There's the victorious adventurer, risen from the depths of the dungeon with treasure in hand, rewarded with riches beyond compare. No time for bragging, though; we have a lot to do." Without even looking up, Finn pointed toward the back of the room. Colm settled himself in front of the Door of a Hundred Locks and unpacked his bag. He looked at lock twenty-four again, the one he had probably practiced more than any of the others. He glanced over his shoulder at Finn.

"Sorry I'm late," he said. "I ran into Ravena."

"A rogue never *runs in* to anything," Finn chided, hawk's nose angled over a flask. "We tiptoe. We skulk. We creep. But the only time we ever run is when we are getting *out* of something. Was she impressed by your victory, or simply bitter that you won?"

"She congratulated me," Colm said. "Though I think maybe she was a little jealous."

"Of course she's jealous. I imagine every trainee in the whole castle is envious of you right now. That was quite a feat you pulled down there. Most impressive. Even Tye Thwodin took note."

Colm laid his picks out in front of him, carefully aligning them next to one another. Hook. Claw. Tooth. Needle. Rake. A tool for every occasion. Even a pin for his hair. Ready for anything. In his sack he came across the discarded sheaf of brown paper that had once held a leaf. Looking at it made his stomach turn. He wondered if anyone else had thought to bring stimsickle with them. He wondered if anyone else had read the same chapters in *The Rogue's Encyclopedia*. Maybe it was common knowledge. Or maybe Colm had just been fortunate. "Did *you* know that stimsickle can cure paralysis?" he asked over his shoulder.

"I think I heard that somewhere, yes," Finn said absently. The rogue was sifting and pouring, the liquids in his glass vials shifting colors, belching smoke. "Though I've mostly heard it used for constipation. I suppose the two are related." The rogue turned and smiled.

Colm took up Celia's hairpin and twirled it between two fingers, watching the butterfly flitter around his thumb and back again. "And did you know that goblin trap makers almost always include a fail-safe in their designs, to protect themselves?"

"Even my grandmother knows that," Finn said. "I believe we are back on lock twenty-two."

"Lock twenty-two," Colm repeated, leaning in and inspecting the one in question. It looked tricky, but no trickier than the conversation he was trying to have. "It's just . . . it's quite a reward, you know. Going into a real dungeon with Master Thwodin and the rest. And the promise of real treasure. I wouldn't want anyone to think I didn't earn it. That I cheated somehow."

Finn slumped back in his chair, abandoning two smoking green tubes. He sighed impatiently, then turned to face Colm. "Did *you* know that someone sneaked into Master Merribell's office two nights ago and acquired a jar of Magic Dan's Anti-Magic Paste?"

Colm knew what *acquired* meant, at least in rogue-speak. He felt his face turn red. "I might have guessed," he said.

Finn leaned on his elbows, his fleckless blue eyes unblinking. "In order to cheat, everybody has to be playing by the same set of rules, Colm. But they don't. The world doesn't work that way. Your friend Lena, she follows a warrior's code, and Serene sticks to the laws of the druidic order, and Frostfoot— who knows what lunatic voices mages hear in their heads? The point is, we all have our own compass. Even our own rules—yours and mine—aren't absolutely steadfast. They're tough, like steel, but even steel can be shaped, bent, molded to fit your purpose, transformed into a sword or a fork or a key or a trap. There is no single rule that is absolutely indisputable.

Some just bend more easily than others."

"But we weren't supposed to have help," Colm whispered.

Finn threw his four-fingered hands in the air. "Nonsense! You were *absolutely* supposed to have help. If I've taught you anything, it's that you can't be expected to succeed all by yourself. We all need *somebody*. Even Ravena Heartfall. Even you. Even me."

Finn stood up and walked over to where Colm sat by the door and dropped to his knees, placing both hands on Colm's shoulders and staring him in the eyes. Colm followed the curving path of the scar along his cheek. "Listen to me. You succeeded in that dungeon because you are a gifted rogue, a fast learner, and a good companion. It wasn't anything I did. Understand?"

Colm nodded. "I understand."

"Good." Finn looked past him at the door. "Lock twenty-two."

Colm turned back to the door and tried to concentrate. Finn went back to his desk full of vials and resumed his mixing. Every minute or so one of them would whisper a "Gentle" or a "Just a little more." When Colm picked the lock and said, "Got it!" Finn said, "Not quite, but I'm close." Colm massaged his hand and swiped at the drop of sweat angling off his nose, while Finn reset the door for lock twenty-three.

The next one opened in even less time. The idea was that they got harder as you moved around the door, but to Colm they almost seemed to get easier. He was beginning to see how they were all related, the same basic ingredients exploded into a thousand permutations. He could draw on everything he'd learned so far to find out what had changed, what subtle mechanical shift made this lock different or more complicated than the one before, like telling eight sisters apart simply by the sound of their laughter. Once he discovered the difference, he exploited it, digging around, probing every angle until it all clicked and the door swung open, revealing Finn's musty boots.

Colm thought about the times he had helped his father out in the barn. It seemed no matter what Colm did, his father ended up coming over and correcting it somehow, silently making an adjustment, resetting a heel or redoing a stitch. He never said anything—never chastised Colm for his shoddy work—but Colm never got the feeling that he had really accomplished anything, even when the sun set on a row of freshly mended boots. Seeing Finn's tattered spares behind that door, though, Colm felt different. Whole somehow. Colm let the pick drop and turned to his mentor.

"Did you get it?" Finn asked, holding up a liquid concoction so clear it made the flask look empty.

"Yeah. Did you?"

Finn grinned in satisfaction. "Almost," he said with a sniff. He put down the container and admired the open door. "I'm not sure you even need me in that dungeon of yours. Pretty soon Tye won't even pay to keep me around anymore because he'll have you," he joked.

"But you *are* coming," Colm prompted. "You're not going to make us go down there by ourselves. Master Thwodin said it was your idea."

"Of course it was my idea. What better prize could there be than the chance for us to go after some real treasure together? I thought you, of all people, would appreciate such an opportunity. I'll be right beside you the whole way," Finn assured him. "After all, I have a promise to keep."

"And Master Thwodin said you had one picked out already. The dungeon, I mean," Colm said.

"I have one in mind, yes," Finn replied.

"And . . . ?"

"And?"

"And it's going to be worth it. Trust me."

By the time Finn let him go, Colm was late for dinner. But he wasn't the only one. Serene was apparently still training with Master Merribell. Quinn had gone with her to see the cleric earlier and had described, in the vaguest terms possible, his unfortunate run-in with Magic Dan's enchantment-eating paste. Master Merribell informed him that there was no instant cure, but there was something he could drink that would speed up the process of getting his magic back. There was only one unfortunate side effect.

"I've peed more times in the last five hours than in my entire life," Quinn explained. "There can't be anything left. I'm going to shrivel up like a raisin."

"Do you feel more magical, though?" Colm asked.

"I feel . . . I feel . . . ," Quinn muttered, then quickly rose from the table. "Excuse me."

"As if that boy didn't have enough problems." Lena sighed, bringing her bowl to her lips.

When Quinn came back to the dining hall, he was accompanied by Serene, both with mischievous looks on their faces. Serene glanced around the room, then pulled everyone at the table close together.

"I think I've found a way to teach Tyren Troge a lesson," she whispered.

With an uncharacteristically devilish grin, the druid produced a small earthen jar from her robes. "It's specially formulated for people with big heads," she said.

She explained what she had in mind. It wasn't complicated, but it was a little tricky. And there was a high chance of getting caught.

"Who's going to do it?" Colm asked.

All eyes looked at him.

"Stupid question."

They had to wait until nightfall, until the moon cast a pallid glow over the castle gardens and seeped through the muddy glass windows. The thieves' sunrise, Finn called it, their busiest hour. Not that there were any thieves in Thwodin's Legion. Not really.

"And you are certain this will work?" Colm asked again as

334

he peered down the empty hall.

"Absolutely," Serene said. "I picked the ingredients from Master Merribell's garden and whipped it up myself. It might not last long, but it *will* make an impression."

Colm led them down the hall, hissing at them to take lighter steps, especially Lena, who seemed to clomp along like she didn't have a subtle bone inside her. Halfway there, he put up a hand—he thought he heard voices coming from the kitchen. Whispers only, but he had attuned his ears to pick up on such things. The one voice was gruff, almost assuredly Fungus. The other was quieter, much harder to make out. Colm brought his finger to his lips. Getting caught skulking around by the gnarled-knuckled cook wasn't part of the plan. Colm motioned the others around the dining hall and into another corridor, the muffled discussion from the kitchen fading behind them.

"This is it," Quinn said.

They grouped outside Tyren's door. Lena took her post as a guard at the end of the hall with the express command to hoot like an owl—and not bellow like an enraged lunatic barbarian—at any sign of danger. Colm removed his picks and started working the lock, undoing it in a matter of seconds. He wasn't entirely sure why Tye Thwodin even bothered having locks on the young dungeoneers' chambers when the masters were training those same dungeoneers to undo them. Only the one on the treasury door was impossible to pick. "We're in," Colm said. Serene handed him the jar, half full of cream the color of seaweed.

"You have to use all of it for it to take full effect," she said.

"And I just rub it on his feet?" Colm questioned. That was perhaps the most frightening part of the whole affair.

Serene shook her head. "It needs direct contact with the skin. I just thought feet would be safest."

Colm nodded. Truthfully, he didn't want to touch any part of Tyren Troge. He looked over at Quinn. The mageling, dressed uncharacteristically in black robes per Colm's instructions, was wringing his hands. "You ready for this?" Quinn nodded. Colm turned the handle and pushed the door open.

The moon shone through the only window, providing a faint light to navigate by. The room was the same as the one he and Quinn shared, except there was one fewer bed; Tyren had the space all to himself.

Perhaps because he snored even louder than Quinn. For once, though, Colm welcomed the sound. Colm slowly approached the bed and deftly peeled back the covers near the bottom, where the lumps of Tyren's feet stuck up like boat masts.

They were still stuck in his shoes. Colm frowned and pointed to the boots. Quinn shrugged. They had already come this far.

Colm handed the jar of ointment to Quinn and bent over the boots anchored to Tyren's feet, slowly undoing the laces of one, tugging at them gingerly, like coaxing fishing worms out of the dirt. When he had the ties plenty loose, he gave the boot a gentle pull and it slipped off easily.

Colm flinched. The smell was palpable. A musty fog that emanated from between the sleeping boy's meaty, sweaty toes. Quinn covered his face with his hands. Colm squinted, eyes stinging. They had talked about slathering both feet in the stuff— for it to have maximum effect, Serene said—but Colm didn't think he could. He would just use all the cream on the one foot. One hairy, disgusting foot, with its cracked yellow nails and that patch of green fuzz growing between the last two digits.

Quinn handed Colm a pair of gloves, the same kind Finn wore to hide the fact that he was missing fingers. Colm pulled them on, then snatched the jar from Quinn's trembling hand. The mageling was dancing.

Hurry, he mouthed, making the word with his lips. Then he crossed his legs and started rocking back and forth. Colm dunked two fingers into Serene's jar and reached out to the sleeping boy's cracked yellow heel. He paused.

He had survived an attack by thugs on the road to the castle. Had survived Renny's dungeon not once, but twice. He had been inches away from spikes and lightning bolts and giant scorpion tails. But he was fairly certain Tryen's crusty foot would be the death of him.

Beside him, Quinn let out a little whine and crossed his legs even tighter. He really needed to go.

Colm closed his eyes and started rubbing.

★ ★ ★

The next morning, the dining hall was buzzing with rumors. Something had happened to one of the members of the guild. A curse. Or a disease. Whatever it was, it must not have been *too* serious, judging by the occasional snort of laughter that accompanied the whispers. Colm looked over at Quinn, both of them barely corralling the smiles that threatened to give them away. All four of them sat and waited.

The buzzing stopped. Colm turned around, though he already knew what he would see. He just hadn't realized he'd have to stand to get a good look.

Tyren Troge paused in the entrance of the dining hall, stopped by the collective gasp that met him there. It was unmistakably him. The same pitch-black goatee. The ice-cold blue eyes. The unibrow. Everything.

Just all of it three feet lower than usual.

"He shrank," someone at the table next to Colm murmured. "He's barely the size of Master Bloodclaw!"

"But his head is so *big*!"

It was true. Tyren's head looked gigantic compared to the rest of his greatly compacted body. Serene's salve had worked beautifully to shrink everything except for his already too-large head, which now seemed to wobble precariously on top of his dainty shoulders. Maybe Colm should have used both feet. Or maybe started at the top.

Then again, he thought, it was probably even better this way.

Tyren gave an oversized scowl to everyone in turn as he shuffled through the dining hall, barely able to walk in boots that were much too large for him, his pants bundled and bunched at the ankles, tunic billowing well past his knees. He looked like one of Elmira's rag dolls dressed in Elmira's own clothes, his head bobbing with each step. Colm was certain he was going to tip over, his skull planting into the stone like an anchor and his reed-thin legs sticking out like flagpoles. But Tyren managed to take one wobbly step after another, head lolling this way and that, till he stopped at Colm's table.

"This isn't over," he said. His voice sounded squeakier. Almost mouselike.

"Go pick on someone your own size," Serene said. Tyren balled his tiny hands into tiny fists and shook them, then turned away and shuffled toward the back of the room, ripples of laughter chasing after him. He stormed straight into Master Bloodclaw, the two of them actually bumping chests.

"What happened to you?" the goblin asked, giving Tyren a long once-over. Then he took one hand and measured from the top of his head to the top of Tyren's and smiled with satisfaction. The goblin was taller by an inch.

The shrunken warrior fumed and circled around the smiling goblin, retreating to his table, where even his own friends seemed to be laughing at him. All except for Ravena, who turned and looked at Colm, eyebrows raised. She seemed to be asking, *Now do you feel better?*

Across from Colm, Quinn Frostfoot chewed his food

339

contentedly, seeming to savor each bite. The enchantment from the shrinking ointment wouldn't last more than a day. And it could still be several more days before the mageling could cast spells again. But for this one moment, at least, it didn't seem to matter.

Colm looked back at Ravena, as if to say, *Maybe I shouldn't, but yes.*

Yes, I do.

After all, they might all be part of the same guild, but Quinn was a member of Colm's party. He was almost like a brother. Like family.

And you don't mess with family.

At the table in the back, Tyren's head got too heavy for him for a moment. The sound of it hitting the table filled the room.

Quinn grinned. "Best. Foot rub. Ever."

14

ANYWHERE AT THE WRONG TIME

By the next day, Tyren Troge's body had stretched back to normal, though he still stumbled when he walked, as if he had to get used to the redistribution of bones and muscle. His head also seemed slightly smaller than the rest of him, as if he would never quite be in proportion again.

Quinn waited for retaliation, keeping even closer to Lena when the four of them were together and making Colm sniff and taste all his food ahead of time. That is, when he wasn't back in the lavatory, getting Magic Dan's out of his system.

It was also the day that Lena received a letter from her father, asking her when she expected to delve into her first dungeon. She happily wrote back that it would be much sooner than expected.

It was on that same day—the day Tyren got his body back to shape and Lena heard from home—that Colm did the seemingly impossible, picking six new locks in record time, Finn egging him on, Colm ignoring everything the rogue said, focusing on the cold metal that soon grew warm in sweaty hands, the sound of minute gears clicking, the smell of Finn's old leather as he opened the door. His fingers were rubbed raw, his joints stiff. He was afraid his back had developed a permanent hunch. As lock number thirty unhinged and the door fell open, Colm nearly collapsed, exhausted.

Finn whistled and stroked his scar. "Incredible. It would take me the better part of an hour just to pick that last one. I've never seen anyone get through them so fast."

"Not even Ravena?" Colm asked. She had been a member of Thwodin's Legion much longer than him, after all. Maybe long enough to work through every lock on the door already.

"Being good at everything usually comes at the expense of being great at nothing," Finn answered. "Even she couldn't do what you just did."

Colm arched his back and heard things snap and pop. His father made the same sounds when he stretched and bent. It was in the bones, Colm guessed.

"Why don't you take a break?" The rogue fished around in his cloak and pulled out a plum, tossing it to Colm.

Colm sank his teeth into it, the juice seeping out and stinging the sores on his fingers. He pressed his aching back against the floor and stared at the ceiling as Finn leaned over his desk. The rogue was busy scratching away at a piece of parchment. Colm's instinct was to steal a glance—to gather information, like every good rogue should—but this was Finn. The man who had saved his hand and his life and his father's reputation. Also the same man who taught him how to pry. He would most certainly catch Colm peeking and then lecture him on why he got caught. Colm wasn't in the mood for a lecture.

Instead he took a deep breath and gazed around the room, at the maps with their circles and lines and indecipherable scribbles. At the shelves of books, including the other two volumes of *The Rogue's Encyclopedia* that he hadn't been asked to read yet. At the door with more than half of its locks still unbeaten. And even after all of those, there was still one more.

Colm looked in the corner, at the chest that simply sat there gathering dust, untouched since the day he'd arrived. The simple shiny box with its single lock that Finn had never been able to open. How could something so simple be so confounding? From the outside it was just a hole, but the insides obviously held such complexity, such minute intricacy, that even after years of trying, the estimable Finn Argos hadn't been able to pick it.

What would it take, Colm wondered, to solve this dusty puzzle? He had been fiddling with Finn's confounded door for well over an hour. Every muscle in his hand had seized with cramps, and his eyes were going cross. The last thing he wanted to look at was another lock, especially one that was impossible to crack. Better to just close his eyes and forget about it.

343

But as soon as he did, one eye snapped open and found the chest again, its silver plate reflecting his own face back at him. He glanced over at Finn, but the rogue was still hunched over his desk, deep in thought.

He didn't even know what was inside. That was the thing that Colm couldn't get out of his head. With the door it didn't matter—just Finn's crusty old boots. The point was the lock itself. But this was different. There could be anything in there. Well, not *anything*. But something remarkable. Something more remarkable than boots, at least. Imagine having something like that sitting beside you your whole life and never knowing what secrets it held.

Colm quietly sat up and pulled his lockpicks over to him, then scooted closer to the chest, keeping his back to Finn's desk. He ran his hand along the cold, smooth metal, trying to sense some semblance of magic, but it gave off no vibration, no aura or crackle of energy. It was foolishness, he knew. He still had over thirty locks on the door, including some of the toughest that had ever been dreamed of, but the more he thought about it, the harder it was to resist. It was as if the chest was mocking him. *If you don't want to know what's inside, what are you even doing here?*

He couldn't stand it anymore. He grabbed his smallest pick and hunched over the chest, silently exploring the lock's inner workings, the delicate mechanism that kept its jaws clamped tight. From the start, he could sense that this lock was different—its insides more like a labyrinth than a tunnel. He imagined it as a dungeon in miniature, almost impossible to navigate in the darkness. And he was blind, like Bartholomew Plink, the first dungeoneer to avoid the ogre's hole. He had to feel his way around, but it seemed even his finest pick was too large to worm its way through the maze of tiny gears and levers, hammers and tumblers, that comprised the lock's delicate composition. He would need something even smaller. Something thin and pliable, capable of weaving and bending, molding and maneuvering, but without breaking. He had no such pick. The only thing he could think of that was even the right shape and size was . . .

Colm reached into his sack and pulled out Celia's hairpin, studying it carefully. No thicker than a bristle on a brush, but longer than any single hair he could pluck from his own head. It couldn't possibly work. It was much too fragile. He wasn't even sure exactly what kind of metal it was made of. It would be one thing if it had some kind of magical properties, but the Candorlys had never owned anything magical in their lives. Odds were he would try to force it through and it would snap off inside, making the nearly impossible completely impossible. Then what would his sister say?

And yet he found himself deftly threading the hairpin through the tiny black aperture, eyes closed, navigating on touch alone, pausing at the slightest sign of resistance, working with trembling fingers. He felt the pin maneuver through the curves, felt the subtle shifts, the most minuscule tremble at the end of the pin in his hand.

345

And he imagined himself back down in Renny's labyrinth, navigating the dungeon, weaving his way through one corridor after another, stepping delicately, dodging traps, listening around corners, ferreting out his path until he came to the end. Colm licked his lips and pressed his eyelids closer together, blocking out even the sound of Finn's scribbling. Holding his breath until he thought he might pass out.

Colm had wound his way through four of the lightest pins he'd ever manipulated, and the fifth was perhaps the most difficult he'd ever encountered. But soon it too gave way, and he felt the hairpin twist slightly. Then he heard a series of *click*s, barely perceptible, like somehow hearing your own eyes blink. He froze.

"Did you just do what I think you did?"

Colm turned to see Finn staring at the chest, eyes wide. Colm nodded. "I think so."

"But how did . . . ?" Finn stammered. "I mean . . . they said it was unpickable. For two years I've been trying . . ."

Colm started to hold up his sister's pin, then thought better of it, tucking it under his leg instead. Celia had given it to him, after all. It was a treasure. Her only one. Not that he thought Finn would take it from him, but what was his was his. "I don't know," Colm said. "I just followed my instincts, did everything you taught me."

Finn covered his mouth with one hand, as if he was afraid of what he might say. He just stared at the unlocked chest.

"Well?" Colm asked, giddily, pushing it toward him. "Aren't you going to open it?"

The rogue shook his head. He looked almost shocked at the idea. Or maybe he was simply so surprised that Colm had done something he never could. "You solved the puzzle, Colm Candorly. You get to see what's inside."

Colm nodded, wiped his hands on his knees, then put one on either side of the lid. He wondered if Finn would share it with him, whatever it was. Wondered if half of it would have to go to the guild. His stomach twisted. He closed his eyes, afraid to look, then opened them, more afraid not to. He nearly fell backward.

"What?"

It was empty. Not empty like the chest in Renny's dungeon, which at least held the one silver coin and an awful poem, but actually empty. Colm leaned over the chest, dumbfounded. Maybe it was an illusion. Maybe it only *appeared* to be empty, but when you stuck your hand in, you buried it inches deep in gold. But a sweep of his hand along all edges of the box only kicked up motes of dust.

"There is nothing. It was all a complete waste of time."

Colm looked imploringly at Finn, expecting a look that shared in Colm's disappointment. Instead the rogue had a grin that was just starting to unwind. He wasn't looking at the empty chest or its opened lock. He was looking at Colm.

"I have to disagree," he said.

That night, after everyone else had gone to sleep, Colm lay in bed thinking about the dungeon, now only three days away, and Finn's promise that there would be plenty of treasure to go around. At dinner, and even after, he and the others had discussed what they would do with their share, Lena describing a new set of practically seamless armor she had seen advertised and Quinn talking about buying a bigger house for his parents. Even Serene, who had once told them that gold is no replacement for the enormous bounty that nature provides, described how she would like to one day own her own farm and raise rabbits. Everyone had their own reason for being here, but none of them was at a loss when it came to thinking of ways to spend imagined loot.

But the more Colm lay in bed and thought about mountains of gold, the more he came back to Finn's empty chest. Something about it didn't seem right. How could Finn not be upset? For two years, he had been trying to open that chest, and for what? Just to find it empty? And yet, instead of being filled with disappointment, Finn's eyes had sparkled with pride. He had called Colm a genius, said that they were destined for great things. And yet the chest itself held nothing. An empty promise.

Colm lay in bed and listened to the sound of the owls loosed from their cages up in the rookery, taking to the night sky, off hunting. Through the open window, he could hear the cicadas and the hushed whisper of tree boughs tussling with the wind, the whistle winding its way through the cracks in the castle's stone.

And above all this, he heard the shout, followed by the *clop* of hooves on stone.

Someone was coming. In the dead of night. To the castle that nobody knew the way to.

Just go to sleep, Colm told himself. *Whatever it is, it's none of your business.* But he could still hear the hooves pawing on the stone, the rider dismounting, verbal exchanges. He couldn't *keep* himself from listening. He listened for the locks undone, the front doors creaking open.

Colm sat up straight, cursing Finn Argos for making him so high-strung and curious—though to be fair, the curiosity had been there long before they met. Still, the rogue had only made it worse, he was sure. Colm quietly slipped out from under his covers—there was very little he didn't do quietly anymore—and donned a cloak but ignored his boots. On smooth floors, bare feet were best. The ball of blankets that contained Quinn didn't move an inch as Colm opened the door. He whispered for the mageling not to worry. He wasn't going to be gone long.

Colm sneaked down the vacant halls, past the shut doors, skirting the pools of light from the torches out of habit, ears perked for the slightest sound, until he found himself standing just outside the great hall, peering around the corner at the two figures standing inside the castle's main entry. Colm recognized both of them instantly. The one by his yellow mane, dressed in too-tight satin pajamas that didn't quite cover his hulking frame. The other by his swords, one resting on each hip, the man himself almost completely concealed by his hood.

The ranger had returned.

349

Colm pressed his back against the wall and crouched down, careful to stay in the shadows, wondering what Finn would say if he caught him here. Would he be angry at Colm for snooping or admire him for his stealth? Colm wasn't sure, but he could easily imagine the rogue doing the exact same thing. Tye Thwodin was speaking softly, but his gruff voice carried down the cavernous hall; Colm had to strain to hear Master Wolfe, though. He could see the ranger's face set in a scowl. It didn't take long to discover why.

"An assassin?" Master Thwodin rumbled.

The ranger nodded. "Ambushed me outside Saddle Hills. There was no doubt of his intent. His dagger was poisoned. Quality stuff. He was not some random thug."

Tye Thwodin pulled on his beard. "Did you get a name?"

"I'm afraid he was all out of breath by the time I got around to asking," the ranger said slyly. "I asked around at some of the thieves' guilds, but nobody would take responsibility. But I did learn something. . . ."

Colm watched as the ranger leaned in close and whispered in Tye Thwodin's ear. The flame-bearded founder frowned, his eyes narrowed.

"Best to keep this to ourselves for now, until we know for certain. After all, someone out there clearly doesn't like you very much."

"Lots of people don't like *you*," Wolfe countered.

"But you don't see them trying to stab me in the back, do you?"

"Only because they know they'd have to get through me first," the ranger replied coolly.

Tye Thwodin looked as if he was about to say something else, but the ranger brought a finger to his lips, then quietly drew one of his swords. "I'm not sure all your mice are in their holes," he said.

Colm quickly ducked back around the corner and stood up slowly, keeping his back to the wall, then started to tiptoe down the hall, toward his room, heart thundering in its cage. He wasn't sure what the ranger would do if he caught Colm spying. Better to just not get caught. *Ready for anything. Guilty of nothing.*

Colm turned the corner leading to the boys' dormitory.

And ran straight into Anywhere, the tip of the sword leveled square at Colm's chest.

Master Wolfe stood in the middle of the hall with his hood thrown back, chin scruffed, black hair curled nearly into knots, and clothes layered with mud and dust and something darker. Two iron-gray eyes held Colm in place. Those, and the point of the ranger's sword.

"Hello, little mouse," the ranger said in a hoarse voice. "You're up late, aren't you?"

Master Wolfe lowered his blade, but he didn't sheathe it. Colm wondered what wolves did to little mice. He had a guess. "Sorry, sir, I was . . . um . . ."

"Sneaking around? Eavesdropping? Or just searching for buried treasure?" The man's voice was calm, but Colm could see the flash of anger in his eyes. *Maybe wolves just ignore mice,* Colm though. *Maybe they consider them not worth the trouble.* But it didn't look as if Grahm Wolfe was going to let him scurry off. Colm thought about the assassin who couldn't give the ranger his name because he was dead already. At least Colm got the courtesy of being asked questions first.

"Nobody buries their treasure, Master Wolfe. They just stash it behind locked doors," Colm murmured.

The ranger smiled. "So just sneaking, then?" he concluded.

"Practicing, actually."

Colm turned to see Finn standing at the other end of the corridor, blending with the shadows. The rogue's voice was casual, ho-hum; he seemed to be fussing with a button on his shirt. "It's part of our training."

The ranger's scowl returned. "In the middle of the night?"

Finn shrugged. "Every good rogue needs to know how to work at night. I was just showing Colm here how to walk in shadow—out of light, out of sight—though obviously he still has a lot to learn." Finn looked at Colm for confirmation. Caught between the ranger and the rogue, Colm took three steps back toward Finn.

"Yes, sir," he said. "A lot to learn. Sorry."

Finn sniffed dramatically. "Of course, it *might* help if you took a bath every once in a while, Colm. I could smell you from a hundred yards, and I'm not half the hunter Master Wolfe is."

"It's been a while," Colm said apologetically. He turned and offered a weak smile to the ranger. Grahm Wolfe didn't look amused.

"There are plenty of shadowy places in this castle to skulk about during the day, Master Argos. Perhaps you should save this lesson for another time."

"Certainly," Finn said. "He's probably learned enough for one evening anyways. Why don't we call it a night, Colm, and pick up where we left off tomorrow—if that's all right by Master Wolfe?"

The two men gazed at each other across the corridor. Colm could hear the thunderous footsteps of Master Thwodin coming toward them through the great hall. Finally the ranger pointed down the hallway. "Scurry off, then. Quiet as you came."

Colm turned back around to Finn, who nodded curtly. "It's all right. Master Wolfe isn't going to eat you," he said.

Colm shoved his hands in his pockets and walked slowly down the hall, keeping his head bowed. As he passed alongside, though, the ranger reached out and put a hand roughly on his shoulder. Colm felt his whole body seize. He stared straight ahead, waiting for something terrible to happen, but Master Wolfe didn't say a word, only squeezed. It didn't hurt. If his father had done it, or Lena or even Finn, it might have been a comfort. But coming from Master Wolfe, it felt like something else. A message of some kind.

A warning.

The ranger let go with a little push, and Colm quickstepped

down the hall with his head bowed, looking back only once, to find Finn and Grahm Wolfe still staring at each other.

Colm disappeared into his room just as Tye Thwodin rounded the corner, demanding to know what was going on, but with the door shut, he couldn't hear a thing.

Even with his ear pressed against the crack at the bottom.

That night, Colm dreamed—as he often did—of riches. Glorious rivers and lakes of gold, as far as the eye could see. Glittering landscapes of jewels and gleaming arms and armor, and chests of coin deep enough to sit in, stacked from floor to ceiling, each and every one unlocked.

But he also dreamed of wolves.

15

LYING BEHIND CLOSED DOORS

olm woke suddenly, sheathed in sweat, to find a pair of hands on him. Through the bleary lens of sleep he could just make out a figure looming over the bed.

He was sure it was a wolf.

He was certain he was about to be eaten.

"Wake up!"

Colm scrambled, clawing his way free of the blanket, free of the hands that held him, falling onto the floor with a muffled thud, reaching for his sword, his legs still tangled in the sheets. He blinked once and focused, finally, to see Lena standing over him. He took a moment to calm himself and appreciate the fact that he wasn't about to die.

"Still haven't lost your knack for falling," she said. Colm smirked up at her. "Aren't you cold?" she asked.

He looked down, realized he was only in his underpants, and quickly wrapped the untangled tail of the sheet around him. "You shouldn't surprise people like that," he barked.

"You should try waking up earlier," Lena said, sitting on the edge of the bed in the space Colm had recently vacated. She was already plated in armor—not that that was unusual for her, even early in the morning—but Colm also noticed that her hair was brushed. Lena never brushed her hair. He assumed barbarians didn't believe in it as a practice. Colm rubbed his eyes with his knuckles, wiping away the sleep, feeling his heart begin to slow. He was about to ask her what she was doing charging into his room when the door opened and more people barged in.

"You missed breakfast," Quinn said, tossing a biscuit that bounced off Colm's chest and landed at his bare feet. He was followed by Serene, who looked away and smiled when she saw Colm wrapped in the sheet, his pale shoulders poking free. She set two oranges on the desk by the window. They were both dressed already, Serene in pristine white robes, her black hair twisted into braids, Quinn looking much the same as ever in purple to match the spot of jelly on his chin. Something was up. Colm could tell by the looks on their faces. Finn had taught him to read expressions, flickers of eyelids, batting lashes, the way the mouth screws and twitches, the way a nose crinkles or cheeks cave. Telltale signs.

That, and Quinn was wearing a knife.

"What am I missing?" Colm asked, sitting up straighter.

356

Quinn looked at Serene. "Do you want to tell him?"

She rolled her eyes and nodded toward Lena, who was biting her lip, about to burst.

"Right," the wannabe barbarian said, then paused to take a deep breath. "Okay. So." Another deep breath. "Apparently Master Wolfe came back in the middle of the night last night and had a talk with Master Argos—I have no idea what they talked about, it's not important. What *is* important is, after *that* Master *Argos* talked to Master *Thwodin* and convinced him that it would be better to go on our adventure *sooner* rather than *later*, while Master Wolfe is here to accompany us. So Master Thwodin apparently had a talk with Master Wolfe and Master Wolfe agreed and told Master Stormbow, who told me, and *I* got to tell *them*, and now we are all here telling *you*. Isn't it *exciting*?"

Colm felt his head snap back and forth as Lena proceeded to shake him all over again, the sheet almost slipping free.

"Wait, what?"

He was sure he had heard her correctly, but he was having trouble piecing it together. Last night it certainly hadn't seemed like Finn was too happy to see the ranger, let alone eager to invite him along. In fact, standing in between them, Colm had felt a certain iciness. And it wasn't the first time.

"But we aren't supposed to go for two more days," Colm protested.

"Make that two more hours." Lena looked at her feet. "I hope I get to slay something bigger than a scorpion. Maybe

357

like a chimera or even a giant. Do they have giants in dungeons, or are the ceilings too low?" Her voice trailed off.

Colm shook his head. *Headed into the dungeon now? With Master Wolfe?* "But we haven't really trained together since the trials. I still have over half the locks on the door, and Quinn still doesn't even have his magic back yet, do you?"

The mageling shrugged. "Master Merribell says it should come back anytime now, and if we have to choose between me having my magic back and having Master Wolfe by our side, I know which one *I'd* prefer. Besides, Lena let me borrow this." He pointed to the intricately engraved, silver-handled dagger at his side. "She calls it a looking-at dagger. But I think it works just fine." To demonstrate, he actually managed to cut himself just pulling the knife free of its sheath. Lena stared for a moment at the drop of blood welling up on Quinn's fingertip, then turned back to Colm, unfazed.

"I thought he wasn't supposed to carry one of those," Colm said.

Lena leaned in and whispered. "I don't actually expect him to use it. It's just for peace of mind. Besides," she added, straightening up. "He's got us. And I, for one, am *more* than ready. It will be nice to finally step foot in a real dungeon." Her eyes sparkled like her armor.

Colm returned her smile, but he felt uneasy. It wasn't like Finn to change plans on a whim; the rogue was nothing if not methodical. Then again, maybe it wasn't his call. Maybe this was really Master Wolfe's doing.

For some reason, that idea made Colm even more anxious.

"Do you not *want* to go?" Lena asked.

All three of them were looking at him. *Staring* at him. Waiting for him. He could see Quinn pleading with his eyes. How could he say no?

"Of course I want to go," he said. "Are you kidding? This is what we were made for."

"Exactly!" Lena said. "So hurry up and get dressed. We'll meet you in the hall." Lena headed toward the door, Serene following her. The would-be barbarian turned back and pointed. "And you better eat that biscuit before Nibbles beats you to it," she warned.

Colm looked over at Quinn, who nodded, confirming that his breakfast was in imminent danger.

Colm hoped it was the only thing.

As Colm laced up his boots, his apprehension slowly gave way to excitement. Lena was right, of course. Not about the biscuit—Colm managed to scarf that down before Quinn could grab it—but about this being their chance, *his chance*. To see if he was as talented as Finn seemed to think he was. And to see if there was a way to step outside the life of a shoe-sole stitcher, to dip not into the pockets of nobles, but into the deep caverns of the earth, returning with not just coin, but a story. It wasn't enough simply to have the gold, Colm thought. Not if you couldn't be proud of how'd you'd gotten it.

It was hard to listen to the masters spin their own tales and not think about what his own might be. He wondered what they might say about him. Colm Candorly. The rogue who picked the unpickable lock and ventured into the dankest, most detestable dungeons, battling the most nefarious creatures, disarming the most notorious traps, and coming out rich as a lord. It was better than Boy Who Fell Off Things. What if he became famous? Stories, Colm knew, moved faster than feet. Faster than horses. They moved on whispers. He wondered if someone might mention his name as far as Felhaven. If his mother might be standing at the market and hear about a young rogue who had picked his way to riches. If, someday, he would pass by the nobles in the town square and have them nod in respect, or even look away out of fear. It was possible. It was more than possible. It was a promise.

Colm checked his bag once more. It was probably unnecessary. Finn would be with them, after all, and while it was true that there was one lock Colm had picked that Finn hadn't, there were hundreds more the other way round. Finn had been lockpicking when Colm was still learning to button his pants.

Pants that he now stuffed with a hairpin and a silver coin.

"I'm n-nervous. Are you nervous?" Quinn said, splitting the hide of an orange—one of Colm's oranges—with his looking-at dagger.

Colm nodded. "But there's nothing to worry about. Remember what Finn said, that very first day? What's the most important thing we need? The thing that we always have?"

360

Quinn knew the answer, though he didn't say it. Instead he wrapped his skinny arms around Colm and hugged him the way Celia always did, with his head on Colm's shoulder. When he was finished, he held up the orange. "Wanna split it?"

They finished the fruit on the way, following the corridor— the same corridor from which he had listened to Wolfe's and Thwodin's whispers only hours before—to the great hall, where Lena and Serene were waiting for them, standing next to Finn. The rogue was wearing his studded leather, his ivory-handled blade, and his smile, complete with two armored teeth.

"Look at you," Lena remarked, giving Colm a once-over.

Colm looked down at his clothes. Shirt and pants. Black cloak. Father's boots. "What? This is what I always wear."

"Exactly," she said with a sigh. "When we get back, I'm going to have to teach you a thing or two about your wardrobe. Do you even own a pair of greaves?"

"Are those the things that cover your elbows or your buttocks?" Colm asked.

"You're hopeless."

"He's a rogue," Finn said. "Our idea of armor is being where the sword isn't. Preferably behind the person wielding it."

"So you can stab him in the back?" Quinn asked.

"So you can take his gold while he's not looking," Finn answered. "Sorry to spring this on you so suddenly," he continued, looking specifically at Colm, "but sometimes everything falls into place and the door opens unexpectedly. Does everyone have what they need? We can't come back just

361

because you left your good-luck charm in your other pants."
He winked.

Colm felt in his pockets for his silver coin, half expecting it
to be gone already. But Finn hadn't taken it this time. Maybe
they were done with that game.

"Very well, then," he said. "The masters are waiting for us."

Lena tugged on the rogue's sleeve. "It *will* be dangerous,
won't it?"

"There will likely be a few surprises," Finn answered.

Quinn tugged on the other. "But not too dangerous?"

"Not half as dangerous as you, Mr. Frostfoot."

Finn led them past the dining hall, stopping only briefly
to mention something to Fungus, who was busy boiling up
lunch. "Probably a good thing we won't be here," the rogue
whispered from behind his hand, pointing toward the steaming pots. "Apparently Fungus caught some rats in the cellar.
The stew will have some chew to it this afternoon." Serene
covered her mouth with both hands.

Colm quickened his step to stand beside Finn. "You're sure
I'm ready for this?"

The rogue offered a reassuring smile. "Any single reserva-
tion I might have had about bringing you along was quelled
the moment you unlocked that chest of mine. You are as ready
as you need to be."

"And Master Wolfe," Colm began hesitantly. "Lena says it
was your idea to bring him along?" He gave Finn a sharp
look. It was a suggestion. The kind of look that passes between

people who know more than they let on. Colm's way of saying, *You can tell me if there's something I should know.*

Finn just nodded—unconcerned. "Having Grahm Wolfe with us will make this easier, I promise."

Finn pulled up in front of a large door that sat directly across from the armory. Colm was a little surprised Lena didn't duck inside to snag an extra mace or something. After all, she was only wearing the one sword today.

"Welcome to the war room," Finn said, then threw open the door to reveal a circular table and several chairs, half of them already filled. Herren Bloodclaw was there, and Masters Velmoth and Stormbow, the one looking sour as always and the other as neatly decked out as Lena in a fine set of chain mail, her sword slung across her back, as was her preference. Master Fimbly was fumbling around with several pieces of parchment, mumbling to himself.

In the corner stood the ranger, staring out the window at the overcast sky. Just seeing him brought a lump to Colm's throat.

Tye Thwodin stood in the center, stuffed into his gaudy golden armor. Smashy Two lay across the table, taking up most of it so everyone else barely had room to set their hands.

"There's our budding adventurers," he said. "A fine-looking party. And so *young.*" He reached out and ruffled Quinn's hair so roughly, Colm was afraid he'd snap the boy's neck. "Just think, Renny, you won't be the shortest one this time." The goblin sniffed and slouched in his chair. "Come on, then.

Gather round. Let's get the boring stuff over with so we can go skull splitting."

Grahm Wolfe took the seat on Master Thwodin's right. Colm sat between Finn and Lena, as far from Master Wolfe as he could get. Only Master Fimbly remained standing, holding up a map. On closer look, Colm could see it was the layout of a dungeon. Their dungeon.

"Number one hundred and twenty-seven," the old man said. "Located beneath the Harbinger Hills in the North Sea corridor, approximately forty leagues from here. A standard multichambered stone affair. Asymmetrical branching pattern that, when last mapped, took on the shape of a leaf, as you can see." The old man traced the figure on the parchment with one crooked finger. Colm studied the honeycombed network of passages, trying to commit to memory every door and corridor, every nook and cranny, but it was impossible to keep it all straight. The dungeon looked huge. Much bigger than the one Master Bloodclaw tended beneath their feet.

Master Fimbly continued. "This particular stronghold was held by goblins for hundreds of years, until they were driven out by none other than our own Master Thwodin, accompanied by yours truly, nearly twenty years ago, isn't that right, Tye?"

"Drove them out like the gutless sheep they are," Tye Thwodin proclaimed, then glanced apologetically at Renny. "I didn't mean you. You have very nice guts," he said. "We emptied the place of all that glittered and left it as a home for the rats and giant spiders."

"*Giant* spiders?" Serene whispered.

Colm raised his hand to get Master Fimbly's attention. "Excuse me, sir," he said, loud enough for the old man to hear. "But if you took all the treasure already, what's the point of going back there?"

All eyes looked at Finn. The rogue cleared his throat and looked across the table. "Recently, Master Wolfe has uncovered ogre tracks coming in and out of the entrance to dungeon one hundred twenty-seven. Furthermore, there have been reports of raids on the nearby villages, suggesting there are actually some new bits and baubles to be recovered."

"So, the gold we're going after likely came from these raids?" Colm asked.

"Wouldn't that treasure belong to the villagers, then?" Quinn added.

"What's ours is ours," Tye Thwodin said curtly. "We aren't in the charity business."

"If there is coin to be had, then it's likely the ogres are hoarding it all here." Master Fimbly pointed to a large circular room near the top of the leaf shape.

"What are those little skulls drawn all over the map?" Serene wanted to know.

"Those are traps," Finn said. "At least, that's where they were the first time around, according to the records from Master Thwodin's expedition twenty years ago. Most of them are probably disabled by now, rusted or disenchanted from neglect. Ogres are big and strong, but they aren't terribly smart. Their idea of a trap is usually to wait around the corner and hit you with a rock. That said, we should still be careful."

Tye Thwodin grunted dismissively. "A handful of ogres, some twenty-year-old traps, and a potential for some real coin at the end. I think you've picked an excellent dungeon for these whelps to cut their teeth on, Master Argos. In fact, it's hardly worth our trouble. Whaddya say we just let the little ones take care of this themselves, and the rest of us go find a nice tavern to spend the afternoon."

Colm looked at Finn—the rogue looked concerned for a moment. Then Tye Thwodin slammed his large, hairy fists on the table, strong enough to make it quiver. "Joking, of course," he said. "The guild can't very well get its share if you all die before you make it out!"

"Of course not," Finn said dryly.

"Well, then, what are we waiting for?" The founder of Thwodin's Legion turned to Master Velmoth. "To the regurgitator!"

Tye Thwodin stood and everyone else followed. Quinn tugged on Colm's arm. "What the heck is the regurgitator?"

It didn't take long to find out.

The regurgitator was just Master Thwodin's less-fancy word for the Crystallarium, the room where all of the guild's teleportation crystals were kept. Colm had seen drawings of it in the books Quinn begged him to look at, books that Quinn had read twice over and probably Ravena Heartfall had too. He knew the Crystallarium was off-limits to everyone except master-class dungeoneers, and that anyone caught trying to use it without permission was kicked out of the guild.

He had no idea where the jewels had originally come from. He knew that it was Master Velmoth's job to tend them, to ensure that their magic was working properly and that they had enough power to get you where you wanted to go, but it was the ranger's job to set them, inscribing the runes that linked each crystal from one point to another. That way, when the time came to raid a dungeon, you didn't have to travel the hundreds or thousands of miles on horseback or ship to get there. You simply chanted the phrase that opened the crystal's gate and held on tight. Once you were there, you slew your monster, gathered your loot, and then used the same crystal to return. It was wizardry of the highest order. And it was the only way Tye Thwodin and his charges managed to raid so many dungeons in so little time, filling the treasury so quickly.

The chamber itself was little more than a circular vault, devoid of windows or proper furniture. A few empty trunks stood by the door. An alphabet of strange symbols was etched into a ring at the center of the room. Torches burned along three walls, providing light that was reflected off the dozens of crystals lining the shelf along the back wall, creating kaleidoscopes of color along the ceiling and the floor.

"I'll get the key," Master Velmoth said, heading toward the back wall, but Wolfe had already beaten him to it.

"Number one hundred twenty-seven," the ranger said, handing it over.

"Number one hundred twenty-seven," Velmoth repeated.

"Excuse me, Master Wolfe," Finn interrupted, "but I believe this is the crystal we need." He took a slender amethyst from the shelf and held it out to the mage, whose ears, Colm noticed, were completely back to normal.

"So it is," Master Velmoth replied. "Thank you, Master Argos." The ranger cast Finn a piercing look.

Tye Thwodin rubbed his hands together. "Still sure this is the one you want now, Finn? We could always pony up and go tackle that harpies' hive again."

"I think this one will do just fine," Finn replied.

The rogue stepped into the circle of runes, and it immediately erupted in a low ring of purple fire to match the crystal's hue. The other masters stepped into the circle as well. "Well, come on, then," Velmoth prodded. "It's not going to hurt you."

Colm stepped tentatively into the violet ring, feeling a surge, his hair standing on end. He reached out and took Lena's left hand, his four fingers interlocking with all five of hers, falling right into the spaces she made for him.

"We simply rode to the castle the first time, Quinn and I," she whispered anxiously.

"It's all right," Colm whispered back. "It's not that bad. It just feels like your whole world is being torn apart and then slowly pieced back together."

"Oh. Well. If that's all." She held on even tighter. Finn took Colm's other hand, holding the crystal in his right. Across the circle, both Serene and Quinn had their eyes shut.

"Stay close to me," Finn said. Then he muttered something under his breath, words that Colm didn't recognize, just as he had back in the forest outside Felhaven.

The crystal blazed even brighter.

And the regurgitator expelled them, hurtling them out of the castle and into the darkness.

Colm was still holding Lena's hand when he emerged, or reassembled, or whatever it was called, everything blinking slowly back into focus, the world reshaping itself before him, the purple light receding into the shadows. He still felt dizzy and disoriented, but he had known what to expect this time, at least, and it only took a moment to recover his balance and catch his breath.

There was a sudden burst of light, and Colm looked to see Master Velmoth holding a bright orange globe that hovered above his open palm, casting an enormous umbrella that illuminated the walls around them—the same spell Quinn had failed to cast in the last dungeon Colm had found himself in. Finn and Master Wolfe both lit the torches that they had brought, bathing the whole party in their collective glow.

Lena looked at Colm once and then pulled her hand away, kneeling down and helping Quinn, who was on the floor, doubled over, losing his breakfast.

"There's always a heaver," the goblin said, standing over Quinn, shaking his head.

"Give the lad a break," Master Stormbow said, bending to help Quinn to his feet. "I seem to recall *you* vomiting all over yourself the first time you used a crystal. *And* the second."

The goblin huffed. Colm looked around, first just counting bodies to see if they had all made it. Lena and Quinn and Serene. Masters Velmoth and Stormbow. Thwodin and Bloodclaw. The ranger, of course. And Finn, who was crouched beside a stone pillar, running his finger along a rune that had been etched into it near the bottom.

"Master Wolfe, are you certain this is the mark for dungeon one hundred twenty-seven?" he asked.

Grahm Wolfe begrudgingly eyed the spot on the stone where Finn was pointing. "It must be," he snipped. "I don't see any of you traveling halfway across the world to find these places."

"Grahm's uncovered more dungeons than any ranger in history. Can't be expected to remember them all," Tye Thwodin remarked. "Besides, the only marks that matter are the ones we make on an ogre's ugly face, am I right?"

Lena nodded eagerly. Serene and Quinn huddled close together. Master Stormbow peered into corners with narrow eyes. The goblin kept sniffing at the air. There were actual monsters in here. Actual traps.

Actual treasure.

Though at first glance it really didn't look very different from the tunnels beneath the castle. The walls were darker, carved from a different kind of stone, but the floor was just as hard, the ceiling still dripping. The only real difference was the smell. The guild's underbelly smelled musty—the aroma of damp dirt that isn't unpleasant so much as old. This dungeon still had that same earthiness, but there was something else underneath, something sour, something *rotten*.

Tye Thwodin took a deep breath and rubbed his armorplated chest like a man about to sit down to a feast. "It *has* been a while," he said rather loudly.

Finn put up a finger. "It might be best if we don't draw the whole family of ogres down upon us *immediately*. Perhaps we could try to exercise some stealth."

Tye Thwodin looked at Finn and snorted. Even his snorts seemed to echo. He turned to Lena. "How'd we get thrown in with such a bunch of shadow-stalking, nambsy-pants, limpdaggered momma's boys? Let 'em come, am I right, girl?"

Lena nodded. Quinn shook his head vigorously. Tye turned back to the rogue. "Have it your way, Master Argos. We will *try* to be quiet." He turned and gave Lena a sly wink.

Finn shot a look at Master Wolfe, who took the lead, Master Thwodin right behind. Lena tried to shoulder to the front as well but was told by Master Velmoth to stay back a ways, just in case. She ended up next to Colm, fuming.

"Men," she snipped.

Bringing up the rear, Sasha Stormbow overheard. "Patience, Lena. Let *them* be the ones to walk into trouble. I'd like to see the looks on their faces when they step in it all the way up to their knees and have to rely on *us* to pull them out."

371

"Still not sure why *I* had to be here." Herren Bloodclaw snorted. "I should be cleaning up the mess you all made in my dungeon. I've got scorpion carcasses everywhere."

"Renny's not terribly fond of ogres," Master Velmoth whispered over his shoulder. "Turns out they use goblins as footstools."

Colm wondered who *was* terribly fond of ogres. From the descriptions he'd read, there wasn't a whole lot to like. Giant, hideous beasts with gnarled knob noses and sharp, crooked teeth, feet and hands matted with fur like wild animals. They were known to eat just about anything, bones included. Colm stumbled a step, but Lena reached out to steady him. Toward the back, Quinn muttered something to himself, probably testing to see if Magic Dan's had vacated his system yet, or maybe he was just trying to get the taste of backward breakfast out of his mouth. Serene fiddled with the charm around her neck, glancing nervously down every hallway.

"There's something strange about this place," Lena said, keeping step with Colm.

"You mean besides the fact that it is the home of flesh-eating ogres?"

"No. I meant the quiet. I didn't expect it to be so quiet. Did you?"

"That's how rogues like it," Colm said. Though he knew what she meant. The place seemed deserted. Though maybe that wasn't a bad thing either.

Up ahead, the ranger had come to a T. He paused and took

out the map that Master Fimbly had given him. "This doesn't make any sense," he said. "According to the map, we should be standing right in front of the main chamber by now."

"That map's twenty years old," Master Thwodin suggested. "Maybe the ogres have renovated."

"You're a bloody ranger," the goblin snarled. "Isn't finding your way around supposed to be your *job*?"

"You're a bloody goblin," Master Wolfe replied. "Isn't falling on the tip of my sword supposed to be yours?"

"Let me take a look," Finn said, snatching the parchment from Master Wolfe's hand and studying it for a moment. "I think we go this way." Finn pressed his torch into the wall of darkness on the right and continued on. Colm noted a quick glance that passed between Grahm Wolfe and Tye Thwodin, the two of them falling in behind the rogue, the rest of the party trailing behind. He noticed Master Stormbow now had a hand on her sword, glancing from side to side.

They came to a much wider corridor than the others, this one big enough for a wagon to roll through, though everyone still clustered close together. Colm could feel Quinn behind him, clutching fistfuls of cloak. Lena was right. There was something out of place here. The quiet, of course, but something else. Like the ceilings, ten feet tall—plenty big enough for Master Thwodin to pass through with Quinn on his shoulders, but ogres stood nine or ten feet on their own. They would skin the tops of their heads coming through the archways. And the smell, even stronger now, even worse than Tyren's feet.

"This reminds me of the dungeon of Vanom Tarth," Tye Thwodin mused, the only one in the party who didn't appear to be on edge. "Remember that one, Grahm? Wasn't hardly a thing to it until you hit that last chamber and then, *fwoosh,* those flames spit out at you on all sides. We were positively broiled by the time we crawled out of there."

"It was warm," Master Wolfe said, putting his hands against the wall as he took slow, calculated, catlike steps.

"*Warm?* My rump was roasted that day. You could have shoveled it straight into Fungus's stew. And all for what? Seven sacks of silver and a sword as dull as Velmo's sense of humor."

Master Velmoth sneered and was clearly about to say something in return when Master Wolfe raised one hand, the other dropping to the hilt of one of his swords. Then he lowered his hand and crouched down. "It's all right. Just a spider."

"We should let Frostfoot squish it," the goblin said. "It might be as close as he gets to slaying anything today."

"Don't you dare," Serene said, rushing forward and scanning the ground around everyone's feet. "Where is it? Let me have it." The ranger bent over and quickly snatched something from the dungeon floor, holding it out. It was probably twice the size of Mr. Tickletoes, but still nothing like the giant spiders Fimbly had warned them about.

"You're not a scary monster, are you, Mr. Wigglelegs? No, you're not." Serene petted the hairy back of the spider with one finger.

"This *is* an odd group," Master Velmoth remarked.

Quinn squirmed his way up between Colm and Lena, whose smile had turned to a tight grimace. The goblin tossed out that maybe they should go back and explore some of the side tunnels they'd passed, that perhaps they were leaving treasure behind. That's when Wolfe said he could see something just ahead.

A door. Finally. Thick rusted iron, and warded with a simple lock.

"This is it, then?" Master Stormbow asked, tightening her grip.

"You can almost taste it, can't you?" Tye Thwodin said, unhooking Smashy Two from the strap on his back and hoisting it to his shoulder.

"Finally." Lena pulled her own sword free. Quinn muttered some incantations, staring earnestly at his hands, but again nothing happened.

Wolfe quickly stepped up to the door and started eyeing the lock, but Master Thwodin pulled him back. He looked at Finn. "This is what I pay *him* for, remember?"

Finn stepped past Master Wolfe and inspected the lock with his torch. "Tricky, but far from the worst I've ever seen. It might be beneficial to let our junior rogue have a go," he said. "This is a learning experience, after all." Finn motioned for Colm to come up beside him. "Just like I taught you," he said.

"You can do it, Colm," Lena whispered behind him. "Just get me inside, and I'll handle the rest!"

Colm removed his set of picks from his bag and studied the

small opening in the iron door. It looked complicated, but no more so than any of the ones in the tens or twenties he'd already mastered. He pressed his hand to the lock, feeling for the resonance of enchantment, but didn't sense anything out of the ordinary. Colm held up a pick and the rogue nodded; then he carefully inched it into the keyhole. He could feel Finn behind him, draped over him like a second cloak. Lena passed her sword from one hand to the next. She was nearly dancing.

"Just look at her, Grahm," Tye Thwodin remarked. "I think she might explode. Reminds me of you a little."

But Master Wolfe didn't seem to be listening. He was pacing around, running his hands along the stone walls, as if their rough faces were speaking to him. Behind Colm, Finn inched even closer. Colm felt one tumbler drop. Then another. A yelp from behind distracted him, and he turned to see Serene shaking her hand.

"What happened?" Lena asked.

"Mr. Wigglelegs bit me," she said, dropping the spider and sticking her finger into her mouth. A third tumbler dropped.

"I f-feel f-funny," Quinn said, holding his head in both hands.

"Concentrate," Finn urged. "Focus." Colm could feel the rogue's breath on his ear.

"Something's not right here," Master Wolfe said. "These markings aren't the work of ogres. Am I right, Renny?" Colm turned to see the ranger pointing to the wall.

"No ogres I've ever seen. They look like orc markings to me."

"Really. I f-f-feel a l-little d-d-dizzy," Quinn said, leaning up against Lena.

Grahm Wolfe pressed his ear to the wall, then shook his head. "No. Something's not right at all."

The last tumbler fell and Colm heard a sound, but it wasn't coming from the door. It was coming from all around them. It was, in fact, vibrating through the walls. A low, rumbling thunder of footfalls on stone.

Hundreds of them.

The ranger drew both of his swords.

Finn reached over and pulled the handle on the door, pushing Colm through the opening just as both sidewalls of the corridor crumbled away behind them, revealing a dozen more doors, through which peered a hundred red-and-yellow eyes. Colm saw the look on Lena's face, both terror and determination, as she pushed Quinn behind her. Saw an arc of blue light burst from Master Velmoth's fingertips. Heard the harsh whisper of Anywhere and Anytime crossed and the cry of the first orc as it came bursting into the tunnel to meet the face of Tye Thwodin's hammer.

And the door slamming shut, with Colm on the wrong side of it.

Colm turned and pulled, kicked and pounded, but the door wouldn't budge. Somehow it had been locked again. He reached for his bag, for his lockpick set, then realized it was on the other side of the door as well, on the ground where he'd dropped it. Through the keyhole he could hear sounds. Weapons clashing. Grunts. Curses. He heard an explosion, and then another, the sound of a giant hammer slamming against the door, followed by Thwodin's booming voice, commanding Finn to "hurry up and open the blasted thing!" Colm turned to the rogue, who had taken a few steps back. He just stood there. As if he was in a trance. A man possessed.

"What are you doing?" Colm demanded. "We have to open this door!"

Finn reached into his pack. Colm hoped he was going for his own set of picks, but instead the rogue removed the purple crystal that had brought them here. "I'm afraid not."

Colm shook his head and pounded on the iron door. He could hear more muffled shouts from the other side. He pulled desperately on the handle.

"Help me!" he shouted. He felt Finn's hand clamp down on his arm.

"I *am* helping you," the rogue said. Then he hissed an unfamiliar phrase. The crystal in his other hand began to glow. Colm heard Lena call his name.

And felt his whole world come apart.

16

A BROKEN PROMISE

The first thing he felt when he pulled himself back together was the knife in his back.

He immediately reached for Scratch, but it was too late. The scabbard was empty. The sword lay on the ground, out of reach. The circle of purple light that had once held ten dungeoneers now held only two. Colm was on one knee, and Finn was standing behind him. He could feel the point of the dagger nudging him, just below his neck, between his shoulders.

"Take a deep breath," Finn said. "You're a very smart boy. Smart enough to know that a rogue standing behind you with a blade in his hand is a reason to be cooperative."

Colm glanced again at his sword, then felt the tip of Finn's dagger press a little deeper, piercing the thick fabric of Colm's cloak, now scratching at the surface of his skin.

"Use your good sense. I don't want to hurt you."

Colm bit down hard on his lip. That would have been much easier to believe ten minutes ago, before the door slammed shut and Colm had found himself back in Thwodin's castle, leaving his friends stranded in an orc-infested dungeon. On his knees with a blade biting into his back. "What's going on? Why are you doing this?"

"I have a promise to keep," Finn said. "And I need your help to do it. But first you need to move. Come on. Up on your feet." Colm felt Finn's hand under his arm, dragging him up, the other still holding the dagger against him.

Colm felt dizzy, but he managed to stand with Finn's help. "What about the others? You took the crystal. What if they can't find a way out?" He thought of Lena calling to him through the door, of the terrified look on Quinn's face as the walls crumbled and the orcs started tumbling through. "We have to help them!"

"*Help* them?" Finn laughed. "The last thing they remember of you was you shutting the door on them. Tye Thwodin will kill you if he sees you, except he won't be able to, because the orcs will get you first."

"We can't just leave them there!" Colm shouted.

"I know you feel that way," Finn said calmly. "I knew you would find this part difficult. That's the trouble with this whole guild business. You get attached. You lose sight of what's important. You start to believe you owe them some-thing, but you don't, Colm. None of them. What's yours is yours. Besides, there's nothing you can do for them now. As you said, I've got the crystal, and there's no way I'm going back there. I'm not going back into *any* dungeon. Not now. Not ever."

Finn leaned in close, his chin on Colm's shoulder, lips to his ear. "Now move."

Colm considered his options. Finn had taught him plenty about locks and traps, enough that Colm might be able to hold his own against the rogue. But in a physical struggle, it was no contest. Even if he had Scratch in his hand, there was no way he could overcome Finn and get the crystal back.

He had no choice. He moved.

Finn pushed Colm through the door of the Crystallarium and into the corridor beyond. The rogue didn't bother checking to see if anyone was there, moving quickly, surely, leading Colm by the dagger at his neck. Colm considered calling for help, crying out, but it didn't seem as if there was anyone around to hear him. It was as if the entire castle had been deserted.

"Where is everyone?" he choked out.

"Fast asleep by now," Finn said, then forced Colm through another set of doors and down a staircase, careful to stay close to him, mirroring his movements. They took a few more turns before ending up in a familiar hallway. Colm had been here before, of course. His very first day. Finn shoved Colm forward until they were standing at a door with only one lock.

The one lock.

"All right," the rogue said, voice soft but still tinged with a threat. "I'm going to take a step back, and you are going to turn around and we are going to have a talk, rogue to rogue. Understood?"

Colm nodded. Then he felt the tip of the knife ease off. He turned to see Finn, dagger in hand, leaning against the far wall, but not far enough that he couldn't easily tackle Colm if he tried to run. Colm scanned the rogue's cloak, looking for the bulge or outline of the crystal that had brought them back here. "You know why we're here?" Finn asked.

Colm nodded. He had a really good idea, at least.

"But you don't know what it took to *get* here. How long I've waited. What I've done. All for a shot at that." He pointed to the door. PROPERTY OF TYE THWODIN. KEEP OUT. Colm shook his head. He looked at the door and then back at Finn.

The rogue shook his head. "An impossible lock with only one key, guarding what just might be the greatest hoard any creature alive has ever collected, and more than any one man has a right to." The corners of Finn's mouth worked into a frown. "Of course, the only way to get hold of that key is to pull it off Tye Thwodin's decapitated body. So, not being in the decapitation business personally, I made a deal with an unsavory character. A Mr. Gutshank. Prickly fellow, even as far as orc chiefs go, but he has a long history of having his dungeons looted by a certain hammer-toting guild master and was more than happy to negotiate. Tye Thwodin's head . . . in exchange for the key around his neck."

"Finn, listen," Colm said, taking a step closer, but the rogue tipped the knife toward him.

"I'm teaching you something. Please, Colm. Pay attention. This is important. Now *getting* the treasure and getting *away* with the treasure are two different things. Rule number thirty-five. And I knew once it was discovered that I was at least partially responsible for Tye Thwodin's premature expiration, I would be hunted by his faithful dog. So I had to get rid of Grahm Wolfe as well. Unfortunately that man is obnoxiously hard to kill."

Colm thought about the first time he had seen Master Wolfe. Being chased by a pack of orcs through the forests outside the castle. Maybe they were some of the same orcs Master Wolfe and the others were battling in the dungeon right now. There was also the conversation Colm had overheard the night before. The night Finn had come to his rescue.

One of many times Finn had come to his rescue.

"Of course, Grahm Wolfe wasn't my only worry," Finn continued. "I had to ensure that the other trainees and masters would be indisposed. I also figured I would need someone strong to help me load the wagon once I made it through the door. Fortunately, the promise of immense wealth is more than enough to convince a castle's cook to quit his day job and become a thief, but not before he suffuses the day's stew with a sleeping draft. In fact, our good friend Fungus should be hitching the wagons as we speak."

Finn twirled the dagger in his hand. Colm looked at the

sword hanging by the rogue's side. He wondered . . . if he was quick, quicker than he'd ever been before, if maybe he could pull it free before Finn realized what was happening. Except he knew how fast Finn was. He knew what the rogue was capable of. At least he thought he did.

"The problem was the key itself," Finn continued, reaching into his cloak and removing his own lockpick set, dropping it on the ground between them. "Orcs aren't exactly honorable, and though we had an agreement, there was always a very good chance they would turn on me as well, and I would be left with nothing—not even my life. But then *you* came along, Colm Candorly, and I realized that I didn't *need* Tye Thwodin's key anymore. I just needed him out of the way. All of them out of the way. And so, with an excuse for the masters to accompany their charges into a dungeon of my own choosing, I simply had to switch the crystals and make sure I escaped when the orcs came barging in. And bring you along, of course. *You* are the key." He nodded toward the door barring the way to Tye Thwodin's fortune.

"So that's it, then?" Colm said bitterly. "You led them all into a trap, but you saved me because you need me to do what you can't?"

"Partly. But also because I made you a promise too. You and your sister. Your whole family. So did you. Don't you see, Colm? This is your chance. Forget those rotten, trap-ridden dungeons. There's enough coin in *that* room to provide for your family for the rest of their lives. And your children's. And their children's.

Why risk your life for Tye Thwodin, giving him half of whatever you find? I'm offering you precisely what you signed on for. One lock. One door. And then we are both kings."

Colm shook his head. "And what makes you think I can pick that lock any better than you can?"

He caught the flash of silver and gold as Finn smiled. "Because you already have." The rogue kicked the leather pouch that held his lockpicks, and it skidded across the floor to Colm's feet. Colm turned and looked at the silver-plated mechanism set into the door.

It suddenly hit him. That's where he had seen it before.

The impossible lock. Except Finn was right. He had done it once before, using something as ordinary as a hairpin. The one that was still in his pants pocket. The lock on the treasury door was identical to the one on the chest in Finn's workshop. Colm remembered what Finn had told him the first time they came down here. *"Failed attempts to pick it can result in death by half a dozen means."*

Finn's voice shifted. For the last ten minutes, he had spoken with that icy confidence that Colm had first mistaken for charm. Now it softened into the voice he had used all those afternoons in his workshop. The one that had convinced Colm to take the journey out of Felhaven in the first place. It was the voice of the man Colm had come to trust. Still, Colm didn't move.

Finn sighed. "Did I ever tell you how I got this scar?" he asked.

"You told me lots of things," Colm said. He tried to be still, to listen for footsteps, voices, anything that would suggest it was more than just the two of them down here. But they really did seem to be alone. Finn reached up and stroked the curving path of white tissue that stopped at his chin.

"I wasn't much older than you when I became a thief. And I wouldn't just pick pockets. I'd steal anything. Food. Horses. Jewels. I was good at it too. Good enough to get noticed by others who made a scoundrel's living. I eventually joined up with a gang, cutthroats and mercenaries. One day whispers came in that there was a man traveling through town with more gold than he could carry. An adventurer. A *dungeoneer.* So the group I was traveling with decided we'd lighten his load. Tracked him to a tavern where he was already half drunk. But it soon became clear that we weren't simply going to pick his pockets. We were going to take everything he had. He was dangerous—you could tell just by looking at him, hulking and battle-scarred and well armed. Odds were, if we robbed him he'd hunt us down and have our heads, but it was too much gold to pass up. We couldn't leave him alive. So one of us would sneak up behind this man and slit his throat. Then the rest of us would empty his bags."

"So, what? You killed him?"

Finn shook his head. "I was supposed to. But I had never killed anyone before. So I panicked and warned the man instead, just as the rest of the gang came for him. He grabbed his hammer and smashed the first thief's face in like a melon.

Then the whole tavern exploded. Everybody fighting everybody. The other thieves turned on me for turning on them, and one of them gave me this." Finn pointed to his cheek, then took a long, shuddering breath. "I could have died that day. I nearly did. And when it was all over, do you know what that man did, the one I warned? The one whose life I saved? He gave me a single piece of silver. Just one. Then he grabbed his sacks full of treasure and left me bleeding on the floor.

"Just imagine it, Colm. Years and years of dungeoneering. Half of every trove, stash, and hoard. Piles of gold ripped from the hands of worthy adventurers and deposited here. Probably the greatest fortune that has ever been amassed by one man, and all he can give me for saving his life is one measly little coin?" Finn pressed his hand to his face, covering the scar. Or most of it.

"He didn't even recognize me, so many years later when he hired me. Even with the scar. I kept expecting it to come to him, but he simply doesn't see it. Not the way you and I do. He thinks he's entitled to it, half of everything. But you and I know better, Colm. We know that if you want your share, you have to fight for it. You have to bend the rules a little. Sometimes you even have to make sacrifices."

"Not everybody's like Tye Thwodin," Colm said.

"No," Finn said. "There are also people like your father, who toil away all their lives just to keep food in their children's bellies, simply because the world has told them they aren't allowed to hope for anything better. Seems a shame that

387

one should prosper while the other one struggles so, don't you think? But you . . . you could change all that. Just one lock. Almost as easy as picking a nobleman's pocket. What do you say?"

Finn glanced down at the lockpicks by Colm's feet, then back up. He had a pleading look in his eyes. And a dagger in his hand.

Colm nodded. "All right."

"All right?" Finn echoed.

"All right," Colm repeated. "You're right. This is what I came for. I've just as much right to it as Tye Thwodin. As anyone. You promise to split it, and I promise to pick the lock and get us in."

Finn put his hand over his heart. "You have my word."

Colm nodded, then turned and looked closer at the lock. It really did look like the other's twin, but Colm knew there was one important difference: The one in Finn's workshop wouldn't burn you or zap you or turn you to stone if you got it wrong.

Finn must have been thinking the same thing. "Remember, you have to undo each pin, every last one, or you won't disarm it. It may feel like you've got it. You might even be able to open the door. But if you don't get all of them, you'll still trigger the fail-safe. Then it's all over."

Colm dropped to one knee and fished out Finn's tools, laying them all out before him—then, with a subtle movement that any rogue would be proud of, he reached inside his pocket and removed his sister's keepsake. He pressed close to the door so that Finn couldn't see exactly what he was doing, holding one of Finn's picks in one hand and the pin in the other. He felt the butterfly's slender tail slip in easily, just as it had on the empty chest before.

Colm felt it, that same sensation as that day on the square, the day this had all started. That feeling of exhilaration and danger, the knot of worry twisting round inside him as he tried so desperately to convince himself that what he was doing was right, even as he untied the purse strings of strangers and slipped their coins into his own pocket. He closed his eyes, weaving the pick through the maze, trying to find his way. He sensed the first pin fall. He could feel Finn standing behind him.

"One giant circle, Colm Candorly. What goes around comes around. The orcs steal the gold from hardworking people, people like your family. The dungeoneers steal the gold from the orcs. Tye Thwodin steals the gold from his dungeoneers. You steal the gold back from him. It's the first rule. The only rule, really."

Colm maneuvered the pin, needling, digging in, till he felt the resistance give way. The second pin fell.

"You might feel guilty for a while, but I guarantee you, Tye Thwodin wouldn't hesitate for a moment to take your hard-earned gold from you. And the rest of them . . . they are all the same. Besides, the moment you see what's inside, you are going to forget all about the others. You will forget all about

389

Tye Thwodin and Grahm Wolfe. You will forget all about the guild. You will look at those mountains of gold, and you will realize that every problem you and your family have ever had, every problem that you ever *could* have, is already solved."

Colm flexed, tensed, felt the release. The third pin dropped.

"I knew it the moment I met you," Finn whispered. "A pickpocket from a backwater village, down a finger, down on his luck, but destined for greatness. Someone who knows the true meaning of family, the most important thing, having someone you can count on. I knew you, of all people, would understand."

There went the fourth. He could almost hear Finn's quickened heartbeat behind him. If Colm remembered correctly, there were only five. But the fifth one was by far the hardest.

"I made a promise, Colm. I promised myself that when the opportunity came, I wouldn't hesitate. I would take what was mine."

Colm paused. He could feel the resistance, a subtle shock that vibrated up through the hairpin and into his fingertips, working its way along his arms and clear down his spine. He had felt it before. This next part was the toughest, but he knew what he needed to do. He felt the resistance give way.

Colm took a deep breath, then removed Celia's hairpin, tucking it back into his pocket. He stood up and looked at Finn.

"Finished," he said. The realization of what he was doing, what he'd done, made him dizzy, and he stumbled as he stood, but Finn caught him. Colm grabbed ahold of the rogue's cloak for a moment to steady himself, then stepped back. Finn looked directly into his eyes, and Colm knew better than to look away.

Then, finally, a wry, wide grin spread over the rogue's face. Finn tucked his dagger into his belt, then wrapped four fingers around the door's steel handle. "You made the right choice," he said.

He pulled the handle. He turned and looked at Colm.

Colm opened his hand to reveal the amethyst crystal he had just snatched from Finn's cloak pocket.

"I know," he said.

He watched the corner of the rogue's mouth twitch, his eyes narrow and then explode in recognition. Saw him twist and try to pull away, except his right hand wouldn't let go of the door. It was stuck to the handle, fingers already turning to stone.

Colm took a step backward, out of reach of Finn's other hand, though the rogue made no effort to get to him. Instead he tried to pull his stone hand free of the door, but it was no use. The curse he had triggered by trying to open it with the last pin still in place worked its way up his arm to his elbow, spreading quickly to his shoulder and down his side. He tried desperately to pull away as it spread across his torso to his other half, turning him to solid rock, clothes, dagger, cloak, sword, everything. It covered him like a second skin. It was nearly to his neck.

Finn turned and stared at Colm, a mixture of surprise and despair, but mostly just disappointment. "Never make a promise you can't keep," he said.

"There's a difference between *can't* and *won't*," Colm replied.

The petrification spread down the rogue's legs, to his feet, to the boots that looked much the same as the ones tucked behind a different door with even more locks, though none as dangerous and difficult as this. Almost his entire body was made of stone now.

"You're going to make a great rogue someday," Finn said. Then, as the curse inched up his neck, he managed to turn and face the door, the one he could never have opened on his own, and smiled as if he had. As if he were standing inside, looking at all the glorious gold. "It's beautiful, isn't it?" he whispered.

Finn blinked once.

And then it was over.

17

UP IN FLAMES

Colm stood there for a moment, incapable of moving or speaking or even breathing, it seemed, just staring at the unblinking figure of Finn Argos, mottled gray like Grahm Wolfe's eyes, cold as the stone walls all around.

"I'm sorry," Colm said. "I know you, of all people, would understand."

He quickly bent down and reached across Finn's granite feet to grab the lockpick set and tuck it into his cloak alongside the hairpin and the crystal key. He knew he had to get back to the dungeon. There was no telling what had happened to his friends and the other masters. Of course, there was a chance they'd made it out—fought their way through. More likely, they had been taken prisoner. Even more likely still . . .

He had to hope. Trouble was, he wasn't sure how to get back there. Finn had never taught him how to use the crystals, what to say. His only hope was that he would find someone, anyone, who hadn't fallen victim to Finn's sleeping potion. He wound his way up the stairs and back through the castle corridors, bursting into the great hall. He looked toward the dining hall and stopped cold.

There they all were, passed out across their tables, some on the floor, others propped against one another, chins wet with drool. If it weren't for the syncopated hum of their breathing, Colm might have guessed them to be dead. Colm spotted the body of Master Merribell crumpled up halfway between the dining hall and the kitchen, robes bunched around her, snoring fitfully. In her hand was a vial of some kind, its contents emptied and staining the stones in front of her. A remedy or antidote, probably, except she hadn't been able to take it in time. Maybe somebody had stopped her, or maybe Finn's potion worked too quickly. Colm ran over to her and shook her, shouting in her ear, but it was no use.

Colm tried to rouse some of the others, even slapped Tyren across his properly apportioned head, but nobody stirred. He couldn't wait for them to wake. He was probably too late already. Perhaps there was something in the Crystallarium that could help him figure out how to get back.

Colm made his way through the castle, calling down every hall. "Hello! If you're here, I need help! The whole party is trapped in a dungeon! Please!" There was no answer. He threw open the doors of the chamber, with its rainbow array of rare gems along the wall and its circle of purple fire

394

promising a trip to anyone who knew the magic words. He looked around for some instructions, a big, moldy tome full of mystical incantations, anything, but the room contained little more than crystals and candelabras. Colm stepped into the center and held the amethyst in his hand. He closed his eyes.

"Go!" he said.

"Vamoose!"

"Fly!"

"Teleport! Transport! Portalify! Transferus bodius!"

The crystal sat cold and lifeless in his hand. It was useless. Colm called up to the ceiling. "If there is anybody out there who can help me, please!"

He heard a grunted breath behind him and turned.

"Oh . . . fungus."

Two beefy arms instantly wrapped around Colm like tentacles, squeezing, threatening to snap his spine. Colm struggled to free himself but only managed to twist so that it was his rib cage threatening to splinter. His eyes shot around the room and landed on Scratch, only a few feet away. Not that he could get to it now. Colm wondered if there had ever been a more useless sword in all of creation.

"Where's Finn?" Fungus growled, somehow squeezing even harder.

"Not . . . going . . . anywhere . . . ," Colm said, in between heaving gasps. He kicked out with his feet, banging helplessly on the cook's shins. Fungus was nearly Master Thwodin's equal in size. He wasn't a dungeoneer, didn't carry any weapons, but when you have arms thick as logs, it doesn't matter. Colm's vision darkened. His lungs burned; his guts threatened to shoot out both ends as Fungus pressed him closer. Colm couldn't believe it. After all of this, to be crushed to death by the cook.

He heard a soft thud. Then he felt everything go limp as those giant hairy hands released him. Colm flopped to the floor, the air rushing back in a great, long, rasping gasp. He turned to see Fungus standing there above him, a stupid, confused look on his face, eyes rolling up into his head. He wavered for just a moment, then pitched forward like a felled tree, Colm barely managing to roll out of the way as the body of the cook landed with a shuddering thunk.

Colm shook his head, feeling the blood rushing back to all the places it belonged, then looked at the figure standing over Fungus's prone body. She was more beautiful than he could ever imagine, with one eyebrow cocked, eyes like pinholes, mouth set in a determined scowl.

"You want to tell me what's going on here?" Ravena Heart-fall demanded. In her hand she held a sword, the hilt of which had taken down the hulking cook with a blow to the back of the head. "Where is Master Thwodin? Why is Fungus trying to kill you?" The tip of that sword was pointed at Colm. She didn't trust him.

He couldn't blame her.

Still gasping for air, he reached into his pocket for the crystal and held it up for her to see. "Finn. Betrayed us. Sleeping potion. Treasure. Trap," he croaked, rubbing his bruised chest. It was the highly abridged version, but she seemed to get the idea. Ravena lowered her sword.

"And the others?"

"Dungeon. Orcs. I don't know."

Ravena nodded, as if she hadn't expected any less.

Colm was finally able to take a full breath again. "The last thing I saw was the whole party being surrounded. Then Finn transported us here. We have to go back." Colm held the crystal out to her, then drew back. "Wait a minute," he said, suddenly suspicious, "how come *you're* not asleep?"

Ravena stared at the unconscious body of Fungus in disgust. "Have you ever seen me eat *anything* that man cooks?" She snatched the crystal from Colm's hand and stepped back into the illuminated circle. "How many orcs did you say there were?"

"Hundreds," Colm said.

"And how many can you handle?"

Colm considered the question carefully. "Three."

"That's more than I thought you'd say." She pointed to the sword still sitting on the floor. "Three with or without that?"

"With, probably," Colm said. He picked Scratch up by its paw, then grabbed hold of Ravena. "Wait a minute. I don't know what to do."

"That's all right. I do," she said. "It comes with having to do everything yourself."

★ ★ ★

They appeared the same place as earlier, except this time the halls were all well lit and no longer quiet. The trap had been sprung, and the dungeon seemed to have developed a heartbeat, a steady thumping that rebounded from every stone.

"Drums," Ravena cursed.

"And drums are bad?"

"They are preparing a ritual."

"You mean like a sacrifice?" Colm asked.

"Well, they're probably not celebrating Master Thwodin's birthing day."

Colm hadn't realized Ravena Heartfall had a sense of humor. He'd kind of assumed she had used some spell to have it removed. She handed the crystal key back to Colm, who tucked it away. "I trust you at least learned how to walk quietly?"

Colm nodded. That part he could handle. With any luck, maybe they could sneak past the first hundred guards, leaving only three hundred or so for her to fight. They crept side by side, swords leading the way, constantly glancing behind them but following the dungeon's heartbeat. Sometimes the percussion was accompanied by the sound of feet clopping across stone, and they would duck into the shadows as a patrol stomped by. One group of orcs carried a set of iron pikes ten feet tall.

"For the heads," Ravena explained. She wasn't being funny this time.

They ducked down two more halls, Colm wishing he had

Serene's chalk numbers to go by, trusting Ravena's instincts even though he was the one who had been here before. At one point they reached a corridor that was darker than the others, and Ravena muttered something under her breath, her fingertips suddenly glowing with a bright white light that spread out in front of them.

Colm let out a squeak. "I forgot you could do that," he whispered. Cast spells, pick locks, and clobber cooks. He wondered if she could talk to spiders as well. "You really are talented."

"Let me ask you something," she whispered back as they inched along the hall, pausing in between breaths to listen. "During the trials. That lock on the chest. How did you get through it so fast?"

"It was Finn," Colm admitted. "He made me practice it. Over and over."

Ravena nodded. "I knew he liked you best," she said.

"I trusted him," Colm said bitterly.

"Maybe he trusted you too."

Colm was about to say something to that when the sound of shouting—human shouting—from a chamber ahead caused them both to stop, their backs pressed against the walls in between the halos of the torchlights. The voice was clearly agitated.

"When I get out of this cage, I am going to rain steel on your leathery little hides! I am going to unleash a whirlwind of wrath so furious you will turn inside out just trying to see where I'm coming from! I will stick you so full of holes, your friends will use you to pan for gold!"

"Lena?" Ravena whispered.

Colm nodded.

"I won't even *need* my sword," the voice continued. "You can keep it. I'll just shove my hands so far down your orcish throat that I'll pull out what you had for breakfast last week and feed it to your friends!"

There was a clang of metal on metal, followed by a grunt. Colm heard a gruff and unfamiliar voice say something about wanting to eat the loud one first, and Lena's voice suddenly went silent.

Ravena pointed to the open archway the voices were coming from. "Stick close and follow my lead." Colm put a hand on Ravena's shirt and trailed behind her, both of them keeping to the shadows and craning their necks to get a look inside the room.

They were there, the three of them—Lena, Quinn, and Serene—locked in separate steel cages suspended from the ceiling. Lena had been stripped of her weapons, though that wasn't stopping her from trying to chew through the metal bars. Serene had her knees pulled up and one hand thrust through both her cage and the one beside her, resting it on Quinn's head, running her fingers through his wild hair. The boy was curled fetal, eyes closed. His whole body shook.

Colm started to get Lena's attention, but Ravena pulled down his arm and nodded to the other side of the room and the six orcs standing there.

She held up three fingers and pointed at him. Colm looked at the orcs, at least twice the size of a goblin, battle scarred and uglier than Fungus even, many of them with necklaces of polished white bones hanging from their necks. Maybe three had been a little ambitious. He shook his head and held up one finger. Ravena rolled her eyes. Then she closed them and mumbled something under her breath.

Suddenly the room started to fill with smoke, billowing up from the floor in thick white clouds. Climbing up the walls, reaching even to the suspended cages. The orcs drew their swords and axes, spinning around and sniffing at the white fog, but in three heartbeats the room was filled with a haze as dense as packed snow, impossible to see through. Colm felt Ravena brush past him, tiptoeing into the room, then lost sight of her altogether.

"Ravena!" he hissed as loud as he dared, but he got no response. He groped around the floor beside him. Then he heard the orcs cursing, heard scraping, something hitting the wall. There was a series of grunts. One orc shouted, knocked something over. Colm took Scratch and jabbed into the fog tentatively, afraid of hitting Ravena but hitting nothing after all. There were several more *thud*s from different places in the room, a long groan, and then silence.

In the space of another breath, the smoke started to disappear, absorbed back into the walls or the ether or the floor, revealing the bodies of all six orcs stretched across the stone, their attacker throwing her braid of black hair behind her again. She glanced over at Colm, who couldn't help but stare. "What? You never learn how to fight with your eyes closed?"

Colm couldn't even pee with his eyes closed. Not and still hit the bucket.

Ravena sheathed her sword, bent down to retrieve a set of keys from one of the orc's belts, and started unlocking the cages. Serene was speechless. Quinn was out of it. Ravena threw the keys to Colm to unlock Lena's door.

They looked at each other through the bars. Colm offered her a weak smile. She didn't return it. He opened the door to her hanging prison. She punched him.

A right hook across the jaw, sending him spinning backward.

"Where have you *been*?" she shouted. "Do you have any idea what has happened to us? We were ambushed! There were hundreds of them! And you just slunk through that door and *locked* it behind you, like a coward! We could have been *killed*. We *were* going to be killed. They were going to *eat* us! Do you understand? *Eeeaaaat* us!"

"Good to see you too," Colm said, doubled over and holding his chin in his hand.

"It wasn't his fault," Ravena said. "It was Finn. Something about treasure and a trap. I didn't exactly get the whole story."

Lena looked to Colm for confirmation. He nodded.

"Oh, I see. Are you okay?" she asked, suddenly concerned.

Colm shrugged. "Well, my *jaw* hurts now." He looked at

Serene, who had Quinn leaning against her, eyes shut, body still convulsing. "What happened to him?"

Serene shook her head. "He's sick, but it's not like anything I've seen before. He's burning up. Poison, maybe? But I don't have anything to give him. They took our weapons and supplies."

Colm went and put his hand on Quinn's forehead and jerked it back. The mageling's skin sizzled at the touch. He was drenched from head to foot in sweat, and yet he continued to shiver. "It's all right," Colm whispered in his ear. "We are going to get you out of here. I have the crystal. Hopefully it has enough juice left in it to get us back."

"Except this isn't all of us," Serene said.

"We don't know where they took the others," Lena added. "But apparently the orc chieftain knows Master Thwodin personally. Said he was going to put them all on trial and then execute them."

"Some trial," Ravena said.

"If you were an orc and got your hands on the dungeoneer who had spent the last twenty years stealing your gold from under your ugly nose, what would you do?" Serene retorted.

"We have to find them," Colm said. He turned toward the door.

"Wait. I'm not going out there unarmed." Lena moved from one fallen orc to another, picking up each of their blades and giving it a swing before dropping it to the ground in disgust, muttering something about balance and tang. Finally Colm

just bent down and picked up the sword of the orc lying closest to him and shoved it at her.

"Is it pointy?" Colm asked.

"I suppose," she said.

"And how do you handle an orc?"

"Stab it," she said.

"Then let's go."

Lena sighed but took the sword, then growled when both
she and Ravena tried to squeeze through the entry at the same
time, each trying to take the lead. Finally Ravena stepped
back and let Lena through. Rule number five.

Colm helped Serene with Quinn, nearly dragging him
along as they worked their way through the dungeon, following the pounding and thrumming that echoed off the
walls. They avoided the larger corridors, sneaking through
side tunnels, peeking into open chambers to find them all
empty. Apparently the whole tribe was gathered together in
one place. Colm didn't think that would make rescuing the
masters any easier at all.

The drums grew thunderous. Colm could feel the vibrations in the walls, like the hum of an enchanted lock. "We're
close," Lena said, wrinkling her nose. "Nothing like the smell
of a thousand orcs crammed in one room." She led them
through a narrow archway and down a steep staircase, then
through another hole in the wall. Suddenly the din grew
overpowering, and Colm found himself staring into a chamber easily twice the size of the great hall, completely awash in

club-brandishing, skull-necklace-wearing, growling, spitting, snarling, stinking orcs, all dressed in bits of leather and iron, studded with spikes and hooks, each one more vicious-looking than its neighbor.

"That's a whole lotta ugly," Lena said. Serene, surprisingly, didn't argue.

The mass of orcs was writhing and undulating to animal-skin drums thumped with polished leg bones. Whose legs, Colm didn't want to know. And in the center of it all, on a circular stone platform raised high enough for all to see, stood the largest orc of them all.

"That's him," Serene said. "Gutshank, they call him. He was there when we were captured. He was the one who said we'd be on tonight's menu."

Colm didn't need an introduction. You could tell Gutshank was the chief by the full plate of armor, scarlet-stained steel that he had probably ripped off one of his victims. He also wore a dragon on his head. Or at least the skull of one, minus the lower jaw, to make room for his own knotted face.

"And look there." Serene pointed.

On the stone stage, lined up in a row, kneeling before the orc chief, were the masters of Thwodin's Legion. All except Herren Bloodclaw, who was bound at the wrists and stuck in a wood cage barely tall enough for him to crouch in. They all looked to be alive, though the giant ax that Gutshank was leaning on suggested that condition was only temporary.

"I guess the trial's over," Lena said.

Luckily, Colm thought, the swarm of creatures before them was so preoccupied with the impending execution of their prisoners that they didn't notice the small pack of fledgling dungeoneers hiding in the shadows at the back of the vaulted room. "All right," Colm said. "We need a plan. There's all of them." He indicated the horde with his short-fingered hand. "And the five of us."

"Four," Serene said, nodding toward Quinn. She was right. The boy was barely conscious. If he could be certain how much power was left in the crystal, Colm would teleport Quinn back to the castle and leave him there, but there was a good chance such a trip would use up whatever energy the jewel had left and would leave the rest of them stranded. It was only guaranteed to make one round trip, after all, and it had already made one and a half.

"I can probably take ten," Ravena said, then looked over at Lena, whose face had turned gray.

"Twelve," she said, refusing to be outdone. "Maybe fifteen."

That left only a few hundred or so. Colm turned to Serene. "What have you got?"

The druid shook her head, started reaching into the pockets of her cloak, to the few small vials and packets of powder that her captors hadn't stripped her of. "Let's see . . . I can heal gout and shrink warts. Sorry, Colm. I'm not really cut out for the whole taking-out-a-throng-of-bad-guys thing."

"That's all right," Colm said. "We don't need to take them out. We just need to find a way to free Master Thwodin and the others and get out of here."

"If we could get down there without being noticed, we might be able to hold them off long enough for you to release them," Lena proposed. "Then we would only need to clear a path."

"*If* we could get down there," Colm repeated. But he wasn't skilled enough to move through hundreds of orcs without getting noticed. Slipping by his sisters was one thing. His sisters weren't usually armed with spiked clubs. They could try disguises, but none of them were near ugly enough to pass for orcs. Still, there had to be *something*. He scanned the room until his eyes fell on a couple of large, dome-shaped steel cages along the back. He tugged on Serene's shirtsleeves.

"Are those what I think they are?" he asked, pointing.

She took one look and shrank back, grimacing.

"You can't possibly—" she started to say.

But Colm was already dragging her in that direction.

"I can't do it," she hissed, refusing to go a step closer. "It's terrifying!"

Colm switched Scratch to his less sweaty hand and gave Serene a reassuring touch on the back that was actually more of a push. His idea wouldn't work without her. She was the only one who could pull it off.

"Think of it like Mr. Tickletoes, only a hundred times bigger."

"That is *not* Mr. Tickletoes!"

Colm looked at the giant spider skittering about in its oversized cage, its glassy black eyes reflecting the flash of the torches, its long, spindly legs tapping against the bars of its prison, its bloated, hairy black abdomen rocking up and down. She was right. Compared to this thing, Mr. Tickletoes was adorable. Colm wasn't even sure what orcs used the giant spiders for, unless it was to torture prisoners. Or maybe they just had questionable taste in pets.

"You can do this, Serene," Lena whispered. "I know you can. You just have to talk to it."

Serene took a gingerly step forward. The giant spider in the last cage scuttled around to face her, its furry mandibles working furiously on the steel bars. Serene began mumbling to herself.

"This is just like back at the Grove. 'It's just a bear,' they said. 'Just another of nature's beautiful creatures,' they said. 'Just talk to it,' they said. But do you know how big bears are? Have you seen their claws? And those jaws? It had rabies, I'm sure of it. And this. There's no way. That thing was twice my size. *This* thing is twice my size . . . *ewwwwww* . . ."

"You can do it," Lena whispered again, but Serene just turned and glared at her. On the center podium, the drumming had reached a feverish tempo, the heart of the dungeon about to burst. Chief Gutshank was walking back and forth behind his prisoners now, as if taking stock, measuring necks, deciding which one to start with. Colm saw Serene kneel in front of the cage and look up at the gigantic spider. He could

408

see her face in its four biggest eyes. She turned back to look at him, and Colm nodded. She shuddered and faced the spider again. He heard her whisper something to it, then louder, a language he couldn't begin to understand.

But the spider understood. At first it raised up, arching its abdomen and raising its two front legs through the slats in its cage, but as she continued to talk, it lowered itself till, finally, it knelt down to her level. Almost as if it were bowing.

Serene turned to Colm, a surprised smile on her face.

"What did it say?" Colm asked.

"It said that if we let it out of its cage, it will do what we ask."

"How do you know it won't eat us?" Lena asked.

"Because the orcs are the ones who stuck it here to begin with," she answered.

Colm wasn't sure he could trust a giant spider, but the last hour had proved he wasn't always the best judge of character. Besides, he trusted Serene, and she said it was all right. Colm stepped to the cage, keeping a wary eye on the creature's jaws. He pulled Finn's picks from his cloak and found one that looked like it might work. There was hardly anything to the lock; it took him less than ten seconds to undo. The door swung wide and the spider scurried out, stretching itself to its full height, taller than Colm by a head. For a moment he was certain he was about to be sucked dry, but the creature quickly bent down again, four of its legs curled beneath it. It made a strange clacking with its jaws.

"It says to get on," Serene said.

Colm scrambled onto the back of the spider, trying not to pull too hard on the thick hairs that sprouted from the creature's body, then motioned for Ravena and Lena to do the same. When all three were aboard, Serene whispered something else to the spider, then reached up and petted the slope of its head, just above its jaws.

"Take care of my friends, Mr. Fuzzyfangs," Serene told it.

"Watch over Quinn," Lena said, looking at the mageling left in the shadows with his back to the wall. He wasn't shivering anymore. Colm didn't know if that was good or not. He wrapped both hands around the spider's thorax, Lena wrapping both her arms around his. Serene whispered one last thing into the spider's ear, and the creature suddenly crawled toward the cavern wall.

And then straight up it.

Just like riding a horse, Colm told himself. *A horse with giant fangs and eight legs that eats flesh and hangs upside down.* He held on tight as he could as it scurried along the jagged stone. It was almost to the ceiling when the drumming suddenly stopped. Colm glanced down to see that the giant orc with the dragon-skull head stepped forward, holding his ax above him. The orc's shouts reached up to the ceiling, where the giant spider had attached its silken thread.

"Behold, my brothers and sisters," the orc chief bellowed. "The pack of murderous thieves!"

There was a tremendous cheer from the frenzied crowd of

orcs. Chief Gutshank gave Tye Thwodin a swift kick in the back, causing him to topple forward. No one bothered to look up. If they had done so, they might have seen Colm about to tumble off the back of the spider, which was slowly descending along its own crystal-silk thread. Ravena and Lena were both pressed up behind him, digging in with their heels.

"For continued crimes against all orckind," the dragon skull continued below them, "I, Gutshank, chief of the Bloodtooth Clan, sentence these trespassers to death!"

There was another wave of hollers, accompanied by the banging of weapons on shields and helms. Colm could see the whole lot of them clearly now. Master Stormbow straining at her chains. Master Velmoth trying to shake free of a collar that glowed a soft blue and must be stifling his power somehow. Tye's muscles bursting through his torn shirt. Only the ranger didn't seem to struggle, though Colm was certain he saw Master Wolfe glance up briefly, then cast his eyes back down to the floor.

"But who should be first?" Gutshank roared. "Do we start with the wolf?" He kicked the ranger hard enough that he toppled over. "Or the lion?" The orc chief held his ax above Tye Thwodin's head, but the crowd began chanting the ranger's name. *"Wolfe. Wolfe. Wolfe."* He remembered what Quinn had told him once—that there were plenty of nasty things that would love to see Grahm Wolfe's head on a pike.

They were about to have their chance.

Colm heard Lena gasp as Master Wolfe was forced to his

411

feet by two other orcs, then pushed to the edge of the platform in the center and back on his knees. It took three orcs to hold him down. Another stood by with one of those ten-foot pikes, ready to collect the ranger's head once it rolled free. The orc chief raised his ax again and gave it a few practice swings, whipping the already frenzied crowd into a froth. Down below, Tye Thwodin made another attempt to escape, but with his hands and feet in chains, he was easily subdued by the trio of orcs guarding him.

The spider was still fifty feet away, descending slowly, no doubt used to sneaking up on its prey. As a rogue, Colm could admire the approach, but they were out of time.

"We need to do something!" Ravena hissed from behind him. The drummers suddenly took up their pounding again. Colm saw the chief take his ax in both hands, raising it above his head. Heard the collective growl from the many hundreds of orcs who were watching. He saw a few of them with their fingers pointing up toward the ceiling.

He heard Lena say, "Hang on!" Heard the metallic tang of her sword coming free.

Then he said good-bye to his stomach, leaving it somewhere in the air above him as the spider's silken thread snapped, severed by a blow from Lena's sword.

They dropped the full fifty feet, the spider landing awkwardly, several of its legs buckling underneath it, but its otherwise soft body cushioning the blow for its three passengers. Both Lena and Ravena rolled off its back, landing on their feet, swords in hand. Colm clumsily slid off onto his backside. It was, he painfully realized, his signature move.

The drums stopped, and the cavern was suddenly filled with the growls of a thousand orcs. Their chief turned away from Master Wolfe, bellowing and swiping at Lena, who ducked his executioner's ax just in time. The blow caught the spider instead, taking off one of its legs. Mr. Fuzzyfangs instantly swung around and attacked, driving Gutshank backward and leaping on him till spider and orc were just one giant ball writhing and tumbling across the platform.

Colm saw Ravena beside him, fending off four orcs at once. Saw Master Wolfe strike out with manacled feet, kicking one of his captors clear into the throbbing mob below. Heard Lena's voice above the chaos. "Colm! What are you waiting for?"

Colm pulled the first pick he could find from his cloak and scrambled over to Master Wolfe, digging into the locks that bound the man's hands and feet.

"Hello there, little mouse."

"Hello, Master Wolfe," Colm grunted, shoving the pick into the cuffs around the ranger's wrists, working frantically, faster than he ever had in Finn's workshop. He felt the lever give, and the manacles clicked open just in time. Master Wolfe pushed Colm out of the way of a hatchet's blow, then drove his shoulder into the attacking orc's gut, slamming him to the ground.

"Get the others," Wolfe commanded. The ranger took up

413

the nearest blade he could find and did that little twirly thing that Colm had never learned how to do before launching himself at the swarming mass. Colm worked his way down the line, freeing one master after another, barely undoing their locks before they leaped into the battle. First Tye Thwodin, who let out a lion-worthy roar, then Master Stormbow.

The moment the collar came off Master Velmoth, his eyes started to glow and little bolts of electricity crackled between his fingers. Master Wolfe had joined both Ravena and Lena in a line that held the surging horde of orcs at bay, though Colm could see they wouldn't hold for long. He quickly undid the lock on Renny's cage and helped pull out the goblin.

"Save the goblin for last, eh?" he spit. "I'll remember that."

Colm might have protested, but he was too busy ducking out of the way of thrown spears determined to put holes through him. He drew Scratch and joined the others, forming a little knot in the center of the hall, the masters and their apprentices felling orcs by the dozens, but still barely holding their ground. Lena and Ravena fought side by side, grunting in admiration.

"Nice octave."

"Thanks. Nice flunge."

"I've done better."

Master Velmoth was doing his best to create a fissure in the ground to give them some space, but his concentration was broken by the fighting around him. Even Herren Bloodclaw was fiercely engaged, swinging a sword that was much too large for him, wreaking havoc on the kneecaps of the nearest orc.

"We've got to make our way back to the tunnels," Master Wolfe said. "We need to clear a path."

That had been the plan, but Colm couldn't see how it was possible now. Not unless Master Velmoth could conjure wings and fly them out. They were too greatly outnumbered. Colm saw Master Stormbow stumble. Saw Tye Thwodin's borrowed sword splinter in two from a blow, the guild's founder resorting to head butting the orc that had split it. Watched as Lena stepped in front of Thwodin, protecting him long enough for him to find something else to swing.

Behind him, Colm heard a screech as Chief Gutshank emerged from beneath the carcass of the now-dead spider, his dragon-skull helmet gone, his arms and legs bloodied, but his ax still in hand. The spider's body quivered, its legs curling. Colm took Scratch in both hands, held it defiantly before him.

He'd told Ravena he would at least get one. Might as well make it a big one.

Gutshank raised his ax, mouthful of yellow teeth and bloody foam, charging for Colm. Screaming. Leaping. Swinging.

And then, quite surprisingly, exploding.

The fireball hit the orc chief square in the chest, driving him backward, clear off the platform and into the crowd below. Colm turned to Master Velmoth, expecting to see the wizard in full bloom, casting spells right and left, but the once-bunny-eared mage was clutching at a wound on his side, being protected by Master Wolfe, who was clashing with five orcs at once.

Five orcs who were suddenly scorched by a wall of flame.

Followed by another searing fireball that sizzled through the air, splashing into the cluster of orcs at the front of the surge. Colm saw Lena glance up at the far wall of the vaulted chamber, to the brilliant orange light bursting out of the shadows like a sunrise.

It was Quinn.

And he was on fire.

Standing on a rocky ledge, robes fanned out behind him, hands reaching for the ceiling as if he was pulling down the heavens themselves. It came from all directions. The flames shot from his eyes and his ears, from his fingers and his mouth, scorching the air, creating plumes of plummeting comets with bright orange tendrils that rocketed forth, striking the ground, leaving smoking craters in their wake. They went everywhere, these balls of bright flame. Colliding with the ceiling and the cavern walls, smashing into pockets of orcs, knocking them backward. The mageling was erupting, every bit of pent-up magic that had been stifled by one heavily iced roll finally being unleashed in a great and furious conflagration.

Colm watched in awe as the orcs were driven back, howling in retreat, escaping into tunnels behind them, leaving an open path back the way they'd come. Colm saw Serene beckoning to them from the other side.

"Time to go!" Tye Thwodin bellowed, leading the charge,

416

striking out at the few orcs who hadn't had the sense to escape from Quinn's rain of fire. Colm ran behind Lena, watching as the very last fireball was spit from Quinn's ear, whizzing in a circle before harmlessly sputtering against the wall just as the whole party made its way across the floor of the chamber to where Serene stood, waiting for them, urging them on.

The mageling looked down at them from his little precipice and belched a bit of smoke.

"I feel better now," he said.

"That's great," Lena said breathlessly. "Now please get down here before you hurt yourself."

On the other side of the vaulted room, several hundred orcs were slowly coming to the realization that Quinn had finished his onslaught and were preparing to charge all over again.

"What do you think?" Master Stormbow posed. "Stay and fight?"

Lena nodded eagerly, but the ranger shook his head.

"Rule number thirty-seven," he said. "Never take on more enemies than you have fingers to count them on." Another reason not to miss the one he'd lost, Colm thought. "We'll come back another time," Wolfe added. Then the ranger led them back through the tunnel and up the stairs, where they met up with Quinn. He had scorch marks on his arms and white ash thick as snowfall in his hair, and his face was beet red, but at least he was smiling. Behind them, they could hear the war cry of the orcs swarming, clamoring, pouring into the tunnels. Colm fished in his pocket for the crystal and handed it to Master Wolfe.

"I hope it works," he said.

"Only one way to find out."

Everyone gathered around in a circle, instantly clasping hands.

Everyone except for Tye Thwodin.

The founder was standing at the entryway to a small chamber, eyes glazed, mouth open. Colm ran to get him, pulled on his armored sleeve, then took a glance into the room that Master Thwodin stood before.

He had to put up a hand to shield his eyes. The view was blinding.

Gold. Piles of it. Mounds and heaps. Not even in chests. Just pushed together in hills that reached up the corners of the room. Here was the orc's stash. The very thing they had come for. The very thing *he* had come for.

"Just look at it," Tye Thwodin said. "Isn't it gorgeous?"

Colm stood beside him and looked. It was gorgeous. So much gold. Enough to bury yourself in. He could almost hear it calling to him. *Colm. Colm.*

"Colm!"

He blinked twice. Then turned to see Lena reaching out.

"Colm, come on!"

"I already got what I came for," Colm said. Then he dragged Tye Thwodin away by the back of his armor. Away from the chamber with its golden piles and back into the circle of dungeoneers pressed close together. Behind them, the shouts echoed off the walls.

The ranger held the key with one hand and reached out for Colm with the other. In a moment, the corridor would vomit a wave of teeth-gnashing, ax-waving monsters. If the crystal was out of power, they would be stuck here, with barely any room to fight. And this time the orcs probably wouldn't even bother with chains and cages. They would go straight for the pikes.

Colm grabbed hold of Lena. He watched Master Thwodin push into the circle on the other side. He felt the ranger's hand on his shoulder, giving it a squeeze. Master Wolfe said the words just as the first wave of orcs appeared. Colm looked across the room at Ravena. Then he shut his eyes and thought of home.

18

THE BEST PART

The chair was uncomfortable. Almost painfully so. It dug into every muscle, forcing Colm to try and sit on as little of it as possible, so that he was nearly standing. This was intentional, he knew. He wasn't here to relax. He was here to prove his innocence. To prove that he wasn't a traitor and a thief.

The traitor part he was sure of, at least.

Colm stared at the eyes staring back at him. There were a few empty seats behind the crescent-shaped table. Master Merribell was busy trying to prepare enough food for a hundred hungry guild members who had slept through their last meal, and she had dragged Master Bloodclaw with her to assist, for which Colm was exceedingly thankful. Not that Colm was afraid of him, but the goblin had a way of making anyone uncomfortable. The only other empty seat was the last one on the right. Colm blinked at the four masters who remained.

"I told you," he said again, "I had no idea Finn Argos was planning to rob the guild."

It was true, but it was a rogue's truth. The kind of truth that required the right perspective. Did he know what Finn was up to? Colm had trusted him more than any of the masters sitting across from him. The man had saved his hand and then his life. Had taught him how to pick locks and disarm traps, to stop and look and listen. He had taught Colm the rules. And the corollaries to the rules. He had taught him to see the things that nobody else could see.

Except Colm hadn't looked hard enough.

"So you would have us believe that you spent weeks learning how to disarm the lock on the guild treasury, weeks spent under the tutelage of Finn Argos, sometimes spending hours in his sole company—a man who specifically found and recruited you, no less—and yet you claim to have no foreknowledge of his intentions to burgle the guild and have its founder and several other dungeoneers led into a trap and murdered?"

Master Velmoth was posing the questions. Master Fimbly fumbled with his quill. The ranger stared at Colm with a grim expression—he hadn't said a single word. Colm shook his head for the fortieth time. Master Velmoth's eyes rolled.

"You have to believe me. I had no idea what Master Argos was planning. I knew that he didn't like Master Wolfe and that he was . . ." Colm tried to think of the right word. Jealous? Greedy? Ambitious? Truthfully, he had been all of these things and more, but those things weren't exactly discouraged here—in fact, the more he thought about it, they almost seemed like prerequisites. He could still remember the look on Tye Thwodin's face as he stared at that room of gold. He had seen that same look before.

Besides, Finn had also been so many other things. There was a time when Colm couldn't look at any of the people sitting across from him and see past their stories. They were heroes. Larger than life. But now, at least, he knew better.

The mage opened his mouth to speak, but Master Wolfe cut him off.

"Pardon me, Master Velmoth," the ranger said. "Mister Candorly is not the only one who underestimated Finn Argos. I admit that I too was blind to his intentions. We cannot fault the boy for being beguiled by a man who made his living on subterfuge and deception. Besides, anyone who would knowingly forfeit his share of the guild's treasure and venture back into an orc stronghold to save all our hides is worthy of our leniency. Perhaps even our thanks."

Colm's face flushed, and he looked down at his boots. Of all the people to stick up for him, he expected Grahm Wolfe to be the last. Master Stormbow nodded her agreement. Then Tye Thwodin slapped his hands on his knees with a sound that made Master Fimbly drop his quill.

"Colm Candorly," he bellowed, "it is my judgment as Head

of the Legion that Finn Argos attempted to manipulate you to his own ends and that your ultimate refusal to aid him—and your heroic actions that followed—absolve you of any wrongdoing in the matter."

Before Colm could so much as sigh in relief, Master Thwodin leaned across the table. "You should know, however, that I've already commissioned to have the lock on the treasury replaced, and that I plan to stick a dragon inside for good measure, so I would think twice before you go opening too many doors around here, understood?"

"Yes, sir," Colm replied, coming to the realization that he wasn't going to be thrown in jail or kicked out of the guild. He was going to keep all his fingers. The rest of them, at least. "And what's going to happen to Master Argos?" He wondered if it was possible that Master Merribell, or even Master Velmoth, could reverse the curse that had turned him to stone.

"Finn Argos has paid the price for his treachery," Tye Thwodin said. "He will serve as a reminder to anyone who has thoughts of betraying this guild or me. As for you, you will just have to train on your own until we find a suitable replacement. You might take the time to work on your swordplay. Or your judgment of character."

"Actually, sir," Colm said hesitantly, "I was thinking of taking some time away. I'd like to go see my family."

The masters exchanged looks. Then, after a moment, Master Thwodin nodded.

"You know the rules. You are welcome to go, and you are

welcome to return, though you'll have to leave anything that doesn't belong to you here, including that little needle of yours."

It took a moment for Colm to realize he was talking about Scratch and not Celia's heirloom, tucked back into his pocket. "Yes, sir."

"And if you *do* come back," Tye Thwodin growled, "know that I'll have my eyes on you. That will be all."

Colm stood and bowed and retreated to the door before the founder of the dungeoneers could change his mind. As he left, he heard Master Thwodin grunt, "Now that that's settled, let's get down to some serious business. Who are we going to find to do the cooking?"

Colm stepped out and closed the door behind him, pressing his back against it. That could have gone much worse.

And it might have, he thought, if they hadn't already had the man responsible.

They found Finn right where Colm had left him, of course, though Master Thwodin had already promised he would be moved to the front garden, right by the gate. The rogue had gotten what he deserved; that's what Tye Thwodin had said, but Colm wasn't so certain. Maybe he should have said something about the scar, about the single coin given to a young thief so many years ago that had been such a small price for saving a life.

Then again, maybe that was just another story.

Colm nearly tumbled backward as the door opened behind him. There, framed like one of the many drawings of him that existed in books already, stood Master Wolfe. He was holding a leather pouch.

"Master Thwodin wanted you to have this," he said, handing over the sack. Colm took it hesitantly in both hands. He knew instantly what was inside. It reminded him of how his pockets had felt that day on the square, the heft of each step, as if his feet were anchored to the ground.

"Master Thwodin did?" he repeated, not sure he had heard right.

Grahm Wolfe shrugged. "The man simply can't help himself. He somehow managed to grab a handful of the orcs' stash even as you were pulling him away."

Colm nodded. He couldn't help himself either; he had to take a peek, opening the sack for only a second. It was all gold. No silver.

"Of course, this is far from standard procedure," Master Wolfe reminded him. "Policy dictates that half of it should go directly to the guild and the other half be divvied up among all participating adventurers according to their rank. But seeing how little there actually is to go around, Tye decided to just let you have it . . . minus his ten percent, of course."

Colm didn't know what to say. There was enough here for each of his sisters to get a few new dresses apiece, for his father to buy new tools for his workshop, for his mother to stock the pantry before winter. It wasn't a fortune, but it was a start. And yet, looking at it, he felt light-headed, almost nauseous. "I'm not sure I should take it," he said, holding the pouch between them. "I'm not sure I deserve it."

"Those are two different things," Grahm Wolfe replied. "But if you don't, someone else will, and there's a good chance you need it more." He pushed the gold back toward Colm. "Now if you'll excuse me, I need to talk to the others about a return trip to that dungeon. I'd like to get my swords back."

Colm nodded and stuffed the pouch in his pocket. It felt heavier than it should have.

Breakfast was unusual, at least by guild standards: runny eggs, charred bacon, something that might have been a biscuit but was better suited as ballast for boats—Colm suspected the goblin was to blame. Looking at his plate, he found himself almost wishing that Fungus was still in the kitchen and not locked in the *other* dungeon down below, awaiting his punishment. Supposedly the cook was going to be shipped to some hive off the north coast and sold to pirates for a life of indentured servitude. It was either that or fight to win back his honor in a duel with Master Wolfe. Not much of a choice.

"This is really good," Quinn said, scarfing each dish in turn.

Colm smiled and pushed his plate over, giving the mageling seconds. He'd certainly earned it, after all. Though the furious whispers traded throughout the castle halls concerned them all, it was the image of Quinn Frostfoot, blowing like a volcano and unleashing his wrath upon a swath of screaming orcs that seemed to garner the most attention. Highly embellished tales were told of Lena and Ravena rampaging through throngs of monsters, of Serene leading an army of giant spiders on a cavalry charge to break the enemy's ranks, even of Colm dueling the orc chief—one version of which had Colm taking the creature's finger as a souvenir that he supposedly kept hidden in his pocket. But the stories they told about Quinn didn't even require exaggeration. What's His Face . . . You Know, the One Guy had become Quinn "Flame Thrower" Frostfoot, Scourge of Orcs and Savior of the Guild, though Colm still sometimes called him Nibbles.

"I get a new sword today," Lena said. "To replace the one the orcs stole. Master Stormbow says I can pick out any one I want. Though, if I'd prefer, she will craft me one herself, and then I can name it. What do you think a good name for a sword would be? I'm thinking Bloodgulper."

"Eww. . . . Why do you always have to be so barbaric? It's always Beheader or Gutspiller or Orc Hacker. Why can't you just call it, I don't know, Merryblade or Mr. Shinyface?"

"Sure, Serene. Just imagine a barbarian going around screaming, 'Feel the wrath of Mr. Shinyface!'"

"I don't know. Sounds kind of scary to me," Quinn remarked through a mouthful of burned bacon.

Colm didn't say anything. He was perfectly content to just sit there listening.

"I like Gutspiller, though. I'll have to remember that one," Lena mused.

"Master Velmoth says he's going to try something new today. It's these little tongue exercises, never been done before. He's calling it speech therapeutics. I just hope I don't light him on fire again." Colm started to reassure Quinn that that wouldn't happen but stopped himself. He was trying to be better about not lying to his friends. And with Quinn, there simply was no telling.

"Did you hear what's going on with Ravena?" Serene whispered. "Apparently she wants to train to become a ranger. Master Wolfe says he might take her on as an apprentice."

"*Gut*spiller . . ."

"Personally I can't imagine that kind of life, being alone all the time, though since I can talk to pretty much anything, I'm never *really* alone. . . ."

"He says that maybe back in the dungeon I crossed some kind of threshold and won't have a problem anymore, though I'm sure as soon as he starts yelling at me, I'll start stumbling over my words again. . . ."

"Out in nature, surrounded by the trees and the grass and the clouds . . ."

"Maybe I could carry *two* swords . . . Bloodgulper *and* Gutspiller. Or maybe Veinsplitter . . ."

"Because it really is beautiful, how you're out there, just listening, and you feel like you're suddenly a part of something bigger than yourself, and you realize just how connected you are, you know? How much everything relies on everything else. . . ."

"Brainbasher! No. That's really a better name for a club. Brain*dicer* . . ."

"I don't know. I just think it's going to be all right, you know? Colm? Are you still with us? Colm?"

Colm looked at his friends, all three of them staring at him, suddenly concerned.

He nodded. He was still with them. For a little while more, at least.

"Actually, there's something I've been meaning to tell you," he began.

Colm stood in the front gardens, waiting for his horse to arrive.

There were no charged crystals close to Felhaven, so Master Wolfe agreed to take him on hoof. It was a long journey—they would have to ride through one night and almost into the next—but there were reports of a potential gorgon's nest not too far from there that the ranger wanted to investigate. Colm could ride with him to the outskirts of town, taking an already-charged crystal with him so that he could come back to the castle whenever he was ready. The ranger would teach him what to say.

Colm had said good-bye to most everyone already. He found Master Stormbow in the armory, and she had taken Scratch back, promising to keep it safe for him. Though it hadn't been put to much use, he had still grown fond of the sword, and it felt strange walking without it thumping annoyingly against his hip. Master Velmoth had offered him a look that was slightly less of a scowl than normal, and Master Merribell had given him a charm that she said gave good luck to travelers. Master Thwodin, apparently, was tucked away in his treasury—making sure nothing was missing, but Colm didn't feel like he owed the man a personal good-bye. He wasn't sure he owed him anything.

Colm had to admit he was surprised when Herren Bloodclaw ambled up to him on his way out the door and head butted him in the stomach. Colm hunched over with a groan. Herren nodded curtly and then rambled off. Colm would later learn it was a goblin sign of respect.

"I wish he'd head butt me," Quinn muttered as they stood together outside, in the shadow of the castle's largest tower. Behind them, Serene was talking to the butterflies, trying to convince them that Lena wasn't dangerous. Eventually she persuaded one to land on Lena's finger, and the would-be barbarian actually let it sit there without trying to squash it. She reached out and showed Colm what she'd caught—a pair of bright blue-and-purple wings that almost matched her eyes—then sighed as it flittered away at the sound of approaching hooves. Colm looked to see Master Wolfe astride his gray stallion, trailing a much smaller and noticeably less-spirited horse by the reins.

"That's my ride," Colm said.

"I can't believe you're leaving us," Serene said, pulling her cloak tighter. "You do realize it won't be the same without you. *We* won't be the same."

"Yeah," Quinn echoed. "What about Harry Herfgold's

theory of proper party conflagration or whatever it is? We need you. You'll probably come back and find us locked out of the castle, waiting for you to open the door."

"Just try pushing it first," Colm said. Nobody laughed.

Serene bowed her head and said a blessing for him while Quinn wrapped both arms around him and squeezed as tight as he could, which was still only a third as tight as Fungus had when he'd tried to break him in half. Colm's ribs were still sore.

He turned and looked at Lena, standing several paces away with her back to him. She wasn't wearing any armor for once, and she looked strange without any shining links or plates attached to her, like a turtle without its shell. He stepped up beside her, remembering the first time they'd met—how she'd almost killed him with a rock. How he'd thought she was pretty. And frightening. He still did.

"There's something I've been meaning to tell you," she began as he stood close. "But it's difficult, so be patient. I want to say . . ." She took a deep breath. "To say . . . thanks. You know. For, um, for, you know . . ." She let it escape with a sigh. "For rescuing me."

"Wow," Colm replied. "That *must* have been difficult."

"Well, I mean. Let's be honest," she instantly backtracked, "I actually did *most* of the rescuing. You just got the process started by freeing me from that cage. Which I was about to find a way out of anyways."

"Sure," Colm said.

431

"Right. So. You know. Thanks for doing your part."

"Anytime."

Lena looked back at the other two, who were huddled close together. "Did you say good-bye to everyone?"

Colm thought about it. Everyone who mattered, he guessed, save for one. He had looked all over the castle for Ravena but couldn't find her. That probably meant she didn't want to be found. He could appreciate that. "You're the last," he said.

"Sometimes it's all right coming in last, I guess," she said. Then she leaned in and kissed him lightly on his cheek. Her lips were dry and the kiss felt rough on his skin, but he didn't mind. "Don't stay gone long, okay?"

"I'll try. But no promises," he said.

"You're a rogue. I wouldn't believe them anyways."

Master Wolfe called for Colm to hurry. Colm waved good-bye to Quinn and Serene again. "You'll look after them, right?" he asked. Lena nodded. "Your father would be proud of you," he added.

"Yours too," she said. Then she stood up a little straighter and put on her warrior face, stoic to the last. "You better go. I'm already jealous enough that you get to ride alongside the second-greatest dungeoneer ever." Colm guessed he was looking at the first. *Someday, maybe,* he thought.

Colm smiled, then slowly turned and walked to where Master Wolfe was waiting. It took two tries for him to get on his horse—it had been a while since he'd ridden anything with four legs—then follow Master Wolfe out of the gardens toward the outer wall and the fields and forest beyond. As they trotted away, Colm looked back, just once, to see his party huddled together in front of the home of Thwodin's Legion, holding tight to one another as they watched him go.

They weren't alone. Looking down on the gardens from the battlements, standing against a backdrop of thin, white clouds, Ravena Heartfall waved once, then turned and vanished back into the tower.

"There are two good parts to any journey," Grahm Wolfe said, bringing his horse up beside Colm's. The ranger looked odd with only one sword hanging from his side. "The setting off and the coming back."

"Which is the best part?" Colm asked.

Master Wolfe shrugged. "That all depends on why you leave. And what you are coming back to. For me, I'm always happy to see home again."

Colm pictured his home, wondering what it would be like. To sleep in his hammock and hear his sisters twittering in the next room over, to smell his mother's cooking, to listen to his father's grumbling. "If you like it here so much, why are you always off somewhere else? Why don't you stay?"

"Why don't you?" Master Wolfe shot back. "Probably for the same reason. You're still looking for something."

Colm couldn't argue with that. "And what are you looking for?"

"Something I lost a long time ago," the ranger replied.

"Treasure?" Colm guessed.

"You might call it that."

"Is that what you and Master Thwodin are always whispering about?"

"If we wanted you to know, little mouse, we wouldn't bother with whispering," Grahm Wolfe said with something that could be mistaken for a smile, though with the ranger it was hard to tell.

They approached the wall hedging the gardens and passed through the front gate and into the grassy fields beyond. Ahead lay Velmoth's Rock, as it was now called, jutting obnoxiously out of the earth like a thorn in its side, a reminder of the time a war band of orcs was foolish enough to follow the ranger home. And there, off to Colm's right, sat another stone reminder. Colm asked Master Wolfe to stop, for just a moment. There was one last thing he needed to take care of.

The man only looked like a semblance of himself, as if a sculptor had had to conjure him from listening to a description. One hand was still only missing a finger, but the other hand was now missing all of them. They had apparently broken off at the knuckles when Master Thwodin had wrenched them from his treasury door. One foot had a sizeable crack that threatened to work its way up the leg. But he was still smiling, at least.

Colm walked up to the rogue and dug into his own pocket. The one on Colm's right held the purse full of gold that Tye Thwodin had given him. The one on the left held a single coin. Colm wasn't sure who the coin belonged to anymore, not really, but he felt like he owed this man something still. He placed the silver coin at the foot of the statue and then stood there for a moment in silence, as if he were making a wish. "What's yours is yours," he whispered.

Colm remounted his horse and turned to Master Wolfe, who was also looking at the statue of Finn Argos guarding the outer gate. "They wrote a song about him once, you know?"

"They write songs about everybody," Grahm Wolfe replied.

The rogue stood in the shadows.

Night had dropped like a hammer's blow, setting a veil over the land. The road into Felhaven was narrow, hard to follow at times, but he was comfortable in the dark now, so long as it wasn't absolute. As long as there was that sliver of moon, the smattering of stars. He knew where he was. There was the expanse of plowed fields, stretched wide and stitched together with fence lines. The familiar smells. Farm smells, not pleasant, but comforting in the memories they brought. He had certainly smelled worse.

He was alone. The ranger had said farewell a ways back, showing him what he needed to do to return. He hadn't even bothered to say good-bye, only "Till next time," spoken with an almost ominous certainty, a sureness the rogue didn't share. Still, he shook the ranger's hand when it was offered, just as he had the hand of the man who had taken him from this place what seemed like ages ago. Then the ranger turned and went back the other way, taking the extra horse with him—property of Thwodin's Legion. Rules were rules.

More or less.

So the rogue had made it the rest of the way home on foot, keeping out of sight, more out of habit than anything. The house was asleep when he arrived, everyone tucked in. He picked the front lock easily and just stood there for a moment, savoring the breath, the scent of honey and lilacs and burned wood and glue. Then he set his little trap and escaped back into the shadows, closing the door less than softly behind him.

He stood in the darkness and waited.

Watched as each of them emerged, dressed in their nightgowns, converging on the dining table and the treasure it held.

"What is *that*?"

He listened to his father's booming voice, peered through the window at the man's wide red face, blooming big eyes, and pout-lipped expression. They were all together, staring at the leather purse, its contents scattered across the table, gleaming in the firelight.

"It's money, Papa."

"I *know* it's money, Cally!" the old man shouted. "How did it *get* here?"

Rove Candorly looked from daughter to daughter and then to his wife, who propped herself against the wall, eyes wide, hand to her mouth. Nobody answered. No one dared say it out loud. He watched as Celia stepped slowly to the table, taking up the silver butterfly in her hand, then ran to the window, pressing her face against it, looking into the shadows.

436

He should go inside, he knew. But as soon as he showed his face, the crying would begin. The smothering, lung-crushing embraces. The sound of snot wiped on sleeves. And the look on his father's face, that trace of doubt, as if it was too good to be true. As soon as he stepped out of the shadows, there would be stories and explanations and what-ifs and even-thoughs.

And it would be harder, so much harder, to say good-bye again.

Because he would have to. Eventually. He had had a taste of it, and it was inside him now.

Finn was right. He had seen it with his own eyes.

There was so much more where that came from.

ACKNOWLEDGMENTS

"I don't believe anybody makes it in this world alone."

I'm no ranger. I'm barely a passable bard. So there is no way I could have ventured into the depths of *The Dungeoneers* without my stalwart party of fighters, magicians, and rogues by my side. First, many thanks to Quinlan Lee and the rest of Adams Literary for recognizing the story's potential and for making me a part of their guild. It's nice not to have to tackle this all on my own. I'm happy to share the stash.

As for Walden Pond's Legions, much credit goes to Debbie Kovacs, my devoted champion, who is truly outrageous, and to Danielle Smith, whose work on the novel continues long after it's published, along with the trio of marketing mavens at Harper—Jenna Lisanti, Emilie Polster, and Caroline Sun. Thanks to Jon Howard, Renée Cafiero, and Laaren Brown for watching my missteps and disarming the linguistic traps that I riddle my manuscripts with, and to Katie Fitch and Amy Ryan for shaping the words into a tangible treasure. For the richly adorned depiction of my band of heroes descending into the depths on the cover, thanks go to Dan Santat. And for his wit and roguish charm, not to mention his unerring guidance, mentorship, and support, many thanks to Jordan Brown, who shows me there are always more doors to unlock and waits patiently while I fumble with the picks.

Finally, thanks to my friends and family, specifically my parents, who scrabbled to make ends meet so that I could grow up and go on these adventures. To my wife, Alithea, who shows me the beauty in all things. And to my children, Nick and Isabella, who are the greatest treasures I could ever hope to have.